"A new
originality
. . . a goo
laughs . .

"The most audaciously delightful detective
teaming is that of Rayford Goodman and
Mark Bradley. . . . It's a savvy, slick and
very wise look at Hollywood . . . a charm."
—*St. Petersburg Times*

"A meticulously observed Hollywood milieu
and a cast of always surprising, colorful
characters . . . Any writer who can make me
laugh out loud on almost every page has
both my respect and gratitude."
—Bernard Slade, author of
Same Time Next Year

"Realistic, funny . . . the plot is intricate, the
pace quick, and the secondary characters are
all as enjoyable as Goodman and Bradley.
Reading *Best Performance by a Patsy* is like
driving a vintage car that has been updated
for the '90s—a touch of the old, a touch of
the new, and a mightily enjoyable ride."
—*Greeley Tribune*

"AN AUTHOR WORTH WATCHING."
—*Library Journal*

"GRITTY . . . A REFRESHING APPROACH TO THE MECHANICS OF TELLING A STORY." —*Indianapolis Star*

"A best performance by one of Hollywood's wittiest comedy writers . . . Cutler has created a monumentally mismatched pair of investigators—guys who don't even like to be in the same room together. I'm crazy about them . . . and I predict that mystery lovers everywhere will be too."
—Gene Thompson, author of *Murder Mystery*

"A FUNNY, LIVELY MYSTERY." —*Richmond New Leader*

"PLOTTING AND STORY LINE ARE SOME OF THE BEST I'VE SEEN. . . . CUTLER IS A TALENT TO WATCH." —*Lambda Book Report*

BEST
PERFORMANCE
BY A PATSY

Stan Cutler

AN ONYX BOOK

ONYX
Published by the Penguin Group
Penguin Books USA Inc., 375 Hudson Street,
New York, New York 10014, U.S.A.
Penguin Books Ltd, 27 Wrights Lane,
London W8 5TZ, England
Penguin Books Australia Ltd, Ringwood,
Victoria, Australia
Penguin Books Canada Ltd, 10 Alcorn Avenue,
Toronto, Ontario, Canada M4V 3B2
Penguin Books (N.Z.) Ltd, 182-190 Wairau Road,
Auckland 10, New Zealand

Penguin Books Ltd, Registered Offices:
Harmondsworth, Middlesex, England

First published by Onyx, an imprint of New American Library,
a division of Penguin Books USA Inc.
Previously published in a Dutton edition.

First Onyx Printing, March, 1993
10 9 8 7 6 5 4 3 2 1

 REGISTERED TRADEMARK—MARCA REGISTRADA

Printed in the United States of America

PUBLISHER'S NOTE
This is a work of fiction. Names, characters, places, and incidents either
are the product of the author's imagination or are used fictitiously, and any
resemblance to actual persons, living or dead, events, or locales is entirely
coincidental.

BOOKS ARE AVAILABLE AT QUANTITY DISCOUNTS WHEN USED TO PROMOTE
PRODUCTS OR SERVICES. FOR INFORMATION PLEASE WRITE TO PREMIUM MAR-
KETING DIVISION, PENGUIN BOOKS USA INC., 375 HUDSON STREET, NEW YORK,
NEW YORK 10014.

If you purchased this book without a cover you should be aware that this
book is stolen property. It was reported as "unsold and destroyed" to the
publisher and neither the author nor the publisher has received any payment
for this "stripped book."

For my father, who waited
a hundred years for this . . .
and my mother, who couldn't.

1

Rayford Goodman

Between Doheny Drive and Sunset Plaza, north of Sunset Boulevard, after you go a mile or two straight up, you come to a bunch of bird streets—Tanager, Thrasher, Blue Jay. That's where I live, way up in the hills, in one of your basic Hollywood drop-dead houses. It's got a pool, putting green, and a view that won't quit. Unless it does. Which means it's either snowcapped mountains to the east and Catalina and the Channel Islands to the west, or a fat smog-cloud four feet away. Depending whether the Big Producer in the Sky's on hiatus or into reruns how it used to be before we hooked into progress.

He flashes the old look just often enough you realize it's not too dreary a place to hang around waiting to see how life's gonna work out.

To be honest, the actual physical plant's a bit run-down—could use a little attention—the word "seedy" comes to mind. This is partly due to things haven't exactly been booming in the Hollywood–Beverly Hills private-detective business. And that Luana, my erstwhile wife of twenty-four years, cleared me out pretty good before taking off in search of I think it was selfhood—or the perfect orgasm. Something in that Donahue-Winfrey area. Sort of pissed me off. In the words of W. C. Fields, "She not only didn't leave a note under the cookie jar, she didn't leave the cookie jar."

You'd probably think, as a private detective I could've gotten a cheap divorce—being it wasn't that hard to get the goods on her. But she had two things going: (1) I didn't want it generally known, hitting, as it did, on my macho professional image, and B) I was in the middle of dying, so it tended not to be my first priority.

My name is Ray Goodman—Rayford, actually. I'm

fifty-eight years old in a town where forty-year-olds look twenty-two—want to talk about if there's a God? I'm 5-foot-11¾ (getting the picture?), weigh 210 (center of gravity lower and lower), and it's been fourteen months since the elephant sat on my chest and clued me in on not living forever. At UCLA Medical they taught me the words "myocardial infarction"—several times. Then the word "angioplasty." And it got to be a standoff, give or take a nitrogylcerin now and then.

So that's why at seven o'clock in the morning I was in my sweats, getting ready to walk the two fast miles I'm supposed to every day in order not to die anymore.

But first I had to get rid of Julie, who, it turned out, wanted one hundred dollars for cab fare.

"Gee, Julie, that sounds a little steep," I said. "For cab fare, I mean. Seeing you have your own car."

"The going rate," she replied.

"For actual *going*. Would you consider fifty?"

"I'd like to, Ray, but you know Hollywood. Once you break your price . . ."

"Still, fifty bucks. For a *nap* . . . ?"

"Well," she said, "seeing it's you. A repeat client."

She saw my embarrassed look.

"Not to worry; you'll do better next time."

"Thanks, Jules," I said. "And next time, come what may—in a manner of speaking—it's retail."

Julie was a bouncy little number, about 5-foot-4, who I sincerely doubted topped a hundred pounds, fully clothed— which wasn't often. She definitely qualified as a spinner. She had short blond hair, kind of ratty punk— we're talking cute rat—and not what you'd expect to be my style. But she was such a kissy-face up person that even suffering the shorts was worth every penny on good company alone.

On top of which she was my connection with the latest what's happening. Perfect example, she decided one day the way I dressed was a crime against nature. So we had to go shopping on Melrose Avenue, where they have those trendy secondhand shops and find me something that was with it. So, you know what's with it? My old Sy Devore suits and wide ties! Good thing I never cleaned my closet.

Now you gotta know I really hate haggling, especially with her. But it was sort of an acquired survival skill learned the hard way from my dearly departed.

So I peeled off a fifty—which meant separating it from the twenty—and slipped it twixt her boobs. Then I kissed her sweet cheek, and with a wave of the hand and a twist of the tush, she was off—richer and wiser.

For my part, I crossed to the garage and saddled up my big old '64 Cadillac Eldorado convertible. Another bonus from Julie. The old wreck used to embarrass the hell out of me, but with new Beverly Hills basic wheels going for something in the neighborhood fifty large, and me without cutting the grass money, I was stuck with the old heap. Turned out, I was wrong. Julie put me straight. What I had there wasn't an old junk, but a dulled-out gem, basic diamond in the rough. All it needed, the minute I came into some serious money, was spring for a first-rate paint job, and shazzam!—we'd be talking classic. Which with a loud ratch-grind I forced into gear—the transmission being classic too—backed out the garage, and eased on down the hill.

Around Thrasher, Oriole, down Doheny, cut right to Sunset Hills Road, around back of Hamburger Hamlet, over to Hillcrest, and parked just shy of Sunset Boulevard.

I started my walk with a new guess how much the mansion on the corner would go for, settling on eight to ten mil. I said good morning to the two Old Cockers ambled along every day kidding themselves they were exercising, nodded at the Shuffler—a definite post-stroke victim—and leapt out the way of the Flailing Jogger, bumping into the garbage cans set out for collection today.

It will come as no surprise garbage cans in Beverly Hills are not *garbage* cans. They're these monster mini-wheeled, hinge-lidded jobs look like Gucci designed them. You really got the feeling there was stuff in there you'd still like to have.

I set off at a good pace, which I had a fat chance of maintaining, since I kept forgetting it was therapy and not a walk. But I did manage at least till Alpine. That was where the crazy Arab sheik had taken that grand old elegant house and turned it into a plastic green eyesore, with pubic-hair-painted statues—a definite no-no in Beverly Hills, where most pubic hairs got nipped by electrolysis. It'd become a big tourist attraction before either the alleged artwork-thieving chauffeur or *someone* with a plan burned it down. To either hide a heist or collect some insurance, or likely both. Now it made a very expensive empty lot.

It was about here I usually ran into the high-stepping Fast Walker, with the speedy lurch, head tilted to one side, looked like a botched hanging. He kept trying to sell me some mind-blowing walking shoes only he knew about. I think they *were* mind-blowing since he never remembered we went through all this almost daily.

And there he came—and away I went.

"Hey, wait, you walk a lot?" he called after me. "You gotta hear this!"

Wrong.

So, past him, and the sheik's empty lot, another two blocks to Beverly Drive, across the street from the entrance to the Beverly Hills Hotel. That was where in a few hours I'd be "doing lunch" with Mark Bradley at the Polo Lounge—one of my favorite places, although not too much lately, for reasons of mostly money.

Bradley was the guy Pendragon Press had assigned to write my autobiography. All Hollywood autobiographies are written by other people. After all, if we were really writers, nobody'd be *interested* in our autobiographies. I'd been told he was an up-and-coming, relatively talented guy who'd probably do a slick-enough "as told to" job, since he'd already done them for the likes of Joanne Whorley (*Deeper Than a Dimple*) and, I think, Benji (*The Actor and the Dog*), or something. Anyway, I was getting a good enough advance, which I only needed like air. And whatever publicity came out of it'd either get me some more cases or at least minimum pay on talk shows. Besides being the only offer I had.

Beverly Drive made it exactly one mile of my two-mile hike, so I turned and headed back. To my surprise, the endorphins were beginning to kick in, which I could tell because I was starting to vague out—almost like meditating (hey, didn't we all try that?)—which I found usually only happened during the last quarter mile. I was cruising pretty good, a little pressed, breath coming a bit hard, hands swelling. All in all, good signs of cardiovascular activity. What started to slow me down, though, was the little bells going off at the sight of a young black guy running full out, with a stride looked like he could keep it up till Pacoima. Nobody in my day *ever* was that kind of shape.

Basketball tall, lanky and loose, he had on three-hundred-dollar shorts, a two-hundred-dollar T-shirt, and over designer socks another couple hundred worth what *my* generation used to call sneakers. Plus he was carrying a very slick weight—brand name unknown—in one hand, and a real trendy Walther nine-millimeter in the other.

There was a time, not so long ago, police considered anybody on foot in Beverly Hills "suspicious"—why'd anybody *walk* when they could ride? And if that body was of the black persuasion, even *in* a car. So to see a black guy, not only on foot, but running—formerly practically a felony confession—and that black man on foot, running, and packing a *gun* . . . ! Well, either what's-wrong-with-this-picture or the times they were a-changing, as the song goes.

I got a definite feeling it wasn't the song when he raised the gun and aimed it at my head.

I waited a microsecond for instinct to kick in and do something about my reflexes. But there was a lot of nothing happening.

They say the first thing to go is the legs (I always thought it was the wife). But my total everything-went was really scary.

Then suddenly I got a thought. It was a real nice thought. The kind gives you back your breath.

Of course: it's Hollywood! Movies . . . location . . . a picture! They're shooting something!

Only partly right. They *were* shooting something, but it was bullets, at me. When the pair of slugs went whistling past my ear—they *do* whistle—I found myself thinking it'd been a real long time since I'd been shot at. Maybe I was doing better than I thought.

The good news was it didn't look like he was going to

actually kill me, since no more bullets seemed to be zinging my way.

The bad news was he *still* kept coming.

One thing I knew: I wasn't about to outrun Carl Lewis here, so I figured I might as well turn and make a stand.

In that tenth of a second before contact, it seemed there was something definitely familiar about his face. But I didn't have time to dwell on it.

He was maybe mid-twenties, and in Olympic condition. But he didn't have my experience. He didn't have my knowledge how to use somebody's strength against him. My savvy on the subtle shifts of weight that threw the other guy off-balance and opened him up for a sucker punch. All the great pro moves . . .

He knocked me on my ass.

Not exactly the plan.

I popped up and aimed a karate chop at his right wrist. The wrist wasn't there anymore. It was at the end of a fist at the end of my nose. I wound up for a hope-and-a-prayer shot to the solar plexus. There's a reason they call it a hope and a prayer—it doesn't work. I got bopped in the eye.

In fact, it kept up like that, a whole lot longer than necessary to make the point, I thought. He took every round, and did everything but sing the head bone disconnected from the neck bone, the neck bone disconnected from the shoulder bone. I really hated it.

But finally he stopped, maybe just to catch his breath.

I tried to look menacing—at least not to cringe.

"This be a warning," he said in an offbeat quiet voice.

Okay, better than punching. *Much* better than shooting. A warning.

"What," I replied. "That young studs with designer togs who work out all day instead of making an honest living can take down flabby old guys twice their age with a heart condition?" I figured a little sympathy bid couldn't hurt.

"Just . . . let it go, mon. Bes' be you drop it." Which had to be Islands—Jamaica, maybe. Like that.

"Doan push you luck, mon. Take de message."

With which he dusted off his duds and loped quietly away.

Let what go? I wondered. Bygones be bygones? The attack? Something else? Experience suggested "something else." But what? I love when they give you a message and you don't understand the message. And who did he remind me of?

I continued my walk, wondering, too, if a continued walk really counted as an exercise day. Considering the interruption, I had my doubts. On the other hand, if a lot of bruises and shortness of breath was any clue, this was a workout.

I gave myself full credit for the walk, eased into the soon-to-be-classic Caddy, popped it into low, and rattled up the hill on home.

2

Mark Bradley

Lord knows it hadn't been an easy assignment from the beginning, but now, three long, depressing, soul-numbing months later, I had finished the last chapter in the "autobiography" of game-show hostess Bambi Blain. For reasons comprehensible only to her hairdresser and legwaxer, Bambi had shot to overnight stardom as the cohostess of *For Love or Money* and become America's latest TV semisuperstar. Her face, somewhat sweet and void of expression, and her body, considerably curvy and *full* of expression—if you liked that sort of thing, and I didn't—were plastered on the cover of every magazine, tabloid, and billboard from here to ennui.

The project was fraught with peril and envy right from the start. At Pendragon Press every red-blooded scribe with even a modicum of lead in his implement had wanted the job of getting Bambi Blain down on paper— or anywhere else. That is, everyone except myself, which is exactly why Richard Penny, the sage, if somewhat gross, founder and president of Pendragon Press, awarded the assignment to lucky me.

"I know you won't let anything *stand* between you and Bambi," Dickie had said in his most lascivious tone three months before. "Plus which, the two of you will be just like sisters. And everyone knows sisters tell each other *everything*."

Well, I had done my reluctant best, but sister or not, Bambi didn't have a lot to say, and even less without cue cards.

She had roughly the IQ of a kiwi—the fruit, not the bird—which, I guess, all things considered, was about par for a twenty-two-year-old game-show hostess from Indiana.

Now, after ninety endlessly vapid days and nights, *Bambi Blain: The Dear Speaks Out* was finished. And so, nearly, was I. In addition to being utterly exhausted, bored beyond canonization by talk about dress lengths ("They should be modest and almost daring") and middle-American morals ("I don't believe in trial marriage on the first date"), I also desperately needed to spend some time with the *guys*. Enough girl talk! I mean, my God, did anyone really *care* what Bambi Blain's personal hygiene was, or whether her pads were mini or maxi?

"Of course they do," Dickie had said with gusto when I suggested deleting the reference. "America eats that up."

Some things even *I* won't respond to.

At any rate, this was the moment I put the finally finished manuscript on Dickie's desk, and not, I might add, without a certain amount of pride.

I had done a professionally good job, and that mattered to me. My deal with Dickie was that I'd do four "as told to" books of his choice, after which he'd give me six months to finish my novel and then publish it— no matter what he thought of the commercial possibilities. The wages of art is hack.

Dickie weighed the manuscript in his hand and pronounced, "Feels good."

"Feels good to be *rid* of," I replied.

The phone rang. Penny grabbed it, without so much as a suggestion of apology, the least of his faults. I considered myself lucky he didn't spit into his wastebasket. We don't call him Penny Dreadful for nothing.

"Go ahead, it's your nickel," he said quaintly, to whomever.

I guess this might be a good time to tell you a little about myself and how I arrived at this particular stressful point in my misguided life. My name is Mark Bradley. I'm twenty-eight years old, basically honest and sincere, or at least as sincere as anyone can be in this kind of profession. On the other hand, I'm not dedicated to perfection. I procrastinate a lot, like most writers, and I smoke a little pot every now and then when reality starts to loom too large. But all in all, I'm a decent-enough preppy-Yuppie kind of word-processor-for-hire. I have sandy brown hair, hazel eyes that incline to green when I'm aroused—they tell me—and I rather like clothes. None of that writerish corduroy and leather-patched-elbows stuff for me. I work out at six in the morning three days a week at the Sports Connection on Santa Monica Boulevard, so I'm in pretty good shape. For a writer, I'm in *great* shape.

I kind of suspect I'm not going to be the next Hemingway—or even the next Kitty Kelley—writing these peeka-boo bios, but who knows for sure? Maybe it will karmically lead to something better. At least that's the plan.

I make my home in West Hollywood, a newly incorporated city comprising primarily impoverished old ethnics and affluent young gays. It has the singular honor of being the only city in the nation with an openly gay mayor who once posed nude for gay-porno magazines. What a piece of work is man.

My condo's on the corner of King's Road and Willoughby, in the heart of what the homosexual population calls Boys' Town—and the rednecks call the Swish Alps—a large white upscale building complete with underground security parking, a swimming pool on the roof, and a dimly lit mini-gym in the basement where the homowners exercise this and that.

At any given time, day or night, there are fussy old queens walking fussy little dogs back and forth on the block while the younger, body-by-Nautilus boys jog by in a blur of Fila shorts and Reeboks. It's sort of heaven.

"Well, fuck you too," said Penny, hanging up the phone gently, with a smile that suggested complete satisfaction at the depth of communication he had achieved.

"I think you'll like your next assignment," he continued, as if there'd been no interruption at all. "Finito on the girl stuff. Which should please you. No more Bambis."

Good.

"And no more no-brainers."

Terrific.

"What I'm offering you now, I say in all sincerity, is only the opportunity of a lifetime."

Uh-oh.

"The chance to really dredge up all the dirt on one of Hollywood's greatest scandals."

Too much buildup.

"To combine, at one and the same time, an artistic, literary docudrama full of historic significance, with the immediacy of an as-told-to autobiography!"

Oh, boy.

"Rayford Goodman," I replied in a small, appalled voice, desperately hoping I was wrong. I had read the Pendragon press release announcing his signing.

"You got it, babe—and it's very close to my heart. This is a big story, a story full of highs and lows, ins and outs, ups and downs—"

"Backs and forths?"

"—and it cries out for our very best writer," he added in his customary subtle way. "One I feel confident will handle the book with a kind of heroic dignity."

Heroic dignity? Ray Goodman?

"Shit, Dickie," I tried, even knowing it was futile, "you *know* I'm not interested in writing about some over-the-hill detective with a macho beer belly and a probable attitude toward gays bordering on the psychopathic."

"So maybe he hates fags. What do they say, guy hates fags, maybe he's a latent himself, right? So then if you're both fags, what's the problem?"

"I'm going to explain one more time," I said, even as I spoke knowing it wouldn't make any difference. "I don't appreciate this assignment, under any circumstances. But what I don't appreciate most of all is you calling me a fag. I *am* a fag, and if I choose to call myself by that name, that's fine, but no one else—unless he too happens to *be* a fag—is allowed. Period."

"Boy . . . sensi-tiiive! I thought you guys were proud! You have parades and everything. Isn't there like Gay Pride Week?"

"*Gay* pride, not fag pride."

"Oh, we're making a big thing over semantics? I'm antisemantic myself!" (Chuckle chuckle.)

"Besides," Dickie continued, "Goodman has no idea of your . . . sexual orientation—better? You don't look like

. . . an alternative life-styler—I'm getting *good* at this—so most probably he won't even find out. Right? Right."

It was as good as I was going to get.

Dickie handed me a huge envelope of press clippings and photographs. He hardly needed to bother. As much as I personally might dislike Rayford Goodman, the man—the womanizing, past-it, boozed-out private-eye antithesis of everything I stood for, who hadn't done anything newsworthy since 1963—I certainly had heard and read about his most famous case.

Of course I was hardly born at the time, but my mother had followed the whole affair intensely, and I guess a certain amount of interest had sort of osmosed itself into me. The American Beauty Rose murder *was* one of the major sensations of the sixties—to say nothing of mother. So I did have a basic familiarity. One was forced to admit, Ray Goodman had, to his credit, single-handedly solved the whole mess. For a brief shining moment—or brief shining year—he was the hottest thing in Hollywood. In fact, nothing quite that exciting happened again until Richard Gere took off all his clothes in *American Gigolo.* I jest.

Still, the thought of an intense daily association with this troglodyte gave me the willies.

As I considered how to frame my refusal, Penny's phone rang again.

"Yeah, who?" he demanded, and settled back comfortably, giving no indication of a desire to cut the conversation short.

I reached inside the envelope and pulled out the clippings. The first one immediately, and somehow emotionally, pulled me back to 1963. It read:

LOS ANGELES STAR EXPRESS
August 2, 1963

SEPIA STAR STABBED!
Rita Rose Murdered on Set!

Gory Crime Halts Million-Dollar Production

Hollywood—Just as filming on Pinnacle Studios' "Gone to Carnival" was about to commence at seven o'clock this morning, the bloodstained nude body of Negro actress Rita Rose was discovered on her satin-sheeted dressing-room couch. The glamorous cafe-au-lait singer-dancer had been stabbed "numerous times," said Chief of Detectives Edward Broward, "the immediate cause of death being said aforementioned stabs."

Asked whether there were any clues or suspects in the slaying, Broward replied that an intensive investigation was in progress and would continue "until there is a conclusion to this barbaric act and the alleged perpetrator is apprehended." The murder comes as a distinct shock to the motion-picture community, which had been free of scandal for many years.

Commenting on that very fact, studio head R. Symington Lefcourt said, "It's a shock, a very terrible shock, and a great loss to all Americans, regardless." Lefcourt further stated, "We will, of course, close down production. Out of respect—and till we can recast."

Next was a clipping dated August 3, detailing how the Hollywood community mourned its great loss, with several very dignified statements quoted, and ending with a salacious lick of the lips as apparently the industry was abuzz with rumors of wild parties involving prominent celebrities and the late Brown Bombshell.

Dickie seemed to be getting a bit impatient.

"We can if I say so!" he said so, listened a moment, then terminated the conversation with his customary, "Well, fuck you too!" Only this time he slammed down the phone.

"Dickie," I began, but he raised a finger to halt me, pushed an automatic dialer.

"Marvin," he yelled, "you know what that son of a bitch Farrell had the nerve to answer back to me . . . ?" By which time I had dipped back into the file.

LOS ANGELES STAR EXPRESS
August 4, 1963

AMERICAN BEAUTY ROSE
BURIED IN LAVISH CEREMONY

Costar Dubie Dietrich Faints

Beverly Hills—Police struggled with hundreds of fans and sensation-seekers as the body of Ebony Lovely Rita Rose was laid to rest today. With the crush of fans and co-workers alike pushing in upon him, an obviously distraught Dubie Dietrich collapsed and had to be carried from the chapel. Miss Rose's other costar, supercomic Harry Light, gave a glowing and tearful eulogy to "this bright luminary, this fallen star, this brief candle that has flickered and gone out." Last to speak was studio head R. Symington Lefcourt, who said, "She was a champion for her race and a credit to the business. In honor of living proof—alas no longer—of the American ideal of equal opportunity for all, we shall go forward to continue to shoot "Gone to Carnival" and will dedicate this picture as a lasting monument to her memory."

What a corker, this guy. Surprising that he missed a beat in honoring her: it didn't have to be just a picture in her memory, it could have been a "soon-to-be-released-in-a-theater-near-you" picture.

Meanwhile, Penny seemed to have calmed down somewhat as he said, "All right, six weeks? You get the book in six weeks."

I sure hoped he didn't mean the book he wanted *me* to write.

"Mark Bradley. He's right in my office. He can do it," he added, dashing that little hope.

I raised a hand weakly in protest, but he merely swung his swivel chair around, affording me a glimpse of the back of his head—no pretty sight, I assure you—from which had obviously been removed the plugs that formed the hairline in front.

I turned to another clipping.

This one, also datelined August 4, detailed the coroner's findings of "large quantities of foreign substances which had been ingested prior to the subject's expiration." These turned out to be marijuana, cocaine, and heroin, which evidently came as a big surprise to the folks at the time. There were no signs of forced entry, as it were, but evidence of sexual activity shortly before death, in fact activity aplenty, there being residue of "more than one semen type."

At last Dickie hung up, this time sans "fuck you too," from which I gathered the deal was set.

"Dickie," I said, "I really have considerable doubt that I—"

But he quickly resumed, with no loss of enthusiasm or gain of sensitivity.

"Mark, sweetheart, I know Goodman's not your cup of cappuccino, but you gotta admit it's a fascinating case, and it beats the shit out of what you been doing. I could say, 'Give it some thought; sleep on it and let me know tomorrow,' but I'm not going to change *my* mind, so what difference does it make what *you* think?"

Pretty irrefutable logic.

"So, okay, we're on the same wavelength, so to speak. I know this is going to be a great book, both commercially and artistically."

"One hopes."

"And not only artistic, but quick—I need it in six weeks. Absolute deadline."

"I see no reason to linger," I replied.

Penny nodded, glad to have the artistic niceties out of the way.

"You got lunch with Goodman at the Polo Lounge, one o'clock today. And just because it's expense account doesn't mean you have to eat like a pig," he concluded with his customary touch of class.

3

Rayford Goodman

I try hard not to get old inside. I know anyone remembers when a stamp cost three cents, and they delivered the mail twice a day, tends to have a not-like-the-good-old-days attitude. But, however I tried, it was hard not to miss the class, the old sparkle and grace used to be Hollywood. I mean, dammit, here I was pulling up to the Beverly fucking Hills Hotel, what's waiting out front? Skinny-legged guys with big bellies in baggy shorts and toy shirts, with their broad-beamed old ladies and doughy daughters and sulky sons. The whole motley group waiting on their damned twenty-thousand-dollar Jap economy cars so they could go "have a nice day." And isn't "nice" something wonderful to shoot for?

I noticed I wasn't doing too good at not feeling old and obsolete. So I took a couple breaths—stress kills—got my ticket from the parking guy, and went on in.

I had to admit, inside it was still the Beverly Hills. A little busier, little more noise, but not all that much. The old dame still had a dance or two left.

I guess what was really bugging me was realizing how long it'd been. It just wasn't my scene anymore, and I sure wasn't its. And maybe being a mite crabby had something to do with every bone in my body ached from my little morning equal-opportunity punch-out.

I made the little right, then duked left, and there she was—the old Polo Lounge. Still the same, no matter what was happening outside. Now, what was the name of the midget maître d' again?

He wasn't there anyway. Maybe semiretired. A full-size snob was, instead.

"Goodman," I said.

Banker's eyes.

"Ray Goodman," I added, since no bells seemed to be ringing.

"Excuse me," he said, turning to greet some TV guy I remember vaguely seeing in a cop suit on a motorcycle. "Mr. Estrada, so good to see you. This way, please."

"Uh, Goodman," I repeated to a stiff back *heard*, all right, but wasn't admitting it. The guy's show had been off for years, for Christ sake. Things definitely weren't going my way.

I sucked air, remembered the time this happened to Bogie, who took it pretty personal. And the bailing-out and paying-off that all took.

But I wasn't Bogie. And now, even poor Bogie wasn't. I found myself sighing. For him, me, both. I told myself not to do that, and turned to see a slim young guy half my age separate himself from a Bloody Mary at the bar and cross over to me.

"Mr. Goodman?" he said. I nodded. "Mark Bradley, Pendragon Press?" I nodded. "Your biographer."

We shook. Firmly. Too firmly. More like a statement. Terrific, just what I needed—a pastello.

"I'm trying to get us a table, but I don't see the regular guy," I said, faking a friendly smile.

The new regular guy came back.

"My table, please?"

"I'm sorry, Mr. . . . umblerf . . . but there's nothing just at the moment . . ."

As if even bothering to fluff me off had been an effort, he started to turn. As if removing his teeth would be enough, I started for his arm. Bradley stepped in.

"Excuse me, excuse me?" he said. "Mark Bradley?"

"Oh, yes, of course," said the fuck, and right away led us to a good table.

"Come here often?" I asked en route.

"First time," said Bradley. "It's my boss who has the franchise."

We were seated. *Very* good table. I'm aced.

"Enjoy your lunch," said the new guy snidely, guaranteeing I wouldn't. Lo, how the mighty had fallen.

A waiter came over, took my order for vodka-rocks,

Bradley's another Bloody. At least it wasn't a banana daiquiri.

We sneak-eyed each other. I lit a cigarette. He looked annoyed, clearly not liking it. Hey, neither did my doctor. I put it out, found myself sighing again. Got on with it.

"So you're the feller gonna do my autobiography," I said.

"I'm the As-Told-To," he replied.

Okay.

"Know much about me?"

"A bit."

"Into ancient history, are you?"

"Well, my mother was a great fan of yours."

Walked right into that, didn't I?

"And," he went on, tapping a folder, "I've got a lot of research, which I haven't had a chance to thoroughly digest . . ."

"You gonna eat it?"

He ignored that, went on, "Though, of course, as always, it's the man I'm interested in."

I'll just bet, I thought.

The waiter brought the drinks.

"Shall we wait before ordering?" asked Bradley.

"No, let's order another round right now," I answered.

He smiled. At least he had a sense of humor.

I circled the glasses with my finger, high-signing the waiter, who didn't need all that much encouragement to get refills. At these prices, tips were fat.

Turning back to the business at hand, I asked, "How we gonna work this?"

"We'll talk; I'll ask questions. It's different every time."

"So you're not a virgin," I replied. "You've done this before."

He gave me a look part weary, part control.

"I've done practically everything before," he said.

Don't I guess.

"How long's it gonna take?"

"Till it's done. Depends on the degree of hostility and resistance."

I relaxed, smiled. Salty little bugger.

"Though the truth is," he went on, "we're under a little pressure. My boss wants us to wrap this up in six weeks and publish it right away."

"Why, I supposed to die or something?"

"Actually, I don't know why there's such a rush, but those're the orders."

Well, sooner the better, far as I was concerned.

Bradley looked around, checking out the clientele.

"How do you separate the dealers from the eaters?" he asked.

"Well, the power-lunchers tend toward salads and fruits," I replied—and couldn't help adding, "no offense."

"It starts," he said.

"I guess you did take offense," I said.

"You're fucking well told," he replied.

"Hey, live and let live's my motto," I said.

"I'm sure."

But before we could follow this up, at least enough to clear the air, which was what I meant—in order to get a working understanding, I like to think—the waiter brought us the reorder, and I decided instead let it drop.

"What'd you get from the research?" I asked.

"Well, I'm through the crime, Rita Rose is murdered; the general reaction. *Gone to Carnival* closes down; then it gets almost funny. They bring Dietrich in for questioning and then ask Lefcourt, the producer, if, considering his star's been murdered, and one of his costars is under suspicion, this doesn't spell finis to his movie. Know what he says?"

"I don't remember."

"He says, 'It don't spell finis, but it don't spell good either.' Wonderful?"

He laughed.

"Wonderful," I agreed.

"Anyway, the police let Dubie go for the time being, and that's when Pinnacle hires you."

"Yeah? How's that read?"

He pulled out the clip, read:

LOS ANGELES STAR EXPRESS
August 10, 1963

RAYFORD GOODMAN TO THE RESCUE!

**Famous "Hollywood Eye" Hired to Make
Independent Investigation**

Beverly Hills—In a move some considered supportive of Dubie Dietrich, and others interpret as belief in his guilt, Pinnacle Studio head R. Symington Lefcourt today commissioned dapper P.I.-about-town Rayford Goodman to "hurry up and get to the bottom, no matter where it is."

Goodman, long known as "Fixer to the Stars"—the man all Hollywood turns to when there's trouble, and who, somehow, always manages to get them out of it, quickly agreed to take the case "in the best interests of our community."

Asked whether this move signified a lack of confidence in Dietrich's innocence, Lefcourt replied, "I have every confidence. I have every confidence I'll be alive tomorrow too, but I still carry insurance."

"That Lefcourt was a pip," said Bradley.

"A little egotistical, I admit, but he did make good pictures."

"So, as I knew, you were the one he called. Did he think at the time you'd find somebody else was guilty? Or destroy the evidence? Or what?"

I didn't care for that tone.

"He thought I'd 'fix it,' " I said. "That's what they called me, right—'Fixer to the Stars'?"

"Hey, *I* didn't say it," he answered. "We're in this together."

A thought somehow didn't thrill me.

"Okay," I said, having to say something. "Go on."

"The next clip goes like this," he said, finding it.

LOS ANGELES STAR EXPRESS
August 12, 1963

DUBIE CHARGED IN ROSE MURDER!

Comedian Arrested at Studio

D.A. to Press Charges

Hollywood—Funster Dubie Dietrich, earlier questioned and released, has been arrested and charged with murder in the slaying of beauteous party girl Rita Rose!

Voicing outrage and strong support for his second banana in the spectacularly successful "On the Sea to" movies, Harry Light, America's number-one box-office star, had this to say: "I know Dubie Dietrich. He's a family man. He's a churchgoing man." Reminded of numerous arrests for disturbing the peace and drunken driving, Light amended, "He's a family man. He's a churchgoing man. He's a man with a drinking problem." But in the strongest terms, Light insisted, "I don't care about any of that, Dubie Dietrich is no murderer, and I stick by him!"

Studio bigwig R. Symington Lefcourt, asked whether he, too, "stuck by" Dietrich, replied, "Let justice take its course."

Bradley laid down the newsclip, reached for another. "Let's forget the papers," I said, stopping him. "You can do that later. Why don't you just talk to me? Go on, ask whatever's on your mind . . . I'll answer."

"Okay," he said, "after Dubie's arrest, was Lefcourt still interested in having you go forward? It doesn't seem like it, unless Harry Light had some influence . . ."

But before I could answer, there was a sudden burst of excited noise in the room, and when I turned around to see, it turned out the Old Legend himself had shown up.

"Speak of the devil: ladies and gentlemen, Harry Light," I mock-announced, as if it was necessary, Harry's face being just about the most famous in America. The country's most-loved top comic, superpatriot, buddy of bankers, and peer of presidents. "Also a family man, a churchgoing man," I added.

On his short but powerful body was a month's wages' worth of cashmere and silk. As always, he had a deep tan, both on his craggy face and in the stripes on his noggin between the wispy strands of hair he combed straight across out of his ear. With what looked like about fifty Chicklets where normal people had teeth, I don't think he could close his mouth. For sure, not many ever remember seeing Harry not smiling. Which might be less he couldn't close his lips than having two hundred million tended to bring out the genial in a person.

Bradley and I watched, together with everyone else in the room—star and gazer alike—as Harry paraded through the room to his table. Here and there he gave a wave, a wink, or, for a special few, an actual word. The royal procession certainly got your attention. As he spotted me, he smiled even more, and crossed right over. Looked like I was gonna be one of the special few. That'd show the bastard maître d'.

"Rayford Supersleuth Goodman." He beamed, giving me a big hug and laying down one of his trademark kisses on the lips.

As I reflexively pulled away, he added, "Don't worry, you can't get AIDS, I'm wearing a condom."

"Hi, ya, Harry—good to see you."

"Did you hear when they asked Phyllis Diller what size bra she wore, she said thirty-two long?"

More smiles. I introduced Bradley, my "autobiographer."

"Yeah, Mark Bradley," he replied. "Didn't you have something to do with my book?"

"I worked on it a little," said Mark, who it turned out had done some rewrite on Light's fourth autobiography, *Let There Be Light*—patriot, statesman, entertainer extraordinaire. But the truth was, he *was* all that. And cut through all the corny stuff, was a lovable guy in there, got to us all.

"Great to see you, Ray," he said, turning the big caps back on me again. "Been too long. By the way, you know the girls are eating here today too."

Wondrousness. My ex and his ever-loving Sally. Gonna be a long lunch. And where else but Hollywood would a man and his wife be eating in the same restaurant at different tables?

"Really like to see you two get together again. Marriage is the backbone of the nation," he said.

"And divorce is the funny bone," I replied.

"I mean it, Ray," he said. And did, too.

"The family that lays together . . ."

"Bubby," said Harry, "it's Hollywood. A little mistake . . ." Repeated over and over?

"Hey, you know me, master of the marital arts."

"Look," he said, "it's a dirty job, but somebody has to do it," punching my arm and winking, wanting to be sure I knew he was kidding. Then he added, "Call me," giving his patented left-hand salute and crossing to the next port of call.

We watched him work the room a bit, my already-dragging spirits sinking. I knew there wasn't a snowball's chance in Palm Springs we'd finish our business before Luana showed up.

Trying not to notice the cloud all but raining on our table, Bradley went on, "So it looks like Harry was really practically the only one who stuck by Dietrich, right?"

I nodded, back to the business at hand.

"Even I didn't think Dubie was innocent at first. But Harry never wavered, I'll say that for him. He believed in Dubie, and he deserves a lot of credit because he took a lot of heat for it."

"And where is Dietrich these days?"

"Last I heard, still at some pricey Rambler's Retreat, tranked to the tits."

"You'd think once he was off the hook, he'd've been all right," said Bradley. "After all, *he* knows he didn't do it."

"Well, he always was a little late for lunch. It was amazing he could work at all. Plus no secret he was into dopes of all nations. The whole thing was I guess just too much."

At which point the waiter showed up with another round.

"Whew," said Bradley, "you better understand I'm not going to be able to keep this up and get a lot of work done."

"I didn't order it."

"Compliments of—" began the waiter.

"Ah, Harry," I said.

"—*Mrs.* Goodman," continued the waiter, indicating

my svelte ex. She'd slipped in slyly—she was good at that—and now nodded at my bare teeth, which *she* might think was a smile, but I promise you was a snarl. Sally Light, too, raised her champagne glass. They were both so glad to see me.

No big surprise, after Harry'd paid his personal respects, the maître d' suddenly couldn't do enough.

"May I personally take your order, Mr. Goodman?" he slimed.

"Not now," I said, waving him away, taking a little shot: "I'm just so glad to be off my feet."

"But we better eat soon," said Bradley with a touch of difficulty. "If I'm supposed to function . . ."

"You're functioning," I mumbled back, being in no shape to toss the first stone.

Encouraged, he took another sip.

"Your wife doesn't appear to be bitter," he noted.

"No," I replied, "I got custody of bitter."

"What was the problem?" he asked.

"Nothing you'd understand," I said.

"Was that a sexual slur?" said Bradley, "slur" getting a little hard to say.

"Probably. But mostly getting a little personal, even for a biographer. At least on a first date."

"Last I heard, I was just supposed to ask you anything."

"Well, anything doesn't mean *any*thing. Use a little discretion. Especially things you don't know anything about."

"Meaning relationships?"

"Between nonconsenting adults."

"Hey, if the pope can counsel about marriage . . . Besides, I happen to have a job to do," he said, I thought a little touchy. At least the pope wasn't touchy.

Then, not exactly doing his case much good, he added, "And my sessual orientation doesn't enter into it."

Ah hah, can't hold his liquor.

"But your sessual orientation does enter into it. Sextial. Sex-u-al."

Can't hold *my* liquor.

"I really fail to see—"

"You fail to see, you fail to see. This is the story about a man—me."

"Right."

"In what you might call a tough profession."

"That I'm not equipped, because of my nature, to write about? You being a 'man'? And me not?"

I tried not to say it, but I couldn't not. "Real men don't eat men," I said.

"Jesus," he said. Not your snappiest comeback, either.

But I did feel a little sorry. I didn't want to *hurt* the guy. "Iss the chemistry," I tried to explain. "You know that. Got to be a *pair*, to collaborate. Truth, now, would you say we're a match made in heaven, the hitter and the homo?"

"No," said Bradley, getting angrily to his feet and raising his voice even more angrily. "I would say we're no pair at all. And you definitely don't need a collaborator," he said, getting *really* loud as he finished off, "to go fuck yourself!"

With which he glared back at the stares of the movers and shakers and started stiffly and unsteadily off. I grabbed his jacket tail.

"Sit down, Bradley," I said as he kept pumping his legs, trying to get some traction. "I was just testing."

But he wouldn't listen, just kept pumping and getting nowhere.

"Lemme go!" he said intensely, though a lot quieter, and a lot redder with embarrassment.

"Come on," I said, reeling him in, finally sitting him down. I wasn't feeling too proud either. "Come on."

He sat as he'd flopped, lopsided, glaring at me.

"You're okay," I said, trying to be nice.

"Yeah?" he replied, still pissed.

I had to give.

"I'm sorry," I said.

That wasn't going to be enough.

I *was* sorry, though.

"Tell you what," I said.

"Yeah?"

"I admit one thing."

"Admit one thing."

"You got ball," I said.

"Ball?" he asked.

"It's a start," I explained.

4

Mark Bradley

Killing Dick Penny wasn't going to be enough. When I got done cutting him into blue-pencil-size slabs, it would take a lot better detective than Rayford Goodman to put the pieces back together. How on earth could he have expected me to work with this Neanderthal? Or was it perhaps Dickie's idea of some cruel practical joke to make me more amenable to the next Bambi Blain?

What we did, by tacit mutual consent, was stop talking for about forty minutes, instead eating a leisurely lunch. This achieved three things: it calmed us down, gave us the strength to continue, and sobered us up.

By that time there wasn't a table to be had in the Polo Lounge, and the hypothetical-deal figures were up—in multiples of ten million—to the stratosphere. Evidently sipping mineral water—now that so many had discovered eschewing luncheon martinis somehow gave them an advantage over their opposite numbers—was as emboldening as the erstwhile beverage of choice.

The snatches I heard now seemed to deal in multiple-picture deals, turnarounds, cassettes, pay TV, and first refusal on their firstborns. I guess just plain making a picture passed with the appetizer.

Harry Light continued to hold court at a large table, with a contingent of ready laughers. He was telling a really funny Buddy Hackett story—but with attribution, I noted. The bigger they are . . .

Sally Light, a short, dark, energetic woman who seemed to have availed herself of every known plastic-surgical procedure and as a result now had that chic death's-head look indigenous to Beverly Hills, was seated off to a side with Luana Goodman, who was one of those oh-so-pale-ash-blond, classic center-parted types that are either very old money or very expensive hookers. (Somehow old money didn't get my vote.) The two were locked in an intimate huddle, swapping gossip that got significantly less sotto with the second bottle of Dom Perignon. Snippet:

"She says she plans to have a baby—can you believe it?—since she's only *forty*," said Sally.

"Give me a break, her *hysterectomy's* over forty," responded Luana.

Then they quieted down conspiratorially into the secret stuff—probably confidential shopping intelligence. Highly doubtful they were exchanging recipes.

It seemed about time to test whether the gift of speech had been restored to me.

"Okay, Goodman, let's have another go, shall we?" I said with a clarity that pleased me. Working out sure enhanced recuperative powers.

He nodded. "Okay, pally."

Pally?

Though it wasn't as if I didn't feel a stronger apology was still in order, I had to deal in reasonable expectations. Maybe we could settle for a wary civility.

"Why don't you just tell me about your professional life in general—before Rita Rose," I said tentatively. "By the way, you don't mind the tape recorder, do you?"

His recovery was evidently less complete than mine.

"Hell yes, I do. In my experience it gets in the way of those little off-the-records," he said.

"All right," I replied, "if you feel it'll bother you. Though it's for your protection too. That way an off-the-record is *on* the record."

"Why the fuck you *ask* me?"

"I can live without it," I said, and turned off the machine. "You were saying . . ." I suggested in what I hoped was an ingratiating manner. We were sure off to a wonderful start.

He made an effort.

"Well, in those days I more or less rode shotgun for the studios. I was the one called to arrange an abortion, go-between for someone in hock to the shylocks, pay off or scare off the gigolos and hookers, or bail out some star fruit nabbed in the Union Station men's room with dirt on his knees."

Oh, shit.

He saw me fight back my annoyance.

"Hey, guess we all have pictures we don't put in the family album," he added, to my surprise showing a suggestion of sensitivity. "And, 'course, that was before . . . you know, it was more acceptable."

I could see how "acceptable" it was.

"Mostly staying in the background, behind the scenes."

"But Rita Rose changed all that."

"Yeah, I became a sort of media darling—for a while."

The busboy removed our dishes, and the waiter hovered.

"No dessert for me," I said.

The waiter knew his customer. To Goodman, directly: "An after-dinner drink, sir?"

"Yeah," said Goodman, tentatively, as if the idea had never occurred. "I'll have a bowl of brandy."

He raised his eyes, I shook my head. The waiter knew that, in front.

"Remy," added Goodman.

"Okay, so when did you get on to Danny Pagani? Did you find out he did it first, or find out Dubie didn't?"

"I decided Dubie didn't. First, because that's what I wanted to find out. But second, because it was logical. Dietrich, those days, was so whacked-out, so weak from all the dope and booze, I couldn't believe had the strength to do it. Don't forget, we're talking multiple stab wounds—something like thirty-four wounds. Plus hacking and awful stuff the papers never really went into. Remember, too, Rita was a kid from the streets, pretty tough. And a dancer, in great shape. It just didn't figure, Dubie, who must have weighed about a hundred and ten, being able to handle her. Then there was the sex. She'd had sex—I can't believe Dubie was up to that either, in a manner of speaking."

"She could have had sex before. Actually, it appears there was more than one partner, anyway."

"Well, that's true."

"Besides, didn't Dubie confess?"

"Yeah, and he might even believed it at the time, being in withdrawal. Hell, he wasn't even sure what his name was. But there's another thing, the coroner's report said the wounds were inflicted by a left-handed person."

"That's almost too pat," I said. "My God: 'Inspector, aren't you overlooking the obvious, that the killer was left-handed?' "

"Look at all the baseball players; lots of people are left-handed."

"I don't follow baseball."

"Right, I forgot."

Temper.

"My roommate does, though. He follows *all* sports."

Unworthy.

"Anyway, the point is, you determined it wasn't Dubie."

"Other reasons too."

"Which were . . . ?"

It would have to wait, as the waiter came with what was the largest pony of cognac I'd ever seen. More like a *horse* of cognac.

Goodman didn't disappoint me by sipping.

"That'll peel your paint," he said, pointing at the nearly empty glass—a signal the waiter didn't miss.

At least I was enjoying the thought of Dickie's anguish when he got the bill.

But I had a hunch that was probably going to be a lot less than Goodman's as the ex-Mrs. and Sally Light, finished with lunch, decided to stop by and pay their disrespects.

We rose, he with notable reluctance.

"Well," said Goodman with a failed smile, "if it isn't the Maiden of Mitchelson."

"Hello, Rayford," she said sweetly. "How're tricks? And I use the term literally."

They didn't waste any effort on preliminaries.

"I still like honest tradespeople. You pay your money and you get—"

"Heaven knows what, these days. And who," she continued, "is this incredibly attractive young man?"

"Pardon me, where're my fucking manners," said Goodman ingenuously.

"Luana Goodman, Sally Light—Mark Bradley. He's my bookie."

We said hello.

"Aren't you the writer who helped out on my husband's book?" asked Sally.

"Yes, as a matter of fact. We met at your house," I said.

"I thought I recognized you."

"I'm flattered you remember."

"It's the lips, I never forget lips."

"Luana's good at that too," said Goodman.

"Speaking of lips, did you get my drink?" asked Luana.

"Yes, thank you," said Goodman. "It was a nice way to end four months of sobriety."

"That'll be the day. Well, just wanted to see how you're getting on and all."

"Don't worry your expensive little head I'm holding out any money," said Goodman. "He's paying."

Luana acknowledged the jab with a pleasant smile.

"Nice meeting you, Mark," she added.

I said it was nice too, and they left.

Goodman sat down, simultaneously turning for help, unnecessarily, as the waiter, no doubt experienced in the angst of casually met exes, was already bringing a fresh drink.

Goodman stared off in the direction of his dearly departing.

"Why do they do that?" he said.

"Ask the pope," I suggested. "No, sorry. I think 'touching base' is the applicable phrase—to keep in touch."

"For Christ sakes, why? We could be friends, we'd still be married. Hey, I'd settle for neutral. I'd settle for just not getting nagged into another coronary every time I see her. Why are they so cruel?"

"I'm not sure I'm best qualified to answer that."

That seemed to take his mind off himself.

"Didn't you ever . . . you know . . . were you always?"

"Oh, I did, but I wasn't up to cruelty, I quit when I was still into clumsy."

What did I know about the wiles of women?

Unless mothers counted, I thought, but decided the conversation—to say nothing of my life—had already veered too far.

5

Rayford Goodman

We fell into a sort of exhausted silence. What he was thinking, I had no idea. What I was thinking: I'd been some kind of asshole. I mean, not real bright to get bombed out of control, then go out of your way to insult your biographer. And that wasn't enough ammo for openers, go show yourself a pussy-whipped wimp when the old ex dropped by for a pin-pricking blood-check. All in all, no large chance I'd make the finals of the David Niven charm-off.

Maybe we ought to just scrub the day.

"I wonder if there's any big use our continuing this interview at this particular time," I ventured, being a big believer in the cut-your-losses school of foot-mouthing.

Wasn't going to be that easy.

"Well, this being one of the days of the week out of the six we have, doesn't leave us a lot of leeway," was his answer.

"True, true. Look," I said, feeling I might be getting a little sloppy, "I'm sorry about . . . everything."

"Well, I don't hold you responsible for *every*thing," he said. "Tiananmen Square, for example. But thanks."

We exchanged sincere looks. (Tiananmen Square?)

It was getting on toward two-forty-five, and the guys who actually had jobs were beginning to drift off. Harry Light and company still camped around the big table, Harry still holding forth. Looked like he could forth the rest of the afternoon. But otherwise, the room had definitely lightened. When Luana and Sally left, it got super definitely lighter.

Bradley and I exchanged more sincere looks. He figured, rightly, the next move was his.

So he continued, "Okay, we're back in 1963 . . ."

So I continued too. "Sixty-three. You, of course, didn't know Rita Rose—"

"Not unless she baby-sat around."

"She may have." I laughed. "There isn't much she missed in that short, lusty life. God, was that a beautiful woman. That was the sort of great thing about Hollywood, too, the old days. They had a license—the regular rules didn't apply. When you were that gorgeous, or that special, it was okay to drink, or take dope, or fuck friendly animals. You sort of had a right. Which of course was before the whole world discovered they could do the same things and get away with it even more. But those beautiful people, you have no idea, they had a shine to them. Like they were lit inside."

"But you were always there to settle the scandals—when they got out of hand."

"More or less. Some just . . . Time settled them. Like when Rita plain disappeared for four months, earlier in sixty-three. I couldn't find her. Nobody else, either. She just up and came back from wherever, and no explanation. Stars could do that sometimes."

I remembered too, and I wasn't at all sure I was willing to share *this*—the time I'd been sent out by the studio to get rid of Rita's latest leech, the spoiled-rotten son of one of Central America's longer-running dictators.

Fulgencio Fuentes, Jr., supremo numero deuce, wasn't used to taking orders. Hell, he wasn't used to taking suggestions, or advice, or, that matter, particularly good care of himself, being at the time in his early twenties with less than a year to live. Of course, if the Ferraris hadn't gotten him, the revolution would've.

I met this primo example of power corruption when, after Rita didn't show up for shooting the second day in a row on *South Sea Siren*, they sent me to check how bad the trouble was.

I'd driven up her old aerie on top Mulholland Drive. It really was like some sort of nest—a cantilever kind of Frank Lloyd Wright job. It was all airplany angles, glass and wood with the brightest white tiles, trimmed with even brighter Moroccan blue in case you otherwise'd miss noticing the place.

Nobody answered the chimes I rang for some time, so

I had to let myself in. Usually I would've gone around back to find an open window. Except around back in this case meant scaling a fall-away drop hundreds of feet at about a forty-five-degree angle. Pass on that.

Besides, tools of the trade, those days, I always carried a portable letter-inner. And the front-door lock wasn't all that sophisticated.

I knew I was in for the full treatment when the first thing I heard was the crack of a whip, followed by a sexy moan. I sort of expected a deep villain laugh, like in the movies, but instead got a kind of silly high-pitched cackle.

I headed toward the action.

It wasn't too big a surprise to find Rita, spread-eagled, nude, and handcuffed to the posts of her bed. And there was Fulgie, whip in hand—one hand that is, with the other he was entertaining himself—standing over her.

"Okay, drop it," I said, which I admit was a slightly confusing command.

No matter, he didn't drop either.

I knew I was going to have to get physical, and I didn't mind a bit. I don't exactly know why, but I hated this guy on sight. I mean, I know why, in general—he was a goddamn pervert. But then, so were half my clients. Only with him there was something so really rancid you definitely didn't feel any big contest between good and evil.

Physically, he was short, and you kind of expected fat. But actually he was more sloppy thin—skinny-legs-and-potbelly-style. Also prematurely jowly, with a strong hint there'd be plenty fat later on. He had a big banana Spanish nose, frizzy hair, and, for the moment, a diamond-inlaid gold tooth. Rounding out this adorable picture was a weak chin, washed-out eyes, and oily skin. As if even his pores couldn't stand him.

What the hell she wanted with him, God only knows. You'd have to be a masochist just to *date* the guy.

I may have done my share of hitting, but I can honestly say I didn't often take pleasure in it. This was different. Plus the situation was clear. What it called for was me to go punch away at his pouty little mouth. I did just that, with not too much holding back, tell you the truth. I didn't stop, either, for the threats, or when they changed to bribes, or got sloppy and whimpery. I just kept punching till more punching was just gonna get in the way of him going, which, after all, was step one.

So I stopped hitting, helped stanch the bleeding, recovered his bejeweled tooth off the floor, and escorted him out—though not before he'd promised Rita to keep in touch.

We both watched him go. Rita, for whatever crazy reason, sighing.

"Sorry about that," I said, a little strangely, since I wasn't the one got myself into this. To say nothing of not being all that sorry anyway.

I had a feeling she wasn't either. In fact, she laughed.

Still naked, still cuffed to the bed, still clearly there by choice, she laughed.

I'd run into more than a little degeneracy in my time, but it still made me nervous, Rita laughing. What made me even more nervous was Rita laughing naked.

Rita practically fully clothed had become a star, getting past the common prejudice of the day to climb the Hollywood heights, as they say. Naked, she was an even bigger star—did the world only know. She had the kind of breasts you couldn't buy in those days. You could, but they didn't move or move anybody else. Traveling southward was an actually concave midriff, which I've always been a total pushover for. And below that, slim hips that ran to a deep, perky keister she kept . . . moving . . . sort of. It was like an idling slow grind, in case there was any call to shift into action.

I looked into her eyes, which had incredible whites. I remember they were unbelievably bright—blue-white. So much for the windows to the soul. But what really loosened the loins were her irises, you just never saw anything like that. They were so light you'd swear actually gold, though they must really have been very light brown—in the way Elizabeth Taylor doesn't *really* have violet eyes. There was invitation, and challenge, and a cocky sureness that carried a lot of put-down with it. ("Who wants to belong to a club would have me for a member?")

I might, even then, have resisted the obvioso offer, wasn't for her skin.

Her skin, her skin, that skin . . .

Start with color; there'd never been a color near like that. It was almost like a backlit gold—gold should look that good. You kept thinking if you tried harder you'd be able to see through it. Then there was, besides this inner glow, a kind of gleaming fine layer of sweat—just in case you were into highlights. And that was just the looking part.

The touch?

Send in the poets.

There's nothing to compare it to. Marble, velvet? Don't begin. The only thing I can say, let me put it this way: how many *touches* you think you'll *remember* after twenty-odd years?

I did remember, too—though very faintly—it was my job to get her to the studio and back to work.

But if they'd waited two days, what possible harm could another hour . . . ?

It was one of the nicer perks of my profession.

"Rita," I said, "I'm going to get you out of those handcuffs . . . before you can say Jack Robinson."

But first, there were those lips to kiss, those breasts to lose yourself in, that crazy lap to quiet.

I don't recall she ever *did* say Jack Robinson.

"Beat me, fuck me," was more what she said, dialogue never being her strong point.

I did the best I could with the tools at hand.

"Where did *you* go?" I heard a voice asking. It was Bradley, pulling me back to the present, the Polo Lounge, the interview.

"Sixty-three was an incredible year—all around," I answered evasively, rearranging myself in my chair as I realized I had a bad-timing erection. Bad-timing, of course, given where and when, but not really all that unwelcome, also given how seldom it seemed to be happening lately.

"Rita Rose," he prompted.

"Her death was a loss to us all," I said, trying to muster a little dignity, the while tugging my shorts. Listening, David Niven?

"So I gather," he remarked, as I felt myself flush, either blushing or pre-strokal.

But as I'd thought back—hell, time-traveled—there was something nagging at me, something nibbling at the edge of my memory. Damn, what was it?

"Since we are in sixty-three, and that was the year of the murder—don't worry if I skip around—let's say, okay, you determined it wasn't Dubie, despite the fact he'd been indicted for the killing."

"Right. Once that was settled in my mind, that he didn't, I mean, it's kind of on-the-nose, but it was a process of elimination—"

"You couldn't eliminate everyone in Hollywood."

"Well, in spite of her reputation—pretty well deserved, I admit—she didn't know *every*one in Hollywood. And, of course, I didn't just open the phone book. I was able, through her driver, maid, security people at the studio, telephone records, to get a list who-all she saw in her final twelve, fifteen hours of life. *Then* it became a process of elimination."

"And that list?"

"Well, Dubie—"

"Right . . ."

"Her secretary/companion/dope connection, Karlin Williams—or Carkeys, as she was known. She went missing, by the way, probably OD'ed by now. Which doesn't mean couldn't have done it. She was with Rita most of that time, but not a likely suspect, since Rita was her meal ticket. Believe it or not, Lefcourt himself paid a late visit to her dressing room. Which, also by the way, was where she was the entire time, far as I ever knew. Though I quickly eliminated him. Even if she was blackmailing him or something, no matter what, Lefcourt wouldn't ever kill a star of his the middle of production. Then there was her mother, Mama Rose, herself pretty whoopee in those days—just as religious now—not a very likely suspect either. Plus there was the husband they always had they'd married before making it or knew any better. In this case one Harley Williams—Carkeys' brother, by the way—who I'd bought off two years before, when it was time to dump him. Before she got really big and he got really expensive. He'd dropped by too, supposedly for a spot of dope and a financial fix. So naturally he lingered in my mind more than a little, being

both a mean and vicious type, and with no more reason
to be bitter than the Beatles' original drummer.

"Wait, wait," said Mark, frantically making notes.
Then, finally, "Yeah, okay."

"Harry, who hadn't been shooting that day, but was
at the studio with Sally, who was overseeing redecorating
his dressing room. So she, naturally, was his alibi.
Though he was covered separately by his dresser, man
named Arthur Rollins. And Rollins by him. And that,
at first, seemed to be the list, till I later discovered
Danny Pagani slept over the studio the night before, busy
editing his latest porno flick."

"Ah hah, and you knew Rita'd made a porno with him
earlier on?"

"Not at the time. She'd been paying him off, it turned
out, both with her body and her bucks, ever since the
good times started to roll. Which gave *her* a motive, but
not, on the surface, him. Why I didn't get onto him right
away, even after I found out. Because, even if selling the
porno might have meant more bucks than holding it back
and using the threat of it for blackmail, he always had
time to go that route if and when the gravy train stopped
rolling entirely. But even then, why bother killing her?
I didn't find out the real motive till later."

"But that was what nailed him?"

"No, it was the dog that didn't bark. He hadn't
checked *out* of the studio. That's what made me suspicious. The reason he couldn't go past the security guard
was his arm was broken and his face all scratched and
bloody where Rose'd fought back. We found that out
after the cops nabbed him. We never did find out how
he got off the lot."

"But all in all, enough to get Dubie off the hook, send
Pagani away for life, and get you started on life-styles of
the rich and famous."

"More or less," I replied with mixed feelings, remembering the rush I'd got from winning at the time, but still
with that nagging feeling. Something was trying to remind me of something. What, what, what?

But then I had something more immediate to think
about as the Polo Lounge went total pin-dropping dead
silent—when Danny Pagani walked in.

6

Mark Bradley

I can honestly say I don't remember ever seeing anyone look more thoroughly abashed than Rayford Goodman when Danny Pagani entered the restaurant. It was also indicative of some kind of powerful behind-the-scenes goings-on that there hadn't been a word in the papers about any parole hearing, much less actual parole. One assumed an escapee didn't choose the Polo Lounge as a hideout.

Another amazing thing was that the crowd, except for the initial shock, settled down immediately and seemed quickly to accept Pagani as just another celebrity. It was almost as if by killing one of their own he had *become* one of their own. Or was it, perhaps, devoid of any immediate emotion—once notoriety had been recognized and dismissed—because it had all happened so long ago, and to another generation? But there were some contemporaries in the room—Harry Light, for one—who, to my amazement, seemed to proffer some sort of greeting to Pagani, though that could have been reflex, since he apparently greeted *every*one. And, of course, Rayford Goodman.

Goodman took another moment to traverse several degrees of shock, then recovered sufficiently to comment.

"In case you're the only one here doesn't know," he said, "this is the guy I sent up for life."

"I do know. Both the guy and the fact he was sentenced for life. Life being, I guess, a rather more elastic term than I thought."

"I seem to remember very clearly the words 'no possibility of parole,' " Goodman added.

To which I replied, "Well, maybe the judge had his fingers crossed. Or they didn't say 'Simon says.' "

I was recounting all this to my roommate, lover, friend, cohabiter, and fellow sexual outlaw, Brian Alexander, that evening at our sumptuous and trendy digs.

Brian was a few years younger, a few inches taller, and a few dollars lighter, with a little more hair and a little less wit—which all worked out just swell.

For the time being, he was working at the Beverly Center, selling costly African doodads to mostly Asian tourists. That was not his ambition. His ambition was to be an actor in the movies. Selling Bantu baubles was what he did at the moment, but not what he *did*. And I had every confidence he'd make it . . . given a little luck. Maybe a lot.

Just now, we were in the kitchen of our stylish condo, in preproduction of our dinner, a chore we regularly performed in tandem, since neither of us liked doing it, surrounded, as in all the rooms, by photographs of us in other tandems: skiing, tennising, swimming. Brian at first refused to assume any responsibility for meals, on the grounds he was nobody's little woman. I didn't put up with that on two grounds: cooking being a feminine occupation was stereotypical, and stereotypes tended to be counterproductive, given our bent, as it were, and two, I was just as cute as he was and didn't have to take that shit.

That's why it was two by two and side by side.

So there we were, together both, Cuisinarting away, zapping dem veggies, in preparation for the wok-ing to follow. Technology teamed with tradition.

"I don't get it," he said. "There was no question. Pagani was tried and convicted, right?"

"Right."

"And sentenced to life imprisonment."

"With no possibility of parole."

"So?"

"So, I don't know. I do know he walked in bold as brass with some big CBS guy, who, it developed, was in charge of long-form."

"My God, they've got vice-presidents for *that* too?"

"Long-form, as you well know, is two or more hours of mini-series, so the inference was clearly—"

"That they were going to do a picture on the same subject you're doing a book on."

"More or less. I mean, the bio is Ray Goodman—the whole Ray Goodman. But what's Goodman without the Rita Rose murder? And if they're tackling that for TV, with the cooperation of Danny Pagani . . ."

"Things are not good for our side. Gimme the garlic press."

"You know, that must have been why Penny's pressing to get the book out in six weeks—to beat TV and/or cash in on it."

"But how would he even know?"

"Oh, if anybody'd know, he'd know. Between 'fuck you too's, he does a lot of listening and a lot of finding out."

"And/or maybe it's more common knowledge than you think, which would tend to indicate you don't necessarily know it all."

"That's a possibility too. Though not a speculation that's particularly attractive coming from you, from whom I would expect greater loyalty, sharing, as you do, quarters, and other intimacies, with one of the greater investigative reporters of our times."

"My, Mr. Woodward, aren't we testy today," he replied. And then, after an almost awkward pause, while we both hastily retreated from further hindrance to our bonding, "These button mushrooms too?" he asked, snatching up a handful from a saucer and dangling them over the Cuisinart.

Those button mushrooms actually being the replacement buttons for my Armani blazer, I couldn't but conclude we were at least even.

"Thanks, why don't we just go with the porcinis?"

"Well, in that case, my culinary chores are completed," he said, turning his attention to a beaker of martinis, the sight of which gave new meaning to the words "conditioned aversion."

But Brian hadn't, more or less, matched drinks with the likes of Rayford Goodman most of the afternoon. He'd been working in the real world. I swallowed my bile—which I was also pretty good at—and, deciding amends ought to include some quality time, gave him my full attention.

Referring to his job at the mall vending Watusi chatchkes, I asked, "And how were things at the kraal today?" (Showing an interest.)

"Give me a break," he replied. "You're the one with the fascinating life—"

"Yeah, Bambi Blain—"

"—*now*," he amended. "Come on, so? Danny Pagani walked in, then what happened?"

Hell, I tried, and he was right, I *did* lead a more interesting life.

"Well, after Goodman turned fifteen shades of purple," I continued, "Pagani spotted him, and without a moment's hesitation, walked right over."

"Jesus!"

"Goodman tried to pull it together, and figured he better strike first, albeit weakly. The exact words were, 'Danny Pagani, as I live and breathe.' "

"To which Pagani responded?"

" 'For the time being.' "

"Whew, nasty, nasty."

"Everybody sort of hung around, waiting for things to deteriorate. Then, weirdly, Pagani turned civil and introduced the guy from CBS, Rick Deerfield, Deerhunter, Deargod, something—"

"Who then said . . . ? I'm getting all the George Burns lines."

"*Rick* allowed as how they were, indeed, going to do a docudrama based on the Rita Rose story, called, with network originality, *The Rita Rose Story*, in which they were going to expose quote 'the *true* story.' "

"Let me guess, Goodman discovered a new shade of purple?"

"Two—one when it turned out what Dearboy meant by the true story was, 'We're taking the position Mr. Pagani was framed . . .' "

"And the other, Gracie?"

"When Goodman said, 'How does that affect me?' and Pagani said, 'You mean after I sue you for five million dollars?' "

"Aiiii."

"Exactly. Goodman got really pissed. And he really sounded off. I mean, it wasn't just Pagani and Deermeat—that you'd expect. But he leveled the whole room, the way the assembled moguls accepted this creep. Exactly what was wrong with Hollywood, in his view. First they'd dumped Dubie, without a minute's thought to loyalty—a little dramatic license, since most of these guys weren't even in grade school, let alone running Hollywood, at the time. They crucify a good man, and one of their own, and then here comes a convicted stone maniac killer, and all they feel now is jealousy they didn't nab him first for a two-parter."

"He said all that?"

"More. He was just getting wound up. The payoff, as best I can recall, to the effect that 'the lot of you're a bunch of mealy-mouthed wimps who'd break bread with Adolf fucking Hitler if it meant some kind of rating during sweeps week, and I say fuck all of you!' "

"I'll bet *that* went over big."

"Well, it got their attention. And for a minute there I thought he was going to carry the day. Unfortunately, he lost a little credibility when he passed out and fell off the chair."

After dinner and our customary argument over who cleaned up ("You clean up." "*You* clean up.") and our customary compromise (*I* cleaned up), Francine Rizetti arrived, to revive fagging spirits.

"Francine, you heterosexual twat!" I exclaimed, embracing her.

"Mark," she responded, mocking me, "I don't appreciate your calling me a twat. I may *be* a twat—shit, I *am* a twat—and if I choose to call myself by that name why, fine. But no one else may call me a twat unless they too . . . and considering who I'm talking to, you may have the right, so forget I said anything."

Francine was sort of average in height, kind of pretty in a way. That is to say, not a total show-stopper, though she was a lot better than someone you'd describe as having "nice hair." For one thing, she had an impressive figure—what you might call on the buxom side with broadish hips, pronounced buns (though a tidy waist), noticeable, even formidable breasts, and *also* "nice hair." I'd once called her "butterball"—I *like* butter. The dialogue went:

"Butterball? Ripe, maybe, lush, perhaps, nubile, certainly—but butterball? That's on a par with 'pleasingly plump.' "

"You have nice skin. Alabaster."

"Didn't he M.C. *Omnibus?*"

That was the essence of Francie—above all, she couldn't resist a joke. Crazy about her. A credit to her gender. Real winner in a lot of ways.

Unfortunately, relationships with men weren't one of them—present company excluded, in the strictest sense of *relationships*, but you know what I mean. At thirty-six she was unmarried, unencumbered, and unenthusiastic. I guess that would be the most depressing aspect of her misfortune with men, that she no longer tried. I guess, too, maybe after you've done everyone from poets to linebackers and *nothing* works, you tend to get the idea it may not be for you. I don't mean to say she was promiscuous. She wasn't really, in terms of her times and longevity on the playing fields. It's just if you don't settle down in your mid-twenties, the numbers do tend to pile up.

At any rate, when her last great attempt—with a man considerably her junior—had crashed six months ago, with the cad in question departing (she thinks) for greener pastures, in reality (I think) for someone of the gay persuasion (which she says I say about *every*one), the result, either way, was a blow to her self-esteem and a blot on her escutcheon. And the outcome was to retire from the lists.

In a selfish way, this worked to my advantage, because Francine was my main researcher at Pendragon, and, being painfully undiverted, was able to devote her full energy and considerable ingenuity to my projects. To give you an idea:

"Since I knew you were going to meet Goodman today, I figured you'd concentrate on personality, a sense of the guy, et cetera, so I got going on history, most especially the Rita Rose case, or American

Beauty Rose, as it was sometimes called. But before I go into that . . ."

"Yes?" I asked eagerly.

"Give me a goddamned drink, assuming you don't have any serious drugs in the house."

"You know we don't do drugs," said Brian, just a touch blue-nosedly. "Grass not included," he added.

"Which we don't have any of at the moment," I said, pouring from the pitcher of martinis.

"And may not get again," added Brian, who really preferred I do *nothing* of the sort.

"A little self-righteous," said Francine, "given all that seed-spilling and stuff the Bible has *plenty* to say about."

I handed her the martini.

"Okay, okay, you guys. Whatta you know, Francie?"

"Well, for one thing," she said, downing the martini in one continuous swig, "have you any idea that Danny Pagani got out of the jug this morning?"

"Yes, I do—we actually met . . . over lunch, much to Goodman's chagrin."

"Wow! All right, here's the thing: there was a closed meeting of the parole board, which is unheard-of—and may actually violate the law, for all I know—at which Rita's *mother*, can you believe it, testified *for* letting Pagani out!"

"Why would she do that?"

"Why, indeed. That, me boy-o, is not a research question, it's an investigative-reporter question. I haven't the foggiest, but I'll tell you something else that'll knock your sex off: she was brought to the meeting, and apparently coached, or supported, anyway, by Harry Light! Who, himself, I understand, spoke at great length and very persuasively *for* paroling Pagani."

"Harry Light did that? He was practically prosecuting attorney, I thought."

"Not exactly. If you read back through the press, and the trial, and all that, Light was always *for* Dubie. But when you really examine it, that didn't necessarily mean he was *against* Pagani. Mostly, he was mum on the subject."

"Which could also explain why he sort of almost greeted

Pagani at the Polo Lounge today when he showed up. It registered at the time as a little strange . . ."

"But not as strange as testifying on his behalf at a closed parole-board hearing, which my sources seem to indicate also convened at his say-so, or at least after he exerted a lot of political influence."

"Curiouser and curiouser."

What did it mean? Here was a killer being let out of jail on the say-so of the victim's *mother*. At a hearing arranged for him by the friend of a man who was falsely accused of the same killing!

At which point the phone rang, and a soft, velvety, somewhat Caribbean voice informed me he would break every major bone in my body if I didn't stop writing the Ray Goodman book.

7

Rayford Goodman

No damn use complaining. There was no Hollywood. Gone, that's all. They still made movies. So did Toronto. Maybe more. So, naturally, the support system mostly plain disappeared.

Bad enough no more Ciro's, no Mocambo, Romanoff's, Brown Derby—I couldn't afford 'em anymore anyway. But Schwab's drugstore I really missed.

The thing about Schwab's was, there I had an *office*. I could get my messages taken, use the pay phones, get mail. And also eat relaxed. Not that the food was all that good, mind you. In fact, it sort of sucked. But you could dawdle over it. It was understood you might be there half the day, meet people, do business, or just plain sober up. Try dawdling over a bromo today somewhere.

I suppose, truth is, it may not have been as good as I remembered. Let's face it, the clientele was mostly a bunch of losers, with a couple major exceptions: Harry Light, Sidney Skolsky, Lana Turner (maybe), Steve McQueen. Hell, I don't know, all I can say is I miss it. Gone.

Which, basically, is why Bradley and I were taking a breakfast meeting instead at what they *called* Greenblatt's, where they had moved—the *real* Greenblatt's now being an improv-comedy-audition store of some sort.

We were sitting in the upstairs room—opposed to the stand-up counter on the first floor—which wasn't too heavy on ambience. But you didn't go to a delicatessen for ambience. The original was a no-kidding-around, smell-the-garlic *delicatessen*. Of course, that was so successful they had to expand and change it. The second

55

one tried much harder *for* ambience. And instead got to be a lot more caviar than carp.

In the old days you never got a tray from some precious cute slim guy who said, "Hi, I'm Jeffrey and I'll be serving you today," and you immediately wondered what. You got served—called "waited on" then—by a fat, sweaty, wisecracking, regular guy behind the counter. The way God intended.

I was working on an artery-damming mound of double-whipped-cream-cheese-and-lox-on-a-bagel, soda on the side. Bradley was nibbling a liverwurst and lettuce on white, glass of milk, and an occasional bite of pickle with a knife and fork. Really liked to get down and dirty.

"Goodman," said Bradley, wiping a bit of mayo from the corner of his mouth and getting down to business, "I received a threatening phone call last night, the gist of which was my continued good health directly depends on quitting the book."

"Yeah?"

"Now, I may not be the most beloved writer in America, but I can't think of anyone who would go to such extremes just to keep me from writing a book."

"Oh, I can," I said, halting his bepickled fork in midair. "For one, Dearborn, the CBS guy. Since their show's taking the tack Pagani was innocent, you can be damn sure they're not going to be including all the evidence. If *we* do, and worse, beat 'em to the punch, they're not going to look too good."

"You don't honestly think a network *executive*—"

My laugh seemed to convince him I did. "Or, more likely, Pagani himself could have had a hand in it. For the same reasons, plus another—they might cancel the project altogether. Which'd mean Pagani loses everything: being a celebrity, the money, the works. He's an obvioso suspect. And most times it does work out the logical guy is the perp."

"But I should tell you, this definitely wasn't Pagani's voice. It had an accent, sort of Caribbean—probably black."

"Well, he don't have to have done it himself. I think it'd be safe to say Pagani'd know more than one guy he could call on. But there're other black people involved in this too—Rita's ex-husband, Harley Williams, for one."

"What would his motive be?"

"He could have been the guy stole the jewels."

"Jewels? I didn't know anything about jewels."

"Yeah, Rita had what she called her 'walking-around gems,' worth at the time over a hundred grand. In the tumult, they sort of went missing. And, what with the gory murder and the whole big scandal, didn't rate a high priority. Plus, when the D.A., in his wisdom, decided to pin the rap on Dubie, who didn't have any jewels—or even all his marbles—that fact sort of got swept under the rug."

"But what'm I supposed to do?" said Bradley.

"You're supposed to tell me. And trust me to protect you. One of the things I'm good at." As I could see this didn't totally set him at ease, I added, "I don't think it's a serious threat."

I could just imagine how ape-shit he'd go if he had any idea I'd actually been shot at.

"I'm not exactly used to this kind of thing."

"Don't worry, we'll find out who's behind it."

"But how soon?"

"Soon enough, I promise. Think of it as added color."

But since his added color seemed to be dead white, I tacked on, "Take my word, you're not in big danger. You ever hear anybody got killed over a book?"

He considered this, nudging his pickle around the plate. I said, "Listen, I'm sorry, but we're going to have to keep it moving. I don't have a lot of time before my next appointment."

"What next appointment?"

"Well, it just came up. An assignment. I *do* work, you know." Which is generally true, although not especially lately. Which is also why I'd welcomed the call earlier from a Mr. Cedric Adderley, owner of BHBM—Beverly Hills British Motors—to meet and discuss a matter "causing some distress and financial loss." That was the usual and/or combination for people to call private eyes. He'd be here in another few minutes.

"I know you work, it's just, time is so limited for us."

"Hey, then we better make the most of it, right?"

"Okay," he said, realizing no point spending whatever time was left arguing. He opened his notebook, took a fast read, and got back down to business.

"You more or less eliminated Dubie, Lefcourt, whoever, right? What convinced you it was Pagani?"

"Well, a lot of it was circumstantial, of course—though there were hairs and semen samples. Hard evidence, in a manner of speaking. A big breakthrough was when I found out about the porno Rita'd made for him years before. There'd been rumors about a porno, but there always were about sexy new movie stars. This time happened to be true. As luck would have it, or maybe not, considering how it came out, Pagani didn't have enough money to distribute it at the time. And what with other business—meaning mostly dope dealing—he'd forgotten all about the picture till she hit it big.

"But when she did, the wheels started turning. This was the big score for him, the chance he'd been waiting for all his life. And he wasn't hardly the kind to pass it up. So, then came the blackmail, heavy and regular. I'll give him credit, he had a knack for knowing just how much the traffic would bear and how often to go for it. We established that through various regular withdrawals Rita'd made, plus appointment books, and like that. Only all of a sudden, in spite of being cool so long, and nipping just little bites, came a time Pagani desperately needed some really serious money."

"I heard something about that. Didn't he blow a coke deal or some such? And lost both the money and the coke?"

"Right. Which he had to make good or be dead, since what we're talking about is mob guys he was in to. No question he was in big trouble. In fact, I got the feeling he was almost glad to go to jail—for a while, anyway—rather than face the music when he couldn't pay back. But that was later. The point was, at the time he was desperate. He *had* to have big bucks. Rita was the only possible source, and the way I see it, she just wasn't going for it—other than maybe the usual blackmail. For sure not the whole ball of wax. So he pressed harder. But she'd had it with him, constantly bleeding her.

"He got physical. What else? She fought back, you can

be damn sure. Remember, she was very strong, very much in shape. And from a background where girls didn't just cave, they fought—with fists and nails and bottles and whatever was handy."

"So she hit back," said Bradley, picking up the thread. "And apparently pretty well, since when the cops picked him up next day he was all swollen, black eye, scratches, and with a broken arm—"

"His *right* arm, which probably got broken early on. So when the pressure built, and he got crazier and crazier, and used more and more pressure, he had to do it with his left."

"All well and good. Let's say he was pressuring her, fine. Let's say she fought back. And it got out of hand. And he killed her. I understand all that. What I don't understand is why then tack on all the gory stuff?"

At which point Slim Jim Jeffrey dashed by, and picked up the tray in full flit. I called after him/her/it to get me some coffee and cheesecake as he flew off, with that incredible energy those guys always seem to have.

"Was Pagani an out-and-out psychopath, or what?" continued Bradley.

"He may be a psychopath, I don't know, but that wasn't why the cutting and slicing. That was trying to cover."

"He wanted it to look like a psychopath did it?"

"He wanted it to look like Dubie Dietrich did it. Let me clue you to something. It was an open secret less than a year before, Dubie, who'd been bothered a long time by a yapping French poodle next door, one day was on a terrible dope-and-booze binge when the pooch started up and wouldn't quit.

"Given his condition, it must have seemed to Dubie like it was barking back of his eyes. Anyway, during what the doctors and the police decided by and by to call a blackout—after I'd done some behind-the-scenes influence-peddling and palm-crossing—he did some god-awful things to that dog before, during, and *after* he killed it."

"Yich," said Bradley.

And here zipped Jeffrey with the cake and coffee.

"Yich, yich," agreed I, responding to Bradley. But Jeffrey seemed to think I meant him, or the cake, or who the hell knew?

"Ssomething ssteaming ssomeone?" he asked sibilantly. I guess he liked to live dangerously.

"Not a thing," I said with my best liberal smile. "This was a personal yich, not a food yich."

He gave me a fish eye and left. I should have, but couldn't help asking Bradley, "What is it with the S's with those guys? What does sexual preference have to do with saying 'ssseriously sssweetheart'?"

"I thought we weren't going to do this," said Bradley.

"Just trying to understand."

"Don't," he warned.

I held up a hand in surrender. He took a deep breath, continued: "Back to business"—with an almost inaudible S.

"Shoot."

"Didn't you say Pagani hadn't checked out of the studio?"

"Right, he didn't. But he had to have gotten out that night—the police searched every inch. My theory is he left in the trunk of someone's car—"

"Your *theory*—it wasn't proved?"

"Nope. And whose car, I never found out either. But it was obvious he wouldn't want the studio guard at the gate seeing him in that beat-up condition and later being able to testify after they found Rita's body. So either with someone's help, or maybe just plain hiding himself, he must have got out in a trunk."

"But you didn't really know," said Bradley.

"I didn't have to know."

"Well, look, no offense, but it seems to me with the jewelry missing, with Carkeys missing, with the likelihood, or possibility anyway, some sort of accessory was involved getting Pagani out of the studio, also never identified, there were an awful lot of loose ends."

"What do you mean, loose ends?"

"Questions that didn't get answered."

"What difference did it make? Once you got the guy, that answered the *big* question. The rest was details."

"True . . ." he said, sounding less than convinced.

"Only?" I prompted.

He didn't seem to want to answer.

"Only what?" I repeated.

There was a long silence. I remember I had time to notice a bit of pickle wedged between two of his otherwise perfect teeth, as I started to get a little bit annoyed.

"I'm getting a funny feeling."

"What do you mean, funny feeling?"

"Just that—a funny feeling."

"Well," said I, maybe a touch what they call these days insensitive, "I guess judged by normal standards, you should be used to funny feelings."

He looked at me, but could tell I didn't mean anything. He let it pass.

"*S*something's bothering me," he said.

"See, you did it, too—'*s*something.' "

Looking back, I guess he misunderstood my natural curiosity. The way I knew was, he picked up his glass of milk and poured it over my head.

There was such a thing as *too* much balls.

As I briefly considered decking him, he rose indignantly and started out. And before I could stop him, and maybe apologize—I guess he *was* somehow insulted—the *other* guy I'd come here to meet, Cedric Adderley, arrived and asked if I was by any chance Rayford Goodman.

With milk dripping from my eyebrows, I allowed as how I was.

Cedric Adderley was about six-foot-one, weighed about a hundred and sixty—or twelve stones and a ha'penny. He was all angles and bones, tweedy to the max, with something less than a shock—maybe a surprise?— of fine unruly hair falling into one eye. He had that look of a third cousin to someone rich the English liked in their car salesmen.

After I'd got him settled down, body-blocked the waiter into standing still long enough to take an order for tea . . .

". . . and one of those peculiar American breadstuffs you call English muffins . . . ," I popped into the gents, wiped my face, and ran a comb through my milk-enhanced hair. Hey, some people shampoo in it. Satisfied I looked halfway respectable, I hurried back.

"I suppose there's a perfectly reasonable explanation . . ." he said, referring to my damp jacket.

"Not really," I offered.

"Reticence—a fine quality. Discretion must be very important in your work."

I accepted that. "Now, then, Mr. Adderley, you have a problem?"

"You do like to plunge."

"Your money."

"Quite. Well, as I explained, I own BHBM—"

"Beverly Hills British Motors. Mostly Rolls-Royce, right?"

"Really *only* Rolls-Royce—specialization makes for excellence, what?"

"Didn't say anything. So you own BHBM—"

"—from whence someone's been stealing parts. Which on a Rolls can be quite substantial, don't you know. Which on a Rolls on which I'm not getting the *job* can be *pain*fully substantial."

"You got somebody's not only stealing parts, stealing the jobs too?"

"Well, yes, the one would have to go with the other, don't you see? One can't bring his broken motor car with the replacement parts in hand and ask me to repair it. They come in, they need work, then I don't seem to see them again. Plus it eventuates I'm missing the very parts they require."

"So, you've got an inside job and an outside job depriving you of an inside job."

"Exactly."

"And you'd like me to find out who the guy is stealing the parts and who else is doing the jobs—and get rid of them."

"Well, getting rid of them would almost certainly follow of its own inevitable accord."

"You've considered normal security measures, inspecting employees' cars as they leave, and so forth?"

"Yes, whoever's doing it is doing it after hours."

"And you have an alarm system."

"And a dog, and all the usual things."

"Okay."

"But the 'usual things'—commercial security, a watchdog, seemingly secure storage, et cetera—are all subject to the scrutiny and analysis of whoever's doing this, don't you see. So, I do believe what's required is someone sort of undercover."

"I see."

"I'd like you to come work for me, as a mechanic."

"No. Not the way. First place, I'm not equipped, I don't know enough about it—"

"Or you could work in the office—"

"No, no—wrong approach."

"Quite. As you say. And the right approach is . . . ?"

Jeffrey brought the tea.

"Since this stuff can only work if your customers are in cahoots—"

"Cahoots?" he asked, sipping the tea.

"Collusion."

"Ah. 'Ah' being in reference to your word, not the tea, which is quite indefensibly dreadful, by the way."

"Sorry. As I was saying, since I'm not equipped to work from inside, maybe I can bring it off working from outside."

He raised a blond eyebrow.

"If I was to become a customer. Say I got a car with a problem, and someone approached me—"

"Yes, but you must realize I have lots of customers, and not everyone is approached."

"But suppose I was a customer looked like he'd like to save a few bucks, definitely insisted on saving a few bucks—"

"It still seems to me like a roulette; you mightn't be approached."

"Well, maybe not right off. But the only way to lick this I can see, is establish myself. If necessary, come in more than once. Might have to work it over a period of a few weeks, even."

"Yes, well, that would be quite expensive, wouldn't it?"

"Could be, could be not. I wouldn't charge you my regular daily rate, since I wouldn't be working on it full-time. Give me, say, fifty dollars a day on retainer. Let me bring a car around, get known, talk to folks. See what develops. Then I'll come up with a plan."

"Seems rather vague."

"Right, it is. I don't know exactly how I'll work it, but I will. Fixing problems is my business. Unless you got a better idea?"

"Very well," he said. "We'll have a go."

"One thing else . . ."

He looked up from his barely touched English muffin.

". . . you'll have to lend me a car."

"Yes, I can see that. Well, I've a Silver Cloud in the lot out back here I just picked up on consignment for an out-of-town customer—"

"Perfect. And it needs some work?"

"Well, it may not. Let's go outside and see if I can't 'find' something wrong with it."

"Heavens, you can't mean you'd deliberately damage a car?"

"Not irrevocably."

"One thing else. I got a beat-u . . . classic Cadillac, which I'll have to swap you for your car. Why don't you, to make the whole thing more believable, take it with you and give it one of your fine British paint jobs? You know, as a cover."

"But it's not even British."

"You could say you're doing it as a favor."

"For whom?"

"For me'm, actually. Make something up."

"I don't see what it has to do with this case."

"Well, what it does, it gets me to *take* the case. You didn't think I was going to do it for fifty dollars a day?"

"All right. What color is it?"

"It's red, but what I'd like you to paint it is anthracite gray."

"Anthracite gray."

"Yeah, that seems like this year's color."

Which is how I came to turn the keys of my classic Caddy over to Mr. Adderley. And how come, after he'd done a bit of negative doctoring, I left Greenblatt's driving a beautiful black-and-sand Rolls-Royce Silver Cloud II—with a whole lot of smoke coming out its expensive tailpipe.

8

Mark Bradley

Not surprisingly, Dick Penny was on the phone as I burst into his office.

". . . I read the galleys, and the galleys are shit," opined Richard. ". . . well, fuck you too," he characteristically responded, slamming down the phone, as was also his custom.

Again following form, apparently totally unaffected by the exchange of hostilities, he rearranged his snarling features in what, for him, passed as a smile.

"So, big guy, how's it going?" he asked.

"Little guy, it's going, that's how it's going—you got me doing it. I'm quitting."

"No, you're not," he said confidently.

"I am. I told you I wouldn't get along with that geek, and I don't. He's insulted me over and over again, absolutely cannot let go of his obsession with homosexuality. He's a real primitive throwback, and I hate his guts."

"Great, that'll give you a good slant for the book."

"There is not going to *be* a book. Correction, there is not going to be a book from *me*, because I absolutely, positively won't spend another minute with that creep."

"Sure you will, it's your job. And your ability to put personal feelings aside to perform that job, which you do so splendidly and professionally, is one of the most admirable qualities about you."

"Oh, don't give me that shit."

"I have other kinds of shit, if you prefer," said Dickie amiably.

"I don't want any kind of shit, I just want off."

Penny rose, circled around his desk, and headed over. I had the dreadful feeling he was going to embrace me and breathe cigar breath into my face, but he had the good grace to stop short of that.

"Bradley, you're a pro. You're a pro and you're gay. You're a gay pro. If you have to give up one or the other, don't give up the pro." With which he patted my arm, turned back to his desk, picked up the phone, and screamed at the operator, "Get me farmelok." Or that's what it sounded like, anyway.

I hoped I never stayed with him long enough to get to understand him, even in English.

But what the hell, it didn't matter if he agreed with me or not, if he accepted my resignation or not. He'd get the message when there were no pages and no Bradley.

I left the room and headed for my office to clear it out. I knew well enough he wouldn't allow me to stay and turn down an assignment like this, so I wouldn't stay, that's all. And if he didn't want to publish my real book, then to hell with that too.

When you worked for someone like Richard Penny, the last thing you wanted to face was the prospect of *continuing* to work for him over the years. Accordingly, it was the only job I'd ever had where I absolutely did nothing to personalize the office I was assigned. There was not one photograph, not a doodad, not a toy, not a *cup*, of my own. In fact, quite the contrary, I kept a packed shoulder bag with a change of shirt, underwear, socks, and tape recorder, plus an updated passport, to allow myself the impression I was so free I might just flee the country on impulse at any given moment. Or if not on impulse, on, say, a sudden irresistible assignment—*Time* magazine had discovered only I could cover an insurrection in Outer Mongolia, with that incredible combination of moxie and journalistic excellence that so informed my days.

That might be your basic pipe dream. But what *was* reality—I didn't have to take Ray Goodman's shit by way of Richard Penny's shit.

So I figured I'd just pack up and leave. Only there was nothing, really, to pack up. Yeah, I could take yet another ream of paper and yet more office supplies, but I'd already swiped enough to supply the most prolific writer the rest of his life. So what was left, I guess, was to just leave.

I sat down. I wanted to remember the *joy* of leaving, I didn't want to just rush through it. Leaving shouldn't be that casual.

Francine popped her head into my office.

"Oh, you here?"

"No, it's sort of an afterimage, like those infrared photo impressions of folks departed the English keep trying to prove ghosts exist with."

"I made a simple friendly remark. I see no call for scathing sarcasm, especially when you have to go that far for it. Do I have your leave to enter, my liege?"

I gestured to come in.

She closed the door, sat down in the chair facing my desk, pulled out a bottle and straw, and starting laying out lines of cocaine.

"Couldn't you at least do that in your own office?" I asked.

"First place they'd look," she replied logically.

"You really shouldn't, you know."

"Oh, Christ," she said between snorts. "Nothing more righteous than a reformed sinner."

"Reformed for a reason, Francine. Nobody quits any dissipation on moral grounds. You quit when it doesn't work. And coke doesn't work most of all. It's a gyp. It gives you an edge, to begin with, and then you spend all your time and diminishing energy trying to catch up. Him that borroweth muth repayeth."

"Thank you, Reverend Davidson."

"All right, but I warn you, you'll wake up in hell—"

"—with all the rest of the interesting people."

"And the *second* reason: it's not chic anymore. Nobody does drugs who's anybody. It's become middle-class, darling. I mean, it's even getting gauche to go to Betty Ford."

"That bitch—couldn't hold her drugs, so everybody else had to stop partying? Please!"

"I'm only offering a little friendly advice, with the best of intentions, having nothing to do with morality, only with what actually works."

"Okay, sermon noted, collection to follow, *now* can we get to why I came in here?"

"Certainly, Francie, my door is always open to you."

"Your *mouth* is always open." With which she addressed a folder she'd put on my desk, and consulted some notes.

"According to the trade papers, *Variety* and *Hollywood Reporter*, as well as the L.A. *Times, Herald Examiner*, and so forth, there were persistent rumors that Symington Lefcourt was in big trouble with *Gone to Carnival* before the Rita Rose murder and Dubie Dietrich getting arrested for it, and the whole megillah. Further, according to 'heard around town' and 'a little birdie told me,' he apparently started the picture with only about two-thirds of the financing, and continued published innuendos suggest he wasn't about to come up with the final third!"

"Whew," said I astutely.

"So, when you think of it, Rita Rose getting offed and Dubie getting busted, well, either event would have triggered an insurance payoff to the producer of the picture—giving Lefcourt a hell of a motive."

"If he'd just collected the insurance and not gone on to make the picture."

"Which, of course, he should have." She laid a clipping before me, with the headline "GONE TO CARNIVAL GOES TO TOILET."

"But with all the publicity when Dubie got off . . ." She put another clipping in front of me.

**NOTED DETECTIVE RAYFORD
GOODMAN SOLVES CRIME!**

DUBIE DIETRICH FREED!

"Never had a doubt," says noted producer R. Symington Lefcourt.

". . . and the subsequent ease in raising the final financing, Lefcourt couldn't resist the opportunity to exploit"— and here she affected the hoarse, street-kid-pedantic voice of Lefcourt—" 'dis great tragedy which has so afflicted all our hearts—in honor of which production will henceforth go forward on *Gone to Carnival . . .* ' "

"Which was about the biggest mistake he ever made," I continued, "inasmuch as at least seven people went to see the picture when what's-her-name replaced Rita Rose."

"A total flop, which was all poor Dubie needed to suffer 'nervous exhaustion'—on what appears to be a permanent basis."

"Nervous exhaustion also and mostly brought about by putting various hazardous uncontrollable substances in his stomach and his nose and his *ears*."

"Will you, for Christ's sake? Anyway, the thing you're overlooking, by concentrating on your fucking crusade . . ." And here, with a defiant look at me, she paused, first laying out two more lines of coke. Then, sniffing them, with exaggerated aaahhhs informing me of her pleasure, she at long last continued. "What you're overlooking is that Lefcourt deciding to make the picture didn't take away from the fact that *originally* having an insurance-proof reason *not* to make it seemed his only way out of financial disaster."

I thought about this for a moment. Made sense. And made Lefcourt a good suspect, since he was definitely on the lot that night, was known to have visited Rita, and was only ruled out on the assumption he wouldn't hurt the chance to go forward with the picture. It was never considered he might want to halt it for the insurance. There was just one thing wrong with Lefcourt being a suspect: who needed one when Pagani had already been nailed and proved guilty? I reminded her of this fact.

"What's Lefcourt's problems got to do with anything, given Pagani?"

"Given Pagani," she agreed, just the trace of a Mona Lisa smile at the corners of her lips. (Just the trace of powder on her nostrils, for that matter.)

"All quite interesting, I'm sure," I said. "And for someone who might be investigating the case, say, writing a book about its principal protagonist, *very* interesting. But inasmuch as I've only this very day, not ten minutes ago, resigned from the entire enterprise, it don't concern me, dolling."

I could see she was stunned. I could see the thought of losing me was devastating. I could tell, because she said:

"Does that mean I get to move into your office?"

I carried my pitiful, though somewhat-larger-than-planned, cardboard box of belongings to the car. I *had* decided to take some additional stationery, envelopes—the big kind, especially—folders, tabs for folders, stapler, staple-remover, Scotch tape, Scotch-tape dispenser, and two dozen cone-shaped paper cups I couldn't possibly ever use. Revenge is a crooked path.

This I put into the trunk of my upscale BMW, opened the door to the driver's seat, hurried in, and for the thousandth time lost the race to punch in the numbers aborting the alarm. Digital dexterity is not my forte.

I turned on the ignition, slipped the car in gear, and eased on out of the parking lot, not without, I might add, a poignant backward glance at what had been, for three and a half years, my home away from home. I guess, be it ever so shitty, there *is* no place like home.

Then, with a sigh of determination, I headed toward the first half-day of the rest of my life.

I parked in my designated spot underground at my upscale condo, noted Brian's trendy classic MG at rest alongside, indicating he was home, opened the trunk, took out my loot, and walked to the elevator that would take me from my upscale parking lot to my upscale actual condo.

My hands full with the carton of Pendragon swag, I turned sideways and punched the doorbell with an elbow.

Nothing happened. I knew Brian was home. Since he had to work Saturdays, he got Thursdays—and besides, his car was home, so he had to be too. I leaned on the buzzer again.

I could hear it sounding inside. Well, maybe he was in the john. I started to put the carton down, to fish for my keys, but as I leaned over, my hip pushed against the door, and for the first time I noticed it wasn't on the latch.

I could feel my blood run cold. I don't know why—it could have been carelessness, it wasn't the biggest breach of security ever committed, but somehow . . .

There was a trail of blood leading from the hallway, past the den-office, and to the bedroom, whither I forced my leaden legs to proceed and where I found him—my most horrid nightmare manifest—tossed in a corner, like a pile of old rags, his grotesquely swollen head wedged under the TV stand.

For what I guess was only a second, but seemed an eternity, I thought I really would be unable to move to his side. And maybe I wouldn't have been able, only he moaned, immediately upgrading it to my *next*-to-most-horrid nightmare.

"Brian, Jesus!" I muttered, crossing quickly and kneeling beside him. "Wait, wait, first let me call an ambulance."

I dashed into my den-office and, hi-tech upscaler that I was, had only to punch a single digit into my memory phone to activate my prerecorded order for the paramedics. When they'd gotten the basics—address, apartment, et cetera—I got on live and answered their questions about his condition. Then I dashed back into the bedroom and cradled him in my arms.

"The paramedics are on their way, you'll be okay, it's okay."

"Could of fooled me," said Brian through lips so swollen it was amazing he could talk at all.

"Don't try to talk," I said.

"Talk okay—laughing hurts."

"What'd they take? I told you never resist, *stuff* isn't worth getting beaten up about."

"No robbery . . . about the book . . ."

"Oh, God, they went after you to get to me?"

"Don't think they knew wasn't you. Queers look alike."

"Who was it?"

"I didn't get the names."

"I mean, could you describe them?"

"I'd describe them as vicious."

"Well, I'm glad to see they didn't knock the sense of humor out of you. Tall, short, thin, fat, white, black?"

"Average. Funny masks, hats, gloves—like a bad Artists and Models Ball."

"You're not going to be able to tell the police a thing?"

"They don't care for literature. Exact quote, 'Just a sample if you don't stop writing the book.' "

"Jesus, Brian, I'm so sorry."

"Me too," he said, wincing with pain, his face hugely swollen and discolored. "Just when my skin was clearing up," he concluded.

I knew he'd concluded because he passed out in my arms.

9

Rayford Goodman

I was just backing the Rolls carefully out the garage when the florist truck pulled up. If he wasn't blocking my way, I wouldn't even have stopped. Cinch he wasn't bringing *me* anything.

How wrong you can be.

After giving the driver a piece of my mind, getting in the way of us folks with serious business, he gave *me* a tasteful floral arrangement would add distinction and grace to the finest home.

After all that yelling, I was so embarrassed I forgot to tip the guy. Which I guess was all right; somehow he didn't seem to expect it from me.

I took the flowers into the garage, put them down on top of a garbage can, and found two cards. The first one said, "Water me, I'm thirsty!" The second read, "You don't know any better, but I do. Sorry, Mark."

I left the bouquet in the garage, artistically arranged on top of a garbage can, got back in the Rolls, and started down the hill.

For sure I didn't expect to work with the kid anymore. We just plain lived in two separate worlds. At least. Maybe four.

But the funniest thing—here I'd lived all these years, and you know, it was first time anybody'd ever sent me flowers.

You know what else? It felt kinda nice. In a manly, at-one-with-nature sort of way, of course. Hey, flowers aren't by themselves necessarily feminine. I mean, I'd say *plants* would be more masculine, somehow—cactus, even better—but really, nothing *wrong* with flowers.

I hit Sunset Boulevard at Sunset Plaza, hung a left, then another quick left into the Union 76 station, and

over to the full-service island. I knew they were trying
to eliminate service altogether by charging another thirty
cents a gallon just to pump it for you, but I felt it was a
move had to be resisted. Even when they extorted another three-bucks-plus every time you loaded up. Lord
knows they weren't im*proving* service anywhere. Every
improvement was something improved it for the im*prov-
ers* by saving on labor. But you had to fight a rearguard
action, even if it cost you—or the guy whose expense
account you were on.

The Armenian hose jockey came over—what was this
thing for gas the Armenians seemed to have?—smiled
his gold, lead, and silver smile, which, also given the
green of his unbrushed teeth, was a little like Moroccan
jewelry. But I'll say this for the extra thirty cents a gallon, they didn't rush you by giving good service.

"What we got here?" he asked, circling the Rolls.
"You trade in the Caddy?"

"No, I'm just sort of . . . driving this for a while."

"What happened to the Caddy?"

"It's being repainted. The Rolls is a loaner."

I thought that was funny, but the guy was taking it
serious. I could tell from his next remark.

"Good thing, 'cause this piece of shit fartin' smoke."

Who asked him? I told him to fill it up with super—I
finally stopped saying ethyl—and let me worry about the
smoke.

"Better put in the additive," he said, "before that big
old piece shit quit altogether."

What the hell did Armenians know about fine cars?
Starving, maybe, that they were famous for.

I told him okay on the additive and to check the body
fluids whilst I crossed over to the Ben Franks fast-
foodery next door.

Ben Franks'd gone through a lot of changes down the
years. Not so much physically—I think it'd been redone
once. Though it was hard to remember from what to
what. A counter's a counter and a booth's a booth. More
its clientele. I remember a time when it was just working
folks, a smattering of show-business hopefuls at breakfast, then hippies, then another, different bunch of

straights, then punkers. It always seemed to be "in" with one crowd or another. I guessed it was a moneymaker.

I headed back toward the pay phones.

It was sort of an impulse, really. Somebody sent you flowers, you were supposed to thank them.

They told me at the office Bradley either wasn't in yet or wasn't ever coming in, they weren't sure.

I called him at home. Got him. He said he'd been trying to reach me. I said thanks for the flowers. He said piss on the flowers—something much more important had happened and how fast could we get together?

So much for sentiment.

I said I was less than ten minutes away, but I had some business, could I pick him up and he could drive with me while I took care of it? He said he could, he would, and good-bye.

I left Ben Franks—without finding out what and who was "in" at the moment, though it did look like an awful lot of hillbillies. I crossed back to the Union 76, paid my ransom for Full Service, and got back in the double-R. The hell with the Armenian, it felt damn good to sit on that expensive leather and look at that wonderful hand-polished cherrywood dashboard and catch the stares of the riffraff wondering: Who's that?

In fact, I gave a big smile to a busload of tourists staring at me, and nodded knowingly, as if to say, "Right, I'm *him*!" Let them go crazy trying to figure out who the hell "him" was.

You are what you drive, they say, and *I* felt like all kinds of a winner sitting in that Rolls.

Right up to the moment the cop pulled me over and gave me a ticket for exhaust pollution.

Bradley was waiting outside his condo at King's Road and Willoughby, clearly impatient, as I pulled up. He looked right past me, expecting the Caddy.

"Bradley!" I called. I almost called "Hey, sailor," but there comes a time you *do* learn some people have no sense of humor.

I apologized for hanging him up, explaining about the cop. I also explained I was on a case that had to do with replacement parts of Rollses and had to drop the car off and see if someone took the bait.

So, instead of the Beverly Hills British Motors folks driving me home, why didn't he follow me in his car, I'd drop this off, and we could take it from there?

He said fine. I gave him the address and took off in a cloud of costly smoke.

Beverly Hills British Motors was one of those places where all the mechanics wore spotless white coats with their names embroidered tastefully over the right breast (I made a Clyde, an Ian, and a Ruppert) and carried lots of pens in the left pocket.

It amazed me people could work around cars and have no grease on them. Maybe the servants did the actual work.

I had brought the sick Cloud in at the prearranged hour—with Adderley on purpose away. That left a clear field for anyone wanted to approach me.

A Ron did. Ron was not English. There were no surfer limeys I knew of. Ron was local product all the way— California to the shiny blond hair, sparkling white teeth, and the kind of body you only got when you had as much vanity as discipline. He was probably thirty, and would also probably look the same for another fifteen or twenty years. I didn't much care for Ron.

"Hi, yuh," I said, popping out of the old equipage. Meanwhile Bradley pulled over in the BMW and parked.

"Sir. Nasty bit of exhaust you've got there," said Ron, as if it was news to me. As if I didn't know somebody putting on an English accent.

"That's why I'm here. What do you think it is?"

"Oh, I wouldn't be able to say straight off. You'll have to leave it, Mr. . . . ah . . . ?"

"Franks. Benjamin Franks."

"Yes, Mr. Franks. Let me just write you up."

He took a blank invoice, had me go through an address/phone-number thing, which I kept legit, since I was hoping whoever was working the scam—and I already full-bore suspected old Ronny—would contact me. Then he wrote down the symptoms: "Exudes excessive emissions."

"Okay, how much it gonna take to *de*exude excessive emissions?" I said.

"I really couldn't say at this time," he said at this time.

"All right, but don't start nothing without calling me. I don't want to spend an arm and a leg on this."

"Sir, I don't set the pricing, but I can promise you an estimate first."

"Just, I don't wanna finance nobody's vacation to the old country."

"Very well, sir," he said. "I quite understand."

"Be sure you fucking quite. I don't mind paying what's fair, but I don't like to be taken advantage of." With which I left, before I overacted anymore.

Sitting cozy in the passenger seat of Bradley's BMW, I told him to just drive west while we talked. I wasn't ready to risk sitting down with him anyplace that served throwable food just yet.

He told me about finding Brian all bloody and beat up, and I felt really bad. I had promised to protect him—and his—and mistakenly made light of the threat.

"I owe you a hell of an apology," I said. "I just didn't believe anybody could be that serious about stopping a book. Especially a book about stuff everybody knows."

"Well, maybe whoever's behind it figures when you go over the ground again you'll find something you missed first time out."

"Well, isn't that what they call 'academic' now?"

"What do you mean?"

"I phoned your office. Sounds like you already quit. So, whoever wanted there to be no book got his no book."

"That was before. I quit because I couldn't stand you."

"Can't hear *that* too many times."

"And I'm sure you weren't too crazy about me either."

"That was before you sent flowers. But, yeah . . . Anyway, you know, enough is enough. Forget the book, your life's worth more than any book."

"You don't understand me at all. And *they* don't either. I won't be terrorized, and I won't let *mine* be terrorized. There's not a chance in the world I'd quit the book now!"

"All riiiight!" said Iiiii. "In which case, keep on west, till you get to Barrington."

"Where're we going?"

"I think it's time we checked out Mama Rose and found out why in hell she'd want to help Pagani get paroled."

"Good idea. But even higher on my list while we're at it, can we also find out who the fuck's doing this to me and make them stop it?"

"You got my word on that," I said.

And to my amazement, he gave me a good-old-boy punch in the biceps.

"You're my man," he said.

A guy sends you one lousy bunch of flowers, he thinks he owns you.

There are some surprisingly beautiful houses in that whole Westwood/Brentwood area. And some even more so because the outsides aren't showy. A whole lot of property is hidden in back, out of sight of the street and your casual thief.

It's not exactly what you'd call an integrated area. The most liberal real-estate attitude is sort of: I'm dead set against prejudice. What I always say, any spook's got the two mil, let him move in.

Well, it was clear this spook had the two million as we turned and went through the driveway gates and up a real long way to the front door. Bradley stopped, and we were halfway out the car when a sour-faced seven-foot black guy looked like he'd mastered *The Wit and Wisdom of J. Edgar Hoover* bass-voiced us to, "Please return to your automobile, gentlemen."

We learned further this was private property, no ingress or egress permitted without specific written authorization, and that to the best of his knowledge we possessed no such authorization. Would we therefore depart at once, understanding that ourselves and our license had been photographed and entered into the security computer.

The shit went down like that for about two or three minutes till I told the dude I recognized him both from his playing days as backup center with the Chicago Bulls and his bodyguard days with Sly and the Family Stone when one of my accounts was the Forum. So please cut the crap, we'd broken booze together on more than one "coordinating security" occasion.

"Then how come I don't remember you, man?" he asked.

"Because, Dwayne, you probably got more brain damage than me. Now, go tell Mama Rose her old boyfriend Ray Goodman's here and like to boff her brown bones."

There was a fairly long wait while he stared at me before managing to dredge up verification from his memory.

"Ray," he said, "yeah, right." Then scored a little more in the dignity department by adding, "It's not Dwayne, it's Delayne."

I nodded at this valuable information, and he went off to see if Mama Rose was home to the likes of us.

While we waited for Delayne's return, I filled Bradley in on Mama Rose.

"Rita Rose learned wildness at her mother's knee. The old lady, who, in those days, was herself only in her late thirties, took a backseat to no one when it came to partying. We're talking Olympic class here. If it was made of flesh she fucked it, if it was made of powder she snorted it, if it was made of weed she smoked it. Naturally, her only daughter having been taken rich didn't exactly slow her down. If she was wild when she was poor, you can imagine how she was with what came her way out of all that movie loot."

Delayne returned and said Mama Rose agreed to see us, though we weren't to stay too long or in any way whatsoever *bug* her.

That seemed reasonable, so we agreed. He said: then follow him.

He took us around the outside the house—which we never did enter—and around back to the pool area, and finally, around the lake-size pool, and to the pool house itself.

He pushed a button activating some serious chimes. An electronic click told us the door'd been unlocked.

"You can go in now," said Delayne.

I thanked him, pushed the door slowly open, and we entered.

I don't know what I expected. Well, I do, I suppose— a pool house with, say, a bar, a couple changing rooms, a fireplace, a pinball machine or two—Hollywood poolhouse.

No way. This was a chapel. The windows were stained glass, only instead of saints, the portraits tended to be of Rita Rose in various costumes from various pictures. Then there was an altar, an organ, and candles by the hundreds. It was a shrine, really, dedicated to the memory of her late daughter and the continuing glory of God—sort of in that order.

Under the circumstances, I immediately guessed "Mama Rose, you jelly-roll-crazed sex pump" might not be the coolest greeting.

"Hi, it's Ray Goodman, Mama Rose. How *are* you?" I said sedately.

"Son," she replied, "I'm a sinner sufferin'."

"You're looking good," I lied through my teeth. She was now in her mid-sixties, with a ravaged face and body that looked like she'd led exactly the kind of life she'd led.

"I'm looking as the Lord choose me to look."

"That we all do, Mama."

I introduced her to Bradley, and as they exchanged how-do-you-dos, I had a chance to check things out a little more. The walls were covered with photos—again mostly of Rita, but not all—as well as Rita's plaques and awards. It's amazing how much good a big box-office star does for society, judging from the awards and citations they're honored with. Then, on a table the length of the room were a bunch of other tokens, scrapbooks, mementos, all mixed in with icons and religious paintings. Possible Rita Rose'd become a saint while I wasn't looking?

As I examined this semireligious exhibit, Mama asked, "Have you found your soul in Jesus?"

"Well, Mama, I guess I still have *some* to go," I allowed.

"Don't you wait too long, now, son—the wages of sin be death."

The wages of sin had kept a pretty fancy roof over my

head as long as I could remember, but I wasn't going to argue. I understood this soul-searching and soul-finding. It was the old Cecil B. DeMille formula. I'd seen it in half a dozen of his movies.

(Heshy takes his trusty donkey, leaves town and the virginal Rebecca, roams the fleshpots of all the mideast heathen good-time spots, fucks anything that moves, and some things that don't, drinks the drinks, eats the eats, and when he's totally burnt out and finds the orgies a little more than he's up to, so to speak, gets his ass on his ass and splits for home and Rebecca, respectability, and the comforting arms of religion.)

There's nothing more reformed than a swinger who can't party anymore. So let it be with Mama Rose.

"I got a feelin' it ain't old time sake bring you calling," observed Mama Rose astutely.

"Mark, here, is doing a book on me, like an autobiography, and naturally Rita's part of it," I offered by way of explanation.

"My daughter rest in the bosom of Abraham."

She rested in a lot of bosoms.

"Amen, Mama. She's gone to her reward." I really hoped God would be more charitable than that.

"And there she remain, with the peace of the newborn."

"Right on. I was looking at some of these pictures. It must be a great comfort to have so much of her still all around you."

"This wadn't her home, you know—she never live here."

"Still, her spirit's here, you can feel it. And, of course, I guess she must have paid for it."

"Hah, that's a laugh. The way that child carried on, she barely made it Friday to Wednesday."

"Then I guess you've . . . done well on your own."

"The Lord provide."

"Though in his wisdom, he provides sometimes better for some than others."

It was then Bradley felt he ought to get a little work done on his own.

"Mrs. Mama Rose," he began awkwardly, "I was a

little curious about your appearing before the parole board on behalf of Danny Pagani."

It wasn't a question she was comfortable with.

"The parole board?" prompted Bradley.

"The Christian thing to do."

"Still . . ."

"Plus, weren't entirely my idea," she said finally.

"Right, Harry Light's, I bet."

"Harry Light . . ." she began, then evidently thought better of it. "The Bible teach forgiveness be divine."

"Well, forgiveness, yes, but still, wouldn't you also say it's kind of remarkable for the mother of a murder victim to plead for her daughter's killer to be released?" asked Bradley.

"Did not Jesus on the cross—?"

"Well, sure, Jesus," I interrupted. "But we're not Jesuses. Hardly." Then, hoping I'd disarmed her by my pious aside, slipped in, "I'm still sort of floored by all this loot you've come by. Was it insurance—you have a whole lot of insurance on Rita Rose?"

"The Lord provided . . ."

"Yeah, but the part he didn't?"

"Well, he did, you see, because, Mr. Lefcourt, you know Mr. Lefcourt . . . ?"

"Yep."

". . . he took out whole batch of insurance, to cover whatever picture she was on. Somebody put that notion to his head, don't you know. And Rita all the time made sure while he was at it to also cover us."

"Who's 'us'?" asked Mark.

"Well, me and . . . Rita and . . . whoever."

"You have other children?"

"No, I was never blessed again. Well, I really done been almost blessed a couple other times, tell the honest truth. But it wasn't the right time, or the right man, so, you know. Then, after a while, I guess I just wasn't able to be blessed no more."

During which I kept looking at the pictures in the room, and I'd come on one really fascinated me. It was a picture of Harry Light, with a very warm inscription: "To Mama Rose—I'll be there for you always."

"That's Harry Light."

"Sure is."

"You still see him?"

"We keeps in touch."

"You have your own friendship, separate from Rita?"

"Through the years, Harry and I been very good friends. He been a rock against the tide."

I wondered if that rock had something to do with paying the freight on this costly mausoleum. And if the rest of the house was anywhere near as expensive, we were talking real good friends. And if the old rock was part of it, why?

I figured I'd be able to find out more about that, investigating Harry through other channels.

Bradley, meanwhile, had also been studying the photos, and was now apparently caught up on a particular shot, pantomiming me to look. I did.

It was a five-by-seven of Rita with a baby, or rather two-thirds of a five-by-seven, the rest having been torn away—the most likely guess being because that part showed someone didn't want a picture of himself in that particular domestic setting.

"Mama Rose," said Bradley, "when was this picture of Rita with a baby taken?"

"Oh, that'd be 1963, in there."

Naturally, naturally, of course, dummy—the missing months when Rita'd disappeared without a trace and returned without an explanation—having a baby!

And, naturally, naturally, of course, that piece fitted somewhere nice and added something more than just a little extra incidental info.

"What happened to Rita's baby, again?" I asked, supercasual, like I knew but it skipped my mind.

"Well, at the time, you know—it warn't like now, everybody havin' babies by theirselves. Those days you were some sort of scarlet harlot or something, especially you was in the movies. So we figured it best to send the baby off to live with relatives for a while."

"Sure," I said, a growing suspicion that I couldn't leave unsatisfied: "Down south?"

"The islands—I have an aunt still in Jamaica."

Bradley and I exchanged looks—he because his telephoned threat had been from a "Caribbean," me because my in-person punch-around had been likewise. Though I hadn't told him about that yet.

But if the heavy behind the heavy goings-on was, in fact, Rita's son, why would he be protecting the likes of Danny Pagani by trying to have the book suppressed? You'd think he'd *want* his mother's murderer nailed all over again.

Unless somehow his grandmother was involved in it. After all, his mother died when he was only a few months old. He didn't know her, except as an object of scandal. His grandmother was the one he was close to—she'd be the one he owed allegiance. But how could she be involved? Maybe the answer to that was in how she *really* came by all this money. By which time I spotted a picture of the guy, grown up. No surprise it was the young dude with a gun who'd done me on my health walk.

I pointed to his picture. "This is him, right?"

"That be Rafeel," agreed Mama Rose.

Which should have satisfied me generally. Even if I didn't know why, I now knew who. But there was still something missing. In a strange kind of way, I didn't feel any more satisfied than when I'd come.

"I'd like to meet Rafeel," I said. And didn't say "again." "Ask him a couple things."

"Oh, Ray, I knows I can *trust* you. There's so much been so heavy on me—"

But before Mama Rose could say *what* those heavy things were, Lelayne drove me crazy by coming in and folding the hand.

"Time fo' yo' prayers, Mama—the Reverend be here mos' anytime now." I noticed he had one dialect for us and another for her.

Mama looked disappointed—too.

"But we was havin' such a nice visit . . ."

"Best you be sayin' yo' prayers now, Mama," said the big guy, a little heavier than I could ignore.

"You all right, here?" I offered.

"I be fine," she replied. "The Lord is my shepherd, I shall not want."

"Because if you're not, you have friends."

"It my *friends* be the trouble," she said.

"Now, Mama," said Delayne, "don't you be gettin' yousef all riled up, now . . ."

"Ah knows when I'm *riled*," she said, her voice rising.

"Our *Father*," said Delayne

"Don't you be—"

". . . which are in heaven!"

"Hallowed be thy name," they said together as Delayne turned Mama Rose toward the altar and jerked his head, definitely inviting us out.

There was a lot more here. But we weren't going to get it today.

10

Mark Bradley

The trouble with emergencies was you didn't have the leisure to choose the really chic hospitals. You always wound up at Cedars/Sinai, being rushed on a gurney (donated by the Simon Weiss Foundation) through a door (donated in memory of Sarah Finebaum) to the emergency room (a gift from the Friends of Cedars/Sinai) to the tender ministrations of Dr. David Wong (education made possible by the sacrifices of four generations of the Wong family).

That had been yesterday, when, heart in mouth—check that, Dr. Wong!—I'd dashed Brian over for treatment after the savage beating he'd suffered on my behalf, my behalf on Rayford Goodman's behalf, and when you really thought it through, Rayford Goodman's behalf on Dick Penny's behalf.

There were other moments I could remember when things looked bleak, when I wondered how I'd ever find the courage to go on. But none I can remember so dependent on another human. If Brian were seriously injured, how could I stand it? What should I do? How possibly continue?

It was the deepest crisis of my life.

I began to suspect the peak of crisis had passed when, lying on an examination table in the emergency room, Brian observed in a small, pitiful voice, "I have never seen a more hideous combination of colors than the walls of this room."

I *knew* we were home-free when he added, anent the aforementioned Dr. Wong: ". . . and fluorescent lighting is catastrophic for a Chinese."

Now, next day, vital signs stable, wounds wrapped,

ribs taped, stomach lined with painkillers, he had been released.

Together with Goodman, we were down at the desk, checking out, and getting the usual hassle over money.

"What's the beef?" asked Goodman.

"The beef is the usual beef," I replied. "My insurance doesn't cover my spouse, because my spouse is not recognized to *be* my spouse."

"I'm sorry, Mr. Bradley," said the very un-sorry-looking, extremely stout harridan in charge of harassment. And why was it that medical centers, ostensibly dedicated to health, always had enormously fat women all over the place, wheezing and practically dying before your eyes? "But Blue Cross does not recognize an unformalized relationship."

With which, to really piss me off, Goodman seemed to agree.

"They don't pay for girlfriends either."

"Yen," said the wheelchaired, painkiller-zonked Brian, unable to contain himself any longer, "but de ril rithn nor nationshi's enfrmzed z Calfern woan le's fkn frmlz't!"

"Didn't quite get that," said Goodman.

"He said," I said, "the real reason our relationship is unformalized is California won't let us fucking formalize it."

"We take credit cards," said the lady.

"Swell," I said.

"From anybody," she added helpfully.

"No use making a scene," said Goodman, intuiting my anger.

"I don't make the rules," said the fat lady.

"I'm sure you don't," I said, then couldn't resist adding, "though, in which case, I'm surprised those who do don't have one against hiring people over a certain reasonable maximum weight."

Goodman sighed resignedly.

"Oh, they couldn't do that," said fatso.

"Wh' no'?" said Brian.

"It'd be prejudice," she said, whipping the credit-card gizmo over the form and back, handing me my card, and settling down to fill in the unbelievable numbers for the night's medical ransom on a desk I noted had been donated by the Fish Family.

We got Brian home, maneuvered him up the stairs, into the elevator, into the bedroom, into his jammies, into the bed, surrounded by tapes of every movie made in the last ten years.

"All set now?" I asked, putting a crystal carafe of Evian on his bed table.

"Parfer," said Brian, his dope still fighting the good fight.

"Parfer, indeed," I replied. "We'll be inside if you need us."

"Firn," said Brian, falling asleep.

I steered Goodman into the living room, settled him down, debated whether to offer him a drink, decided civility demanded it.

"Can I get you a drink?" I said.

"You crazy? It's ten-thirty in the morning," he replied.

"Right."

"Nobody drinks before eleven."

We settled on coffee.

He followed me into the kitchen. I had all the latest high-tech versions of the earliest hardware—to wit, a monster espresso machine, computer-enhanced—but the thought of putting it all together, then all the cleaning . . .

Chemex was really a good way to make coffee. It tasted swell, and the grounds were contained within the paper filter, the filter lifted almost in one continuous movement to the wastebasket, and you were left with a lovely neat glass container of coffee, sans any residual mess.

So I boiled the water, ground the beans, folded the filter, put the beans into the filter, slowly poured the water, let it drip through, keeping a simmering flame on to maintain just the perfect temperature, and made the perfect brew. At which point Goodman said:

"On second thought, think I'll pass. It's almost eleven."

There were a lot of times I wanted to punch that man.

I took my own cup of coffee, ignored his pointed reference to the time, and headed back to the living room.

There, amid the muted tones of gray, the muted gray eminence that was Rayford Goodman settled into the muted gray and mushy pêche pillows and looked at his watch.

"Well, now," he said.

"You want a *drink*?" I said testily.

"No, no," he continued affably, "I just thought we ought to continue—seeing Brian's okay and all."

"All right."

"So how you want to go about it? You want more background stuff? Where I was born and raised, that kind of shit?"

"The basic stats I more or less have on file—"

"Okay, so what's next?"

"I think it's pretty clear—we've got to solve the mystery of Rita Rose."

"What mystery? It's solved, Pagani's guilty. Case closed."

"Well, there's no case closed if they're beating up Brian to get me to stop writing about it, even investigating it. That sounds pretty active to me."

"So what do you want to do?"

"We've got to dig deeper. Somehow or other, we're starting to annoy people."

"And if you dig deeper, you'll annoy more."

"But we'll find *out*—"

"We already know!"

Then he sighed. He knew I was telling the truth, even if he couldn't yet admit it.

"Let's consider," I continued. "What did we learn from Mama? We learned Rita Rose had a child. Okay, nothing so unusual about that. *But*, no pictures of Papa around. Could, or could not be significant."

"Significant," said Goodman. "If the father wasn't known, or someone didn't give a damn, there might not be a picture. But since there was a picture, with someone's face torn out, you've got to figure it was someone a person might recognize."

"Right, good, okay. Further, we learned Lefcourt took out apparently huge amounts of insurance on Rita—over and above what he'd recover for the movie—with Mama Rose and Rita Junior, Rafeel, the beneficiaries. Why?"

"She probably made it a condition. You think Eric Dickerson invented the idea of 'renegotiation'? Sports stars learned that crap from movie actors."

"Still, I'd like to interview Lefcourt," I said, wondering who Eric Dickerson was. "Don't forget, he was there that night too."

"With the most to lose . . ."

"Not necessarily. If he collected that much in insurance for Mama Rose, he damn sure got plenty for Symington Lefcourt. We know he collected enough to recast the picture and restart."

"Which in theory only made him even, if he'd stopped there. In reality, he broke a lot less than even, losing the whole wad when the new *Carnival*, without Rita Rose, turned out to be a total bomb."

"I'd still like to talk to him. Maybe he could supply one or two missing pieces."

"You keep saying that. There are no missing pieces! I solved the case."

"Okay, okay, but I need to recreate it for the book, in detail. It's the heart of your story. Maybe Lefcourt has a *detail* or two. Can you set it up?"

"No problem," said Goodman.

Problem, it turned out. He called the studio, wasn't able to get through to Lefcourt, wasn't able to get through to Miss Eldrege, Lefcourt's octogenarian secretary emerita, wasn't able to get through to Miss Kay, Miss Eldrege's fiftyish perennial "trainee"—got shunted from station to station, put on hold, ultimately disconnected.

"I'm starting to get the feeling they don't want to talk to me," he said finally, continued: "Okay, tell you what let's do meanwhile. If it's all right to leave Brian, why don't you and me tool on over to the Rolls place. I'll quick-check that, then we'll go take a ride visit Dubie Dietrich at Mental Mountain. See what we get out of him. How's that grab you?"

Grabbed me as reasonable. I checked on Brian—out cold, sleeping the sleep of the deeply doped—and left him a note.

Back in the living room, I asked Goodman if there was anything I could do for him before we left.

"Well," he said, "it *is* eleven o'clock."

I pulled the BMW up to the front of the Beverly Hills British Motors and parked.

"This won't take long," said Goodman.

I watched him meander or maybe lope—there was at least a suggestion of John Wayne to his walk—through the open garage door, where he was joined by a blond sort of prince with appropriately regal buns.

His highness handed Goodman an invoice of some sort, which he needed only one look at before exploding with rage.

The princeling merely shrugged with a haughty indifference. Whatever the trouble was, he neither cared nor was about to help.

Goodman shouted some more and tossed back the paper. The prince shrugged some more and tossed Goodman his keys.

Goodman got into the Rolls, belched smoke—the car, that is—drove out, pantomimed me to follow.

He turned the next corner, then the next, found an empty parking spot, beckoned me into it.

I parked, locked, and joined him in the asthmatic Rolls.

"So, what was that?" I asked as he pulled away.

"That was my little outrage act. Adderley did something or other to the motor. It's a simple fix, but an expensive part. The plan calls for me to bring it in. In Adderley's absence, somebody—still don't know who—"

"Tell me it's not the blond," I implored.

"Probably is," said Goodman.

Trouble is so sexy!

"Anyway, somebody makes an estimate. The estimate is sixteen hundred and fifty dollars. I'm outraged. Not paying prices like that. My outrage is loud enough anybody in the garage wants a sucker for a cut-price fix can hear it. My phone number's on record. The next move is whoever's the villain."

I found this a little less than engrossing. I suppose even brain surgeons have some dull cases.

Near Ojai, where everything's called some kind of oaks, there's a place named Shady Oaks. Shady Oaks is silly city; the conservator-enforced residence of Dubie Dietrich.

Goodman got cleared at the gate—they apparently knew him—and drove us up a long, long driveway through and under some . . . shady oaks! He parked in a visitor's spot and turned off the ignition. This, somehow, didn't immediately communicate itself to the motor, as for another minute or so it continued to belch smoke and do its automotive St. Vitus's dance.

We were met by a rather startlingly beautiful, chicly slim brunette nurse of no more than thirty summers. When you're talking big-money health care, the employees ain't fat. She greeted Goodman by name, took mine, which she entered in a Gucci-leathered notebook, and indicated a spot under a particular oak about fifty yards away at which the former funnyman apparently dozed in what looked to be a Lamborghini wheelchair.

"He'll be coming around in a minute or two. We gave him a mild stimulant so you could chat."

Goodman thanked her, for a moment obviously considered a discreet goose, decided decorum was the better part of strategy, and led us over.

Dubie was hardly recognizable as the knockabout comic I'd seen in all those "On the Sea to" movies. His thinning hair had achieved its ultimate thinning, at least on top. As if to compensate, he'd let the sides grow inordinately long. Not satisfied to look merely foolish, he'd colored them a kind of orangy Grecian Formula, the effect of which was clownlike, in the Emmett Kelly school of sad clowns. Which I'd never liked, by the way. I never could understand what was supposed to be funny about sad-faced grotesques.

Goodman gently shook him.

"Dubie? Dubie? It's Ray Goodman. Hello, there."

Dubie barely opened his sad, sick eyes. Hard to imagine we'd get anything out of this joker.

"Anybody home?" said Goodman.

"Nobody but us schizos," said Dubie.

I guess I was wrong.

"How ya, gumshoe, how's the dick business?"

"Limp," said Goodman. "How's it for funnymen?"

"A million *laugh*," said Dubie.

Goodman introduced me, told him we were doing a book together, said I was anxious to meet him.

"Hello, Mr. Dietrich," I said.

"Mark would like to ask you a few questions, if you're up to it, and have the time."

"The time, I've got," said Dubie, "but I ain't been up to it since I tried gumming one of the nurse's tits and they took out my prostate to teach me a lesson."

"Truth?" I asked.

"Who the fuck knows?" said Dubie, laughing.

Suddenly he sat up straighter. "Boy, you ought to come here more often. They shot something up my ass feels awful good."

"Maybe we ought to talk before it wears off."

"Whatever. I'm game for anything."

"Okay, Dube," said Goodman. "In that case, let's go back to that night, the night Rita died—would that be too painful?"

"With what I got in me at the moment, lopping my balls off don't even sound painful. So whatta you wanna know?"

"Who was there?" I asked.

"Who was there? Who wasn't? Harry was there . . ."

"Right."

". . . with Sally." Goodman nodded. "And Rollins, his dresser. Lefcourt was there—my new godfather. Turns out he's my conservator."

Goodman and I exchanged looks.

"He pays the bills?" I asked.

"I don't know. I'm incompetent. Or is that incontinent? Both, I think."

We gave it a laugh. He needed to know he had an audience.

"Harley Williams was there . . ."

"Rita's ex-husband," prompted Goodman.

I knew.

"Carkeys was there. Naturally, they wasn't all there at

once. Well, Carkeys was usually wherever Rita was—if
only to hold her dope. *I* was there—I think to get a hit
or two. Not too clear. I mean, I'm sure that came into
it—Rita and I did that pretty regular."

"What about sex?" I asked.

"What about it?" said Dubie. "I seem to remember it
was fun."

"Did you and Rita . . . that night?"

"So they say. No big deal, with her, or for her. It was
a big deal for me. That girl . . ." His voice faded in
pleasant reverie.

I noticed Goodman seemed to be nodding agreement.
I had a feeling the only one she might have missed was
Edward Everett Horton—for reasons I could guess.

Then he sort of pulled back out of the past, continued
the recounting, albeit somewhat hesitantly. "I remember
. . . who else? Uhm, Pagani, I think."

"Sex?"

"I don't know. He was leaving."

"You saw Pagani *leaving*?"

"Yeah, sure."

"Why didn't you say so?"

He seemed a bit slow in answering, or maybe it was
just professional timing. "Nobody asked me," he said.
And then abruptly fell asleep.

Goodman shook him once or twice, called his name,
but couldn't get a rise out of him. He turned to me.

"I *would* like a little more," I said.

He agreed, found the nubile brunette nurse, beckoned
her over.

"See, sweetheart," he said, "Mr. Dietrich seems to
have nodded off."

"Well, I suppose that's that, then," she said.

"Well, it *could* be," said Goodman, "only we need to
ask him a few more questions—for this book on my life
Mr. Bradley here is assisting with."

Assisting, shit!

"Which is going to make me a whole big bunch of
money, and real famous, but I won't ever change, or
forget the little people who helped along the way. Especially those who're dynamite-looking and really worth a
shot at." Incredibly, this seemed to interest her. "So,

honeylips, whyn't you just give him another taste of that joy juice?"

"Oh, I couldn't do that," she said, I swear leaning against Goodman. "It's not good for him."

"Tell you what," said Goodman. "Would a hundred dollars be good for him, you hold it?" With which he reached back in a clear indication I give him the hundred. I did. (Fuck Penny!)

She smiled, took the bill coyly—just barely short of tucking it into her bodice—reached into a pocket, pulled out a syringe full of good feeling, and we turned away discreetly as she opened Dubie's pants, found a withered cheek, and sent the message home.

This time Goodman did pat her ass, which she didn't seem to mind in the slightest—doing nothing to upgrade the sensual-nurse stereotype. They exchanged eye promises of good times to come, and she departed.

It didn't take long for Dubie to come around.

"Hey, now, where were we, or are we?" he said. "I'm not exactly kidding, you know. But I figure I'm all right as long as I can remember the word 'Algerheimer.' "

I really didn't know if he was kidding or not; decided on a half-smile.

"We were talking about Rita, that night, all the people there," I cued him. "Who do you figure really did it. Pagani?"

"The guy I always suspected most is *me*—that's why I confessed."

"You still think it was you?" I asked.

"I don't actually fucking *know*, of course. It was my *style*, they tell me. I'm totally whacked, you understand."

"Well, at the time you were doing a lot of drugs," interjected Goodman.

"I ain't doing a lot of drugs now, and I'm still whacked. I keep feeling little pieces of my mind signing off. Brain damage. I'm what they call a recovering addict. Some recovering."

"You sound pretty good," said Goodman.

"That's 'cause right now I'm *on* drugs. Doctor drugs. Still, I *am* better than some. At least I'm only insane. Three-quarters of the rest of the vegetables in this loony bin just sit around rehearsing death."

We needed to keep his mind from wandering before the shot wore off.

"But you must have known you didn't do it when they let you out," I said.

"Oh, shit, I just figured that was the old studio fix. I guessed the gumshoe here took care of it—especially when he set up Danny Pagani to take the fall."

"I didn't set up anyone," said Goodman, with some force. "Pagani was guilty."

"Don't shit a shitter," said Dubie. "Rita Rose was alive and fairly well—although a bit banged up—when Pagani left."

"How do you know?"

"I saw Pagani, who was a lot worse off than her, beat-up and bloody-faced, get into the trunk of Harley's car . . ."

"Didn't that strike you as odd?" I asked.

"Shit, buddy, being conscious struck me as odd in them days. Whew!" he said, enjoying some reflexive harmonic of the shot.

"But you saw Pagani driven off, and *then* saw Rita Rose still alive?"

"Sure. Absolutely," he said. "I think."

With which Dubie's pharmaceutical good times came to an abrupt end, as his head slumped to his chest and he joined the company of those rehearsing death.

Back in the wheezing Rolls, on the highway, after the very long silence, I finally said, "Well, Ray"—I figured maybe it'd soften things if I called him Ray—"we accomplished a lot today. There's one thing I'm absolutely convinced of."

"Which is?"

"Now, I hope this doesn't upset you."

"What could you say could possibly upset me?"

"You busted the wrong guy. Danny Pagani never killed Rita Rose."

That's what could possibly upset him. In fact, it went over so well, I thought Goodman just might kill *me*!

11

Rayford Goodman

What was this, what the hell was this? Who *needed* this? The whole idea of doing the book was to do something good for me. Not to aggravate me. Or drive me crazy.

I really wanted to belt the bastard. It was all I could do to *keep* from belting him. In fact, there were only two things kept me from doing it. I outweighed him by a full person, and two: there was an outside chance he was right.

But how the hell could I have been wrong about Pagani? He hardly even denied it. And was such a slimeball. And had such a strong motive. Plus all the physical evidence. There were semen samples (which sounded like a freebie for a sailor), wounds, and the broken right arm. Which'd make him use the left. Which is what the forensic people said: wounds inflicted from the left. How could it *not* be Pagani?

These were the thoughts followed the beat of my flapping feet as I trudged my weary miles next morning on Sunset Boulevard. Doing the don't-die shuffle.

I had dumped Bradley yesterday on the street where he'd parked his car—around back of the Rolls place— and driven away without a word. Which I still think showed a lot of restraint, all things considered.

Now I could feel my soles slapping the pavement angrily as I passed the eight-million-dollar house, the Old Cockers, the post-stroke Shuffler.

I walked on, head down, still angry, pissed-off angry. Who needed such a smart-ass kid to upset the apple cart?

And what kind of health walk was I on when I was burning mad? Stress, look out for gut-busting stress.

God damn! Good luck in this wonderful world of aggravation.

Then, oh, shit, just what I needed, here came the crazy High-Stepping Fast-Walker who was going to try to sell me those fucking walking shoes again. I tried lowering my head and walking past him, but he blocked the way.

"Hi," he said. "You do a lot of walking?"

"We been through this," I said. "A lot. I like my shoes. My feet like my shoes. I'm not interested any more shoes."

"Oh, but these are really wonderful. They're computer-designed."

He said the magic words. A great selling point—computer-designed. How about shoemaker-designed? Computers sure weren't making *my* life any better. The goddamned bank couldn't even cash a check when the computer was down, which was only about eighty-percent of the time. Tell me about computers.

"What do you say?" the Fast Walking man said.

"Thanks just the same," the talking-between-clenched-teeth person said.

"But you don't know how wonderful these shoes are," he went on. Like ol' man river.

"No . . . no . . . no . . . thanks," I said, glaring at him. "I don't *want* them!"

He was a very slow study.

"Your feet will thank you."

"Watch my lips," I said, "I do not now, nor in the near future, far future, nor so long as the grass shall grow and the rivers run, want to buy your fucking shoes!"

He formed a disappointed O with his lips, considered whether this actually *was* my last word on the subject, and incredibly still wondered.

"This is probably not a good time for you," he said.

And before it got seriously nasty, he spotted another potential customer across the street and light-stepping fast-walked on and over. I knew with a tooth-grinding certainty I hadn't seen the last of him. Maybe it was time to change the route.

Where was I? Quitting, quitting, definitely quitting the

book would solve a lot of problems. Right away, for openers, I wouldn't have to see Mark Bradley anymore. Wouldn't that make for brighter days? Even more important, I wouldn't have to go on undermining the main accomplishment of my life.

And, incidentally, wouldn't have to deal with whoever definitely didn't want the book written. Though it wouldn't do a whole hell of a lot for my self-respect.

Walk, walk. Trudge, trudge.

I hit the turnaround point across the street from the Beverly Hills Hotel, did just that, and headed back toward the car.

A mile to go, and a lot to think about. If it wasn't Pagani . . . Shit, it *had* to be Pagani! All right, cool it, say it wasn't. If not him, who then? Back to square one and the whole damn cast of characters, that's who then. Could it really have been Dubie after all? No, I didn't believe that.

I walked on.

There was no point in this. I'd been over it and over it. Everybody else was accounted for.

Well, in a way, accounted for *if* Pagani was guilty. I still couldn't believe he wasn't.

Walk walk, trudge trudge.

Lefcourt, Lefcourt—all that insurance. No sense to it, though. Oh, some, in a way, but he *lost* by it, in the end.

For that matter, crazy maybe, but . . . Mama Rose seemed to have made out a whole *hell* of a lot.

Harley Williams? If Dubie was right, and Pagani got smuggled out before Rita was killed, that cleared Williams. He was the guy got Pagani past the gate in the trunk of his car. Also according to Dubie, admittedly not the most reliable source I ever saw. But anyhow, the only possible way Williams could make any money out of Rita would be if she stayed alive. Of course, he had been rejected—thrown out's more like it. But that was long before. No, Williams didn't make sense. As if *any*body's doing a mutilation murder made sense.

Harry's dresser, Arthur Rollins? Hard to figure a motive there.

Carkeys? No sense to that either. Rita was her meal

ticket. Alive, Rita stood for ongoing fun, excitement, drugs, money, men. There'd just be no point, that used groupie offing the golden goose.

So, where was she, then? Why'd she take off? And how'd she stay off so long?

Probably a housewife in some trailer camp in the desert by now. With four kids and a beer-swilling biker old man.

Probably dead of an overdose, more likely.

Trudge, trudge.

Harry . . . No, no, no, no. Why? What possible reason? Besides, Sally was there too, as well as Rollins. Which, right, covers Rollins too.

I just couldn't believe it wasn't Pagani.

Walk, walk.

Trudge, trudge.

Yes, I could.

The chugging Rolls struggled up the hill in second, still laying down its cloud of smoke. I pulled into the driveway, trying not to notice how long the grass seemed to be getting in the yard, and how bad the house needed painting. Damn, I really could have used all that serious money from the book.

I'd left the garage-door opener in the Caddy, so had to get out and manually open the door. Then I got back in the Rolls and pulled into the garage.

The flowers were where I'd left them on the garbage can, but for some reason seemed to have died. Maybe it had to do with not watering them.

I turned to head into the kitchen, stubbed my toe on the lawn mower. Was that a hint from God maybe I should cut the lawn myself? Then, again, I'd had another hint from God with the heart attack. That left a strong-enough impression I wasn't about to start mowing lawns. But thanks for the bruised shin, O You with That Great Sense of Humor.

The rest of the morning went about like that. I went in to shower, and discovered about sixteen jillion termites. They were swarming between the inside glass of the shower and the outside glass looking out into what used to be the rose garden. Before the rose garden turned into the dead forest.

Well, all hillside homes have termites. And anyway, who could afford tenting the house?

I showered—the water starting to run rusty—slipped on a fresh set of sweats, and went down for some breakfast.

No cereal. I took out a frozen pizza, popped it in the microwave, and went to check my messages.

There were four. This early in the morning, that was something.

The first was Adderley wanting to know if I'd had any action for his fifty bucks a day. Which he hadn't paid yet, anyway. I didn't know, had to see first what the other messages were.

The second was from Harry Light's secretary inviting me to a screening at his house night after next. RSVP. Didn't say what the picture was. Joke. The fortunate folks got an invitation to Harry's didn't care what was playing. They were happy just to *be* there.

Interesting. I hadn't been on the A list in a very long time. Hell, I wasn't on the Z list. Why now? I doubted he was so taken by my drunken performance at the Polo Lounge my company suddenly became all that desirable.

The third was from Bradley wanting to know were we on or were we off. And if on, we'd better *get* on with it. Call him.

The last call went like this:

"Cute, your answer phone has no cute message. That's cute. This is a voice out of your past. Recognize it?"

I didn't, really. I recognized I *should* have recognized it. It was female, middle-aged probably, since it was fairly low and the whiskey-and-cigarette sound takes some years to acquire. Also possibly black. Though that, too, wasn't entirely predictable anymore. What was? And it went on, toying in this manner for a minute or two.

"If you think back to a certain time, a long time ago . . ."

I was about to turn it off. Who needed this? I had

enough trouble with straightforward women. Phone teasers? Forget it.

But there was just an edge suggested it wasn't somehow social, might be something.

"Our paths crossed lots of times, though not the most important night of both our lives. Do you know me now?"

No, but almost.

"I have something to tell you that's important. I know what really happened on that certain night a long time ago. I could give you the key—ha ha."

Almost.

"Only I'm so afraid. I can't hang on much longer. I can't keep running and dodging."

Who?

"I'm gonna have to chance it. So tell you what, meet me at Nipper's, eleven tonight. As they say in the old flicks, I'll make it worth your while."

Sure, I'm gonna meet somebody I don't even know who, at some place I don't even know where. Nipper's? I felt pretty sure that was some sort of disco in Beverly Hills. Great combination, coy mystery lady and my favorite kind of place, discos. As you could guess, dancing was really my thing. Got-ta dance! I liked it just better than root canals.

Well, whoever, she had some fat chance I'd be going to . . .

Carkeys! It was Carkeys!

12

Mark Bradley

The locksmith had just finished installing the Fox police lock Goodman had recommended—the floor-to-door bar that I'd never before seen in California, other than in movies about New York—designed to discourage future Brian-bashing (by mistake), or Mark-bashing (on purpose), charging me a totally outrageous three hundred and seventy-eight dollars for his hour and a half's work ("We have to get these from New York") and departing.

I'd settled down at the word processor to bring my notes up-to-date, though hardly sure there was any point to it, last communication from Goodman suggesting I could take my notes and stuff them where the sun didn't shine—his opinion, not mine. I had the machine booted up, my knuckles cracked, and myself halfway psyched to ignore the what-ifs and just get on with it. Instead:

"Maa-rk," came a querulous summons from the bedroom.

"I'm worr-king," I called back.

"I'm hunn-gry."

I got up, left the muted-gray room, and crossed the muted-gray hall to the muted-gray bedroom, where my muted-gray roommate lay abed, wan and tragic, with all the grace and appeal of a pile of sodden laundry.

"Brian, the food'll be here any minute."

"What'd you order?"

"You asked for pizza. Francie's picking it up on her way."

"When's she coming?"

"Soon. Relax."

"How soon?"

"Minute and a half."

"Really?"

"Minute and a quarter. Any second. I can almost hear her footsteps."

"What kinda pizza?"

"The kind you like."

"With everything?"

"Everything."

"Anchovies?"

Too bad the guys who worked him over hadn't killed him. It was beginning to look like I'd have to do that myself.

"Trust me."

"I don't know if I want anchovies."

"Why don't we wait and see? Then, if you don't want the anchovies, we can take *off* the anchovies. But if you *do* want the anchovies, we can still *have* the anchovies."

"What's taking so long?"

Brian didn't make the best patient.

"Brian, I'm working. Please let me work."

"I don't feel well."

"I know."

"But I'm hungry."

"So I gather."

"Usually when I don't feel well, I'm not hungry."

"Fascinating."

"You don't care. I could starve to death."

"Brian, I'm going to kill you. Not an easy death, it will be slow and lingering. The food will *be* here in a second, momentarily, instantly. Meanwhile, take a pill, try to relax. Sleep. A coma would be nice."

"Some sensitivity," he said.

Since the last word was going to be his, I decided to let it be "sensitivity," left the muted-gray bedroom, crossed the muted-gray hall, and entered my muted-gray office.

"Maa-rk," I heard.

I closed the door. Slamming is closing.

But, really, he had taken the beating meant for me. He *was* entitled to some consideration.

"Maa-rk . . ."

Which he was using up fast.

I sifted through my notes. It was slow going. Mainly because I didn't know where to start. Everything about

Rayford Goodman hinged on the American Beauty Rose. The case *was* Rayford Goodman, and if he were wrong, as I was increasingly sure, what was I left with?

Okay, born in Detroit—wonderful, colorful—of unexceptional parents. Family moved to California. Father an "entrepreneur," meaning he never made a living; mother got a defense job at Lockheed. Fascinating? Goodman himself went to Hollywood High, where the yearbook described him as "rooty toot in a zoot suit." His taste in clothes hadn't much improved.

Drafted, he was an M.P. in the army between wars—lots of material there. Later married to Luana Goodman, nee Millhiser, divorced from nee Millhiser, neither then nor now kids, dogs, cats, or interests that would make for anything remotely worthwhile chronicling. No brothers, sisters, surviving relatives. Did the man exist?

It was as if the only memorable thing about his entire life was the Case. Maybe it'd be a good thing if we *did* drop the book.

Great. Now, on top of everything else, I had to contend with what clearly had all the earmarks of an incipient writer's block. Which called to mind the woman plagued with recurring green spots on her thighs, going unsuccessfully from doctor to doctor till a canny specialist diagnosed the cause. "You have a Gypsy lover?" She did. "His earrings aren't real gold."

I guess I know writer's block when I see it.

The doorbell rang.

Thank God.

I crossed the muted-gray room, etc., and to the door, where I had a hell of a time unbarring the newly installed Fox police lock—not especially celebrated for my digital dexterity, you recall—and admitted Francie, carrying the pizza.

"They were out of anchovies," she said.

"You know what my view of that is?" I said. "My view is I don't give a flying fuck about anchovies."

"You don't give a flying fuck, period," she replied. "In the conventional sense, anyway."

"Nobody *cares* about anchovies. Anchovies exist only for people to say, 'Hold the anchovies.' "

"Going that well?" she said cutely.

I smiled. What the hell. She always could cool me out.

"He's terrible. Driving me absolutely crazy. Thank God he's young enough and strong enough that even a broken neck would only take him about a week to get over. Me, a pimple goes six weeks. Otherwise, one of us would have to go to a convalescent home."

"Why don't we feed the fairy?"

"Why don't we, for God's sake, stop already with the gay-baiting?" So much for cooling out.

"Oh, is that offensive? I didn't realize. One just never knows what you can say to people with an alternate death-style."

And as I glowered, getting really angry, she added sweetly, "Give us a kiss. I'll chance it."

Putting her arms around my neck, she delivered a warm, sloppy buss. What could I do? Francine was Francine. Which, all things considered, was mostly pretty good.

So, okay, we went to the kitchen—meringue yellow, by the way, with only gray *trim*. I opened the box, removed a couple of slices of pizza, and put them on a nice black-and-chrome art-deco tray—which, even if unsigned, *I* was positive was a Chase. Then, rather than face the certain carping over the lack of anchovies, I added a liberal sprinkling of beluga caviar as a substitute and took the whole gooey platter in to Brian.

He moaned, groaned, moaned again, and kvetched his way upright, settled the tray on his lap, took a bite, and said, "Take off the anchovies."

I scraped the caviar off the top to the side of the tray.

Not good enough, he wanted them totally out of his offended sight.

I crammed about a hundred and ten dollars' worth into my mouth and swallowed it in a gulp.

Apparently satisfied, he took a big bite of pizza, and while his mouth was full I asked if there was anything else I could do for him. Ignoring the outstretched hand that indicated impending speech the moment his mouth was free, I said in that case we wouldn't disturb him further and quickly pushed Francie out of the room ahead of me and closed the door.

"Seems to be recovering nicely," she said, once back in my study. "So cheerful."

"Right, he's about four laughs."

I took a breath, found I wasn't *that* angry, relaxed.

"So, what's with the book?" Francine asked. "Is it a go or a no?"

"I honestly can't say. On the one hand, it's all falling apart, in the sense that the case just doesn't add up. On the other hand, all this unexpected crap we've stirred up tends to make it sort of fascinating. But on the third hand, Goodman and I have all the rapport of a cobra and a mongoose."

"Let me guess who's who. So, what's going to happen?"

"Ah hah, if I knew that I'd be turning out pages."

"Meanwhile, I don't suppose you have a toot till payday?"

"Francine, I've told you repeatedly, I don't *do* drugs . . . anymore. I have seen the error of my ways."

"Just asking. No need to get upset. I'll just have to use my own."

And she did, laying out four lines, taking four swift snorts, gasping, sneezing, her nose turning red.

"Why do you do that shit?"

"It's the only way I can get to look like Meryl Streep."

I hardly considered that a legitimate answer, but before I could challenge her further, there came a knocking—Rayford Goodman at my chamber door.

"See you got the lock," he said. "Good."

Barn doors came to mind. However . . .

I closed the door, followed Goodman in.

"Okay, let's get on with it," he said. "Are we writing a book, or what?"

In a way it was better than an apology. How many times can you apologize?

I introduced Francie to Goodman, told him she was my research assistant on the project, and asked him what he had in mind.

"I have in mind to show you you're wrong about Pagani . . . I'm pretty sure."

"Pretty sure? The guy spent twenty years in jail!"

"Closer to thirty," amended Francie helpfully, earning a frown from Goodman.

"Let's not quibble," I offered. "What exactly do you want to do?"

"Well, for now, I'd like to follow up a bit on Mama Rose. There's something very weird going on there, and it doesn't really add up."

"Okay, how do we proceed?"

"First, I'd like to find out for sure if she owns that house. It's pretty lavish, and she herself said Rita didn't leave any money. So, even say she got some insurance from Lefcourt, it doesn't strike me it would be enough to support that kind of deal."

"I can do that," said Francie. "I can at least certainly find out if it's in her name."

She crossed to my desk, sat down in front of the computer, cut out my program, and inserted a disk of her own from a carrier she had in her oversize bag, booting it.

"Francine's the local hacker's hacker," I explained. "If it's in a state bank, she'll find it."

"You don't mean money bank," Goodman said.

She gave him a look of contempt—the guy was from the Dark Ages. She picked up the phone.

"I got a buddy downtown I think'll give me the access code to the property-tax mainframe."

"Ah, computer bank, tape, disk, thingo," said Goodman. "Right." To which he added, as if to explain his ignorance, "There was a time a researcher was just a smarter librarian. Not someone heavy into software of the hardware."

Then, tucking the phone between her chin and shoulder, Fran reached into her purse, took out some kind of pill, popped it down. I made a moue of displeasure, to which, characteristically, she responded by whipping out a vial of coke. I managed to get Goodman turned away from her and tried a larger pantomime—a veritable mighty moue—to indicate my opinion that it wasn't the smartest thing to do in front of Goodman.

Francie wasn't all that security-conscious, unfortunately, with a very strong mind of her own, or a drug-

fried brain-damaged mind, so she went out of her way
to pay no attention.

"Why don't we go inside," I said to Goodman, "and
let her make her calls and do her thing—it'll probably
take a while." Judging from past experience, Goodman
wasn't terribly strong on to each his own.

He chose not to make a scene, apparently.

"By the way, just for my own information," he said,
turning back and positioning himself so as to manage not
to see the coke bottle, "why does anybody entrusted with
keeping the access codes secret give them to you?"

"We trade off," she said. "Some I give coke to, some
I fuck." She started pushing the buttons on the phone,
smiling innocently the while, enjoying herself.

She really liked baiting him.

That nonplussed him for a moment; then he plussed
enough to ask, "How do you know which to give which?"

She gave that some pseudo-serious thought, then responded, "If the nose is bigger . . ."

At which point the number downtown rang through.

"Hi," she said. "Records? Is Harold Wittenbrough
there?"

I managed finally to steer Goodman out. I wanted to
kill Francie. The bitch—just doing that to aggravate me.
This was the day for *every*body to aggravate me.

We went into the kitchen, where Goodman sampled a
piece of pizza (if he said *one* word about anchovies . . . !)
and announced there was a new development.

But before he could tell me what, there was a distinct
snort-snort from the other room. He raised his head wearily from the pizza.

"I hate that," he said. "Especially in a woman."

"What's that?" I asked innocently.

"You know what's that—putting that damn crap up
her nose."

"She just has no tolerance for liquor," I said.

"Don't start with me. I don't like working with coke-
heads. I hope you don't do that stuff."

"Heaven forfend," I replied. "The old vices are the
best vices," I offered placatingly. "You were about to
tell me about a new development?"

"I got a call from Carkeys."

"Wow, the elfin and elusive Carkeys!"

"Evidently decided to surface. We got a meeting tonight at Nipper's."

"Fascinating."

"Ought to be. That's a girl's kept very much out of sight for a very long time," he said. "There's gotta be an awful strong reason."

"Maybe the jewels, you think?" I replied. "Suppose it wasn't Harley who stole them, suppose it was Carkeys. That'd be a reason."

"Yeah, maybe, but . . . all this time? First of all, there's the statute of limitations . . ."

"I gather the jewels never showed up anywhere."

"No, and she wasn't exactly the sort of lay-back person'd sit on that kind of money this long. Not likely she stole the jewels. Chances are pretty strong she knew something, and someone knew she knew. Which kept her scared enough to stay hidden to hell and gone somewhere out in the boonies."

"But why's she showing up now, do you think?"

"Maybe he, they, it, are on to her finally, and she'd feel safer sharing whatever she knows. As insurance."

After twenty-eight years!

I was starting to feel like typing.

"By the way," he said. "This Nipper's is a private club?"

"Yeah."

"I'll have to think of someone to call could get me in."

"I'm a member," I said. Somehow this seemed to bother more than please him.

"I just know I'll hate it."

"Only if you hate pretty girls."

"But you're a member . . ."

"I like pretty girls—they're often accompanied by pretty boys. I can get you in."

"Great," he said with a noticeable lack of enthusiasm. "That case, maybe we ought to all go together."

"Sounds like a plan."

He took another bite of pizza.

"Okay," said Francie, joining us, carrying a printout. "The house is owned by the El Pea Corporation. That's

E-l, space, P-e-a. I've got a call in to a friend in Sacramento, who might be able to access the corporate file. Hopefully we'll find out who El Pea is."

"El Pea—'the pea' in Spanish?" I asked.

"No," said Goodman. "That would be El Guisante."

"Maybe it's short for piss," said Francie helpfully.

"That would be P-e-e," I said.

"Not if it was a Mexican spelling," said Goodman, revealing another facet of his bigotry.

El Pea, El Pea . . .

"Hey, how about this," I offered. "Suppose it was somebody being cutsey?"

"Meaning?"

"Initials. The initials L and P."

"The L. P. Corporation," Goodman said.

"For example, Lefcourt Productions?" I suggested.

"Yeah, possible," allowed Goodman. "But if it was insurance money, and due to Mama Rose, why wouldn't she be the outright beneficiary?"

"Francie, would there be a record someplace you could check if there actually was insurance money?"

"I don't see why not. At least if the insurer were a publicly owned company. I can look into it."

"And while you're at it," said Goodman, "maybe we can find out who else might be part of Lefcourt. In the old days there were rumors of mob connections."

"They'd hardly list their names if they were," she said.

"True. But corporations have officers—might be a name I've heard."

"They'd go out of their way to—"

"Just try it," he said sternly.

"Shit," said Francie, heading back to the study.

"And keep your nose clean!" added Goodman.

"*That's* where that expression comes from!" I said.

While we were waiting, Goodman wandered back into the kitchen and took another slice of pizza.

"Good," he said thoughtfully.

I tried a piece. It *was* good. Added the remains of the caviar jar. Even better.

Goodman seemed to be mulling over the recent intelligence.

"There's something . . . I'm just beginning to get a

feeling," he said finally. "It's starting to be something. A little out of reach, but it's starting to happen . . ."

And I, too, felt a sense of heightening mystery, which was exciting, because it wasn't cerebral at all. We hadn't really found anything terribly significant. What I was feeling—what we were sharing—was more an emotional sense of proximity to discovery.

We ambled back into the living room, just in time to hear Francie snort two lines of coke.

"Again?" said Goodman, annoyed.

"Maybe she's got a cold," I offered unconvincingly.

Then the phone rang. I picked it up.

"Francie!" I called, "For you—Sacramento."

We waited. A few grunts from the study—innocent ones—we heard her punching in some keys, followed almost immediately by a printout. She thanked the party at the other end, hung up, and in a moment rejoined us.

"Well?"

"That was my friend in Sacramento."

"*Close* friend?" asked Goodman, somewhat archly, I thought.

"*Bosom* buddy," she replied, looking him right in the eye.

"Any luck?" I asked, getting back to business.

"Uh-huh."

"Lefcourt Productions?"

"Guess again."

"Guess again! I'll break your bones," said Goodman, clearly peeved.

"We were right. El Pea is/are letters. L. P. stands for Light Pictures."

"Harry fucking Light!" said Goodman.

"There was no middle name," said Francie.

"Harry Light!" said Goodman, standing corrected.

"Knowledge is power," said Francie smugly.

"I can't believe it," said I, incredulously.

"Maa-rk!" called Brian irritably.

13

Rayford Goodman

I left Bradley's little nest and stepped into the hallway. From the noisy fiddling going on behind the door, I got a feeling he hadn't quite got the hang of the Fox lock. Another clue was the words "fuck . . . shit . . . piss."

I headed for the elevator, feeling pretty good. We were making progress. I was kind of surprised I was also starting to feel like a "we." I mean, the man wasn't my *partner*, for Christ sakes. But I had to admit he was useful. For that matter, so was Francie—who wouldn't be half-bad she wasn't a doper. A little zaftig for my tastes. I liked skinny women, generally, as long as they weren't *too* skinny in the functional parts. Though I never held it against a woman if she were burdened by a large breast.

That computer stuff she'd done really knocked me out. Punching a bunch of keys, she'd come up with information in half an hour would've taken me days of serious sleuthing. Plus lots of shoe leather and plenty palm grease. Though come to think of it, she wasn't exactly getting the information free either.

I had a feeling those flying fingers were going to put me totally out of business one of these days. I could just see where lots of my cases could be done by computer over the modem, or whatever they called it. But never all. IBM might deal in probabilities, but it didn't get hunches, I tried to convince myself.

When you first got a case, for a long while you weren't sure you were actually going to solve anything. Then, if and when you started getting bits and pieces, and the moon was right, and your luck running, you *might* work it out. I mean, wasn't like there was a *method* to follow. That I knew.

For one thing, I'd never been a cop. If you didn't

count being an M.P., where the most valuable and practical thing I'd learned in three years was watching out drunken soldiers didn't barf on your shoes. My work as P.I. to the Stars was really mostly cover up their scandals or bail 'em out when they got into trouble. Anything that helped the studios protect their valuable property. Most especially the middle of production.

But once or twice there'd been a real mystery. And I remembered how I'd gone first from not-a-clue-in-the-world to a little something. Then a little something more. And finally to a click when it began adding up and that old adrenaline kicked in. After which it got to be kind of a runaway, almost-out-of-control fun.

Right now, of course, all I had was a little something *didn't* add up. And it was about as far from fun as divorce court.

First I had to get over the hump and inside accept it *was* a new case. That the old case cool and clever supersleuth Rayford Goodman cracked so brilliantly hadn't been cracked at all. Worse, I nailed the wrong guy. Double worse, I did all the mistake-making at the top of my lungs, in *public*! I had scrapbooks, tapes, and cassettes loaded with being wrong!

It was no small voice shouting just leave it alone, don't kick the crawly old can of worms.

Not much doubt I'd rather write a book about my exploits as a big public hero saved Hollywood than take out a large double-page ad announcing what a horse's ass I'd been.

Not to mention helping Danny Pagani sue me for five million *because* I was a horse's ass. The *good* news being he'd only collect about seven and a half dollars—after legal fees ate up the car, the house, and the Christmas Club.

Those were the happy thoughts occupied me as the elevator got to Bradley's floor and I got in.

There was a Prissy Old Party inside, together with a tiny overgroomed pampered-looking dog shivering in a corner. The Prissy Old Party gave me a smile.

What the hell, it was the nineties—I smiled back. A small one, no teeth.

The elevator hit One, the door opened. I put my regular scowl back on my face and stepped out.

"Come along, Conan," he said to the dog, which immediately obeyed. Some Conan. "Hold the door, will you, love?" he said to me.

In for a penny . . . I held the door. Out they went, step for step. We weren't in Kansas anymore.

But, God knows why, as I headed for my car, he did remind me I had to phone Julie and see if she was free—and I mean *free*—to be my date tonight at Nipper's.

Which further reminded me, as I got into my "loaner" Rolls, just how much I was looking forward to talking to Carkeys. She'd been there, and the odds were awful strong she'd seen something, maybe *every*thing! At the least, she ought to be able to shed some light. Light. Harry fucking Light! Who'd believe it?

But it couldn't be Harry. For the same reason as Lefcourt: it was his picture too. And once Rita was gone and they had to recast her, *Gone to Carnival* had gone straight into the dumper. After that, there was a year or two Harry wasn't exactly top ten in flicks.

But, of course, he wouldn't necessarily have known that.

Still, you have to wonder, what possible motive?

To say nothing we're talking *Harry*—America's Harry!

Only there it was: Light Pictures. Owning the house Rita's mother lived in—and lived in so richly. Another thing, maybe it didn't entirely eliminate Lefcourt either. There was more than just a coincidence of initials with Lefcourt. They'd been partners in a lot of stuff together through the years besides making pictures. And sharing starlets—I couldn't count the times I'd had to act beard for one or the other. For one thing, between the two of them they owned half the San Fernando Valley. With first mortgage on the rest. So it wasn't hard to picture them in some kind of conspiracy. What was hard was figuring why. Why, why, why?

And what else did we know? Well, now that Harry's name had floated to the top, there was the left-hand business. Harry's left-hand salute was a trademark—caused by a boyhood injury to his right—common knowledge. Who hadn't heard how he fell from the trolley after hitching a ride on back? And got run over—"a terrible lesson, kids . . . that's how you get to be called Lefty"—what a good sport! Someone could have *used* that common knowledge to throw suspicion off themselves . . . Nah, nah, nobody could do that in the midst of a gory killing. They'd have to be . . . what, a maniac? So?

But Harry? *I* was being crazy. Involved, somehow, some way, but actually doing it? Harry?

Well, it was for sure I couldn't approach finding out anything like head-on. I'd really have to waltz on eggs. An attack on Harry'd be like an attack on the flag, the church, motherhood, and All We Hold Sacred. Whatever his part, damn well better get the facts up front. And damn well better be right.

Even then . . .

I hit Santa Monica Boulevard at King's Road and turned left, belching smog. But on impulse, instead of continuing straight where Holloway angled in and heading up La Cienega to Sunset, I bore left and continued on Santa Monica. I decided I'd best do something a bit more dramatic on the Adderley Rolls scam. So far I hadn't had nibble one on my ploy to have the bad guy contact me. And there was actual money I was supposed to be earning.

I continued on through the heart of West Hollywood, slowing at the Sports Connection—to take inventory on the entering and exiting of some of the most awesomely built women on God's earth. To be perfectly fair, God never planned women like these. It took a lot more than seven days and an odd rib to put one of them babies together.

I spotted a pair so absolutely perfect I almost ran up the curb. Be still, my infarking heart.

As I looked in my rearview mirror before resuming speed, I noticed another car had slowed with me and now picked up speed as I picked up speed. Perfectly natural. Probably lots of guys did it, slowing down as they passed the Sports Connection. Why wouldn't the driver of this green Jaguar XKE with the celebrity glass hiding him from view, whose license plate I'd catch if it got any closer?

I kept on, past the bus garage, past the artsy-strangey sculptures that'd replaced the railroad tracks—or maybe made *from* them. And finally, block or two before Doheny, came to Beverly Hills British Motors, where I turned the chugging, shuddering Silver Cloud on into the garage.

I shut off the motor, sat shaking till the suffering machine got the message, opened the door, and got out. I didn't see the XKE anywhere about.

A somewhat surprised Cedric Adderley, looking positively sterile in his white motor-doctor coat—with *shoulder* pads, don't you love Hollywood?—crossed to my side, arching an eyebrow in greeting.

"Well, Mr. . . . ?" he said.

"Franks," I cued him, since it was officially supposed to be our first meeting.

"I see your Cloud has a bit of a problem," he noted astutely.

"Right." I asked was he the owner, and told he was indeed, "informed" him I'd been in a few days before, but they'd given me such a crazy estimate so far out of line I was sure it was a mistake. And would he please straighten it out personally?

He said he would be delighted to look into the matter at once and make whatever adjustments were indicated. With which he went into his office to get my file.

I took the opportunity to case the place and get a line on who might be watching the action. It was a little disappointing. Several sincere mechanics—meaning darker-colored smocks—were actually working on several gorgeous cars. Another guy was doing something with a bank of seriously high-tech machinery looked it could sustain life on Mars. While two others seemed to be mostly busy brewing tea—in the basic, old-fashioned way, oddly. And the only one looked even remotely interested in me was good old surfer Ron-boy, who showed his perfect surfer teeth in a combination smile and sneer.

Adderley returned with my estimate, asked what was the problem, actually.

I told him the problem, actually, was his man thought I was some kind of easy mark he could just con into paying any fucking thing he asked, the crazy bastard having quoted me sixteen hundred and fifty actual dollars!

He read on, nodded.

"Yes?" he said.

"Almost funny, right?" I said.

"Uhm, no, actu . . . that seems about in line," he replied. "Of course, it's only an estimate. Could be less."

"Could be less? Of course it could be less. How could it be sixteen hundred and fifty dollars?" I asked, calculatedly raising my voice.

Adderley understood completely what I was up to, making a scene, clearly establishing I was in the market but not willing to pay the going rate. I was doing everything but say, "Come deal with me on the sly."

"Well, sir," he said, "with this kind of malfunction—exuding excessive exhaust—it might well require disassembly of large parts of the power train, don'tchu know."

"I don't care if you have to take apart a whole choo-choo train, don'tchu know, you can't seriously tell me it'd cost sixteen hundred and fifty *dollars*!" By now I was pretty loud. Outrage'll do that. Certainly those in at least half the garage could hear.

"I'm afraid I don't know what else to say. Our prices are our prices."

I upped the decibels. "It's highway fucking robbery! I'm not going to pay that kind of money. You gotta be out of your mind!" Now the whole garage could definitely hear me.

"Well," he countered, "the final determination is, of course, your own. As I say, it could be less. But I wouldn't want to mislead you: even if it is less, it would only be marginally."

"Well, marginally *this*!" I screamed, showing him the finger.

I did feel it was a touch rude—the man *was* English.

"It's your motor car," he said, ignoring the finger as he turned to go back to his office.

"Sure," I said, "you think you got us over a barrel, we can't get parts anyplace else. But I'm gonna call Rolls-Royce in London, England, and we'll see what they have to say, you holding a gun to my head!" I called after him, actually feeling angry.

"That's your privilege," he called back.

"I fucking well ain't going to fucking pay that kind of fucking money!"

"In that case, Mr. Franks, you're not going to obtain our fucking service," he replied, continuing on into his office.

I got into the car, slammed the door, started up, and—noting I'd had the full attention of everyone in sight, especially Ron—eased on out, damn near blinded by the smoke I was backing through.

Jolly good show.

I drove the old tank up Doheny, hung a left on Sunset, and continued on to the Hamburger Hamlet. There I left the car in front of a sign saying "Valet Parking," which also announced how much the used-to-be-free parking now cost. Plus the welcome news gratuities were accepted. No shit, I thought they'd be insulted. The guy told me I wouldn't need a ticket. They remember Rollses.

The host seated me in the inside-looking-like-outside part, which I liked, gave me a menu, and wished me a nice day. Wish me a nice meal would make more sense, I thought.

But actually, the Hamlet was an institution. They'd been around since the year one, when they actually had a *stand* on Sunset Boulevard. They had grown to a large and very successful chain based, I think, on a single radical idea: people might like their hamburgers some other way than well-done. They were the absolute first, I ever found, to give you medium rare when you ordered medium rare. Plus good service.

In the early days they had black waitresses, all of a uniform cafe-au-lait, all looking remarkably alike. They must have all come from the same tribe originally—or the same mad-scientist laboratory—and all real graceful and efficient.

Along came equal rights and feminism. And with equal rights and feminism, some clever male troublemaker must have sued them for reverse discrimination to open the ranks of waitresses to all comers, regardless of tribe or sex. Result? Now mostly all waiters, all white, and all gay. Progress.

I ordered a number eleven, "Our Greatest Burger"— a large beef patty, bacon, cheddar, Thousand Island dressing—medium rare; fries very crisp; salad with blue cheese. Your basic Cholesterol Special. Plus, a definite two-pounder. Why, I'll never know, but whenever I ate that there I gained two pounds. It didn't weigh two pounds—till you ate it.

While I waited the six minutes it would take, I went to the men's room, where they hid the pay phone. I called my answer machine and listened to myself tell me I wasn't home, and checked the messages. The pool man said I needed a new filtration system, and if I didn't pay pretty soon, a new pool man. Adderley wanted to talk to me, he wasn't satisfied with my modus operandi, don'-tchu know. And Luana's lawyer would appreciate a call-back. I bet.

And like that—nothing that was going to bring in a dollar.

I called Julie, got *her* answerphone, and asked did she want to go dancing tonight at Nipper's. I made clear this was a social invitation, not an offer of employment. I looked forward to the pleasure of her company and as-sured her she could count on my performance this time. That was a lie too; I was no better at dancing than ro-mancing . . . the days dwindle down to a precious few.

Then I came back, ate my perfect number eleven, paid the check, went outside, and there was the Rolls, parked right in front. It was always in front, I'd noticed.

So, getting with the spirit, I decided to spring for a two-buck tip. I gave the attendant a five-dollar bill to make change. In a flash, he pocketed the fiver, said thank you, and sprinted away—hands down winning the fastest Mexican-in-motion award. What the hell, I wasn't going to make a scene over three bucks—you know me. Especially three bucks I could charge to Adderley.

I popped into the car, took a sharp right up Sunset Hills Road, shifted down into second, and out of the corner of my eye spotted the green XKE edging past the intersection. Evidently he hadn't been the simple horny voyeur I'd hoped. He now hesitated, waiting for me to make a move.

I circled the block, coming down on Cory. I didn't see the Jag—maybe a flash of green up the hill, we'd see—turned and went east till I came to the mini-mall where my dry cleaners were. I turned in, parked. I'd be needing my suit tonight. Nobody else in sight; could be wrong.

Mr. Mull had some comment about catching up on the bill. I assured him I had every intention of getting to it the minute my Cayman Islands account completed transfer of funds from my Geneva account. I could see he wasn't totally sold. Considered holding my suit hostage. But in the end my bright, open smile carried the day, as he hit the button, starting the carousel.

Mr. Mull was a dour, skinny, craggy-faced individual, all hard edges and bones. He had deep-set hooded eyes that avoided contact with other people's, purple shadows under and over, a big Adam's apple, and long skeletal fingers with unkempt ridged nails. Like every other dry cleaner I'd ever seen, he looked like a mass murderer. My theory was it had something to do with the fumes.

I hung the suit on the suit-hanging hook in the back of the Rolls, closed the door, opened the front door, and grabbed a peek through the rearview mirror. Then, instead of climbing in, I slammed the door and broke into an all-out dash for the green Jag—on the other side of the lot— that was doing all this following.

But he'd left the motor running, and now popped it into gear, pulling out. I considered racing to the exit to try barring the way. But discretion being the better part of cowardice, and bodies being real bad at barring, I thought better of it, stopped, and turned back. Suddenly I heard a roar, and whirled around to see the Jag backing full bore *at* me, trying to run me down!

I dodged, he dodged. I dodged again, he dodged again. Dodging seemed to be doing the job, till it didn't when I ran out of dodging room, and here he came hunting.

At the last second I leapt to the side and onto the hood of an old Pontiac—glad it was an American car and *had* a hood. The driver slid to a stop, raced the motor a second, considering options. Then, seeing he was drawing a little too much attention for now, he rammed the clutch into forward gear and took off noisily.

The darkened windows kept him from view. All I got was a flash of license plate which looked to be a vanity tag, no numbers. Just what seemed to be AAR, which of course didn't tell me anything.

But Francie could find out. She better. And at this point, I didn't care what favors she had to exchange for it, either.

14

Mark Bradley

There were two reasons Francie and I had gone back to the office. We figured the Fox police lock was security enough for Brian, considering in another minute and a half he'd've needed security from me. The other reason was that Dickie Penny liked to see his writers actually writing. The thinking and the researching and plotting all left him cold. What impressed him were pages, and not only pages, the making of pages.

So we were in my office, showing the flag, as it were, when Penny stuck his ugly face in.

"I don't hear the clacking of keys. You guys working, or what?"

"We're working, Dickie. Even when we're or what, we're working."

"Yeah? How many pages ya got?"

"I got most of it worked out."

"No pages yet?" he screamed.

"Tell you the truth," I said. "I exaggerated—I don't have most of it worked out."

"What's to work out? You got a man's life, you write it down. Where it's exciting, you leave it exciting. Where it's dull, you make it exciting. You never did that before?"

"Well, this one's a little different. The most significant event in Rayford Goodman's life was the American Beauty Rose murder case, I'm sure you'll agree."

"Yeah . . . ?"

"So, hold on to your hat"—Penny tended to bring out the cliché in a person—"it's beginning to look like Goodman got the wrong guy!"

I'd expected this to knock him on his keister, put the roses in his cheeks, at least raise his eyebrows. (See what

I mean?) But nothing. Unless you consider scratching his scrotum something.

"Where'd you get a crazy idea like that?"

Francie indicated a willingness to field this.

"It's sort of developed from a brilliant combination of investigative reporting by Mark, here," she said, "and inspired, intuitive research by yours truly."

"So you don't have any pages?" The guy sure kept his eye on the ball.(!)

"Forget pages for a minute."

"That's easy for you to say."

"If we're right, and we *are* right, there's no telling where the story might lead."

"Yeah, into the toilet. Suppose you are right. So then instead of writing a story about the famous solution by a famous detective of a famous crime, you write about a famous crime and how no one ever solved it, including the writer. Isn't that satisfying? You crazy?"

"Yeah, but suppose we, ourselves, really *do* solve it?"

"Given we go to press in six weeks—more like five now—I can't live with supposes. Sit yourself down, start writing, and write what everybody knows. How Goodman solved the case by nailing Pagani and putting that slimy porno purveyor away. Which suits everybody fine."

With which Penny strode from the room, leaving a sulfurous cloud of vile cigar smoke as proxy for his breath.

"Suits everybody fine, if you don't include Pagani," *sotto voce*'d Francie.

I couldn't understand how *any* publisher could fail to be excited by this new promising way the book could go.

"Can you believe that?" I said to Francie.

"Yeah, considering it might cost him more if we go into overtime. He's got a firm print date. You gotta know with Penny there's no contest between truth and money."

"Well, I'm not writing that other book, period."

At which point Penny stuck his head back in.

"And if you're thinking of defying me, don't defy me. It may look like you got me over a barrel now. But if you ever expect me to publish your great American novel later, you got two chances, slim, none, and none."

With which he deliberately discharged some more hideous cigar smoke and withdrew.

"Was he calling me Slim, do you think?"

"Or None," replied Francie, punching something into the computer. "Give me a minute, I want to get that license plate for Goodman." More punching—a reply; another—another. A beat or two more, then, instead of the printout I expected, she shook her head and shut down the machine.

"There is no AAR. I even tried a number or two around it, 1AAR, and the ever-popular 2AAR and 4AAR. No AAR."

"That'll be reassuring to Goodman next time they try to run him down." And what the hell was I supposed to do with this story?

I crossed back to my desk, checked my watch—who was I kidding? That was it for today. If there'd ever been any chance I'd do some pages, old inspiration-killing publisher-editor Dick Penny'd sure taken care of that. Such being the case, might as well go home, clean up, have a bite, and wait for Goodman to pick us up and take us to Nipper's.

I so informed my research associate and also date for the evening. No argument there. I closed up shop—meaning turned off the lights, next best to pages as far as Penny was concerned—and we started out.

"You know," Francie said, sniffing the horrible air as we reached the door, "I've been thinking of taking up cigar smoking."

"Good idea," I replied. "That way you could get to be a virgin again."

We were in Goodman's loaner Rolls, heading west toward Beverly Hills on Santa Monica Boulevard.

Francine, actually dressed in real clothes, black high-heel boots, leather slacks, leather jacket—first time I'd seen her in anything costing more than a hundred dollars—sat in back beside me. I was decked out in my Armani midnight blue, with the slick silk blue-and-red one-previous-owner-who-only-wore-it-on-Saturday-nights art-deco tie I'd bought at Those Were the Days on Melrose.

Goodman was driving. He seemed to be wearing what couldn't really be a continental suit in an olive-drab color. It was probably just short. Under this he sported an almost white shirt no doubt bought when he was a lot younger and ten or twenty pounds lighter, judging from the tightness of the collar. Which, however, was affording him a high color that might pass for sunburn. On that he'd Windsor-knotted a yellow tie—a remnant from the year yellow was the power color—with a small designer motif I decided not to investigate, since it was more than a little likely to contain a bunch of tiny K-Marts.

Beside him was a hot little number whose name was Julie whom he described as a dear old friend, dressed in leathers and feathers that made Francine's look like a starter kit. Julie's was a here-and-there number with bits of leather vying for space with more substantial bits of flesh. The whole production was bounded on the north by a generous expanse of bosom, at the equator by a tidy innie belly button, and concluding south just millimeters below her obviously valuable vulva. It was basically the sort of thing one sees in the window of Addictions that in your heart of hearts you don't believe anybody actually buys but Cher. But Julie had, evidently, and, I must say, really did it proud. Which I had to admit did set me to wondering if by "dear" old friend Goodman hadn't actually meant "expensive."

At any rate, he now turned down Rodeo Drive, past Little Santa Monica, on down the fabled street, and finally pulled up in front of the Rodeo Collection. Noting an open spot at the curb, he started to pull in.

A valet-parking attendant came over to take the car. Goodman told him he'd just leave it there in the street. The attendant told him there was no parking there in the street. Goodman started to get angry. Why not?—it was a perfectly good spot. There was no paint on the curb to indicate limited parking. He wasn't about to be bullied by special interests.

The attendant indicated a sign on the light standard that prohibited anything but discharging passengers during hours that might be advantageous to valet parking. Goodman muttered at the venality of corrupt officialdom and its susceptibility to the blandishments of special interests. Not in so many words, exactly. What he actually said was, "Fucking goddamn payoff, the son of a bitch bastards," before yielding to the inevitable and surrendering the car.

The Rodeo Collection is sort of a shopping mall—the way rhinestones are sort of diamonds. It's gorgeous. A pair of socks costs the equivalent of a Laplander's annual salary—and I'm talking about the premier. To buy a belt the average American plastic surgeon would have to do an eye and a half. You get the idea. It brings new meaning to the word "exorbitant." I love it.

It was ten minutes to eleven when we arrived at the relatively inconspicuous entry to the disco, before which was an even more unimpressive little table, behind which was a pretty girl, on which (the table, not the girl) was either a toolkit or a money box, and before which was a large-enough guy to make you pay.

As a member I was entitled to one guest free of your basic couvert, and to bring two more, who had to pay ten dollars each—Goodman and Julie. I sensed resistance when Goodman's already rosy neck turned flame red.

"I got it," I said, to forestall apoplexy. "My boss has deep pockets."

"With zippers at the top," added Francie as I paid the tariff and we climbed the flight of high-tech lighted stairs and were greeted by music loud enough to have a wind-chill factor.

Ten minutes to eleven is not prime time in a disco. There were exactly four other people in the place. They were Goodman's ex-wife, Luana, with an extremely handsome young man, and Sally Light, with what was probably the resident gay. At any rate, obvious enough to render the question of adultery moot—which no doubt was calculated.

We were led, I thought at first fortunately, to the other side of the room, where *un*fortunately we were taken to what was clearly the worst table in the place. Since the rest of the tables were all unoccupied, it would seem to call for a bit of a shmear.

Goodman, don't you know, didn't see it that way.

"We'd like that table there," he said, indicating a ringside lounge.

"That's taken," said the maître. "They're all taken."

"Isn't that remarkable?" said Goodman. "Not hardly a soul here, and all these tables are taken. How about over there?"

He indicated a table across the room—near his ex-wife *et al.*, whom I guess he hadn't seen.

"Very well, this way, sir," said the maître, suddenly agreeable, leading us across the empty dance floor and over to the section on the right.

To my surprise, Goodman evidently was aware of the other foursome, nodding pleasantly in passing and offering, " 'Evening, ladies, gents," and continuing on before a barb could be bandied.

We were seated at a tiny table on which was an ice bucket in the shape of a top hat, in which was a bottle of champagne, and beside which was a wine list of champagnes. All of which I took to be in the nature of a hint for the suggestible.

Goodman, hosting expansively, took everybody's orders—which were more mundane. Vodka this and vodka that, vodka with and vodka without.

The waiter approached, was given the order, smiled tolerantly, and explained we were in the champagne section. Which, it developed, meant the choices were limited to champagne. I sneaked a peek at the list—the cheapest bottle went for a hundred and sixty.

Goodman beckoned the waiter to come closer. The music was loud, and apparently he didn't want to shout. The waiter leaned in, pencil poised and eager. Goodman grabbed him by his satin lapel and pulled him down to within an inch of his face. The waiter sensed there might be some difficulty impending. This was confirmed when Goodman informed the chap there had been a slight misunderstanding. What he was dealing with here was not some economy-wrecking Jap bastards. Nor a bunch of escaped Iranians sneaked their loot past the ayatollahs. We were fucking American citizens. Members of the country. *Therefore* we would have four vodkas, one with club soda, one with tonic, and two with just rocks.

The waiter, still sampling Goodman's breath, looked

for help in the direction of the maître d'. The maître d',
knowing a stiff when he saw one, shrugged. The waiter
said, "Very well, sir," and Goodman released his lapel,
even smoothed it down.

"There," he said, smiling. "It's not all that hard to be
reasonable, is it?"

The waiter departed.

"Sorry to put you through that, ladies," said Goodman. "It's just you have to fight injustice wherever you
find it."

"See," whispered Francie to me. "He's a champion of
liberty, when all this while you thought he was just a
tightwad."

The music continued. Sally and her companion, Luana
and hers, got up to dance. I asked Francie if she were
interested in tripping the light fantastic. She said if it was
all the same to me, she'd rather dance.

As we got up, I noticed Julie indicating she, too, would
like to dance. Goodman elaborately pretended not to
notice.

And that's the way it went—for ten minutes, fifteen
minutes.

Some of the people with "reservations" starting showing up; other couples got up to dance.

Goodman kept his eye peeled on the door.

Francie and I had enough dancing for a while, left the
floor—on which Luana and the Gorgeous Guy and Sally
and hers continued indefatigably—and returned to the
table. We were just in time to hear Goodman tell Julie,
"I know I said I was taking you dancing. What I meant
was I was taking you to a place that *had* dancing. I didn't
say *I* was going to dance. Frankly I would dance . . ."

"Only . . . ?"

"Only I'm here on business."

"I thought you said this was a nonbusiness en-
gagement."

"Nonbusiness for *you*. I'm looking out for somebody."

"Number one?"

I liked Julie—she was feisty. She had perk, a bunch of
spunk. Did figure to be a hooker, how else would Goodman come off with someone like her? Although, to be
frank, Luana wasn't exactly chopped foie gras either. I

guess it just goes to show, you can't judge a book by its taste in clothes.

Having given eavesdropping my full attention, I hadn't noticed Francie pulling out her little bottle and ducking down half under the table—which averted suspicion, it only looked like she was giving head—to take a hasty couple of hits.

"God damn, Francie, you got to stop that," said Goodman, and I immediately had a good idea what "that" was.

"Right, next thing you know, I'll be cursing."

"You won't even consider quitting?"

"Nope. I like to dope. Anyway, contrary to whatever you think, it's not that big a thing in my life. I'd rather *do* it every now and then than go to AA or CA and spend *all* my time *thinking* about it and *talking* about it and being with a bunch of scrungy addicts."

"It's great to know you have it under control."

By now it was close to eleven-thirty and the sincere disco crowd had begun to congregate. The tables were mostly full, and filling fast, though there was a noticeable lack of crush in ye old champagne section—a lesson learned.

I left to make a quick call home and see how Brian was doing. He was doing crabby.

I assured him I wasn't dancing at all—not even one. Yes, I *knew* how much he enjoyed dancing. We definitely *would*, the moment he got his strength back. I *was* looking forward to it. We couldn't have danced together here anyway—we'd go to Rage and dance the night away. No, I wasn't having a good time without him. It was work, like overtime. One of those sacrifices I had to make. Yes, I'd be happy to stop off on the way home and bring him a pizza—loaded with you-know-what.

I returned to the table to find Francie and Julie deep in confidential conversation—the best of friends. Francie was gregarious. The coke didn't hurt either, which, judging from the evidence on Julie's nostril, Francie hadn't been selfish with.

"Been to the ladies' room?" I asked.

"Yes, did we miss you?" answered Francie.

Goodman, making wet circles with the bottom of his

glass on the tabletop, had looked away from the door for a moment, so it was I who saw the short, dark, Whoopi Goldbergish woman, wearing a purple cap pulled low over her eyes, which in any case were covered by huge dark-rose-tinted glasses, green jacket collar pulled up. The only thing missing from her incognito kit being a false nose, beard, and a sign saying "This is me!"

"There, I think," I said to Goodman.

He looked up.

"Right," he said, recognizing her, and starting to rise, at which precise point Sally, Luana, and their escorts all converged on the table to add insult.

There followed struggling and harsh words, the last along the lines of ". . . know better than to expect you to be civil," and by the time either of us was undiverted enough to look up, Carkeys was gone.

15

Rayford Goodman

I tried desperately to disengage from my wife, who certainly in the past hadn't been shy about leaving *me*. I managed finally, only got further hung up by the maître d', who, God knows why, somehow got the impression I was trying to run out on the tab. Got past that, and at last dashed down the stairs, to the courtyard inside the mall, and through, out to the street. By which time I couldn't reasonably have expected her to still be there, and I was right, and she wasn't.

The valet parker *was* there, however. Not to go get your car, this was the *in* valet parker. The *out* valet parker was downstairs. But this one might have seen someone.

I described Carkeys, asking if he'd seen a little black woman looked like Whoopi Goldberg, wearing a purple cap, dark-rose-tinted glasses, and a green leather jacket with the collar turned up.

He didn't seem certain. Since that description could fit anybody!

"How many people have come out in the last two, three minutes?"

"Jes' wan."

"Was it her?"

"I'm nah sure . . ."

I pulled out a ten-dollar bill, which he snatched like a gecko gulping a fly.

"Ju min wis porple cop, dork-rose-teen glass, an' grin jacket wis color oup?"

"That's the one."

"Jais, I see her. She come out. Das her."

"And . . . ?"

"An' wha'?"

"Took a walk? Sang a song? Flew away in a helicopter?"

"Es har' to 'member."

I gave him another ten. Graciously. Sure.

"She liv' in grin car—ax key ee."

"Driving?"

"Es har' to—"

I grabbed him by the shirtfront.

"Somewan else dri'."

I let go my grip, thanked him. I was finding out a lot. The way to get ahead in this life seemed to have something to do with grabbing people by a hunk of cloth around the face.

So, whoever'd been trailing me and occasionally trying to run me down was connected with Carkeys. Which was kind of cute, considering one wanted to kill me to keep me from finding out something. And the other wanted to get to me to tell me whatever the something was the other one didn't want me to know. Or was it only a ploy to set me up so the one who wanted to kill me would know where to find me?

Except the green XKE was nowhere in sight. Which meant the one who wanted to kill me didn't want to kill me at this particular time.

I went back inside, by which time my party had left the club and was waiting for me. We went down the escalator to where the *out* valet parking was. I paid the bandit fee and waited the no-excuse-for-it long time while several people who came after us got their cars. After which they finally brought mine. We all piled in as still another guy held the door for me and stuck his hand out expecting a reward for this terrible service. I tried to close it, but he held it firmly in your basic grip of greed.

"Hef a nize day, meester."

I didn't have a nice day, I wasn't having a nice day, I wasn't going to have a nice day. And I wasn't going for another holdup.

The back window rolled down a few inches and a hand snaked out with a five-dollar bill in it. It was Bradley's, of course. The guy let go my door like it was molten metal and lunged at the fiver.

"*Ju* hef a nize day," he amended, laying his good

wishes on the right patron, and not wanting someone who figured the regular charge was plenty highway robbery enough for ransoming his car to have a nice day by mistake.

"Noblesse oblige," said Bradley.

Easy for him to say, he was educated.

I drove out of there, explaining to Bradley I'd either been set up or Carkeys'd been spooked—bad choice of words. The chances of making progress tonight seemed pretty slim, so I suggested we call it a day.

"The chances of making progress with *me* are pretty slim," said Julie. "Un*less* . . . you care to stop and feed my face at say Spago, how's that strike you?"

"I can't think of anything I'd rather do than go hand some smartass stuck-up snotnose with a thousand-dollar suit twenty bucks for the privilege of waiting at the bar for an hour and a half before being allowed to pay four times what a pizza oughtta cost."

"Is that a yes?" asked Francie.

"I can get us in," said Julie.

"Look, you don't understand. I got nothing against paying for things. I even got nothing against paying a premium for going to the head of the line. What I hate is when you pay for it and they spit in your eye."

"I can get us in without getting spit in the eye."

"I'm not goddamn hungry," I said.

True, I was getting to be a grouch. True, I was starting to sound like all old people get to sound. But also true, I had been having people take advantage of me. And shoot at me. And try to run over me. And in general leave some doubt on the odds of my going the distance. And if those kind of things made me a little testy, so be it. Still . . .

"I'm sorry, I didn't mean to bark at anybody. I'm just a little bugged I missed an important connection there. At the moment Spago doesn't happen to top my list of can't-live-withouts."

"Reasonable enough. We understand," said Bradley. "No need to apologize."

"Hey, if we aren't for each other, who will be?" said Julie.

"Earth is a lifeboat, and we all have to pull our oars," said Francie.

We went to Spago.

Later, I dropped Francine and Bradley off at his place and drove back up the hill to mine, where Julie wanted to do it for free, so I gave her fifty bucks to go home and leave me alone.

I opened the front door to go get the paper. It was a nice morning. I had hardly any hangover. How can you, the way they water the drinks at the kind of places we'd been drinking?

And speaking of watering, there was definitely something wrong with the sprinkler system. Some places looked like desert, while others tended more toward the Okefenokee Swamp. I was definitely losing ground on the grounds.

In fact, I was losing ground all around. I'd best get my ass in gear and pull this case out of sewer city or forget living here altogether. (I'd already forgotten I didn't *get* the paper anymore.)

I heard the phone ringing, and went back inside to answer.

It was Francine, thanking me for a lovely time and telling me she'd double-double-checked and the computer still hadn't kicked out any name on AAR.

I couldn't see how that could be, since I'd seen the plate, and I knew it was California.

"So what good's your wonderful computer, you can't come up with a simple three-letter plate?" I asked.

"Well," said Francie in a tone you might use to a backward cactus, "what I'm going to do, Ray, I'm going to assume under the stressful circumstances of someone trying to separate your legs from your torso, it's just possible you made a mistake."

"Hey, I'm only human."

I thought I heard a "barely" but decided to let it pass.

"Therefore the next plan is to set up a program for the computer to follow and see who owns, if not AAR, then BAR, CAR, DAR, and so forth, then the middle letters, ABR, ACR, ADR, then the thirds—you get the idea."

"Okay, sounds reasonable."

"I'll get it going."

"And thank you, Francine—I appreciate it."

There was a pause, as if nobody'd ever thanked her before.

"Well, you're more than welcome," she replied. "Hang on for Mark."

I hung on for Mark. Mark wanted to know if I could meet him and we'd keep working while he got a haircut. I assumed he meant a haircut by the word "stylist." I said suits me. He said would I like one too? Maybe he could get the guy to squeeze me in—for some reason mentioning it cost forty bucks.

I figured he was kidding.

The sign said "Hair Today." I suppose to be trendy. But to me it either sounded like a *People*-type-magazine article or else like half a warning—Hair Today: Gone Tomorrow.

The first person I spotted was Francie, getting a manicure. She waved a wet-nailed hand at me. I guess it was an equal-sex-opportunity beauty-barber.

"Hey," she said. "Just the man I want to see."

"I thought you were working on the license plate."

"I am."

"Hardly looks it."

"Well, technically, the computer is. Even as we speak."

"Oh, I get it, you already programmed it and it's working."

"*Exactement, mon cher.* Now, do me a favor . . . open my purse . . ."

I did.

"Inside that large bottle of . . . vitamin pills, you'll see a big black beau . . . black vitamin B."

I gave her a gimlet-eyed stare.

"Do be a love and pop one into me pore salivatin' mouf, won'cher dear?"

As I hesitated, she added, "I'm taking an oral exam for another degree in less than an hour, and if there's one thing I can count on to make me oral, it's that black mother."

I popped the pill into her mouth. This wasn't the time and place for a lecture on morality. She washed it down with some cold coffee in a container. Anyway, I sort of always admired people who went to college. And those who went to college after they'd already *been* to college, well . . .

She mimed a kiss which, the truth be known, seemed genuine and not her usual cynical put-down. I moved on to the back of the shop and quickly spotted Bradley being done up by his stylist. As expected. What *wasn't* expected, and seemed a fantastic break, was the guy in the next chair, probably also in for a forty-dollar styling. It happened to be none other than R. Symington Lefcourt, the eightyish movie mogul—and one of the original founding gonifs—who'd produced *Gone to Carnival*.

Lefcourt's chair was in a nearly horizontal position, the old guy half-snoozing with a wet towel over his eyes.

I exchanged greetings with Bradley, and then, as if taken by surprise, said, "Say, Mr. Lefcourt! How nice to see you!"

"Whozat?" came the reply under the wet towel.

"Ray Goodman here. You remember me, Mr. Lefcourt?"

"Hrmpf."

"Listen, what a break, running into you. I've been trying to make an appointment to discuss some matters of mutual interest . . ."

"Call my secretary."

"I did, I have, but sort of ran into a little missed communication, with Miss Eldrege, and Miss Kay, and Ma Bell in general. Anyhow, since we're both here, getting haircuts, stylings, I wonder if you'd mind—"

"I mind."

"You do remember me, Ray Goodman? The detective? I've worked for you so many times?"

"Of course I remember," he said, half-sitting up, lifting a corner of the compress. "This is Lefcourt Productions, not Alzheimer Productions. The body may not be Arnold Schvartzer, but the mind is a razor blade."

"I know, and I couldn't agree more. That's why I want to ask your advice, to seek your wisdom . . ."

"Don't shine me on, buddy boy, I've been yessed by the best."

"But if we could talk, for just a few moments . . . ?"

"We could, but we won't. I got a headache. A sinus migraine. Hitler and Stalin should share a headache like this."

He lay back down and replaced the compress.

"And that's all I have to say on the subject."

He crossed his hands on his chest, end of speech.

The subject? I hadn't even mentioned the subject. And now the minutes were rolling by, and my golden opportunity going by the by. The man just lay there, with all that information, those secrets, all those answers!

I had to do something. No way I'd get another shot like this. Desperate-measures time.

"Just one thing, Mr. Lefcourt," I said finally. "I wouldn't bother you at a time like this when I know you're suffering a terrible sinus migraine, but, just by some far-out coincidence, only today I located the absolute, perfect, no-fooling-around, surefire cure for sinus migraines!"

There was a brief silence, then a reluctant grunt. "You got my attention."

"Don't move a muscle."

I dashed over to Francie, took her handbag, and without so much as a by-your-leave opened it up and took out the bottle of "vitamins."

"Black beauty?" I asked, pointing at the amphetamine.

"Gets my vote."

"With your permission?"

"The devil loves company."

"It's for research," I said, taking the pill, dashing to the water fountain, filling a cup, and taking cup and pill over to Lefcourt.

"Mr. Lefcourt, just swallow this and I guarantee in ten minutes you'll feel like a million bucks."

"Mr. Goodman, on bad days I feel like a million bucks. A good day is at least ten million."

I handed him the pill, the paper cup of water, and watched him swallow. Now, if it didn't kill the old bastard, it might just get him talking.

He recovered his eyes, lay back down, and I settled into the chair next to him to wait it out.

Bradley had watched the whole bit with a touch of smugness. He knew I didn't approve of drugs. He also knew I was on the job, and that came first. It wasn't a case of compromising your integrity, it was more like putting your priorities in order. (Right, said the man, selling his mother down the river.)

To my dismay, Lefcourt seemed to have fallen asleep, and now started to snore gently.

I looked at Francie. She nodded her head reassuringly. I guess the message was not to worry. But I *did* remember they gave Ritalin to overactive kids to slow them down. What if this upper made this oldster even downer? But Francie had indicated don't worry. And after all, who was the resident dope expert here?

I stared, watching him sleep, hearing him snore, feeling so frustrated. I wanted inside the man's head—to get to what he had to know. Always assuming, of course, he hadn't gone senile on me.

You've heard of time standing still? It was going goddamn backwards, I swear. Eight minutes, nine . . . eleven—hope on a change of rhythm. Nope on the change of rhythm. Thirteen, fourteen—suddenly two short snorts, a single loud shot, and up popped Lefcourt, snatched away the compress, and leapt out of the chair.

"Works!" he said.

With which he started pacing the floor and roaming the room as he said the following:

"You got here a gold mine. People know about this pill? I'd like personally to invest the vast resources of Lefcourt Productions to make this pill, it's already on the market I know, probably got a patent, certainly got a patent, wouldn't you, maybe we could do a generic, wonderful! What do you want to know? I'll tell you what you want to know, you want to know from Rita Rose. You want to know all the stuff you didn't know when you were doing the right thing by the industry that nourished and nurtured you during the good times and the bad, and has meant so much for this great nation and in projecting the real image of our great democracy abroad. Okay, you're writing a book, I heard you're writ-

ing a book, I know you're writing a book, so what'll the
book be on, you're a Hollywood detective, it'll be on
Hollywood, of course—and I know you will once again
do the right thing, and tell it like it is—that's what they
say these days when they want to express a very one-
sided opinion, tell it like it is. No, like it ain't! Well, like
it is, the way *we* saw it, which, you might say, is nobody's
business—were they the ones putting up millions of dollars on an idea, on a flicker of light?"

Whew, I didn't mind listening, but the thoughts zoom-
ing off in a million directions . . . ! How the hell was I
ever going to steer him into talking about anything might
remotely relate to the case?

"Rita Rose! You're talking Rita Rose, right?" he continued. Maybe there is a god. "Beautiful girl, what a girl.
Anybody's got prejudice could forget it with her. I'll tell
you something, we're talking excellence. Perfection.
Shtup, my God!" Which seemed to take him down memory lane for a moment or two—but he was in the area,
on the subject.

"Why she had to go get killed . . ." There were, to
my great surprise, actually tears in his eyes. Francie nodded again. I guess a crying jag was normal.

"That night! That was a night, if you had to pick one
crazy night out of all the nights! There we were, in the
middle of production, could have been the biggest, the
best . . . we had Rita Rose, we had Harry Light, we had
Dubie Dietrich—ah, Dubie, poor shlep. All that coming
and going, can you have any idea what it was like?"

The question wasn't meant to be answered. I
couldn't've gotten a word in edgewise anyhow before he
continued:

"Who was in that room? I'll tell you who—everybody!
And most was doing it with her, I can tell you. *I* saw
her, must have been ten o'clock, late for me, but a girl
like that you didn't mind missing sleep, you understand
what I'm talking? Of course, one way or another, you
paid. It was quid pro dough—there was complaints, there
was demands. In those days they didn't say demands,
they said they were unhappy, they said so much was on
their mind they couldn't act. It was demands, believe me.
Even so, didn't always give in, you know. She wanted,

you understand, insurance, for example. Lots of insurance. Insurance on her—that I took, to cover the picture, the insurance where Lefcourt Productions was insured. Normal, we all did that. Otherwise couldn't be no *Gone to Carnival* once Rita Rose gone to Forest Lawn. But she wanted should be insurance for the mother. I said sure, you think I did it? No way, Jose. She wanted insurance for what was called 'unnamed child'—she had a child, you knew that? Thought I didn't know, I was just going to insure on the general chance? I didn't insure, either. Said yes, did nothing."

Which meant, of course, that the whole Mama Rose money source was a lie. She wasn't living on insurance— the money was coming from somewhere else. Although it was just possible Mama Rose herself didn't know.

"The husband too, Harley Williams, him we paid enough, believe me. Say, you know, you took care most of it. But still there was no getting rid of him. Him I saw too, that night—when I was leaving, he was coming— that piece garbage wouldn't even say hello on my own lot! I had to work, there was at the time the inventory tax, and we had to decide what was in stock and what was in development, and what money went where, and what got hid where, you know the business—it was already the politicians didn't take care of like they used to. They still took your money, but now they had 'integrity' and 'principle'—oil money. So, of course, that was my alibi, like I needed one, of course, the head of the studio—heh heh—that I was working . . . you could ask Miss Eldrege, oh, lots of my people, the accountants, the vice-presidents, Miss Kay . . ."

I remembered questioning Miss Eldrege routinely back in sixty-three. And she said the late work night he was talking about had been the night before. As a result of which *her* alibi had been she hadn't come to the studio the day of the murder at all. She and her staff were exhausted. So for some reason Lefcourt was muddying the waters now, after all this time. Did it mean he, himself, had no alibi, and was afraid I was going to find that out? Then where was he and what was he doing that night?

"Harry, too, you know, was there in the dressing room."

I was under the impression Harry'd been with Sally and Arthur Rollins all night. Each'd vouched for the other. Which opened up both Harry *and* Rollins. But especially Harry, considering all the other things. And sure, it *couldn't* be Harry, it was all too obvious. But suppose it *was*—like it *usually* was, when it was obvious. . . .

"You know, in those days Harry was a big cocksman, not the elder statesman of comedy like today . . ."

But Harry aside, how would Lefcourt have seen that, if he was busy taking inventory with his staff?

"Mama Rose, I remember too, she was there at least part of the time, because we discussed a recipe my own mama used to make. Then there was, you know, you proved it, Pagani. Him I saw with my own eyes when I happened to stop by the editing rooms and he was crossing the lot . . ."

Which could have accounted for some of the time Lefcourt spent, if he was watching the editing of Pagani's porno. The stuff was just pouring out of Lefcourt. But it was just a mass of information none of which seemed to pin anything down. Everything he said just opened up more possibilities without closing any doors.

"Carkeys, naturally, she was always around somewhere, shlepping, making, doing—like so much there you half the time never even saw her. She's back in town, by the way, I'm letting her stay in Dubie's old place on Laurel Canyon. I have the key. I have everything, you know, I'm Dubie's conservator. I didn't want the job, believe me, but someone had to, there's money now with cassettes, and reruns, plus maybe after you and CBS get done with all the publicity, a nice reissue of *Gone to Carnival*—there could be some money for Dubie, so it was a responsibility I couldn't evade, after all, we are both of the industry . . ."

Nice and neat for Lefcourt, complete control to keep Dubie on ice indefinitely.

". . . and Arthur Rollins stopped by too—at least that's what Harry told me, the two of them met outside Rita's dressing room and went out for a bite, and I forget whether they took . . . no, didn't take Dubie, nobody saw him—why everybody thought he did it at first. Poor shlemiel, he's out, you know. On furlough. Like it's the army, they gave him a pass. My responsibility, he's at my house—the pool house—*in* the house makes me a little nervous, because even they don't say he's cured, they just pump enough tranquilizers to stop the Turkish army, and give him the weekend off, and maybe, all right it was Pagani did Rita Rose, but Dubie sure did that dog, and there is a side of him not very nice. Can't help it, but still . . ."

And he fell silent for a moment. I sneaked a glance at Bradley, who was open-mouth stunned at this explosion of talk, but like me cautious not to break the flow.

"So—you want to get together, you want to talk, you'll call Miss Eldrege, we'll talk." With which he fell back asleep.

I couldn't think of anything else I wanted to ask him. It was going to take me a while to sift and sort what he'd already said. I was really pleased. I didn't even raise a stink when Bradley's stylist guy came over, wrapped a towel around my neck, and started giving me a forty-dollar haircut.

16

Mark Bradley

I was starting to like this detective business. In a way, of course, it wasn't too far different from investigative reporting. Except we'd always used the term "investigative reporting" as a joke when applied to, say, getting to the bottom of Bambi Blain—not that plenty of people hadn't *gotten* to her bottom. But that was another story.

We'd been very lucky with Lefcourt, not only to get to him at all, but to get to him in such a receptive condition—legal niceties aside. We'd certainly learned a lot of things, not the least of which was the effects of amphetamines on eighty-year-olds.

Or, as Goodman so inelegantly put it, "Sure made the old fart spill his guts."

Francie took a proprietary bow, adding the philosophical observation, "There's good and bad in every dope."

Goodman had finished his styling, concluded his bitching about the bill, and we had all left the beauty salon and were back on Canon, crossing the street to where I'd parked the BMW. Goodman was walking with his head canted to one side as if favoring a broken neck, which struck me as odd, till I factored in the slight breeze from the north and reckoned he wasn't risking a mussed hairdo at these prices.

There'd been such an overload of information, it was hard to figure where to start. But it was, after all, Goodman's case, and his call, so as we approached my car I asked, "Well, what's the agenda?"

To which he replied, "I believe the agenda's a Japanese automobile." The man did surprise me from time to time.

We climbed into the car and Francie rummaged through her bag.

"Anybody mind if I smoke?"

I mumbled my customary vague objection, since I knew she wouldn't respect it anyway, and Goodman didn't care.

Let me amend that. Goodman didn't care if she smoked a cigarette. He cared a lot when she pulled out a joint the size of Cleveland and filled the car with enough marijuana smoke to cater a Rastafarian wedding.

"Look, lady," he said. "I don't like you doing that stuff. And I double don't like you doing it in front of me."

"That goes for me too," I said, inhaling as deeply as I could, giving a lift to whatever contact high might be in the offing.

"But what I can't understand most of all is why you take an upper to get up and then take a downer to get down."

"It's not a downer, it's a mellower," she replied. "I'm still heading up, this is just a little sideways. I'll get back to you later this afternoon on who owns the green Jaguar. But now, Mark, if you'll be good enough to drop me off at the corner by the ticket under which is my car, I'll be out and off to take my exam."

And I did and she was—with best wishes and kindest regards.

Goodman opened the windows wide to get rid of the smoke, while yet angling his head to maintain his coiffure.

"The agenda?" I reminded him.

"Okay, first off, Dubie's out, right? And we do have to talk to him again. We now know that Harry wasn't totally, always, opposed to previously established alibis, in the company of Sally and Rollins—I'm starting to sound like Lefcourt. Quite the opposite. We now know for a fact Harry was alone with Rita sometime that night. So our first order of business has to be get with Dubie and see what *he* knows about Harry's being with Rita. And if possible, when—which is very important."

"Isn't it just as important to make contact with Carkeys, now that we know where she is?"

"We will, but first, since Lefcourt's here in town, let's quick swing by his place and check out Dubie."

Which then became the plan.

Lefcourt had, as you might expect, a suitably mogulish mansion on Bellagio in Bel Air. It was only slightly larger than the Colosseum. I couldn't at first observe that, since like many homes in Bel Air, it is completely hidden from the street. The vegetation is so lush and all-encompassing, the impression is that you are on a country lane or, really, driving through a forest. It seems totally uninhabited—which must drive the sightseers absolutely bananas.

One knows one has arrived at one's destination when suddenly confronted by a pair of massive wrought-iron gates stout enough to withstand an assault by a Nazi panzer division—a not totally paranoid possibility at the time they were erected.

Two television cameras ran hundred-and-eighty-degree pans clockwise and counterclockwise simultaneously. A lawyerly worded sign advised us of the presence of killer guard dogs, while another promised equal violence from human guards should we somehow trespass. A car-window-level console offered a means of communication to the main compound, while yet another sign advised us that entry without prior permission fell into the category of fat chance.

Goodman had me cruise right past and pull to a stop about a hundred yards beyond the gates, around a slight turn in the road. That presumably precluded TV observation—but I wasn't ruling out radar and/or other high-tech security devices undreamed in my philosophy.

"Well," I said. "That's an*other* fine mess you got us into. I have a feeling we could breach the Great Wall of China easier than this."

"Oh, ye of little faith," he replied, the while going through his pockets, from which he produced a packet of business cards and a badge. He selected a card, handed it to me. It read "State of California Department of Social Services." The badge said "State of California, Enforcement Officer."

"To the gate," he directed.

I backed the car, repassed the gate, then drove forward, aligning the car with the console.

"I don't think they're going to buy this," I said. "State officials in a BMW?"

"Better than a Rolls or a Caddy."

He got out, walked around the car, pushed the buzzer, picked up the phone. Lights came on, an alarm sounded briefly, and a recorded voice said, "You have just been photographed. Please state your business."

"Hi," said Goodman affably. "We're with the state Board of Psychiatric Counseling Services, and we're here to examine and inspect the accommodations for a Mr. D. Dietrich. May we come in, please?"

"I'm sorry," said the loudspeaker. "Admission is by appointment only."

"Yes, I understand," replied Goodman. "But this is a *surprise* inspection by the state board of psychiatric evaluation." With which he held up both card and badge to the camera. "The purpose of a surprise inspection is to make an evaluation of situation and circumstance without the inspectees making special preparations."

"Yes, well, if you'll make an appointment . . ."

"If we are not permitted ingress, it will be necessary to obtain a court order, which will cancel the medical parole granted Mr. Dietrich."

"One second," said the voice.

We waited a few moments; then a uniformed guard, accompanied by two sentry dogs, rode down the driveway in a golf cart, stopping just short of the gate on the other side.

"Stay, Gunder, stay, Helmut," said the guard to the pair of German shepherds, who, not surprisingly, were good at obeying orders. He walked slowly to the gate, faced Goodman.

"Hey, there," said Goodman, "how's she going?"

"Now, what's all this surprise inspection about, officer?"

"Just that, officer," said Goodman. "Pain the ass, but that's the drill."

"Really . . ." he began hesitantly.

"You ex-P.D.?" asked Goodman.

"Sure—you, too?"

"Sure," lied Goodman. "How's the job here?"

"Okay, good peripherals, low risk."

"Yeah, mine too—no more shoot-'em-up."

"What'd you, twenty?"

"Yep, you too?"

"Bakersfield. Mostly D and D, give 'em a knock on the nog, sleep it off till morning. Easy enough, but pretty dull—except your occasional shooter."

"San Diego, me. Got through without 'discharging the weapon' once. Now all I get's the occasional violent patient. And all the shooting's done with a hypo. Pretty low sweat count. So, let us in, okay?"

"Got a problem with that, sarge. Standing orders from the CIC—without he knows, nobody at no time."

"Hey, I got the city, county, and state says you make an exception for us. Give us five minutes, we go check Mr. Dietrich—the pool house, right?—give him a quick look, and get the hell out. Less mess, no fuss."

"Can't, man, orders. I already stuck my neck out letting in one guy from the studio delivering a script. Might could get hell for that."

"Tell you what, chief—use a little executive discretion here. I'll leave my associate in the car. It'll just be you and me. All's I have to do is set eyes on the guy, I'm gone. You're in the clear, and nobody knows. Otherwise it's half my day in the courthouse, getting the papers and warrants. Then back and serving the papers and warrants. The kind of crap makes me a whole lot less friendly, I promise you. Take my word, your CIC'll be a bunch happier this way."

"Well, I got to see what's holding up the studio fellow anyway . . ."

Goodman took that for acquiescence, turned, and strode purposefully back to me.

"Going to do it alone, Riley. Wait here."

By which time the security guard pushed the button that opened the massive gates. Goodman turned about, scurried through, and plopped himself down next to the growling shepherds.

"Tell Siegfied and Roy here to cool it," he said to the guard.

"Down, boys," said the guard, closing the gate and getting back into the golf cart.

They headed up toward the house. I had to admire

Goodman's chutzpah. *I* certainly could never have talked my way in.

It was a matter of less than five minutes before the golf cart came careening back down, the guard opened the gate, the men exchanged hurried handshakes, and Goodman hastened to the car and got in.

"Move it!" he said, reaching toward the dashboard, then taking his still-empty hand, now cupped as if he held a microphone, back toward his face and bellowing, "Get me headquarters, this is an emergency!" And to me, urgently, "Go—now!" Which I promptly did, backing out, and heading down Bellagio toward the East Gate.

"What's up?" I said finally.

"Hammersmith is out!" he replied. "Dubie's gone!"

"What do you mean, escaped?"

"Broken window. He was locked in on the second floor. He, or somebody—also departed—pulled all the electric wires out of the appliances, tied 'em together to make a rope, and boom—out the back into the alley. Our Dubie done flew the coop."

"So what now?"

"Now I think we better haul ass over to Laurel Canyon. That's where Dubie's house is, and according to Lefcourt, where Carkeys ought to be."

"Shouldn't we first report it or something?"

"We'll worry about that later. The minute you report, you gotta talk to cops. It'd hold us up."

There was sort of a nice sense of adventure building. I really liked it. A kind of reactive business, I mused . . . something happens, you respond, takes you to something else, you respond again . . .

"Will you get the fuck moving?" Goodman screamed, as I guess musing tended to slow me down.

"What exactly's your main worry?"

"Hey, there's lots of people, including Dubie, think he might've been the one hacked Rita up. So it's not exactly good news he's on the loose. But I also worry in case whatever she saw had something to do with him, he might scare Carkeys away before we got a chance to talk to her. The woman's plenty skittish . . ."

So I hurried. Or tried. Traffic on Sunset Boulevard

west of, say, Whittier moves pretty quickly. But it begins
to slacken around Beverly Drive, then gets slightly worse
till, say, Doheny, after which it really slows down.

We were inching along past Doheny—where Scandia
used to be on the right, then really crawling till we got
to Tower Records on the left, more slow stuff past Old
World, Mirabelle, Nicky Blair's, Le Dome, and by the
time we were approaching Sunset Plaza Drive it was really bumper-to-bumper.

Looking ahead and seeing no clearing, Goodman had
me go up Sunset Plaza, through which there was a connection leading to an extension of a mountain version of
Hollywood Boulevard I never knew about. We twisted
and turned through what was a residential mountain lane
(though called Hollywood Boulevard) and finally came
out on Laurel Canyon, where he insisted I take what
looked like an illegal left and scoot on up.

We pressed on to the turnoff at Lookout Mountain
Road, popped up, and right on Wonderland where
Goodman directed me to a really surprisingly lush
multistory house—not much frontage, but all interesting
elevations and strangely shaped rooms.

"This is it," he said.

"You've been here before," I replied, while looking
for a place to park, never easy in the hills, with the
narrow streets and few driveways.

But he hadn't. I guess detectives and cabdrivers just
somehow know how to get wherever. Me, I was totally
lost already.

"Just pull it onto the lawn here," he said. "We haven't
got all day."

I guess detectives get impatient when they are on the
scent of something exciting.

We sort of abandoned the car, popped out, ran up
what must have been a hundred steps, me, easily, him,
not so—but very determined.

He reached for the door, which was ajar, and eschewing formalities, pushed on through. I followed, equally
hot on the trail.

He seemed sort of driven, albeit asthmatically, as he
prowled swiftly from room to room, level to level, till we

reached what I devoutly hoped (for his sake) was the top floor.

Detectives certainly are tenacious.

He dashed, I dashed, into what I guess was a bedroom. I mean, it *was* a bedroom, I just couldn't concentrate on that part of it. All I could see was the incredibly hacked and mutilated body of Carkeys, gushing blood, and innards and brains and intestines, and gory gory stuff. One fast look and I knew it would haunt me for the rest of my life. I guess detectives get somehow inured to crushed faces and eyes hanging out and . . . I stopped speculating, being far too busy retching and retching over and over, upchucking my guts and . . . Goddd . . . !

17

Rayford Goodman

It was déjà vu—all over again. True, Carkeys, in life, was no match for Rita Rose. But as a carved-up, mutilated corpse, wasn't a whole hell of a lot of difference. And while I didn't have the forensic expertise to know left-hand wounds from right-hand ones, I knew enough about the slimy areas of life to bet the farm this was no coincidence or copycat. We were dealing with the one, the only, the original crazy killer.

I should have followed Bradley's instinct to come here first instead of trying for Dubie. Might have saved her life. Basic oops. And now again, was it Dubie? Sure as hell *looked* like it. Sure as hell loaded the dice. But also sure as hell, not just a little too convenient the only possible witness gets offed by a guy doesn't exactly remember what shoelaces are for?

While Bradley finished puking his fillings out, I went to the bathroom. Since there didn't seem to be any obvious evidence to disturb, I ran a little cold water over a towel and brought it back for him to wipe the cold sweat away.

"Jesus," he said finally. "Sorry about that. Guess I flunked basic macho."

"Not really, it takes a while to get used to."

"How does anybody *ever* get used to it?"

"Lots never do. Just keep taking deep breaths. Better?"

"I guess. I'm talking instead of barfing. We should call the police, huh?"

"Yeah, but let's take a minute."

"The killer might still be around, you don't think we should call right away?"

"Well, if it's Dubie, ain't going to be that hard to find

. . .," during which I was looking beyond Bradley in the bedroom. "Look, you don't want to hang around this room. Whyn't you take a look around out there? See if you can find anything might be helpful. I'll do the same here."

"Isn't that tampering with evidence?"

"Yeah. Go on. Let's take a fast look, then we'll call the police."

"What're we looking for?"

"Ah, if I knew that . . ."

He left the room, careful to avoid looking at poor old Carkeys. I turned back, checked for a purse—didn't see one. I took a quick gander at the body. She wasn't wearing any jewelry—God, also not wearing one of her fingers. Yiich. Didn't spot the finger anywhere, though in all the gore . . . Jesus, how the hell did anybody ever come to this?

Then I heard it—a faint scratching sound—close by. Again, over there—the closet, maybe. Nobody would hide in a closet after this kind of thing, unless . . .

I whipped it open and there was Dubie, huddled on the floor, rocking back and forth, shock clear on his face.

He cowered as I reached for him.

"It's me, Dubie—Ray Goodman."

"Oh, Christ, yeah, man, God—you see that?"

"Yeah, I saw it."

"I wanted to go home, you know? I didn't like staying at Lefcourt's, he kept me locked in. I get enough locked in back at the brain bin, so I took off. You know, kind of a lark, what can they do to me, right? And I hadn't been here so long, I wanted to see the old place. Lots of good times, lots of laughs—lots of hangovers and wishing-you-were-deads too, but you know, my home . . ."

"Yeah, Dube."

"I didn't expect anything. I didn't even know anybody was supposed to be here. They don't tell me things, you know, incompetent. So, when I got the chance, and the guy helped me . . ."

"What chance? Who was the guy?"

"Can't, I promised."

"Jesus, Dubie, maybe that's the one *did* this."

"Oh, no way—very gentle person."

By which time Bradley had heard the commotion and cautiously returned to the room—even possibly to see I needed any help. I shook my head slightly so he wouldn't say anything might break the trend of thought.

His back to the door, Dietrich didn't notice Bradley, who pantomimed phoning. I nodded cautiously.

"Tell me the guy's name," I pushed.

But meanwhile Dubie took a hasty look at what remained of Carkeys, and gagged badly.

"Oh, boy, look at that."

"Pretty awful."

"Listen, Ray, hey—you don't suppose *I* did it?"

"The thought crossed my mind," I answered truthfully.

Which it was clear was the wrong thing to say, as Dubie's eyes rolled back into his head and he fell over in a dead faint.

"Should I help you or go call?" asked Bradley.

Damn, I didn't want to lose Dubie like that—especially before finding out.

"Go call," I said.

But before he could get to it, we heard the approaching siren. Not what I wanted, either. Life would have been a whole lot simpler if I'd been gone, but . . . so be it.

I worked over Dubie, who came around, but not exactly "to."

"Okay, pal?"

No answer.

"Dube?"

Blank nobody-home stare.

"Why don't we all wait downstairs," I said, helping him up and taking him by the arm. "You remember Mark Bradley, my writer?" I cued, hoping to get some light back in his eyes. "Remember?"

He didn't. He didn't anything. But it wasn't going to matter, we'd run out of time.

We got downstairs and to the door just as the squad car pulled up and two officers got out with drawn guns.

"Hold it right there," said the one with lines.

I half-raised my hands in the universal no-harm-from-me way least likely to provoke a mistake.

"Ray Goodman here, this is Mark Bradley, and that's

Dubie Dietrich. You've got a dead body upstairs in the back bedroom."

"Keep them covered," he told his partner. "While I check this out." And he entered the building cautiously— not that I blame him.

"Who discovered the body?" asked the other cop.

"We all did."

"Together?"

"Well, Mr. Bradley and I were together."

"And you?" he asked Dubie.

But Dubie had stopped talking. Maybe hearing.

"Mr. Dietrich has some mental problems, officer. I think we may need a psychiatric social worker, and a lawyer . . ."

"Uh-huh, so what you're saying, he's the perp?"

"I'm not saying anything. I just think this is a little heavier than you think and maybe you ought to get some higher-up help with the investigation."

With which, as if to prove me right, an unmarked police car arrived, out of which stepped my old nemesis Chief of Detectives Edward Broward. The very same who never forgave me showing him up an asshole arresting the wrong guy for the Rita Rose murder. And that very same "wrong guy" was now a pretty obvious suspect all over again. All of which put me in the potential position of asshole emeritus for my having busted a *different* "wrong guy."

"Well, what have we here?" said Broward.

"Chief, these men were all at the door when we pulled up. My partner's upstairs checking out a potential homicide. I've been holding these suspects and/or material witnesses, pending your arrival. All yours, chief."

"So, this time Mr. Hollywood doesn't even wait to be called in. You're way ahead of us, who don't even know there's a murder yet. And I'll bet a juicy sensational one. Only duck soup for a guy like you, right, Mr. Hollywood?"

"Nothing like it, chief, no such thing. Just happened to be interviewing folks for a book, my associate here and I. Stumbled onto this, total accident. I know from nothing."

"All right, then let's start with question number one:

how come no call to the police when you discovered the body?"

"You guys are just too efficient for us amateurs. We were just about to when you beat us to the punch."

At which point the first officer came back, looking badly shook.

"Gory—bad scene, chief."

"I want the area sealed. Call the M.E. Get me, say, six backup for traffic control, another six to comb the area. Nobody goes in or out who's not official, and nobody on the site without my specific authorization. You know the drill."

Know the drill? Anybody ever saw television knew the drill.

What I was wondering: who'd called the cops in the first place? I didn't have long to wonder.

A Rolls Corniche convertible pulled up, and out stepped Harry Light.

"Uh-oh," he said.

"Looks like you had a pretty good hunch, Mr. Light," said the chief.

Pretty good hunch, my ass.

"What's the story?"

"Just got here myself," said the chief.

"Carkeys is dead," I said. "Same M.O.—god-awful. Dubie was here—"

"What I figured. Got a call from Lefcourt, who got a call from his security people that Dubie'd taken off. I figured he might come here and thought it was a good idea to have him picked up by a friend," indicating the chief.

"You didn't know Carkeys was staying here?"

"No, how would I know that?"

"Lefcourt knew."

"Well, Lefcourt doesn't tell me everything. He only called me about Dubie because I was responsible for the weekend pass."

"Isn't that a little strange? If Lefcourt's Dubie's conservator, how come you're responsible—?"

"Uh, Rayford, not now. I don't exactly know what business it is of yours in the first place—"

"I can explain that," said Bradley, sensing a touch of

hostility. "Since we're doing the book, we're naturally retracing all the steps in the first case, and all the people involved, what and who they were then, and what and who they are now, so it's only natural—"

"Yeah, right," said Light. "But, I mean, we can go over these *personal* things at our leisure, understand? We don't have to take up the chief's valuable time."

"Gotcha."

"Anyway, you're coming to the screening tomorrow night, aren't you?" I nodded. "Good, why don't you come too, Mark. Make it a little earlier, say eight-thirty, and we'll get our stories straight . . . that's a joke, chief," he added, smiling.

"Now, here's what," he continued smoothly. "I think I better take Dubie back to Ojai. He's clearly in no—"

"I don't know," interrupted the chief. "It seems to me as a principal suspect we ought to keep him on tap."

"He'll *be* on tap," said Harry forcefully. "If I tell you he's on tap, he's on tap." Then, more congenially, "And we don't know if he's a principal suspect, really. Just . . . the man came to his own house, maybe, probably, just found what you found. But given his condition, I don't see what good it'd do you guys, and definitely not him, to be kept in custody. I mean, you know who you're dealing with, you're dealing with me . . ."

It went on like that for a while, Broward claiming responsibility, Harry straight-ahead paying no attention. By which time the main task force was arriving. Coroner's wagon, M.E., investigative teams—and not far behind, the first of the TV vans.

"Wait," called Harry as one of the police cars started to hem his Corniche in. "We're just going out."

He took the dazed Dubie by the arm and led him quickly to the car, counting on Broward to cop out rather than lock horns with power.

"We'll be running along too," I said, taking Bradley's arm.

"You'll be nothing, until I say," responded the chief, trying to save *some* face.

"Look, you've got a lot of work to do here. You have our statements. If you have any more questions, or we think of something to add, we can call each other."

"You'll go when I fucking *tell* you to go—"

"Or I could stay and talk to the TV people and remind them how it was the first time we tangled assholes."

"Don't leave town," said the chief.

We threaded our way back across Wonderland and down Lookout Mountain, through the obstacle course of official cars, reporters, TV equipment, *et al.* I kept my head down, not wanting to be connected to the current disaster till I at least had some idea what went wrong the first time. And hopefully got to sort out the good guys from the bad guys before taking my lumps for being wrong.

So it was almost an afterimage, an impression, but didn't I, a block or so back, see a green Jag tucked around a corner? Or maybe in a driveway—only with the motor running?

For sure, I'd blown it with Carkeys. The girl definitely knew something big. And for sure she'd been blown away to keep from putting the finger—oops, bad image—on who did what to who when. Yeah, the same M.O. Yeah, that made it a crazy, and possibly, likely according to the odds, Dubie. But the two didn't go together. If she was just being shut up, then the gruesome way she was offed could be a blind. And what about whoever sprang Dubie in the first place? Was he here too?

We hit Laurel Canyon and Bradley turned right and headed back toward Sunset. He was still taking big gulps of air, settling his stomach.

"Life's sure full of ugly, ain't it, buddy?" I said.

"I'll say. Bambi Blain was never like this. But how I'm going to write it all, I don't have the foggiest."

"First we have to see how it comes out."

"If it comes out."

"Oh, it'll come out."

"Well, lots of cases don't get solved, right?"

"This one will."

"How can you be sure?"

"I'm a believer. This is what I do. And I'm good at it—generally. Trust me, I'll find out."

"If nobody kills us first."

"There's that."

We drove in silence for a moment.

"The only thing," I said, "I wish we'd had more time before the cops got there. Maybe we could've found something, to keep us going. Give us at least a direction."

"Yeah," said Bradley, then slyly added, "I don't suppose this might be of any help?" And he pulled Carkeys' handbag from inside his shirt where he'd stashed it all this time.

I practically tore it open. There was a Polaroid of Carkeys leaning soulfully on one hand—a corny shot, flashing a ring. There were some marijuana twigs and seeds. Then a wallet with over four hundred dollars—an amazing amount for a junkie—half a candy bar, lipstick, comb, cigarette papers, matches . . . and a locker key. "I could give you the key—ha ha," she'd said.

"Well . . . anything?" asked Bradley.

I could have kissed him.

Almost.

18

Mark Bradley

Brian had recovered from his assault sufficiently to become ambulatory, which meant he could kvetch and whine whilst on the go, affording little respite for poor beset-upon old me, the object of his discontent, albeit having also inadvertently provided the subject.

What all this thrashing amidst the shrubbery alludes to is the fact I was a smidge stressed as a result of a call from Mother accepting an invitation I hadn't proffered to pop over for tea this very afternoon. That meant we had only a matter of hours in which to remove every trace of Brian's co-tenancy and replace them with suitably disinformationally heterosexual props—an occupation that tended to promote the peeve in Brian, not without some measure of justification.

"I know it seems disrespectful to you," I wimped. "To deny your very existence, so to speak. But you know how it is with Mother. I mean, she not only drinks tea, she *takes* tea—being somewhat less liberated than the Daughters of the American Revolution. I *can't* tell her."

"Whatta you think she'd do if you did?"

"You mean after regaining consciousness?"

"All right, even given the shock. The 'not *my* boy,' 'where have we failed?' 'why are you doing this to me?' whole thing—whatta you think she'd do *after* that?"

"If you think join the Gay Pride Parade you're barking up the wrong tree—which, of course, is no new occupation for you," I replied, removing a batch of his clothing from a closet and dumping it into Hefty bags.

"She's not going to look in your closets."

"Wanna bet? My mother thinks until you're safely married, a boy *belongs* to his parents, especially his

160

mother. She thinks even if you're in the army you ought to still come home nights."

"I told mine."

"Right."

"And you don't see my mother carrying on."

"Once they pumped her full of lithium. Come on, what's the big deal? So you go to a movie for an hour or two," moving to the bathroom from which I removed the second comb, the second razor, the third and fourth toothbrushes.

The doorbell rang.

"Get that, will you?" I called.

"What if it's your mother and she came early?"

"Then just quote me an exorbitant price for the plumbing."

It was, of course, Francie, bag and baggage. She joined me in the bathroom, putting down a second comb, a second razor, a third and fourth toothbrush.

"Thanks, Francie, you're a love," I said.

"Or at least that's the impression I'm supposed to give."

We crossed back to the bedroom, where she unpacked and hung a few things in the closet.

"How'd your exam go?"

"Pretty good. I was absolutely fantastic through the first half, before my tiny little time pills crapped out. But I think I got through okay, all things considered. What's new with you guys?"

So I told her about Dubie's escape, the mad dash to Laurel Canyon, finding Carkeys kaput—the whole thing, including my copping Carkeys' handbag, and discovery of the locker key inside.

"And inside the locker was . . . ?"

"We don't know yet. Goodman's out trying to locate where it is, first of all, but he's convinced we're talking major evidence, once he gets to it."

All this so impressed Francie, she sat down on the bed and started rolling a joint.

"Could you hold off with that till after we do Mother?"

At which point a petulant Brian limped in.

"Since your *girl*friend's here, and my absence is required, I think I'll bug off now—"

"Better than buggering off," said Francie, not helping a whole lot.

"Listen, I'm sorry," I said. "I'll make it up to you," and as Francie opened her mouth, added, "Don't say it." To Brian, "Give me a call about six, okay?"

"We'll see. I might just be halfway between Rage and Revolver about then," alluding to two of the more popular cruising bars on Santa Monica.

I supposed I would have to endure a little snideness.

"When it's convenient," I said, stashing the Hefty bags full of his clothes on the higher shelves.

"I'll expect everything to be cleaned and pressed," he said.

I didn't see where cleaning reasonably entered into it, but figured I wasn't in the strongest bargaining position.

He left in a huff—and if you've ever ridden one of those . . .

Francie finished rolling her joint, lit it.

"And what am I supposed to tell Mother about the smell?"

"Tell her it's musk."

She finished establishing her residence—a drawer full of undies—and I went to the window, where I watched Brian hobbling off just as Goodman pulled up in the Rolls, still belching smoke.

"Goodman's on his way up," I noted as she took a frilly negligee and hung it with studied carelessness on the bathroom hook. Nice touch.

"Tell you a secret," she said, taking a final toke and flushing the joint. "When we were out at Nipper's, on our double date? Rayford's date, Julie, who's not exactly a date but more a professional fun-person, confided to me he's not exactly King Kong in the sack."

"Nice friend."

"Oh, nothing vicious, just the sort of shared confidence that makes going to the ladies' room such a social delight."

"So he's not King Kong. People slow down."

"The way I get it, he's actually more your total no-show. Who'd of thunk?"

Not I. So much for Mr. Macho.

"The *good* news is Julie, certainly qualifying as an expert, thinks it might be only temporary. Brought about most likely by the combination heart-attack-and-ball-breaking proclivities of his ex-old-lady."

"Well, I'm sorry to hear there's *any* problem. For all his gruffness—"

"—there's an endearing teddy-bear quality about the old geezer, I agree."

"Something like that, but don't quote me."

"Me? My lips are sealed."

"So I noticed."

The doorbell rang, and I went to admit Himself, who entered with a decided bounce to his step and a very smug smile (bravely disguising the heavy burden I'd just learned he was carrying).

"I've seen shit-eating grins before . . ."

Francie entered from the bedroom, and they exchanged greetings.

"So?" she said.

"You first," he said. "Did the computer age come through?"

"Uh-huh," she replied. I'd forgotten she was running down the license on the green Jag. "And the locker?"

"Uh-uh."

"Okay, it wasn't AAR, it was A*B*R," she said.

"American Beauty Rose!" I said.

"Wrong," they both said.

Francie graciously yielded to an obviously anxious-to-spill Goodman.

"Arthur B. Rollins," said Goodman.

"Correctamente," said Francie. "How'd you find out?"

"I *figured* it out—by mistake. Since we knew it wasn't AAR, on a hunch I went for American Beauty Rose—A*B*R. So, wrong reason, I got the right plate. Once I had the actual license, naturally I had my *own* sources. Who I didn't have to give my body to, by the way. They told me Arthur B. Rollins."

"A name I've heard more than once," I said.

"Right, Harry Light's dresser. Always there, always invisible, sort of part of the scenery."

"And present the night Rita got offed," I offered. "But wait a minute, he was never alone. He was with

Sally and Harry the whole time. At least one or the other. I seem to remember he and Harry went out for a snack. But nobody so far said anything about him being alone with Rita."

"Just think about it—his whole life, his career's with Harry. He's there socially. He's there businesswise. He's practically family. At the studio he could go wherever he wanted easy enough—including Rita's dressing room."

"The jewels?" I asked.

"Why not?"

"I thought you thought Harley took them."

"I was just speculating. Now I'm speculating it was Rollins took them."

"And killed Rita?"

"I don't say he did that—necessarily. But he must have some reason to be following me around. And he—at least the Jag—was on the scene at Carkeys'. Try this: suppose even if he didn't kill Rita, he was caught stealing the jewels by Carkeys. He split them with her, or paid her off or something. On the promise she'd get lost. Then, when she reneged on the deal and showed up again and contacted me, he got spooked—"

"And killed her!"

"What better time? He knew Dubie was out on a pass at Lefcourt's. He would know anything Harry did. Then say he knew, too, Dubie'd gotten out of there—hell, he might have *let* him out. Remember, 'someone from the studio' visited Dubie, according to the security guy, 'delivering a script.' What script? So, why not him? Which gives you one hell of a hot suspect!"

"So now?" asked Francie.

"So now we find Mr. Rollins and go have a little chat?" asked I.

"No, that'd be premature. We don't want to tip our hand. It's all speculation so far, but at least we know what and who to watch. And of course I gotta find out where the hell that locker is. Carkeys was trying to tell me something. So I'll keep on that and we'll wait for developments. But I promise you, there's not a doubt in this world, there're gonna *be* developments."

Which was the moment the bell rang again.

"Would you get that for me?" I said, putting a familiar

arm around Francie. "That'll be Mother, coming for tea. She's been anxious to meet my fiancée."

"Where *is* Brian?" said Goodman.

"Brian?" I said. "There is no Brian. Francie is my fiancée."

"I see," said Goodman, seeing. He opened the door

"Howjado," he said to Mother. "You must be Mrs. Bradley."

With which he ushered her in, then added, "My daughter and I have been so anxious to meet you!"

He could be a fun guy.

Tea was very pleasant. Mother had orange pekoe and milk, Goodman had Darjeeling and Old Overhalt, Francie—health enthusiast that she was—herbal chamomile and several "vitamin" pills that made her charmingly logorrheic, and I kept my fingers crossed we'd pull the whole thing off. Which, to my considerable delight, we managed to do.

As I walked Mother to the elevator, she expressed her pleasure that I was at last showing a "healthy interest in the opposite sex" and bestowed her blessings, encouraging me to "stop all the gallivanting" and settle down.

"Don't think for a minute you're fooling me," she said, just when I thought everything'd gone so swimmingly.

"I'm not fooling you?"

"Not for a minute, young man. I saw that young lady's negligee in the bathroom. I can put two and two together. But I'm not so old-fashioned as you may think. I know what young people do these days. And don't you think young people didn't have equally strong feelings in the old days, either, which many expressed. Not your father and I, of course. But living together, while I suppose has some value in determining compatibility, is still jumping the gun, and not an acceptable substitute for marriage. Nevertheless, I am very pleased you found someone down to earth, who seems stable and possessed of suitable values. I was half-afraid you might be shacking up with a floozy dope fiend or some such."

"No chance, Mother."

"Good. I like that girl. And her father is an absolute

charmer. Look to the parents when you measure the child.''

''What I always say.''

''Now kiss your mother good-bye.''

Which I did, dutifully, deftly avoiding her lips—Mother tended to be affectionate—and saw the elevator close on her.

With an enormous sigh of relief, I returned to my apartment.

Having shared the charade, Goodman and Francie were hooting it up, reviewing the dialogue that had passed with old mum.

''I kinda thought I'd lose it when she asked if you were on the pill—''

''—you mean when I said 'Which ones?' ''

''All right, all right,'' I said. ''That's enough. Let's say I admit I owe you both a big one.''

''To say the least,'' said Francie.

With which the guffaws settled to chortles, to chuckles, to grins, to the odd sigh of amusement.

''Well, what now?'' I asked Goodman, back to business.

He took a breath and resumed. ''Well, now I want to find out a lot more about Rollins. Which I can do on my own, or whatever—you want to tag along. But first I've got to get in touch with Adderley. I had a call on my answerphone from someone at the garage offering a 'special deal' fixing the Rolls. So the plan's working. A little luck, I should be able to wrap that up before too long and then concentrate one hundred percent on our thing.''

During this I'd strolled over to the window to watch Mother get into her car and leave, which she did. But just as I was about to turn back, I spotted someone jimmying the window of the Rolls.

''Hey, Goodman, I think someone's trying to steal your car.''

Both Goodman and Francie rushed over. Goodman took one look, threw open the window, and shouted down, ''Hey, you—whatta you think you're—?''

But the rest was pretty much obscured by the explosion that destroyed the Rolls in a ball of fire.

19

Rayford Goodman

I debated about lunch with Adderley. On the one hand I really wanted to go to Nicky Blair's—the latest of many Nicky Blair's. This one so successful the odds-on betting was it'd never burn down. But since my client was going to pick up the tab, and the prices at Nicky's were higher than a hooker's hemline, it seemed a little bit bad taste. Plus there was the bad news of the good news/bad news I was going to tell him—the Rolls gone to car heaven. So I figured I better not push my luck. I told him to meet me at Mirabelle's, which is modestly priced and okay if you're more interested in pretty girls than food. Nicky had both.

Adderley had gotten there first and was sitting in the outdoor section facing the street. So I imagine he had some hint of the general area of the problem when I showed up in a taxi. Though, of course, he couldn't know how *much* the Rolls was out of order.

I think it said something about his English reserve that he didn't even bring it up as I joined him at the table.

"Good to see you, Mr. Adderley. I've got a lot to report."

"Yas, well, I imagine," said Adderley.

You don't even begin to, I thought.

But it *would* have to be dealt with, so maybe . . . "Uhm, they make a really nice bullshot here, if you like," I suggested.

"I don't drink at lunch."

"Or beer," I tried.

"At all."

"Why don't we order?"

Which we did, me starting with a tall glass of "just plain tomato juice."

"Sounds wizard to me," said Adderley, which I guess meant good. So we made it two, ordered lunch from a young lady said her name was Marcie and she would be serving us. I excused myself to go rinse my hands.

I caught Marcie at the kitchen door, put a tenspot in her hand, and told her the nature of the service I'd be requiring. It was to put three shots of vodka in my tomato juice and keep it off the bill and make it quick.

I *did* wash my hands. It's always best to keep things closest to the truth, I find. And by the time I returned to the table our efficient little server was bringing the juices.

Marcie put *my* juice down first, unfortunately close to the center of the table, where Adderley immediately grabbed it.

"Uh, that's this gentleman's tomato juice," said Marcie.

"What's the difference?" said Adderley reasonably. "Tomato juice is tomato juice, whether tomayto or tomahto, as the lyric has it." With which he gulped it straight down.

Holding Marcie with a gesture, I did likewise with my own darker but weaker imitation and said, "Why don't we both have another? The *same*."

"*Both* the same?" asked Marcie.

What the hell . . .

"Both."

So what I did, I sort of stalled. The new "tomato juices" arrived—which would make it six shots for Adderley. Poor guy was gonna have a real good time. (I reminded myself to remember to cover Marcie for the money she'd fronted before I left.)

I pointed out several items of local interest—here a breast, there a leg—in the passing scene. That seemed to be the only nonbusiness mutual interest we shared, sports being out of the question with a limey. Finally I figured the time was ripe, and so was he, so I told him.

"First, I had a call from 'an interested party'—which I gotta believe is someone either from your garage or with access to it. The party said he understood I had a problem with my Rolls and guaranteed he could make me a much better deal repairing it than you would."

"The blighter said that?" asked Adderley, with a slight slur, thank goodness.

"That's what the blighter said, or words to the effect. Something like, 'Much cheaper than *that* bloody thief.'"

"That bloody thief called *me* a bloody thief? Bloody cheek of the bloody beggar."

I think when Englishmen come to the United States they feel they have to talk like a cross between Ronald Colman and Michael Caine or we might mistake them for somebody from Pittsburgh. I personally do not believe people in Blighty still bloody talk like that, except maybe to the odd bloody wog. Or maybe when they get drunk on six bloody Bloody Marys.

"So, what do we do now? I suppose make arrangements with the blackguard to get the car to him, in order to nab him with the gooch?" he said, proving my point.

"Well, that *would* be a good plan, but, uh, there's a slight hitch to going about it that way."

"And the hitch itch?"

"The hitch *is*, I'm going to have to ask you to get us a sort of standby car. You know, like when they make a movie, they always have two of everything in case one breaks?"

"Oh, do they now?"

"Yeah, and you see, it's a good idea. Because, uh . . . ours broke."

"I did make notice of your unorthodox arrival. I believe you've something to tell me."

"Yes, well . . ." and, what the hell, took a shot, "I'm afraid it's what we've been expecting a long time, the terrorists. Could be PLO, but in your case, more likely IRA."

"Internal Revenue?"

"The Irish."

"Yass?"

"They're heeere."

"The bounders here?"

I took a deep breath, reached for his hand, grasped it with my sincerest sympathy. "I'm afraid they've sort of, well, blown up your car," I said.

"Motherfucker," he said.

*   *   *

I'd gotten through lunch. Adderley was waiting to check if his insurance covered the car before deciding whether to strangle or merely sue me. Though technically off the case—"You're bloody fired!"—I still checked my answerphone to see if the thief'd called back. I figured maybe a big bust might still work a save. He hadn't. Then I rented a beat-up Porsche for as much as a new Oldsmobile, keeping up the front. Next, I put out some feelers for info on Rollins—Francie doing likewise computerwise-wise. Now I was shaved, showered, and shined for our meet at the screening Harry Light'd invited Bradley and me to.

I didn't have any trouble deciding on the silk shirt. There was only one left. And the tear under the armpit wouldn't show if I didn't take off whatever I wore over it. It was the sweater—the screenings being casual—took a moment's thought. The "new one" Luana'd gotten me about five years ago for Christmas during a rare fit of frugality was mostly made of dead polyesters and definitely leaned toward loser. On the other hand, I did have a cashmere, which, on top of the silk shirt, would lend a nice air of success. Except for being a wide-sleeve cardigan, with a little logo of Arnold Palmer on the chest. Maybe a sport jacket. Casual was no snap.

Bradley arrived and gave me a honk. We had decided to go in his car—since I was on mileage. The BMW was enough down the middle to do it socially.

I gave him instructions to Harry's house. It was in old-money Beverly Hills flats—old money in Hollywood being from the forties and fifties—rather than tonier Bel Air and such. Harry'd always said he wasn't one to put on airs and "move out of a perfectly good twelve-million-dollar house just 'cause I struck it rich."

I was about to lay out the ground rules when Bradley interrupted me.

"Look, we have to talk about this," he said.

"What 'this'?"

"You were practically killed today!"

"Oh, yeah."

"I'm still shaking in my boots."

"Well, actually, it wasn't the first attempt—though the first time I didn't think they were serious." I felt I owed it to him now to level about things. So I told him about the black guy confronting me on my health walk, on instinct *not* telling I now knew who it was. "My reading then was they were just trying to scare us off the project, like when they beat up Brian."

"Yeah?"

"But I gotta admit, they don't wire your car just to scare you. You gotta take that for serious attempted murder."

"And it doesn't bother you?"

"Yeah, it does."

"So?"

"So, we better nail whoever's doing this if we want to get out of it alive."

"But I'm just a writer! Ghosting a book. That's not supposed to include mayhem and murder."

"I guess you could get out of the deal. But I'm not sure it's in time anymore."

"Jesus Christ!"

"You turn left at the light, here."

"And you're not scared? It doesn't affect you?"

"Not including diarrhea and retching? Another block and a half."

But instead, he pulled the car over to the curb and stopped.

"Look, now wait," he said. "I need a few answers, something! For example, who do you think set the bomb?"

"Beats me."

"And was the guy who got killed the guy setting it, or just someone happened along?"

"Well, since he slipped a bent hanger through the side vent, trying to unlock the door, it's pretty clear he wasn't the bomber. The bomber had to've already set the bomb. So it must have been someone trying to steal the car or the hi-fi."

"Still and all, that's not too likely—in my neighborhood."

"Why not?"

"Gay car thieves?"

"Look at Mr. Stereotype. How about the radio was a Blaupunkt?"

"In that case, you're probably right." But it seemed to hit him again. "You could have been in that car! Another minute and you would have been!"

"Another reason we have to solve this thing. Come on, move out, we're due at Harry's."

And he did, still shaken.

"Over to the right. So, one more time, the ground rules: we let on nothing. We have no suspicions, no doubts, no whatever. As far as we're concerned, Pagani did it, period. And, in fact, I'd like to know just exactly where *was* Pagani when Carkeys bought it. Ditto Rollins, hardly notice him, he's just a shadow in the background. The guy you send out for more Fresca—"

"More what?"

"Fresca, a soft drink."

"Never heard of it."

"You gotta be kidding. Fresca, it's a regular popular brand name, like, say, Rinso."

"What?"

"Let's not get sidetracked here. Harry specifically asked us to come early. Means he wants to tell us something. Or make some sort of arrangement."

"About Dubie."

"Probably, which means he thinks Dubie did it."

"Or wants us to *think* he thinks Dubie did it."

"Kid, you're starting to sound like a detective. You turn right here."

Harry's house was California Spanish, not quite as laid-back as San Simeon.

The security guy disguised as a parking attendant handed us over to the security guy at the gate with the clipboard and the gun. Who handed us over to the security guy at the door with just a gun. Who passed us on to the butler. Who showed us through the foyer, past the den on the left, the lavish living room on the right—neither of which I'd ever seen actually used—and around the massive staircase down which, in its original setting, no doubt some spic royalty once trod. Then, just before the grand dining room, seating maybe fifty (more if they got off their horses), turned us right and pointed us to a long covered lane. That led to the house next door, which Harry bought to entertain in so his own didn't get dirty. Actually the building was officially called the Screening Room. Though it was three stories high, and big enough to house the Trapps, the Foys, and half the Kennedys.

"How do you like the show so far?" I asked Bradley as we crossed over.

"I have the feeling there's a few bucks here."

We went down the lane, passed a Lake Superior-class fish pond full of koi.

"These fish cost more than my house," I said.

"Moom pitchers been mighty good to folks," said Bradley.

"And with rich goes lotsa power, so watch it," as we finished crossing and entered the first floor of the Screening Room.

There was a bar large enough for St. Patrick's Day in Dublin. Behind the bar was a bartender—regular size. On a stool in one corner was Harry Light. There was no one else.

Harry rose, his face cracking into a broad grin, and crossed to greet us. "Rayford, Mark, I suppose you're wondering why I've asked you here," he said, aping an Agatha Christie detective. "Welcome to my humble commode." With which he gave his trademarked left-handed salute (hint, hint). Then he embraced us one by one, and slobbered kisses on us both, which seemed to offend Bradley.

"Okay," he said, leading us back to the bar. "Ramon?" he said. "Later?" dismissing the bartender, who looked like the guy who squeals in jail pictures and seemed used to being told to get lost.

Harry changed places back of the bar. "I'll do this myself," he said, laying out three glasses.

"Never lose the common touch, me lads," he continued, filling a trio of thousand-dollar crystal goblets with ice that even looked great. I mean, you ever notice rich people's ice? No bubbles, no air. Like diamonds.

He asked what'll it be and I ordered vodka rocks. Bradley did the same. Harry poured us some gooey rich stuff out of a bottle looked like it came over in the czar's diplomatic pouch.

"Salut," he said, taking a sip from his own, which was

something like lalapalooza water, which I guess must have been hipper than Perrier. Then he immediately re-filled my immediately emptied glass.

"Enough lovemaking, off with the clothes," said Harry. "Here's the way it looks to me. I wanted you here too, Mark, because I didn't want you getting too wild in the book, or going off half-cocked in new directions because of some of the strange things that've been sort of happening."

"Well, it's a little more than 'strange,' Harry," I interrupted. "And a little more than sort of. There's a couple, or maybe just one and a half, attempts on my life for openers. Then there's Bradley's boyfriend-roommate being beat up. And, for laughs, there's Carkeys being severely killed."

"Right. None of which I'm saying isn't important or awful or serious. What I wanted to get to was more sticking to the main thing. Meaning, none of what's happened actually affects what *did* happen to Rita Rose. Right? I mean, if you're writing about the American Beauty Rose, it's still Rita Rose viciously murdered by Danny Pagani."

"Superficially," said Bradley. Harry and I both gave him a look. He was supposed to listen.

"I say superficially," he nevertheless continued, "because if Pagani actually did in fact murder Rita Rose, then why would anybody kill Carkeys to stop her from talking about it?"

"There could be lots of reasons for that," said Harry. "She might have had some information about other things. About who was involved with Rita. About who stole the jewels. About God knows what. It didn't have to be that she had information anybody else but Pagani did it."

"I suppose . . ."

"Or it might be she had even *more* proof Pagani did it and he was afraid that might nix his CBS deal."

"Which you're suggesting is a motive for Pagani to have murdered Carkeys," said Bradley. Again we both looked at him.

"More than, say, Dubie?" I said, knowing who Harry really suspected. "You think Dubie did it."

"I really love that galoot," said Harry.

"That *crazy* galoot," amended Bradley. We both looked at him again.

"Say, kid," said Harry. "We're on the same side on this."

"We want to see justice done."

"Right," said Harry. "Justice. On the one hand, a giant of the industry, who's brought laughter and tears to millions of fans in good times and bad, now a bit down on his luck—who was found innocent. On the other, a sleazy dope-peddling pornographer and blackmailer—who was found guilty."

"And who now, by the way," I said, "has a deal with CBS for a mini-series on the Rita Rose case that'll come out either first or in a tie and knock the shit out of our book. Which was only going to keep me from bankruptcy."

"Well, yeah," said Harry. "I been thinking about that. And it's just so darn unfair to have that happen to someone like you, who's done so much for this business."

Even Bradley knew enough to keep his mouth shut when the bullshit piled up.

Harry married more of Nicholas' perfect vodka to more of his own perfect ice cubes for me, raised an eyebrow at Bradley, who folded with the one drink, then continued.

"Happens, my contract with the network comes due soon. We've been talking. They're very anxious, naturally, to have me renew for my thirty-fourth straight year. I've already made it a provision that they drop their little mini-series on Pagani if they really want a Light in their lives."

So that was going to be the deal. Harry was determined to protect Dubie. To do that we had to write the book stet. The old case stood. The old solution stood. Pagani was guilty. In exchange Harry'd get the competition out of our face.

"I hear you," I said to Harry. "My biggest problem, though, is if I stop digging, how'm I going to get whoever it is to stop trying to kill me?"

"I think if the word got around—my PR people could do it—that the book's not going to stir up any unexpected new dirt, then whoever's nervous would stop being nervous."

"And instead," said Bradley, "my *publisher* would get nervous that he's only going to sell about seven copies."

"Oh, I wouldn't worry about him," said Harry, obviously sure of Penny. "Besides, it could still be an *exciting* book, and we can help there too. Once the old Hollywood press gets on the case—"

"The old Hollywood press didn't do too much for *Ishtar*," said Bradley.

"I didn't expect you were going to be a problem," said Harry.

"Life's full of surprises," said Bradley.

"Look, guys," said me. "Why don't we all just take the matter under advisement?"

"*Strong* advisement," said Harry.

Which was about when Ramon slithered back in to squeal the other guests had started to arrive.

20

Mark Bradley

I couldn't help thinking there was more to Harry's offer to kill the mini-series than mere friendship for Goodman, who, after all, wasn't that much of a friend. Nor, too, did it seem to me that anything I'd heard so far about Dubie constituted a big enough reason for him to interfere so forcefully. The guy'd already been declared non compos, by reason of which he was also basically home-free, even if they ultimately did tie him to Carkeys. Yet Harry'd made it clear he was going to use all his considerable clout to stop Pagani's mini. Something more had to be at stake, something that hadn't come out in any previous investigation, which he wanted to be certain stayed hidden. I was sure of it. Fairly.

Which might have meant, as Goodman had suggested, I was starting to think like a detective, or it could be simple paranoia in this singular age of conspiracy.

I must say, absent the element of danger—which was hard to absent, given the exploding car, the attack on Brian, the earlier one on Goodman, and the warning I'd gotten—it was kind of fun. Being in the home of a legend definitely was fun, to say nothing of the company he kept.

First off, there was the king-jester himself. Having greeted the earliest arrivals, a couple of "working" actors (meaning TV, as opposed to movie stars—you remember their characters' names, but not theirs), he was already "on." "So the guy's impotent, see, and goes to the doctor, and the doctor gives him a thorough examination and says, hey, not bad. First off, it's not psychological, there's a definite physical reason why you can't get it up anymore. And the good news is, there's an operation that can fix you up good as new. It does cost a bit, about thirty-five thousand dollars, but it's guaranteed a hundred percent. The guy says, gee, thirty-five thousand's an awful lot. So the doctor says, tell you what, why don't you go home, talk it over with your wife, and let me know what you decide. So next day he gets a call from the guy and he says, did you talk it over with your wife? And the guy says yes. And the doctor says, yeah? And the guy says he decided to redo the kitchen.''

Then had come Sally Light, such a work of art you almost expected the surgeon would have signed one of her nostrils. Always charming, always elegant, in this case she was sporting a simple little eight-thousand-dollar set of Jewel Parks lounging pajamas and a hundred thousand dollars' worth of casual jewelry. Sparkling, effervescent, she favored each and every guest with a burst of vivacious welcoming chatter, after which she assumed a refined little smile that seemed to distance her from the vulgarity that paid for it all.

The truth be known, she'd come from humble beginnings herself—the former Sally Lewis, of the Las Vegas Lewises. And though she made no particular secret of her origins, it somehow never really registered. The lady was so clearly a lady, despite the fact that, in company with her friend Luana Goodman, she'd been a showgirl. Which, come to think of it, was probably great training for becoming a lady—posture and all that.

She was into the usual show-business giant's wife's obligatory charities, which she seemed to perform ably and enthusiastically. In addition to the drug-abuse things, and the AIDS things, and the actors-who'd-pissed-away-all-their-money-and-become-embarrassments things, because of Harry's super-Christianity (Stars for Jesus), she additionally had Wayward Girls, Starving Africans—the Russians had inherited the Armenians—and other churchly good works as well. She was also good for the odd hundred or two to the occasional over-the-hill showgirl gone to fat.

I had all this on background from the files Francie'd dug up, as well as a fairly extensive reading of the *Enquirer*, *Star*, *People*, and other such impeccable sources of biography.

To this add—more via Francie than the media—under

"Character and Traits," Sally was also a speed freak. It took a lot of energy to do so much good. Francie claimed she could tell almost exactly the extent of amphetamine ingestion in a given subject by the quality of his or her perspiration. (Don't get her started on Nixon.)

Additionally, there was an underpublicized stay at Betty Ford's, as well as a couple of quick encores for recidivism. Or, as Francie put it, "She flunked dope school."

Anyway, in the first wave there were Goodman, myself, Harry, the TV actors, Jack Carter—who, I was reliably informed, was always *every*where—and Jimmie and Cluny Komack, Jimmie, presumably, to check if Harry was getting a better selection of pictures to screen at home. He was. Then came Sally; and for reasons I didn't understand, shortly thereafter, Goodman's ex, Luana, which clearly thrilled him. In addition, what appeared to be Luana's current Significant Other, Roger Meade, who was very handsome and shiny-haired and basically sort of great-looking. Then there was Arthur Rollins, who seemed to have nothing to do with Fresca that I could see, but who, the *world* could see, was a fussy old queen; Symington Lefcourt; his aging secretary, Miss Eldrege; a dapper, graceful gentleman named Armand Cifelli, who someone said was a dancer, or *the* dancer; and most surprising of all, Chief Broward, of the cops. The custom, Goodman had informed me, was a two-drink maximum—over about forty-five minutes. Then all proceeded to the second floor, which, I understood, was almost entirely given over to a near-theater-size screening room.

Goodman, evidently allowed special dispensation, was on his third "tureen of vodka," and making small talk with the buxom TV star whose character name even escaped me—though the tits were familiar. This seemed a waste of good investigative opportunity, but was probably more a show of independence for Luana's sake, given my inside knowledge of his inside indisposition.

Lefcourt and Broward were chatting off to one side of the bar. I scrunched over—a seat or two, close enough to catch a snatch of this and that.

". . . shouldn't of really took him from the jurisdiction," Broward was saying.

"Well, Ojai's not the end of the world. And personally, I don't think you got anything to gain, opening that can of worms."

"The can of worms is already open, for Christ's sake, Mr. Lefcourt. We got Carkeys in the morgue, and worse, in the goddamn papers. It ain't gonna go 'way."

"So I suppose you been questioning Danny Pagani—"

"Can't just go framing the guy."

"But Dubie you could frame."

"The guy's bananas, he's certified."

"My advice, you got Pagani, already a convicted killer, you don't think he's a good suspect?"

"Naturally he's a suspect. The first guy we pulled in. He claims Carkeys was one of the few if not the only one could have proved he didn't kill Rita Rose. He says he has no motive."

"Which naturally you believe."

"We're checking it out. He's also got a pretty strong alibi. We're checking that too. But in my heart of hearts I still believe it was Dubie did it then and Dubie did it now."

"And you want to know what's in my heart of hearts?"

"Well, of course, Mr. L."

"I believe you're due to retire at the end of this year."

"Right."

"After which, considering your long and able service to the industry, you'd certainly have a right to expect those of us in a position to do so would do so."

"Do so?"

"Find an executive position commensurate with your stature. Not just head of security at a studio, but say head of security for *all* the studios. Head of all the heads, you understand my meaning?"

"I certainly do—in general."

"All right, in specific, what we don't need is another scandal in the business. What we don't need is any more remembering of a scandal we once had. But if we have to be reminded of an unfortunate time, how more fortunate we got the right felon and how unfortunate the authorities saw fit to release the momser prematurely."

"But that was Harry's doing."

"Harry, unfortunately, made a mistake. Harry, fortunately, is big enough to get over having made a mistake. You, on the other hand, are not big enough to get over making a mistake. Especially a new one, especially one where it looks like you were trying to recover from one you made so many years ago which practically everybody has mostly forgotten by now."

"Yeah, which they've mostly forgotten, but not totally enough to make me D.A., or mayor, or any of the things I might have been."

"We let you still be chief."

This sobered Broward a bit.

"So what you're saying . . . ?"

"Let sleeping dogs sleep, don't go frying new fish, and enjoy the movie."

On which note Lefcourt turned away from Broward and made his way to the rest room—just as three guys and a girl emerged (cocaine not being *totally* out of fashion).

An interesting turn of events, I thought, wondering why Lefcourt would be so involved in the politics of Hollywood. After all, at his age . . .

Maybe Goodman would have an opinion.

But Goodman was doing his own research, which seemed to be concentrated on ascertaining whether the TV starlet's bosom was surgically augmented or God-given.

"When you do aerobics," he was saying, bouncing lightly on his feet, "you don't feel there's danger of shin splints?"

"No," the lady replied, stepping into the snare. "The idea is to take the pressure lightly on the balls of the feet, while giving at the knees." With which she demonstrated, looking down at her feet. Goodman was looking at her boobs. The feet moved; the boobs didn't.

"Well, thank you," Goodman said. "That answers my question." And he eased off.

I guess if he was going to have a fantasy life, he was going to have it based on the real thing. Or maybe he was just zinging Luana, who was trying hard not to notice him, elaborately enjoying the wit and wisdom of the stud in attendance.

I joined the now apparently aimless Goodman and

asked, "Are we on duty, or just rubbing salt in old wombs?"

"Don't be a smartass. Keep circulating."

So I ambled over to the stud, who'd now moved off to refresh his drink, on the off-chance—or likely chance—and tried to engage him in conversation. This proved not entirely satisfying, as his ability to communicate was a shade less than that of Koko, the signing gorilla. Still, with those muscles and that hair . . . which of course you could say for Koko too.

Evidently Arthur Rollins was of a like mind—to check him out—for he sidled over too.

Small talk was apparently the order of the night.

"Roger Meade here."

"Mark Bradley."

"Arthur Rollins."

"Roger."

"Mark."

"Roger."

"Artie." If ever anybody *wasn't* an Artie . . .

"So, you in show biz?" asked Rog.

"I'm a writer."

"TV or movies?"

"Books."

What a coincidence, it turned out. Each had a swell idea for a book, needing only someone to "put down the words"—Artie's on stars he had dressed, Roger's on stars he had undressed.

Both wore significant amounts of jewelry of a quality and value to have misted Zsa Zsa's loupe. Roger proudly proclaimed all his were gifts—though he was "doin' pretty okay" in his own right, being "in transport," which I assumed meant he was either feeling good or drove a cab. Rollins said most of his were likewise gifts— "John Wayne gave me the cufflinks; Bill Holden the I.D. bracelet" during stints on their respective pictures. But the biggest item, and most recent, an impressively large diamond ring, he had "treated myself to," which had to make one wonder: that kind of jewelry on a dresser's salary?

It went along like that, drips and drabs, chitchatty, till out of nowhere, bits and pieces, hobbies and interests, things I have done out of the ordinary, came the incidental intelligence that Rollins had served as a sapper during the war. Exactly which war, we were both too discreet to inquire. Young Rog thought it had something to do with extracting maple syrup from trees, I was of a mind it had to do with handling explosives.

So now I had a dresser with a green Jaguar, enough money to buy a large diamond ring, and a knowledge of blowing things up.

I could hardly wait to share my trove.

Goodman, meanwhile, was talking to Harry, and by the looks of it, either not getting along too well or merely feeling the heat from his fourth vodka. I headed over on the off-chance he needed reinforcements or diversion.

". . . just wanted to know why you thought it'd be nice to invite me and Luana to the same party," I was just in time to hear.

"Because, good buddy," said Harry, putting his arm around Goodman, "I'm an old romantic who also still believes marriage is sacred to the Big Guy upstairs. And also still happens to think you guys had a good thing going and all you really need is to just sit down together—"

"Some of us didn't believe in marriage even when we laid down together."

"Can't blame a guy for trying."

"No?"

"Did you hear the one about the rabbi and the pope?" asked Harry.

"Hey, Rafe, how's it going?" I interjected inanely, seeing he looked really steamed. But before he had a chance to tell me, Miss Eldrege chose to save things by piping up to Harry:

"I don't know about you, Harry, but I'm an old lady. And if you don't start this screening soon, I'm going to be sleeping halfway through and snoring in Dolby."

Which evidently convinced Harry it was time to start the movie.

"Showtime," he said, and offered her his arm. "Hear the one about the rabbi and the pope?" he said, then, enlarging his audience, "Jimmie, Jack, I was just telling

Miss Eldrege about the rabbi . . .", and they headed for the elevator.

"Sort of surprised to see her here," I said to Goodman. "I mean, she's Lefcourt's secretary, isn't she?"

"Yeah, well, but they've known each other since the year one. On the other hand, they're not exactly in the same social circle. I guess, I don't know. It *is* funny, now I think about it."

"Come on, let's go," said Harry, holding the elevator door.

"I found out some things," I said to Goodman.

But it didn't seem exactly the moment, mostly because Goodman spotted Luana closing in and decided to catch the elevator about to leave in order to avoid her. And besides, Sally came up alongside me and took my arm. Evidently I was being permitted to escort her to the picture.

"So how goes the book?" she asked.

"Pretty well, so far. Still mostly gathering material."

"I guess that's the hard part."

"Yes, it is, though often the most interesting too. One of the hard things, though, when you're dealing with a second person's relationship to a third person, is to get it accurate."

"Well, I haven't noticed accuracy playing an awfully big part in books about Hollywood."

The elevator door was closing in Luana's annoyed face, beyond which could be seen Goodman's relieved face.

"All full up," he said, looking like a cat about to wipe canary feathers off his whiskers.

"We'll catch the next one," said Sally, including Luana in our group.

"I must say," I said, "I think it's kind of wonderful how the community sticks together."

"In what way?"

"Well, loyalty, affection, friendship."

"Sweetheart," said Luana, joining in, "in Hollywood friendship's usually based on who's got what on whom."

"I suppose there's a lot of that too. But I was thinking of Harry and Dubie. It's really rather remarkable what

Harry's done for him. It must be very painful for him to see Dubie so senile."

"Well, in a way," said Sally.

"I mean, you know, working together so long, being such good buddies, and all. I guess, cynicism aside, there's real love there."

"Darling, you're kidding," said Sally as the elevator returned. "Everybody knows Harry *loathes* Dubie."

21

Rayford Goodman

We were watching the latest Vietnam-was-hell movie, with all the new hyped-up special effects—exploding body parts and great mounds of gore. It seemed like they'd tried to cater both to folks thought war was plain insane and to sports fans thought it was some kind of diplomatic superbowl.

It always surprised me Harry kept picking these kinds of movies to screen. You'd think he'd naturally go for comedy. Maybe he didn't like the competition. Yet he'd been friends with other comedians, Dubie for one, to judge by how he'd gone to bat for him.

Anyway, I was only halfway watching the movie—I knew how Vietnam came out. I was seated next to Miss Plastic Boobs, whose thigh, however, felt very real pressing against mine. Further, her fingers were hanging around the seam of my trousers and looked to become friendlier by the minute.

This wouldn't be too hard to do at Harry's. The actual screening room was bigger than lots of today's plexes, and the lighting was dimmer. Then, too, instead of separate seats, there were huge couches ran the width of the room, on separate levels, and lots of soft fluffy pillows to sink into and hide in. So I wasn't exactly unhappy when the busty starlet chose to flop down next to me. Surprised, maybe; possibly even suspicious, but that's my nature—and I had to admit not too put out by the fact Luana noticed it too and reacted by so heavily not-seeing it she might as well taken out an ad. (I've never understood why some women will dump you—and on you— and still think somehow you're supposed to stay faithful even after they've left for private-parts unknown.)

Now here came those little fingers, finding my thigh,

and that shoulder leaning into mine. But I wasn't a young hunk. I wasn't even a producer. Plus her old man was only a row away. So why?

Because I was there. Because I was the only one there—figuratively. Jimmie Komack *was* on her other side, but his wife, Cluny, was on the other side of him. And because there are women who don't know any other way to relate except with their bods—unless and until they got a running part in a series.

But I had nothing *against* being rubbed against. It wasn't as if it was a *good* movie I was missing.

The hand found the inside of my thigh, ever so lightly. It could still almost be an accident—what the White House calls plausible deniability ("What, me, *what*? how dis*gust*ing!).

But then she upped the ante, dangled a digit against my dingie, and right away crossed the line, settling down to some serious fondling. This definitely got my attention, old romantic that I am.

I turned to face her, smiled. She smiled back, beckoned me closer. I leaned in. She whispered in my ear. What she whispered was, "Is this the shittiest camera work you've ever seen, or what?"

You can't get much more romantic than that.

I reached over, took hold of a tit felt like a doorknob, and replied, "I think it's more the lighting." Under the circumstances, I don't think not being entirely aroused counted against me.

She was considering this when I felt a tap on my shoulder and a hot garlicky breath. I figured, uh-oh, the husband, and turned with a hunched shoulder half-expecting a shot, only to find breath and finger belonged to Chief Broward.

"I wanna talk to you—outside," he whispered, indicating outside with a jerk of the head. Broward wasn't very big on subtlety.

I got up, Busy Body starting up too, figuring an invite to an in-depth critique of the film or something—more likely something. I put a hand on her shoulder and gently pushed her back.

"No, sorry," I whispered, pointing at Broward. "This guy's got dibs on me." That crushed her so bad by the time I looked back she was already leaning in toward Komack. Maybe Cluny wouldn't notice.

I guess I hadn't made that lasting an impression. I excuse-me'd down the row, got to the end, headed past the projection room, and followed Broward to the library beyond.

He took a comfortable leather chair, and I settled into the twin across. We were separated by a small copper-topped table. On it were crystal ashtrays and other smoking stuff—which were all over the house, Harry being a heavy smoker. In fact, the only time he *didn't* smoke was when his cardiologist came over. I guess everybody lies to *some*body. I settled in.

"What can I do for you, Ed?" I asked real friendly.

"You can start by calling me 'chief.' This ain't a social call."

Of course we had never been social. Official police somehow never liked private police, even when the latter came from the former, unlike me. Maybe it was the idea you might be making bigger bucks that griped them.

"All right, chief. Your nickel."

"Well, we got us another murder, now, with Car-keys . . ."

"Right. How's it look?"

"Looks wonderful! What the fuck you mean, how's it look? Like everything's under control? Like, relax, folks, good old chief's in charge, nobody getting knocked off but some old semipro doper?"

"I meant sort of, what've you got on the case. Same M.O.?"

With which he semi-calmed down. Jump-y!

"Yeah, it was. That much I'm sure you knew, but the autopsy confirmed it. Same angles, same directions. Ninety percent it's the same killer."

"That's the way seemed to me. And good news too— I'd hate to think there were *two* of them out there. So where was Pagani?"

"Pagani was with his parole officer."

"You'll be able to check that."

"Did check that."

"The exact time? The autopsy establish the exact time of death?"

"Within two hours."

"And Pagani was with his parole officer exactly and for the whole two hours?"

"No, only about forty-five, fifty minutes."

"Ah hah!"

"But in San Diego."

"San Diego? His parole officer is in San Diego?"

"How about them apples, Goodman?"

How about people who still said "how about them apples?"

"Tends to look like maybe Pagani didn't do it."

"Don't it, though? And how about in addition to the murder, your car gets blown up? Just like that, exactly when Dubie's out and running around."

"How about that the *guy* doing my car got blown up?" I said, as usual trying to mislead him.

"How about maybe the guy got blown up was only trying to rip off your radio?"

"For a fact?"

"Based on a few teeth and a missing small-time stereo thief."

Well, now I definitely knew.

"So," continued Broward, "like I say, how about your car getting blown up just when Dubie's out and on the loose?"

"For openers, Dubie couldn't work a light switch, much less plant a bomb."

"You don't think so."

"No, I don't. I'll tell you what I *do* think, chief. I think you'd like to pin Carkeys on Dubie. Because if you could do that, you could make a hell of a case for the fact it was Dubie back in sixty-three killed Rita Rose too. Exactly like you said at the time."

"That's one logical conclusion."

"And what's another?"

"Just follow this line with me for a minute. Who was the one person who profited by the first murder?"

"Killing Rita Rose? I suppose in a money sense, whoever stole the jewels."

"Well, yeah, you could say that, since we don't know who did steal the jewels. But apart from that, seems to me the only one really profited was *you!*"

I kept my temper in check, since bopping police chiefs wasn't good PR, even in Hollywood. So I merely said with your basic frozen smile, "How you figure that, chief?"

"You became a star. You got to be a celebrity, got lots of work. So, follow me more, now you're writing this book, right? And maybe not everybody alive still remembers what a hotshot you were. So isn't it fascinating, here comes *another* murder? Just like the first one—*exactly* like the first one. And, would you believe it, who is right there at the crime scene, Johnny on the spot, but Rayford Starcop Goodman, his world-famous ownself!"

"You *seriously* believe that?"

"I didn't say I *seriously* believed it, it's a theory's all. Just like Pagani being guilty of killing Rita Rose was a theory too."

"Except for two things—not counting how I blew my own car up."

"I'm listening," said Broward, peeling back the shirt cuff from his right wrist to peek at his watch, "but we also better get back inside before we upset Harry."

"Right. The first is, Pagani got *convicted* of killing Rita Rose"—which wasn't my strongest argument, since by now even I was convinced he hadn't done it.

"And the second?"

"I'm not left-handed, which the autopsy says was the hand did the killing. And which, by the way, I notice you are, since by and large only left-handed people wear watches on their right wrists."

"So what's that say? You're losing ground on Pagani, now you wanna make me the patsy?"

"Not seriously, chief. I don't think that any more than you seriously think it's me. So let's stop jerking off." And swapping lies.

But when I went to rise, he put a heavy paw on my shoulder.

"Ain't why I called you out here."

"Riiight. This the place you tell me to stay out of the investigation?"

"Why would I do that?"

"Maybe 'cause you're not all that good at it?"

"You got some big mouth, Goodman."

"I know, but you *do* want me to lay off investigating Carkeys' murder . . ."

"Well, of course, officially you're a civilian . . ."

"Or is it more the point, anything I find out you want me to tell you?" I said, fingering Carkeys' locker key in my pocket.

"No, anything you find out you *better* tell me."

"Right," I said. Wasn't that the way it always went? Watch it, shamus—

"—*or* I'll have your badge."

"Or I'll have your badge" was exactly the way it always went.

I tried to look like I was taking the warning seriously. After all, the chief was getting on, and I wouldn't want to push him into doing anything rash before he retired and had to start paying for his own clothes and meals and girls.

We went back inside.

With all the special effects and the quadraphonic incredible sound of the loudest war of all going on, I had to practically shout "Excuse me" to get the starlet to take her tongue out of Jimmie Komack's ear long enough for me to get back to my seat. What a polite guy!

After the movie we all adjourned to the first floor, where Harry's "couple" served coffee and cakes.

Coffee and cake, too, was a ritual. You were supposed to stay ten to fifteen minutes. After which, if you didn't catch on, the host went to bed.

You also discussed the movie, though somehow you always laid off real downer reviews, figuring that took away from the host's pleasure. Even though he didn't produce, act, direct, or write that particular movie. Unless he, himself, thought it was "the biggest piece of shit I ever saw." In which case, you told the whole truth.

Bradley pssst'd me over to fill me in on the things he'd learned on his own—that Rollins was some sort of explosives expert in the war and that Harry and Dubie weren't really friends. By a long shot. Very interesting. Both.

So I sidled over toward the one person might also be worth sounding, old Miss Eldrege, Symington Lefcourt's secretary. She was standing next to Miss I'll Take Romance—you wanna talk odd couples? Lefcourt had gone immediately after the screening, or maybe during, for all I knew. With him gone it was all the more offbeat for Eldrege to be here. How come? No way she'd be in Harry's social circle. And wasn't *his* secretary. I leaned in to listen.

"I hate war pictures," Eldrege was saying.

"Me too," said the starlet.

"Oh, are you a pacifist?" asked Miss E.

"No, a realist," said the starlet. "War pictures have very few parts for actresses."

I joined the twosome, smiled at the starlet, which she totally ignored—how quickly they forget—and settled next to Miss Eldrege.

"I'm not too big on war pictures either, actually," I said.

"I think Mr. Light just likes them because he's got a lot of stock in defense industries."

"That's probably it."

At which Harry ambled by. "Enjoy the picture?" he asked.

"Loved it," said Miss Eldrege. You don't survive in the business into your eighties not knowing which side your croissant's buttered on.

Harry smiled approvingly and moved on.

"I wonder," she asked me, "if you'd be good enough to call me a cab?"

"I'll do that," said Bradley, who'd quietly joined us.

"I've had to give up driving," continued Miss Eldrege as I put my hand on Bradley's shoulder, holding him back. "Reflexes just go. Had to sell my lovely car, too."

"Was it, by any chance, a green Jaguar XKE?" I asked.

"Why, yes! How'd you know that?"

"Just your basic lucky guess," I said.

"Let me try one," said Bradley. "Did you sell it to Arthur Rollins?"

"You people are uncanny."

"Actually, we're both uncanny *and* canny," said Bradley.

"But you must, please, call a cab for me. It's getting very late."

"We'll do better than that," I said. "We'll take you home."

She insisted we not be put out. We insisted we be. And we won. Though I could tell Bradley's heart wasn't quite in it. "Brian's expecting me," he whispered unhappily under his breath.

"The reunion will be all the sweeter," I whispered back.

After thanking and good-nighting our host, neatly under the fifteen-minute deadline, we slipped out with Miss Eldrege.

We got past the various checkpoints without any trouble, got back Bradley's car. He got behind the wheel while I helped Miss Eldrege into the backseat and climbed in after her.

Somewhere in the past I'd heard a couple of reasons Miss Eldrege had stayed a permanent Miss. "Married to her work," went the more charitable. "The only thing she'd ever marry was gin," went the other. Counting on number two and hoping to loosen her tongue, I suggested we stop for a nightcap, having some small expertise in that area.

I could tell she'd dearly love to but her energy was going fast.

"I have to get up so early," she said.

"Better plan," I continued. "Mark will pull over over there at that package store. I'll just get us a little bottle and we'll have that nightcap at your place. Then if you get sleepy, you just throw us on out and get right to bed. How's that?"

That was peachy keen. Bradley pulled up at the liquor store and I was out in a flash, back in another, and we were off and running. She took the occasion to apologize for giving me the runaround when I'd called the other day. It wasn't her doing, she said, without saying whose doing it was. I let it pass, and before you could say ninety proof we were in her neat old Burbank apartment around the corner from Warner Brothers, which somehow was called the Burbank Studios these days. And before much longer, the good times were rolling, and so was Miss Eldrege.

"Of course, in those days," she was saying on her second gin and "whoa, not too much tonic," "pictures were refined. You didn't see all this sex and all that open-mouth kissing. My lands, can you imagine Clark Gable opening his mouth during a kiss?"

"Didn't he have false teeth?" asked Bradley.

"There, there, see—just the sort of terrible gossip people make up these days. Clark Gable?"

"Maybe I'm thinking about Herbert Marshall," he continued. "Or was he the guy with the wooden leg?"

"You want to wait in the car?" I said. He settled down.

I freshened Miss Eldrege's drink.

"And the language! Heavens, it's just awful."

Fookin' A.

"Say, you know," I said, slickly casual, "I was surprised to see you at Harry's."

"Why's that?"

"No reason, now that I think of it. After all, he's been associated with Mr. Lefcourt all these years, so anybody works for Mr. Lefcourt—"

"Lefcourt? Of course I work for Mr. Lefcourt, but it's Mr. Harry pays the bills—he's really my boss." Then she put a quick hand to her mouth. "That's a secret."

"Mum's the word," I replied. "I suppose we all just naturally thought Harry worked for Mr. Lefcourt—making all those 'On the Sea to' pictures with Dubie at Pinnacle Studios."

"Wellll," she said, handing over her glass for a refill, " 'strue, to a point. But I shouldn't be telling tales out of school."

I fixed her a killer drink which I justified on the grounds this was serious business. The way she knocked it back, I didn't *have* to justify.

"You were saying, Harry worked for Lefcourt up to a point. The point was . . . ?"

"The point was *Gone to Carnival*."

"Ah," I said knowingly, not knowing.

" 'Twas a vurrry big bomb-y. Mr. Lefcourt lost the old homestead on that stinker."

"And Mr. Light bailed him out?" asked Bradley brightly.

"Well, yes and no."

"I thought Mr. Lefcourt owned half the Valley," said Bradley, pushing.

"He did, once."

"So what happened? Didn't Harry bail him out? It's still Lefcourt Productions."

"Maybe it's called Lefcourt Productions, but somehow as the time went by it got to be more and more Harry's, and Mr. Light really owns Pinnacle now . . . Oops!"

"Oops," I mimicked, her coconspirator in harmless gossip. "So, in a way, then, Mr. Lefcourt works for Mr. Light."

"In a way, Mr. Lefcourt kisses Mr. Light's gluteus maximus, you get my meaning."

"Yep."

"I don't believe I have to spell it out. There's no reason for vulgarity. Mr. Light says jump, Mr. Lefcourt says 'Kiss what?' Ha, ha, ha!"

"Has to do everything he says, right? Like, if Mr. Light says, 'Dubie's coming to stay in your pool house,' Mr. Lefcourt says, 'Great idea.'"

"Does a bear defecate in the forest?" said Miss Eldrege.

And, I thought to myself, if Mr. Light says to Mr. Lefcourt, "You and me're going to make us a little conspiracy to cover up what really happened to Rita Rose," Mr. Lefcourt also says, "Kiss where?"

It'd been a well-spent couple of hours, and a worthwhile detour. I was sure Brian would forgive Bradley. I'd learned a lot in an offbeat place and was feeling pretty satisfied when Miss Eldrege suddenly put her glass down and, staring me right in the eye, leaned in to whisper, "Whyn'tchu dump the kid and you and me'll party?"

It was the first time I'd been propositioned by an octogenarian. "Why, Miss Eldrege," I replied. "What would Clark Gable have said?"

"I know what he'd say today."

"Yeah?"

"'Frankly, my dear, I don't give a shit.'"

22

Mark Bradley

Basically, of course, it was a whole lot of fun—screening with celebrities. It sure beat hell out of hobnobbing with the hoi polloi.

It got a little sloppy toward the end over in Burbank, but then, it *was* Burbank.

I had to hand it to Goodman, he did have a knack of getting information out of the oddest places. And strange information it was, too, everything conspiring to make sure the story stayed stet. Everyone, it seemed, with the possible exception of Broward, wanted Rita Rose's killer to remain Pagani. Despite the fact we all knew now, even Goodman, that it hadn't been Pagani at all.

Why would Lefcourt want it that way? Why, for that matter, would Light? Or stranger still, Penny? At first I'd thought money, because of the time element, but really, it wouldn't take me any longer to write the terrific true story than the already-known old and false one— provided I could find out what the true story was.

But what were they going to do about Carkeys? Somebody had to take the fall for that. And for that matter, what had she wanted to tell Goodman? My money was on covering her buns by nailing the actual killer, who she knew had done it and who knew she knew and had, for some reason, decided to cancel the deal they'd had all these years. Maybe we'd find out if Goodman could locate the locker her key fitted.

Now we were headed back over Barham, and from there down the Hollywood Freeway to escape the Valley. Goodman seemed deep in thought, as opposed to being shallow in thought, and relatively uncommunicative.

"What do you make of all that?" I asked conversationally.

"Hmpf."

"Come on, talk to me—we *are* in this together."

He found that reasonable.

"I can't figure it. It's wheels within wheels, with Harry the hub. Only no likely reason to be there. I mean, you got Harry controlling Lefcourt, Lefcourt controlling Dubie and Broward. And either Harry or Lefcourt surely controlling Mama Rose and company . . ."

"And all or none of the above very strongly not wanting us to write this book—or at least write it in any revisionist way."

"And now factor in Rollins. He had to be the guy trashed the Rolls, since Broward says they got an I.D. on the one blew himself up, who was just a small-time thief, like I figured. This time not just to scare us off, but to kill me. Why? Why anybody, but especially why Rollins? For himself, not likely. . . ."

"Well, wait a moment, don't gloss over that too quickly. Why not for himself? Suppose, for example, it was Rollins who killed Rita Rose."

"Don't be silly, Rollins is an old . . . alternate lifestyler. You know what I mean. Rita sure wasn't any fag hag, and sure no way he was boffing her."

"Maybe," I suggested coldly, "he was boffing someone who *was* boffing her—ever think of that?"

"I don't like to think of that," said Goodman.

"There could be all kinds of motives—it doesn't have to be sex."

"You didn't know her. There's a reason that's what first comes to mind."

"Maybe, but there're also the jewels, don't forget," I went on. "It'll be interesting to see if they surface now. One, you have Carkeys, a likely suspect for the jewelry, since we saw one in the Polaroid, murdered. She had at least one of the rings we know of on her finger at the time, otherwise why lop it off? Two, you have Rollins suddenly awash in money. And to that we now know it was Rollins in the green Jag, and we know Carkeys got into a green Jag, a definite connection."

"But what motive for Rollins to try killing me? How do you figure that?"

"I don't. I stop right here. Listen, for a person who

does biographies, I think I'm doing surprisingly well with mystery."

"I admit."

"But there comes a point—which I'm at—where every line seems to go just so far and then makes no sense."

"Well, sometime soon it *better* make sense—for both our sakes."

I hear you talking.

We popped off the freeway at the Hollywood Bowl, cut down toward Sunset.

"Shall I take you home?"

"First stop wherever you can there's a phone—there, at the bar. Let me check my messages first."

"There's also a drugstore, you could check from there."

He gave me a look.

"I'm really able to go into a bar without getting smashed."

I couldn't deny that was on my mind. I pulled up and over to the curb. He went inside to check his messages—one hoped.

I had to start turning out some pages. Time was hugely a-wasting. But how do you write when you don't know what the story is?

Or did I follow where all the fingers pointed and write the sanitized version? Dubie falsely accused, Goodman to the rescue, Pagani nailed? No one could sue, for one thing. Pagani would have to prove his innocence before he could have a case, which he'd never been able to do before.

But now he had the first leg up, being in San Diego with his parole officer at the time Carkeys was getting murdered.

Goodman returned to the car smelling of gin. At least he didn't mix drinks. So much for outraged indignation.

"I gotta get home," he said. "There's an outside chance I can wrap the Rolls thing tonight. The thief left a message he'd come by and make a deal on the repairs. Plus . . . another."

"I sort of expected that case would go by the boards once you'd lost the Rolls."

"Well, I was kind of fired. But the guy's still painting

my Caddy. I figure he might want some money for that
unless I settle his problem."

"Won't you need a Rolls for that?"

"Or to be very lucky."

"And what's the other?"

"Other?"

"Message."

"For some reason I can't figure, my ex-old-lady wants
to see me. I thought once a night was punishment
enough."

I turned west on Sunset and headed toward Sunset
Plaza.

"I've been thinking," I told him. "Just for the sake of
neatness, shouldn't we check on Pagani?"

"What check? Broward says he was with his parole
officer."

"Yeah, Broward—the only one who doesn't want it to
be Pagani."

"You got a point. I guess I could find out who his
parole officer is."

"If it's a matter of public record, Francie could get it."

"Should be."

We drove in silence for a bit. But we had to reach
some kind of decision.

"Goodman," I said finally, "what're we going to do
about this book?"

"I talk, you write."

"You know what I mean. Do we do what we're told
by everyone and his dog, tell the old story? Or do we
follow this through and tell the new, wherever it leads?"

"Well, we don't know the new."

"Are you chickening out?"

"Oh, we've got to find *out*."

"Uh-huh."

"If only to stay alive. Definitely to stay alive."

"But . . . ?"

"But then we'll have to decide whatever makes the
most sense."

"Meaning you have a vested interest in not being
proved wrong either."

"I'm not exactly eager to be shown up an asshole."

"You could become a hero again."

"Or I could become 'was he wrong then, or is he wrong now?' "

I passed La Cienega, continued two blocks to Sunset Plaza, headed up the hill, confronted almost immediately by a huge construction in progress.

"Know what used to be there?" asked Goodman.

"Yeah, wasn't it some kind of like the Garden of Eden?"

"You're thinking of the Garden of Allah—that was over by Crescent where the goddamn savings and loan is now. Here it was something like that, the Sunset Plaza. It was a great old art-deco group of small buildings where everybody lived before they got around to having a house."

"Everybody?"

"You know what I mean. Show-business people, famous ones, too. It was beautiful, had a sort of scalloped pool, the most beautiful pool I ever saw. And the beautiful people around it? Wow."

"A lot of memories?"

"They were giants, pal. They were one-of-a-kinders. Pictures got dreamed up there. Romances got romanced there. Trysts got trysted there. It was really like real Hollywood—you know what I mean? Hollywood today isn't *Holly*wood—it's an embarrassment. These buildings were beautiful. The people who lived there were beautiful. The things they did were beautiful. And now, zip—pygmies where there used to be giants. I really hate what's happening. Is it just getting old?"

"Not at all, lots of us feel the same way. At least you've got memories—I never even knew it at all."

"Buddy boy, be glad you don't have memories. In the quaint phrase of the times, memories suck."

And on this philosophical note I turned into his street and on up to his house.

"You can come in for a nightcap if you want," said Goodman.

God, was he going to get mushy now?

"Thanks, it's late. But I would like to use your phone for a minute, if you don't mind, to call Brian and tell him I'm on my way and see if he wants anything, other than revenge."

So we both got out of the car and went past the un-kempt lawn—which looked like it hadn't ever *been* kempt—and up to the door, where he stopped, and seemed to sniff the wind.

"What is it, what's up?"

"It's nothing, just, I keep a few pebbles in a certain way on the mat. But, shit, you know, could be a dog, cat, a coyote even. I could've got careless and kicked one off myself."

"I didn't think detectives really did things like that."

"Why not, it doesn't hurt to be cautious," he said, opening the door and heading in.

"It only hurts when you ignore it," he continued as we were inside and facing the muzzle of Danny Pagani's gun.

"Close the door," said Pagani.

I closed the door.

"You," indicating me, "over there," indicating over there.

"You," indicating Goodman, "assume the position."

Goodman turned and faced the well, putting his arms overhead against the surface and spreading his legs wide. Pagani patted him down. He wasn't carrying.

"All right, keep your hands on your head. You," indicating me. "Faggot." See? "Rip the cord off that lamp and very, very carefully, since your life fucking well depends on it, tie up the big guy here."

"No," said Goodman. "We're not going to do this, Pagani. No cooperation. You're going to have to do it all by yourself, you want to kill me."

"Fucking right I want to kill you! You send me the fuck to jail for a hit I didn't make, twenty-fucking-eight years! I finally get out, I finally have a chance to make a dollar, you fucking get them to fucking cancel my fuck-ing TV show!"

"Ah hah, that's what's pissing you. A bum rap you can live with, but a canceled TV show . . . !" Harry'd been true to his word.

"Hey, man, I'm gonna break your fucking head. And I'm gonna do serious damage to your boyfriend's head too, just in case he fucking figures he'd like to fucking carry on without you."

No great startling insight, but prison obviously didn't expand one's vocabulary.

"One thing about you, Pagani, you got a bad attitude," said Goodman. "Now, what we're gonna do, I'm gonna lower my hands and we're gonna sit down and we're gonna talk—"

There was an incredibly loud noise as Pagani fired a bullet into the wall beside Goodman's head.

"—or I'm gonna stand here with my hands against the wall, waiting for further instructions," Goodman continued—with considerable sangfroid, I thought.

"Listen," I said, not to be outdone, "don't do anything foolish here. We've been digging up some new evidence that could really be helpful to you."

"Yeah, helpful what fucking way? Give me back my stir time? Give me back my mini-series deal?"

"Well, I mean, if we can prove, for example, you didn't kill Carkeys—"

"How you fucking prove that?"

"For one thing, your being in San Diego at the time."

"I wasn't the fuck in San Diego. I ain't allowed to fucking leave fucking L.A."

Goodman and I exchanged looks.

"Or we could go another way," I suggested.

"Look, faggot, your best way of getting out of this with the least damage is to keep your faggot mouth closed. Get my meaning?"

"Clearly."

"Now, let's start again, faggot. Move your faggot ass over to that lamp, and with your faggot hands—"

And suddenly a furious whirlwind exploded from the landing.

"You son of a bitch!" screamed Goodman, as he seemed to fly through the air, landing on and knocking Pagani down. "Who're you calling a faggot?"

The gun got knocked away but I couldn't immediately locate it, as they started knocking each other about furiously. First it looked as if Goodman had the situation under control. But the years in jail, and by the looks of him a great deal of working out, had put a lot of muscle on Pagani. And he'd evidently learned a lot about fighting too, as he now seemed to gain the upper hand and was punching and hitting and clubbing Goodman.

I found the gun, tried to hit the back of Pagani's head, but he kept moving it, till finally, in rage and frustration, I just plain squeezed a shot off into the ceiling. This had the singularly salutary effect of stopping Pagani from pummeling Goodman.

"I believe it was I he was calling a faggot," I said in response to Goodman's query.

"Well, don't do that no more," said Goodman to the now-semirelaxed and off-guard Pagani. And for emphasis, resoundingly broke his nose.

"Thank you," I said.

"Thank *you*," said Goodman.

23

Rayford Goodman

You broke my fucking nose!" wailed Pagani.

"And you're bleeding on my fucking couch," I said. "Am I making a big scene over that?"

I handed him my good handkerchief. It was either that or really lose the couch.

"What is it with you, you gotta make my life miserable? I never done nothing to you," he complained, holding his head back with the handkerchief pressed against his nose. "And there I wind up doing twenty-eight hard."

"Don't be so righteous."

"Well, he has a point," said Bradley.

"Look, maybe he didn't kill Rita. Maybe he got nabbed for the wrong thing. They did that with Al Capone too, you know."

"Al who?" said Bradley.

I was beginning to hate the whole generation.

"This mutt here was, after all, a pornographer. I'm sure he treated everyone worked for him kindly and generously. With lots of benefits. Free medical, good pension . . ."

"So I made some dirty movies."

"And you blackmailed Rita Rose for all the blood money you could get."

"She had plenty of money."

"So did the guys with the bent noses you double-crossed on the dope deal."

"I regret that."

"I bet you do."

"It wasn't like that. I got fucking involved with some wrong guys fucking robbed me."

"Poor baby."

"I may of been a little out of line here and there, but

I didn't kill Rita Rose. And I didn't deserve no fucking twenty-eight years."

"Considering this and that, and especially your personality, I'd say it was about right."

And it went on like that awhile, till finally I decided I really wasn't going to press charges. Not with Broward in place to run interference. What'd be the point? Anyway, it wasn't really my style. Breaking his nose was satisfying enough.

So we let him go with a warning to stay away from both of us. Or, as Bradley put it: "Face a faggot's wrath!"

After, we tried to figure what the hell Broward was up to. Or was maybe Pagani really *in* San Diego and just teasing us saying he wasn't? Or, wilder even, maybe protecting someone? There were too many maybes. We'd have to get Francie to check it out. (Those computers *were* going to put guys like me out of business. On the other hand, guys like me were practically out of business already anyway.)

Bradley called Brian. Left alone all evening while his roommate went cavorting with celebrities hadn't much improved old Bri's disposition. But Bradley would be allowed home if he brought something scrumptious to eat. I guess food plays a part.

I got a call from "Mr. GoodRolls" saying he'd be right over. That, together with Brian's sulkiness, convinced Bradley to call it a night.

I got a pan of cold water and a dishrag and tried to get the bloodstains out of the couch. Pagani really was a pain. The phone rang. The call went:

"Yeah?"

"Rayford, it's Luana."

"Yeah, Lu. What can I do for you?"

"It's not something I want to talk about over the phone."

"All right, let's get together. Lunch?"

"I tell you, maybe I'm wrong. Forget it."

"You could tell me and *then* I forget it."

"No, it wasn't a good idea."

"Sure?"

"I'm sure. Sorry to've bothered you."

"You didn't bother me."

"I don't think it's a very good policy to try to seduce Harry's guests in front of God and the whole world."

"Is that what you wanted to talk to me about?"

"No, that's just something I thought I might point out to you."

"Thank you, Luana. In the immortal words of Charles Manson, 'So I'm not perfect.' "

"You never could take criticism very well."

"Which is surprising, considering how much experience I've had getting it."

She hung up. No good-bye. Hang up. Just in case I might have been feeling good.

The knock on the door was a relief. Though I always felt a little antsy opening the door on someone wasn't bright enough to find the bell.

It was one of the little tea-makers from Adderley's garage—no big surprise. This one had "Curtis" embroidered over his right pocket.

" 'Evening, mate," he said. I guess even Brits were going Aussie these days. TV for you.

"Ah, Curtis, right?"

"Right's rain. Moind if I come in?"

That was the idea.

"You said on the phone it's a flat five hundred, parts and labor."

"About the size of it."

Of course I didn't have five hundred.

"So what's the drill, where do I take the car?"

"Oh, you don't take it, mate, *I* take it." He rubbed his fingers together. I didn't know people still did that. "The five?"

"I'll give you a deposit now and the rest when it's done."

He thought a moment.

"Three hundred."

"Fifty."

"Three hundred and fifty?"

"Plain fifty."

"Get owwt. I already got the parts."

"Hundred. I guess you don't do the work at the garage."

"Right," he said sarcastically, "I break in nights and work with a flashlight. Fact, I don't do the work 'tall."

"But a factory-trained accomplice."

"Bloke's waitin' this very minute for me to deliver the parts, get right on it."

"So you already got the parts."

"Look, mate, you want this or not?"

"Yeah. Here's a hundred." Which was only a fraction of my working capital—nine-tenths. "The only catch is, I let someone borrow the car overnight."

"Well, I gotta deliver the parts now. I don't wanner leave 'em in the car, without I got no bill of sale, doncher know?"

What I wanted to hear.

"Fine, deliver the parts. But you'll have to come back tomorrow for the car. Unless you want *me* to bring it to . . . whoever?"

"No, no, 'e wouldn't like that 'tall. 'Kay, now." He put the hundred in his coveralls. "But tomorrow you have the car, and another two-fifty or it's no go."

"Roit, mate," I said.

He looked at me funny and left. I waited a beat, then started for the garage, when the phone rang. I needed to give him a minute or two head start anyway, so I answered.

"Changed my mind," said Luana.

"Can't talk now," I said.

"Meet me for breakfast, tenish, Beverly Wilshire."

"You paying?"

"No."

"Ben Franks."

"I'm paying."

"Beverly Wilshire's good."

She hung up; I hung up. I went out to the garage. Bradley's flowers were looking pretty sad by this time. I'd really have to throw them away. One of these days.

I got into the rented Porsche—the Adderley guy's tail-lights were just disappearing down the hill—and got it going. I zoomed out the garage, turned, and raced after him.

Even a little beat-up and old—as who wasn't—the car cornered great, and took the speed with no complaints.

In a moment or two I'd caught up, and had to lay back a little.

But the guy was no pro, and never seemed to even suspect a tail. As he turned left at Sunset and left again at Laurel I realized he was taking me right back to the Valley. Where else would mechanics moonlight?

We tooled up Laurel. He got through the light at Mulholland. I got caught. Then, afraid I'd lose him, I took a chance and shot through the red, lucking out no cops were waiting to jump us early-morning outlaws.

I got old Curtis back in my sights as we both poured down the hill toward Ventura. But a few blocks shy, he suddenly cut west. I kept my distance. Then, where whatever that street is curved back down to Ventura, he again cut left. There a narrow road went back up the hill. I followed, twisting and turning, afraid I could lose him because I didn't dare get too close when we were the only traffic going.

By now he was on something called Sunswept that looked like it didn't get either sun or swept very often. I lagged, as we twisted around and back up the mountain. One more turn, and then . . . gone!

He must've turned up one of the driveways leading back toward the south side, but which?

Since I couldn't see a light, I decided instead to turn off my motor, get out, and listen. And when I did I caught just the tail end of a motor laboring up the hill before it cut out. I made it the next driveway over.

Leaving the car, I followed on foot. The damn driveway was steep—things seemed to be more physical these days. Can't imagine why. I inched my way up very cautiously, caught the reflection of a light at the top. But here came a huge ferocious-looking German shepherd. Great.

The dog barred my way, looking me over, finally gave a kind of bass "woooof." But just when I decided maybe it was tame, it decided to show me its growl. I searched my pockets for some food. The best I could come up with was a couple sticks of gum. I started holding these out, thought better of it, and settled for laying them on the ground.

The dog snarled, sniffed, then snarled less, sniffed

more, and decided to try a bite. He seemed to like it even when he discovered what made gum gum.

With his teeth more or less stuck, I tried a small, cautious pat. He laid down and rolled on his back. Pussycat.

I dug in and continued up the driveway, puff puff. The driveway was only a little steeper than K2.

By the time I got to the top, my heart was beating so heavy I thought the paramedics'd be able to hear it back at headquarters. Certainly the guys up there.

"The guys" turned out to be the Adderley tea-maker, Curtis, of course, and his black-market, stolen-parts, midnight-mechanic coconspirator, Roger Meade—my ex-wife's boyfriend.

Well, he said he was "in transport"—no lie. Now, next morning, as I entered through the grand gates of the Beverly Wilshire, I knew I had a problem.

Luana was going to tell me she suspected her boyfriend was into something a little less than honest and would I look into it for her. And if I said I already had and he was, she'd get all pissy-faced and complain I was a jealous, suspicious bastard always thinking the worst of everybody.

I took the time-stamped ticket from the attendant, and the clock was running. If she picked up the check, they'd validate her ticket, and I'd be stuck with a parking tab the size of the national debt. Ask them to validate both tickets, she'd think I was chintzy. (She always had a lot of ways to get me to spend a lot of money so nobody'd get the right idea about me.) I think it was a dollar twenty or fifty every twenty minutes. Maybe the service'd be quick. And on second thought, if *I* picked up the tab, they'd validate *my* ticket and I wouldn't be out all that much, plus a good guy. Something to be said for generosity.

She wasn't there yet, as it was only on time, so I got "her table" and ordered a Bloody Mary. "In a breakfast glass."

"Ju wan a leetle Blahdy Mairy?"

Considering they might think I meant less of the active ingredient, I changed my mind and said forget it, just hold the celery. I wouldn't be fooling her anyway.

Fifteen minutes, and a second Bloody Mary later, Luana came waltzing in, wearing a zillion dollars' worth of Arab shit from Laise Adzer, looking like prayertime in Tibet.

I rose to greet her and got a Hollywood kiss—her lips missing my cheek entirely. And at no time did any of her body parts touch mine. She did look great, though. I remember when men used to age better than women, but that somehow got buried with Cary. Between furiously working out and constant facial surgery, California women seemed to've gotten the upper hand—or upper chin. Though in fairness to Luana, she was a natural. As much as anybody in Beverly Hills could be called natural. Meaning everything short of nip-and-tuckery.

Anyway, she quickly settled into the prime spot looking out, and I took what was left of my morning "juice" to the other side, facing the wall. My favorite seating arrangement.

An Italian nobleman came over to take our order.

"What're you having?" she asked. And when I told her, told me I shouldn't have that.

"What're *you* having?" I asked. She said she never ate breakfast anymore.

I almost knew better than to ask so why were we meeting in a restaurant.

And when the first fight was over and I had *double* what I was having, I sat back and lit a cigarette. Then she gave me the enlightening news that for a man in my condition a cigarette was equal to a bullet. I said aggravation and fury weren't too hot either.

When our breathing got back to normal, we got down to it.

"Something's been kind of bothering me," she began.

"Go on," said kindly old I, the shamus-psychiatrist. Despite the inevitable skirmishes, I'd earlier made up my mind I was going to really be nice about it when she told me she'd found out her boyfriend was a thief.

"You know about the big affair Friday at the Beverly Hilton . . ."

Didn't sound like she was going to tell me about the boyfriend. "No, I don't know about the big affair Friday at the Beverly Hilton."

"For Los Amigos Americanos, for heaven's sake."

"That's a charity?"

"Five hundred a plate."

"How could I have missed it? What's the charity do?"

"It helps preserve the Spanish culture and language in America."

"You contribute to that . . ."

"Of course, it's vitally important to scads of people."

"Such scads of people you don't have to contribute to it—all you gotta do is *not* contribute to planned *parent*hood. The culture and language'll take care of themselves."

"You always were a bigot."

"Persona intolerante."

"What's that?"

" 'Bigot' in this language so in danger of dying."

"*Any*way," continued Luana. "The theme of the affair is, of course, old California Spanish. Well, you know how little jewelry I have." Did I ever! "So I asked Sally if she had something Spanish I could borrow, and she said sure, since it turns out she wasn't going. And she lent me this." With which she opened her purse and took out a jeweled Spanishy tiara.

"Yes?"

"You don't recognize it?"

"I wouldn't recognize the Hope diamond if *Bob* was wearing it."

"I asked Sally how she got it."

"The same way any wife gets jewelry, nagged her husband into buying it."

"She didn't *nag* him, but you're half-right. Harry did give it to her."

"Okay, seems reasonable. So what's the problem?"

"The problem is, I recognized the piece—it's called the Sierra Tiara and it's part of the jewelry that was stolen from Rita Rose the night she was murdered."

24

Mark Bradley

The dreaded occurred: Brian was already well enough that we had to get back to working out, which I'd graciously sacrificed in order to take better care of him and leave him less alone.

So at six-incredible-thirty in the morning the miracle of recuperation that is given to the young alone having come to pass, a clear-eyed, raring-to-go Brian had pounded on my shoulder and in an insufferably cheery voice urged this old sleepyheaded slugabed to rise and shine.

With that measured self-control that accrues only to the older and more mature, I didn't punch him, pinch him, yell at him, or kick any of his rainbow-hued contusions. I don't pretend sullenness wasn't part of my aspect, but after only the merest indulgence and a light taste of orange juice to jump-start my bodily functions, I permitted myself to be force-marched to the Sports Connection, and subsequently abjectly humiliated on no less than a dozen brutal Nautilus machines.

Following this we did funny things with rubber bands, low-impact aerobics, just a dash of yoga to cool out, and then didn't we feel just wunderbar? Get out of here.

But that was the price you had to pay if your lover was cute, young, and thinner than a Movado.

Then I, stiff, sore, aching in every millimeter of tortured flesh, and he, fiddle-fit, tuned, and honed, returned home, where he leisurely commenced basting his oil-soaked body in the sun whilst I applied just a touch of Retin A and hied myself hence to the office.

I had a quick conference with Francie, set her a computer task, and settled down to a couple of hours of actual work, plotting the book. Whatever the outcome, whether new and startling or old and predictable, lots of stuff would remain the same. I still had to cover Goodman's history, background, family, start in the business, earlier cases, and so forth. So there was nothing to lose by starting. It was some relief to find my fingers remained nimble enough to work a keyboard despite the torture to which they'd been subjected earlier.

The better part of the morning passed productively. It even started to look like one of those days that you make up for all the goofing-off between. Until I received the call from my Jamaican-sounding threatener who said he "hurdit on de grapevine" that while we hadn't abandoned the book, there wouldn't be any "rockin' ob de bo-at." Evidently that was aces with him. As long as we kept to the script, there wouldn't be any need to be "breakin' yu bo-ans, mon." Which I suppose went under the heading of good news.

But good news or bad, it tended to slow the flow. So I was back to and into an elaborate program of work avoidance—really *study*ing the newspapers, for example—when I noticed a squib about Pendragon's forthcoming opus, *Hollywood Eye*. This was the first my writer's eye had seen or my ear had heard of the title of *my* book—goddamn Penny! The plant suggested it would be an in-depth, tell-all tale revealing how supersleuth Rayford Goodman had solved the American Beauty Rose slaying, put Pagani in jail, and saved Hollywood. So the fix was in.

The news put me in high dudgeon—straight past low dudgeon—from whence it was difficult to determine just what my next course of action should be. I suppose I would have to quit. I should quit. If I had a scintilla of integrity I *would* quit. If I had a scintilla of integrity I wouldn't have done Bambi. But at least it was an honest Bambi—to a sanitized degree. Bad enough to do this fluff, but to do it dishonestly?

Or viewed from another angle, what possible difference did it make? Why the hell fight it?

For one thing, Brian had been brutally beaten because of it, Goodman had been assaulted and almost blown up. It *wasn't* fluff; killer or killers was/were out there! That's why the hell fight it!

At which point Francie entered, bearing a printout. She took one look at me and said, "You look like an apoplectic lobster. Judging from past experience, I'm about to be treated to the screaming meemies."

"I am furious!" I said.

"You must be, not to say, 'And if you've ever had even the quiet meemies . . .'"

"Look at this," I said, showing her this. "That chicken-shit Penny."

When lo, himself popped in.

"Now, now, children, is that a nice way to talk about the man who puts groceries on your table and dope up your nose?"

"You really *want* me to write the story stet, no matter what we find, it isn't just money?"

"I wouldn't say it isn't just money, it's just money. And a little fear."

"But there could be big money in an exposé, in a dynamite revelation of conspiracy."

"The operative word there is 'could.' While every book of Harry's is a *lock*, if I'm not being too subtle. And the powers that be have expressed their royal druthers."

"Don't you have any integrity as a publisher?"

He wasn't even offended. He just smiled.

"Get with it, lads," he said.

Lads?

"See, no prejudice here!" And he was gone.

I really felt defeated.

"So I guess you're not particularly interested in what I found out," said Francie.

I sat mute, dispirited.

"Well, Francie, since you went to all that trouble," said Francie on my behalf, "Broward lied, Pagani was not paroled to San Diego, but to L.A. And he was not, repeat not, with his parole officer at the time of Carkeys' murder. At least according to the latest records, which if they were intending to create an alibi would certainly have been altered before now."

"So Pagani told the truth at Goodman's, which means even if he didn't kill Rita, he might have killed Carkeys.

But in that case, why not take the alibi Broward set up for him?"

"Maybe he didn't know about it."

"Or maybe he's a stalking horse, thrown in to muddy the waters," I said.

"Stalking horses stalk, they don't muddy waters. Well, in a way . . ."

"But he could have killed Carkeys. He would have had a motive. It looks more and more as if Carkeys definitely knew who *did* kill Rita. And given she kept quiet and let Pagani take the rap, it might've tended to peeve him off."

"Forgetting," said Goodman, at the door, where he'd evidently been waiting for a break in the conversation, "that it was Rollins—so far we're pretty sure—tried to kill *me*. And *did* kill some poor gay music lover from the neighborhood only wanted to steal my Blaupunkt."

"We don't know he was gay," I said reflexively.

"They got his teeth," said Francie. "They can probably tell from the teeth."

"Which suggests to me," continued Goodman, ignoring this, "we ought to mosey on over to Rollins' and see what comes out when we squeeze."

"Sounds like a plan," I said.

We wanted to be sure, of course, Rollins was home. So I called ahead. Goodman seemed to have the unlisted number of everyone who'd ever had anything to do with any motion picture ever made. I reminded Rollins we'd met at Harry Light's and how impressed I'd been by him, and how, since I was doing a book on Hollywood, I'd really like to interview him. Since he, of all people, knew everybody's dirty linen.

"I not only know everybody's dirty linen, I know what size and in what colors!" said the Dresser to the Stars. "Do come ahead, dear boy."

That being by nature of a straight line, I let it lie, promising to be along in a jiffy—a colorful if outmoded vehicle. I didn't mention I'd be bringing the world-famous Bloodshot Eye as well. Some things are best left as a surprise.

In the car, Goodman brought me up-to-date on the

sudden appearance of one of Rita's jewels, which did nothing to narrow things as far as I was concerned, but did admit was interesting.

"And, of course," he also pointed out, "someone could have the jewels who didn't do the killing. Or even have a connection with it. Or did the first and not the second. Or the second and not the first."

"Thank you for clearing all that up," I said.

We were heading west toward Pacific Palisades, through the main drag, and continuing to the clifftop house of Arthur B. Rollins. It was a marvelous piece of property atop the mountain over Pacific Coast Highway, with a clear unobstructed view of the ocean.

"What a place for a home," I said.

"The old Franklin Pangborn estate," said Goodman.

"Franklin Pangborn," I repeated, the name not ringing a bell.

"Next to the Eugene Pallette place."

"You're putting me on."

"And across from Eric Blore's, within striking distance of Donald Meek's and not too far from ZaSu Pitts's."

"Old actors," said I, getting the drift.

"Every worthwhile house in California was owned at some time or other by an actor. It's a real-estate ploy but true to refer to some shack you want to sell as the Zachary Scott place or Marguerite Chapman's house. Hers is farther down Pacific Coast Highway, by the way, near the Guy Kibbee cottage."

Now, even owned by only a semicelebrity, it was still an awfully nice place as we drove up and parked—right in back of the police car and the dowdy Dodge that spelled plainclothes loud and clear. They ought to have a model named for them, like Dodge Dart, Dodge Colt, Dodge Cop.

"Ever have the feeling that you wanted to stay and yet have the feeling that you wanted to go?" said Goodman. "Durante," he added.

When Chief Broward came out the door, I understood what Goodman meant. "Durante" must be Italian for uh-oh.

"Well, well, what have we here?" said the chief.

"Are we early for lunch?" said Goodman as we got out of the car.

"I wouldn't wait for the host to serve it," said the chief.

Oh, boy, they were dropping like flies.

"Just got here, right?" said the chief.

"Right as rain," said Goodman.

"Doesn't happen to be your second time around . . . ?"

"You mean like returning to the scene of the crime?" I asked.

"Along those lines. Whyn't we go in and have a look?" said the chief.

"I wouldn't mind at all passing on that," I said.

"Your attendance is required," said the chief.

I didn't think they could force you to do that. But on the other hand, I had a morbid curiosity to see if one didn't eventually become somewhat inured by repeated exposure.

I don't mean I thought I'd be totally unaffected, but I wondered if I might this time, for example, not get the vapors.

The chief beckoned; we followed.

The house was peculiar, to say the least. It was furnished in early dungeon, containing an incredible amount of medieval implements of torture. It was definitely the first time I'd ever seen a floor lamp made out of a rack.

"Boy, some fruitcake," said Goodman, which I chose to take in only one of its several connotations.

"Oh, this is just the sitting room," said the chief.

"I'd hate to see the playroom," I remarked.

"Was he really that crazy, or just English?" asked Goodman.

"That's crazy," said the chief. "We knew about him, but he usually stuck to consenting perverts. So, besides the odd missing neighbor's pet every once in a while, we didn't have any cause to intervene. Come on, I'll show you the body."

I couldn't help thinking, as I'm sure Goodman was too, what this did to our theory that he was the murderer.

We passed through a kitchen that looked like it contained eye of newt and wombat parts, and into a service area.

I steeled myself for the sight of slaughtered Rollins, blood and guts galore, and was almost pleased to see that while he was unquestionably dead, the silly old twit—wearing what looked to be June Allyson's old prom dress—had been dispatched so neatly it was almost an exercise in good taste.

What it was, he had this neat little round hole in his forehead.

I didn't throw up or anything.

25

Rayford Goodman

And the good news," I said, "we know he wasn't killed by the same person killed Rita and Carkeys."

"Unless that person was being clever and tried to make it *seem* like a different killer," said Bradley. Now that he had decided not to faint.

"The *bad* news," said Broward, "is how you keep being at the scene of the crime every time there *is* a scene of the crime."

"Oh, we're going to start that crap all over again?"

"Let's just start with why you were here so inconveniently."

So I told him. I told him all the reasons why we'd come to believe Rollins was a very good candidate for murderer-in-chief. How, for one thing, he'd been struck rich. Which tended to indicate the jewels. For another, how he'd tried to make me quit the book, by intimidation. First following, then nearly running me down. For another, how he knew about explosives and no doubt was the one offed my car. And the poor shlub trying to cop my radio. And finally, looking at his taste in hobbies, the kind of murders we were talking about'd be almost like fun and games to him.

"So how come he's dead? Other than you've just given me about four reasons why *you'd* like him gone?"

"Well," I said, "it could be that he did the murders, or maybe say just the first one, for someone else. It could be Carkeys he did to protect himself. So if he did the murder or murders for someone else, it could be that someone else got a little nervous we might be getting onto him. They might have worried we'd torture the truth out of him." The last was a little joke, considering his home furnishings, which included matching iron maidens. The only reaction Rollins'd have to torture would've been to beg for more.

"Or," Bradley continued unasked for, "he could have been murdered by someone who had nothing to do with the other two cases altogether, someone he picked up cruising."

"He certainly was dressed for it," said Broward.

"Well, actually, he wasn't," said Bradley. "I mean, that was a cocktail dress, and here it is noon."

"We don't know how long he's been dead," said Broward.

"We do, to a point," said Bradley. "I talked to him only an hour ago." When would he learn never volunteer things to cops?

"So, in effect, you were the last one talked to him."

"By phone."

"Chief, could I ask you what *you* were doing here?" I asked.

"For your information, though why I should give *you* information I don't know, I was here to question Rollins about Carkeys' murder."

"Uh-oh," I said.

"What uh-oh?"

"I don't like that."

"Why?"

"When you and I start *agree*ing on a suspect, I *know* I'm in trouble."

"Tell you what," said Broward. "Whyn'tchu get the fuck out of here?"

"That's *another* thing we agree on," I said. Out was just where I wanted to be.

So we left old Franklin's place, passed Gene Pallette's, Eric Blore's, and so forth and so on, and headed back toward town. I was really sorry about Rollins getting killed. Not I cared *about* the creep. I was sorry because it meant I couldn't wrap the case around him. And still had a lot of work left to do and didn't quite know how to do it. Or at all. Of course that was always the way. You never had a *plan* to solve a case. You nibbled on a notion here, took a shot there, asked questions, checked a document, hoped someone would tell you. Then it either happened or it didn't.

So, back to the drawing board. Find another way to go.

I lit a cigarette.

"Would you mind not smoking in the car?" said Bradley.

"Yes, I'd mind not smoking in the car. I mind not smoking anyplace. And I'm getting damn tired of people trampling on my rights."

"You don't have any rights."

"I know that," I said. The only reason I'd argued at all was to get in a couple of puffs before I had to dump it.

I threw the cigarette out the window.

"Don't do that!"

"Littering?"

"Setting fire!"

"You must be hell to live with."

"Don't be silly, I'm a pussycat."

I let that one lay there.

It was Bradley broke the ice.

"What do you think we should do next?" he asked.

"I've been giving that a lot of thought, and I think I have the answer."

"And the answer is . . . ?"

"Lunch."

We got back to Beverly Hills and tried La Scala Boutique, which is good for girl-watching, sandwiches, and your basic honest drink. But it was mobbed and I didn't have any special pull there—and not too disappointed, neither did Bradley. So we walked a few blocks over to Prego, which is good for girl-watching, Italian things, and your basic honest drink. Beverly Hills is a town pours generously, not necessarily out of niceness. Just they've noticed sloshed customers tend to tip more and complain less.

I drank my midday mood enhancer while Bradley didn't even drink water—a bit pointedly, I thought. As we waited for lunch, we reexamined everything we'd seen, everything we'd read, everything we knew or even suspected. And the truth of the matter is, there was only one person at every bend of the road.

Who most wanted us to write this thing straight ahead,

no curves? Who convinced CBS to drop their project
with Pagani's point of view? Who arranged Dubie to be
on tap when there might be an opening for a red herring?
Who was it notified Broward Carkeys was dead before
anyone else'd even seen her back at Dubie's house? Who
was it Rollins worked for and owed his whole professional career? Who probably paid the bills for Mama
Rose and company—blood money?—under the guise of
El Pea, under the further guise of Lefcourt Productions?
Who *really* controlled Lefcourt Productions? Who had at
least one piece of the stolen jewelry, which he gave his
wife? Harry, Harry, Harry—no one but you!

Right, it was incredible; right, it was impossible; right,
nobody in America'd ever believe it. But son of a bitch,
it had to be true!

"I find it so hard to believe," said Bradley.

"*You* find it hard? Believe me, aside from personal
feelings, professionally I wish it was anybody *but* Harry.
It'd be like trying to prove Eisenhower was a Nazi spy."

"It *is* a German name."

"Cute. But look at all the signs!"

Instead we looked at a lunch we were both suddenly
a lot less hungry for. That's the nice thing about drinking.
Good news or bad, you don't lose your appetite for it.

"I'm gonna go check my messages," I said, getting up
and crossing toward the phone, catching some incidental
cleavage along the way. It's nice to be on your feet while
women are seated. They did have pretty women at
Prego.

They also had nice hardwood floors—made a good
sound. I always liked walking on hardwood floors in
leather heels. It's strong—a person is passing. You're
making tracks.

I called my answerphone, found I had zilch messages.
Did a lot for my self-esteem, like guess who's the middle
of the universe. Then I remembered I was supposed to
have the Rolls available for Luana's boyfriend Roger in
the Valley today. Of course I couldn't do that. Number
one, there *was* no Rolls anymore, which helped cover
number two, that I was also in no mood for a showdown
with loverboy. To say nothing of three, that I wasn't
even officially on the case anymore.

I called Beverly Hills British Motors and asked for Curtis. Personal? Said employees weren't allowed personal calls during working hours. I said it was personal to me, business for him. Name? Mr. Mercury Ford. Told me just a minute, Mr. Ford.

Curtis got on the phone.

"Hello, Curtis, this is Ben Franks."

"You cryzy, callin' 'ere?" came the urgently whispered response.

"I don't think so, Curtis. Just taking care of business, trying not to hang you up. I thought you'd want to know I can't make the 'test drive' today."

"Well, sir," he said, getting himself together, but clearly in someone's earshot, "you shouldn't orter let the matter go, you could suffer some damage by delay."

"I understand, but I'm up to my ass in other things."

"Yes, sir, but if we order parts expetially for you, sir, and you don't prom'ly permit us to utilyze 'em parts, we suffers a loss which we might hafter pass on to you, sir, you see what I'm saying?"

I saw what he was saying.

"I will get to it very first chance I can—maybe tomorrow. Thank you, Curtis."

"Doncher ferget, naow, sir. In yer own best interests."

That really scared me, threats from a car-parts thief. He didn't know he was dealing with a man'd been threatened by pros.

"I get the picture. Tomorrow," I said, and hung up. I walked nice on the nice wood floor, did various chest checks, and made it back to Bradley. He'd stopped even trying to eat.

"Let's get out of here," I said, calling for the bill.

We split it, and split the place—angry and frustrated.

Outside, the sun was shining. On the tourists looking for movie stars. Who gave up on Beverly Hills because of the tourists.

I didn't have an idea in the world where to go from here.

"You know," said Bradley, "you *assume*, since El Pea owns Mama Rose's house and since Harry controls Lefcourt, that it's Harry. But maybe you're wrong—maybe it's really Lefcourt, just like it looks. Things aren't always not what they seem."

I guess the pressure was getting to him too.

"How does that notion grab you?" he continued.

"It grabs me great, you know why?"

"No, why?"

"Because it gives us a place to go and a thing to do."

"Right, let's hear it from the horse's mouth."

"Or Mama Rose's lips."

"Is that a racist remark?"

"Don't be silly, she's not Mexican."

When we got to Mama Rose's house in Westwood, we again turned into the regal drive, and right on up to the very big front door. And again the deep bong of the bell brought my seven-foot black buddy, Delayne.

"Hey, Delayne, what it is?" I offered, showing lots of teeth.

"What's what is?" said Delayne coldly.

"What is *hap*pening?" I continued, real friendly.

"What is it that you wish?" continued Delayne pointedly.

"My wish, good buddy, is another few minutes of Mama Rose's precious time. There've been some developments in her daughter's case might have some long-term effects on her well-being."

"So 'what it is,'" he continued, "you're here to do Mama Rose a favor and sort of look out for her interests."

"Right on," I said.

"Well, I'm sure she appreciates your concern for her well-being, but last time notwithstanding, Mama Rose doesn't really *see* people anymore. She spends her time in prayer and contemplation."

"Well, I'd like to contemplate just a little with her."

"No way."

"Delayne, don't make this difficult."

"You're the one making it difficult, Goodman—I'm just minding my business. And my business is to see Mama Rose is not disturbed.

"I don't want to pressure you."

He rose to his awesome full height. "Surely you jest," he said.

"There's pressure and there's pressure—everything's not physical. For example, I notice you're packing a gun. Which known felons are not permitted. And after the Forum business, and your stretch, and the terms of your parole . . . Do I have to go on?"

"You could have a very short time to go on, you start threatening me."

"I'm not threatening you, Delayne. I'm asking your cooperation."

He considered this a moment, then mumbled into his walkie-talkie.

"All right—but just for five minutes."

"Sure, pal."

"I'm not your pal."

"Brother?"

"Farther than pal."

With which we were again led around the outside of the main house and around back to the pool area and the pool house. I wondered if anybody actually lived in the main house. Probably just the servants.

He pressed the chime button and again we heard the electronic click unlock the door. He pointed in.

Mama Rose was on her knees, being prayed over by a local takeout preacher.

He was just finishing. "And give us the strength, O Heavenly Father, to accept the greaaat loss of this precious chile so cruelly snatched from our bosom by the eeevil of this world, and gain comfort in the knowledge that she done found eeeternal peace in your house, O Lord, forever and ever, amen."

"Amen," said Mama Rose, and the preacher helped her to her feet.

"Mama Rose," said Delayne, "Ray Goodman here agin wif de boy what writin' his book." Black man spoke with forked tongue—ofay to me, down-home to Mama. "And dis heah, de reveren' Goodpastor."

I suppose with a name like that it was preordained, you might say. Or, on second look, was it a nom de preach? Since he seemed to remind me of a dip I'd help bust years before.

Reverend Goodpastor nodded at the introduction, but his eyes narrowed when he actually looked at me. Helping Mama up, he said, casually averting his face—it *was* the guy—"I'll leave you to talk to your friends. I'll be right next door with Rafeel. You need me, Mama, just give a holler."

And we were left alone.

"They sure wrap her in a cocoon," I whispered to Bradley.

"Don't say it . . ." he pleaded.

"Say what?" I asked innocently.

Mama Rose turned to face us.

"Well, Rayford, have you come to Jesus yet?"

"I'm still on the road, Mama."

"Don't tarry too much. He want you. He longeth for you."

"I understand."

"Who hath not cometh unto him maketh hith eye to cry."

"Don't want to do that."

"Do it, son, save yourself."

"Working, Mama, working. Uhm, listen, remember last time we were here and we were talking about insurance? About the house, and Mr. Lefcourt? And how you said he always took out insurance on Rita and you and Rita's son and all that?"

"Sort of."

"Is that the way you got this house?"

"Why you wanna know?"

"I think it'd help me find out more about Rita's . . . passing. I'm still not satisfied we got the whole truth. I *know* you want the truth. *Was* it insurance money paid for the house?"

At which a cunning look came into her eye, and she leaned in closer.

"That's they tole me to say."

"I thought so," I said.

" 'All just insurance.' "

"But we know better, right?"

"I'm not at lib-ty to discuss," she said archly, reaching for the picture of Harry inscribed "I'll be there for you always."

"Nice picture, don't you think?"

I thought.

During all this there'd been a lot of low but intense conversation in the next room. But now it started to get loud enough to hear. And what I heard was the good reverend Rightpastor whining, "I just lef' her in peace to converse with her friends."

But the answer was even louder and angrier. "Ah tole you, mon, de woman not hab ahny visitors."

"Even old friends?"

"Dey no frens to dis house. Jes bring trouble and dishahmony."

With which he marched into the room. Seeing him in person again, this time without a gun, it was so clear. I couldn't understand why it had taken me so long to place him.

"You met Rita's son, Rafeel?" asked Mama Rose.

"Yeah, I met Rita's son, Rafeel," I said to the woman. And also Harry Light's son, Rafeel, I said to myself.

26

Mark Bradley

It was the guy! It had to be the guy who kept calling and threatening me!

"You're the guy!" I said.

"Yes, he's the guy," said Goodman. "The one called you, the one shot at me."

"And the one who beat up Brian!"

"Who Brahn?" said the guy.

"My roommate. You beat up my roommate!"

And it really started to sink in. All the pain, all the fear—this guy right here. I could feel the hairs standing up on my arms. I could feel my blood boiling. I could feel myself going crazy. Without conscious thought, I grabbed a poker from the fireplace.

"I doan beat up no Brahn!" Rafeel pleaded, backing away.

I didn't believe it. I hardly heard it. My arm, totally of its own volition, just lifted the poker over my head . . .

"Wait a second, Bradley—hold your horses," said Goodman, grabbing me.

"Let go, let go!"

I struggled furiously.

"This fucker . . . !"

"We don't know if this fucker," he replied. "That's why I didn't tell you."

"Lemme go, I'll kill him!"

"I won't let you go till you stop that. Stop it! There'll be time enough for killing when we're sure he's the fellow we ought to kill. Now, cool it!"

I kept struggling a few moments more, but in his surprising grip, my anger waned. I got hold, and when he felt me easing up, he slowly released his grasp.

"Okay?"

"Okay."

"Right," said Goodman. "Now, then, let's start from the beginning." And he crossed over to the picture of Rita—Mother-with-Felon—the one with half torn off.

"Let me take a guess," said Goodman. "What's wrong with this picture? There is a missing person. Who is that missing person? That missing person is none other than Harry Light."

Harry Light?

"His pappy."

"Figured you'd figure," said Mama Rose.

"Figured right," said Goodman. "So, all this, the money, the house, the setup, comes from Harry. Not insurance."

"A man gotta own up t'is respons'bility," said Mama Rose.

"Let me get this straight," I said. "Harry is this guy's—"

"I ahm not dis guy. I am Rafeel."

"Harry is Rafeel's father."

"Das right."

"So all the money for all this—"

"And all the *threats* and all the strong-arm stuff—"

"Not no Brahn."

"Except maybe Brian . . . come from Harry."

"Da' right, honey," said Mama Rose. "We do what Harry say. But mos'ly he say what good for Harry."

"Who did not," I summed up, "particularly care to have it known he'd sired an illegitimate son of mixed blood."

"Drum the dickhead right out the Republican party," said Mama Rose.

"So I get the idea," said Goodman. "Everything you did had nothing to do with . . . the case. It was all because he was taking care of you and Mama Rose. You couldn't risk losing that. So you did whatever he wanted. And what he wanted was to protect himself."

Rafeel nodded. "Papa Harry say scare you off writin' de book, I try scarin' you off. Papa Harry say make de call, I make de call. 'Cause Papa Harry doan wan' you fine out wha' you fine out—mainly me!"

"Which means," I realized, "we're basically back to

square one. It explains everything suspicious we've been learning about Harry."

"With the possible exception why he wanted Mama Rose to help get Pagani paroled, and why he wanted Pagani paroled at all."

"Dat paht I din care for much," said Rafeel. "He make me hep de mon kill me mama. Whyfor I doan know."

"So, okay," said Goodman. "Now we're all clear here. We know what you've been doing. And we know why. But let's be super clear—any more that shit and I'm gonna break your brains!"

He glowered at each in turn. "Any questions at all?"

Nobody seemed to have any.

So we went away from there.

Past the good reverend, past the big security man, and back into the car.

Did Goodman really believe Rafeel had done all the other stuff and not Brian?

"Probably not, he probably did Brian too. But was afraid to admit it. For which I don't blame him. You were a tiger in there."

"I was kind of macho, wasn't I?"

I drove off, feeling on the one hand a threat had been neutralized, but on the other, that we were bogging down again.

"What now?" I asked, not a little discouraged.

"Now, some basics." He took out the locker key we'd taken from Carkeys' purse. "I've got to find this locker and see what's in it."

"What do you think is?"

"My guess is notes what she saw that night. And the name of who it was knew she saw it. Plus, if we're lucky, why whatever their deal was went sour."

"In other words, the solution to the whole thing might well be in that locker."

"You just sounded like Dr. Watson. I think so. Which is why I definitely have to find out where it is."

"And how do we do that?"

"Well, the most likely place is the airport. But there're dozens of buildings have lockers there. Must be a code of some kind. Maybe I can get to someone at the airport authority."

"Can I help?"

"Sure."

"Suppose it's a bus terminal?"

"Don't help," said Goodman.

"No, no, let me—this is a research kind of thing, I'm good at that."

"Okay."

"Want to give me the key?"

"No. Just take down the number," he said. "I might want to go another way meanwhile."

So I did—after borrowing paper and a pencil, two items no self-respecting writer ever carries. Actually, I wasn't going to shlep all over the place with the key in hand anyway. What I meant by being good at that was getting to the person who *was* good at it—Francie. Let her do some electronic snooping.

So what happened, I dropped Goodman off at Le Dome, where there was a guy at the bar he wanted "to check out some important stuff with"—oh, yeah. Then I went back to the office. I figured to do some work while Francie checked out the locker key. But as I was handing her the note with the key's number and description, I spotted some writing on the other side. It said, "Harley Williams, try Sunset Royale." Goodman'd been holding out on me. But his instincts were good, and with all the ties to Harry apparently nullified by the discovery of Rafeel, it was definitely time to strike out in a new direction.

Hey, I'd done a lot of investigating before. This was probably something I could do on my own.

Besides, if I followed this up, I wouldn't have to write yet. Irresistible.

The Sunset Royale was so far east the sunset never reached it. Too, I've noticed, things Royale are usually things crummy. The Sunset Royale wasn't breaking any new ground.

There were a bunch of chains wrapped around the legs of the furniture, and they looked better than the furniture. The only threat to the furnishings I could see was if someone wanted firewood. There were a lot of signs saying what you couldn't do—cook in the rooms, sublet, keep pets. Or live very well. It wasn't much dirtier than an Arab jail, and smelled about the same.

I asked the creep at the desk for Harley Williams' room. He told me he was out. I gave him a finif and said I wanted to borrow his key. He told me to get the fuck out—keeping the finif. I grabbed him by the collar and said I wasn't in this game for laughs. He punched me in the stomach, grabbed me by the seat of my pants, and threw me into the street. Evidently there was more to this tough-detective business than I thought.

I picked myself up and betook my wounded dignity down the street to a greasy spoon—which was more literal than euphemistic—and ordered a cup of java. I turned the cup around, the handle facing left, calculating the odds of catching bubonic plague from a left-hander favored me slightly, and tried a sip. It tasted more like lava than java. It was beginning to look like I might just be a little out of my element.

I told the guy behind the counter I was looking for a black dude, name of Harley Williams. He said, yeah? I said, yeah. He said he didn't know nobody by that name, but if he did, what did I want with him? I said I was a lawyer from Mutual of Omaha and he was the beneficiary of a considerable insurance policy left by his recently deceased great-aunt, a doyenne of the smart set in Shaker Heights. He said to get the fuck out of there.

Being somewhat of a quick study, you didn't have to hit me over the stomach twice for me to catch on. I left—but stiffed him on the tip.

On the street were enough assorted characters to cast *West Side Story, Porgy and Bess,* and a road company of *Little Shop of Horrors.* These must be the kind of people in the know who were constantly referred to as source material for "the word on the street is . . ." so favored by mystery-detective writers.

I casually sauntered over to a senior citizen who looked to be celebrating his golden years as a wino, dressed, this stifling day, in a couple of suits, an overcoat, and a homemade poncho.

"How you doing, old-timer?" I assayed for openers.

"I wonder, sir," he said, opening a mouth from which issued a breath death would gag on, "if you could spare a dollar for carfare so I could go to the Red Cross and give blood?"

"Tell you what," I replied, "I'll give you *two* dollars if you promise *not* to give blood." And I started to peel them off. "And another three if you can steer me to a guy lives around here name of Harley Williams."

"I know him, I know him!" said the old-timer.

I held the money before his bloodshot eyes. "Yeah? You wouldn't just be saying that?"

"No, I know him—he kicks me and takes my money. Nigger gentleman."

"He's black, yes . . ." It didn't seem quite the moment to strike a blow for tolerance.

"Right. That's him over there," he said, pointing down the block and grabbing the five singles.

There wasn't a doubt in my mind I'd been had, but I was going in that direction anyway, so I crossed to a group of clearly ne'er-do-wells, and assuming my hippest look, asked, "One of you cats happen to be Harley Williams?"

You could have knocked me over with an art-nouveau ostrich feather when a mid-fortyish, pimpy-looking person dressed in head-to-toe day-glo took one look at me and bolted off in world-class time!

I checked in with Francine—the key was for a locker located on the ground floor at Delta.

"You're a cockeyed wonder, you know that?" I said.

"Get along with your blarney now, you old smooth-talkin' coke-sacker," she replied.

"Don't start . . ."

"He who puts coal in the bag, you're not going to take offense at that?" she answered ingenuously.

"Not today. Anyway, I know you're just a frustrated bitter old maid whose sere and vacant vagina has withered and her juices dried to dust."

"I call that even," she allowed. "You going to go to the airport now and check out Delta?"

"Seems the thing to do. But first I'm going to go try

to tear Goodman away from the bar at Le Dome. I've also located Harley Williams.''

"Great. You keep that up and one of these days you'll actually have to sit down and write the book."

"Don't forget your station, missy—you're just a literary lackey. *I'll* decide when and what gets written.''

"That's what I told Mr. Penny as he was searching your desk for a hint of some pages—though in all probability also for any loose change you might have overlooked.''

"This really could be a book, Francie."

"Okay, with me—I like it when my work actually gets printed.''

We exchanged acerbic barbs for another moment or two, then bade each other a more temperate farewell.

At Le Dome they told me I had only just missed Goodman, who, after a heroic performance of vodka chugalugging, had expressed a desire to lie down other than on the floor and gone home.

Slowly I turned. Step by step . . .

At his home the door was open, the place had been ransacked, and Goodman was, indeed, on the floor. Only he hadn't passed out, he'd been bludgeoned, judging from the flow of blood and the ugly wound on his head.

I dashed for the phone, dialed 911, and gave the pertinent facts. Those included the exact address, which I had to get by running back outside, only to discover the painted number on the curb had faded—a perfect combination of that disappearing-paint scam those guys operate and cheapskate Goodman's not going for a renewal. I had to bracket the address by those on either side of him. I was then rewarded and relieved to learn the paramedics were en route even as we spoke. You got much quicker service being assaulted in a nice neighborhood.

He was starting to come around. I kept him still, got some ice—about the only thing in his refrigerator that wasn't mutating into penicillin—and held it against his head. And really remarkably fast, the paramedics arrived.

They confirmed my deduction—not terribly difficult, given the condition of the house—that he'd been coshed, advised he go to a hospital for X rays and observation. An attempt at immediate payment was parried by a vacant stare—coshees can be vague when they want. So they merely departed.

I changed his ice pack and gave him a chance to catch his breath.

"You see who did it?"

"Nope—got me from the back. Really embarrassing."

"You feel up to going to the hospital now?"

"No hospital."

"You ought to get that looked at."

"You're looking."

"Serious."

"Not the first time I been beaned."

"Okay. I don't suppose you've had a chance to discover what they stole."

"Well, seeing my pocket is inside out and my wallet's still in my other pocket, I can guess."

With which he quickly touched all pockets.

"Yes?"

"The key. They stole the locker key."

I took a moment, but then I remembered. "Hey, I know where it is, it's at Delta."

"The locker may be at Delta, but by the time we get there I guaranfuckingtee you whatever's in the locker won't be."

A sobering thought. For me, anyway.

27

Rayford Goodman

It was so goddamn embarrassing. I'm supposed to be a pro. How many times can I be taken by surprise . . . and lose? Worse, in front of my biographer. Who I wouldn't let have the key because I wanted to hang on to it—for safekeeping! Feet of clay, man. Really.

We agreed there was no sense him hanging around nursing me. The thing to do was make a stab at the Delta locker. Though now if it *was* still locked, getting in would be a whole nother thing. So the alternate plan became Bradley to hang around, slick and invisible—good luck— and hope to spot whoever was the baddie.

I doubted he'd get there in time. No way he'd get there in time. But I wanted him out of the way here, not being all sympathetic and *supportive* while I worked my way through a probable concussion and a definite killer hangover.

Given the level of stress, it took only about two puffs on the cigarette to start the tightening in the chest that was pretty scary. The angioplasty had pretty much stopped the real chest pains—the ones you had no doubts about. But what was left, whenever you had maybe only gas or something and weren't quite sure, you tended to pop a nitro under your tongue. Just for insurance. It wasn't much fun living semiscared. Of course, I wasn't supposed to smoke at all, or drink hardly. "One one-ounce mixed drink a day is *fine* . . ." Fine for what? So it wasn't that I was living *terrified*, it was just every once in a while it got sort of *nervous*.

My head was really thumping, the throbbing behind my eyes brutal. And whatever little breath I had was coming in short pants—I won't say it. I felt like the pro-verbial last few minutes of a misspent life.

But with my luck, I'd live.

So I'd have to deal with the fact my case was looking worse by the minute. Now, what with the key stolen, and the locker likely cleaned out, I had one less potential clue to work with. A definite net loss for the day.

I went over to the bar. California must lead the world in home bars—which really didn't help develop good habits. Luana once said if we'd torn it out and put a sectional couch instead, we might still been married. The good news, whoever tossed the manse looking for the key hadn't racked up the bar before I arrived as an alternate target.

I cracked a new half-gallon—excuse me, 1.75 liters, don't you love it?—of Smirnie one-hundred. I was fighting a lot of negatives, so I put a few too-much-air middleclass ice cubes into a big glass and poured myself a week's worth of doctor-authorized vodka. Try and make the desert bloom.

The effort cost me a few more breaths. But I'd been there before, and I knew it would help. Well, I knew it would help the hangover part. The concussion I wasn't so sure of.

Oh, boy, it hurt. Of course, hangovers used to be funny—concussions've never been funny—before everybody's *awakening* and newfound *awareness* of the evils of alcohol. Nobody's a heavy drinker anymore. Everybody takes one beer's a goddamn alcofuckingholic *addicted personality*! Me, I'm a heavy drinker. I don't blank out, I don't forget. I'm *sorry* lots of times . . . mornings, mostly. But I don't wake up in strange motels, with strange bedmates, without knowing how I got there.

I refilled my glass, drank some more, picked up one or two things the bastard'd thrown on the floor.

And started back to life.

I went to the answerphone, found an urgent message from Curtis at Adderley's. Good, let him stew he'd stolen a lot of parts for nothing. Another from Francine for Mark, call the office, she'd found something interesting.

Truth be known, I wanted to put off finishing the Rolls business. It looked to be sloppy and pretty much no-win for me. Okay, I could get my money out of Adderley I solved his problem. But busting Luana's chops by busting her boyfriend wasn't going to exactly get me in her good graces. Not that I was looking for a reconciliation, I just didn't want the war escalating.

So I called Francine.

I told her Bradley was off to the airport to check out the locker, but since her message promised something interesting, I thought I'd call in case it also had something to do with the book.

"It does," she said. "In fact, I owe you an apology. You were right to dig into El Pea."

"Yeah, what'd you find?"

"Well, El Pea, as you remember, is the corporation that owns Mama Rose's house—among a great many other things."

"Yeah, Light Productions."

"Which begat Light Enterprises, which begat Light Realty, et cetera et cetera, eventually losing Light as a name and/or even on the board, and becoming, for one, California Citrus Corporation."

"Listening."

"The founder, the base corporation, El Pea itself, has your usual Bank of America-type board of directors, a WASP ten-pack."

"Yeah."

"And so it went, more or less, down the line—the occasional Schwartz (usually an upped accountant) as treasurer, if it looked better on the letterhead. Say on a nondenominational cemetery, Eternal Care Corporation for example."

"Got it."

"But you know, for me it's fun to go deeper and deeper and see where it leads. It's part of my game, my thing, you should pardon the expression. Anyway, out of all the begats, about seven holding companies deep, lo and look out, I came upon Trans-Pacific Import and Export. And on *that* board of directors are several guys respectable, several guys political, and Armand Cifelli, euphemistically identified as entrepreneur-investor in the prospectus, and Mafia capo by whatever's current crime commission."

"Armand (The Dancer) Cifelli. Met him the other night at Harry's—it didn't register."

"Soooo, I would say we have our mob connection you heard rumored about Lefcourt."

"But you say these are Harry Light's companies."

"Yes and no. There's been an incredible commingling with Lefcourt, and in fact a lot of these companies were originally Lefcourt's. I wouldn't be at all surprised if El Pea didn't start out being Lefcourt Productions. The point is, you don't accidentally have Cifelli on your board."

"I understand. That is very interesting, Francine. I don't know where it takes us . . ."

"Probably just makes things more confusing."

"Yeah . . ."

"And lots more dangerous."

"Why more dangerous that I know than when I didn't?"

"Because, old bean, even electronic snooping leaves tracks. Somebody, somewhere, is going to know there have been inquiries made and information excerpted. Which is okay if those knowing are of the Bank of American persuasion. But if they're of the Cosa Nostra faith . . ."

"Got the picture."

"So, if I were you, from now on I'd make a practice of sitting with my back to the wall in restaurants, and stay out of barber shops altogether."

"Really funny, Francine."

She told me she'd been functionally fulfilled dispensing data, and it'd been a gas interfacing me.

So I thanked her for her valuable *input*, and since we were done *networking*—I love that shit—said good-bye.

Since I'd already established Harry's interest in all the goings-on had been innocent—in the sense of the case, not the *love child*—the key now was Lefcourt. I couldn't, obviously, go sound him again. So the way to Sante Fe had to be Eldrege. You can't be somebody's executive secretary for fifty years and not know where the bodies are buried.

I poured myself another double-header and tried to figure how best to shine Miss Eldrege on.

"Miss E.," I said when I'd gotten her on the phone

and to my relief found no leftover embarrassment about the other night, "you know what this weekend is?"

"Passover," she said.

I'd thought she was going to say Easter. I guess Eldrege hadn't always been Eldrege. Probably some lunk at Ellis Island's version of what her real family name had been.

"Passover, right, and also Easter."

"So it is."

"And here's what I thought. Since I'm all alone, and it's my Easter, it struck me as possible you might be all alone for Passover. So why don't we go to the restaurant of your choice and together celebrate Passeaster or Eastover?"

She laughed. "A charming idea from a charming boy. But I'll tell you, despite alcoholic fantasies to the contrary, what I'd really like isn't romancing . . ."

"You sly puss, could've fooled me."

"What I'd like is a little warmth, a little friendship, and a chance to do a little *mothering*."

"Uh-huh," I said noncommittally. Being Hollywood, God knows what she meant by that.

"So my suggestion is, why don't you let me make us both dinner at my place. Seven-thirty."

"Ish, or seven-thirty?"

"Seven-thirty*ish*, naturally. You've lived here long enough, nobody's going to actually say come at ten minutes to eight."

"Seven-thirtyish, can I bring the salad?"

"No, you can't bring the salad, what do you know about salad? You can bring the wine. Beefeater. This is a very good year."

"You got it, love. See you later."

We good-byed and I hung up.

I'd evidently struck oil, catching her on a holiday. That was a touchy time, when a woman who'd opted for a career over housewifery might be all alone and having her doubts. There was a knack to taking advantage of people.

I picked up four more items from the floor. I'd made a tentative plan. If every time I went through a room I picked up three or four things, I wouldn't have to do an actual cleaning-up. A month or two, the house'd be like new. Or like old, really.

I spent a restorative couple hours, easing my pain at the bar and planning for the evening. And first thing you know, it was getting to be time.

I went upstairs, stripped, and dumped my old clothes on the closet floor—which wasn't a part of the cleanup plan. Then I went in the bathroom and shaved—a touchy process, given my bumps and lumps. I decided a steam might help, turned it on—didn't go on. I remembered they'd wanted three hundred and sixty-two-fifty to fix it—parts and labor. Three hundred and sixty-two-fifty, like they really knew *exactly*.

I took a very hot shower, spending a good long time. It did ease the pains, though the water was getting rustier. Hey, maybe one day they'd find rusty water healed things. Just to show myself how tough I was, I ended with an ice-cold rinse, hopped out, and dried myself off.

I decided on the gray slacks. Not too tough a decision, being the only semipresentable ones left. And they did go with everything, no accident. With that I'd wear my nice deep blue shirt I'd gotten at Carroll's the last good year, the blue cashmere socks with the brown suede loafers from Gucci ditto, and my camel-hair jacket.

I put on the slacks, shirt, socks, shoes, etc., but found the jacket was at the cleaners. Keeping things at the cleaners was sometimes a last-minute drag, but it really saved closet space.

I crossed out of the bedroom after picking up the entire contents of a drawer and putting it away—*i.e.*, dumping it back into the drawer. Then I went out the back to avoid having to pick up more stuff, and to the garage, the car, and down the hill, and to the cleaners.

I laid an extra fifty on Mr. Mull to show my good intentions and he dehostaged my camel-hair jacket.

Then I went next door to the Keg and Cork. I love those cutesy names—maybe one day The Fall-Down Drunk? There I picked up the quart—excusez moi, liter—of Beefeater and headed Old Paint out toward the Valley.

Miss Eldrege did a sort of *Reader's Digest* version of the seder, with the egg and the fish and the matzo and the salt and the empty chair—four empty chairs, actually. I learned about next year in Jerusalem—God forbid—as I joined in reading from a booklet donated by Mogen David wine, who didn't want you in Jerusalem, wanted you here, buying Mogen David wine.

It was kind of nice, but a touch sad, since it was supposed to be a big family thing. I guess it was still better I was there than she was alone. She asked me did I want to do anything about my religion. I told her I gave at Sunday school.

She said in that case, the preliminaries were over, and popped the liter of Beefeater.

"Do you want to make some martinis?" she asked.

I said sure.

"Shall I get you the vermouth?"

"Don't need that for me."

"Olives?"

"Don't need that either."

I poured generous portions of gin over ice.

"Martinis," I said. "Lechaim."

"Down the hatch," she replied.

After a while—the second martini—she sighed, put down the glass, and said, "Okay, I appreciate you're a nice guy, but . . . ?"

"But?"

"What do you really want?"

Smart cookie.

"I want to *know*," I said. "I'm not at all sure even when I do know I'm gonna write the book any different, but I gotta know." Like most people being ghost-written, I'd come to think *I* was actually writing the book, the other guy just sort of putting my notes in order. Not that I'd let Bradley know I knew.

"What exactly is it you gotta know?"

"The whole story, what really went down. For example, during the course of my reinvestigation, I've come up with the fact El Pea really owns Mama Rose's house. I also learned how come—Harry being daddy to Rafeel, son of Rita. I also know El Pea, in spite of being Harry Light's corporation, has its headquarters in Mr. Lefcourt's office. You being a guest at Harry's house, I got to figure you also work for Mr. Light."

"Not breaking any confidence to say okay to here."

I poured us another drink.

"You don't have to get me drunk," she said.

"Wouldn't hurt," I replied. "The other night at Harry's I noticed Mr. Lefcourt brought a guest, a man by the name of Armand Cifelli."

"Uh-huh."

"Your basic strange bedfellow, I'd say. I'm sure it's no big surprise to you Mr. Cifelli's in the mob business."

"Mr. Cifelli's in a lot of businesses."

"Right, including some run by Mr. Lefcourt."

"Oh, Mr. Lefcourt doesn't do much running these days."

"Correction, *owned* by Mr. Lefcourt."

"Or owning."

"Okay, you tell me."

"And why should I do that?"

"Well, to help out an old *shaygitz* in somewhat of a jam, counting on the holiday spirit."

"Borderline incentive."

"And maybe unburden yourself?"

"And maybe get myself killed."

"Really think so?"

"Well, I don't really know. I must say I don't consider it likely. And if I miscalculate, what am I really losing? I *am* eighty-one years old . . ."

"Kidding!"

"Come on, don't start that, bubby. At seventy-one you may still have some concern to look sixty-five. At eighty-one you're mostly pleased if you remember the day of the week and whether you already had lunch. But there are things on my mind . . ."

"I thought so," I said, topping off our drinks. "You don't have to *drink* it," I added when she raised an eyebrow.

"First, let me give you some background. You remember when we talked last time I told you how since *Gone to Carnival* cost old Mr. Lefcourt the farm, he'd been more or less in hock to Mr. Light?"

"Right, I remember that."

"Well, it was only partially true, or part of the bad news. I mean he was/is up to his eyeballs to Harry, but he wasn't content to let it lie with that. He resented so much someone who'd worked for him now being his boss that he compounded his stupidity—he let Cifelli in as a counter to Harry."

"Harry must have been furious."

"Harry never knew. To Harry, the fact Mr. Lefcourt was palsy-walsy with an underworld figure didn't seem all that unusual. Lots of Hollywood people hang out with gangsters. You know, who's a celebrity to a celebrity?"

"Right."

"But Cifelli had good use for Lefcourt. It was a fine place to launder money, and Lefcourt wanted money, in the hopes some of his businesses would recover. Which of course never worked out either. Cifelli didn't want successes, he wanted losses to offset. Plus Mr. Lefcourt thought he could become independent of Harry. He didn't stop to figure out how he'd become independent of Mr. Cifelli. And just what he'd do if Mr. Cifelli ever asked a 'favor' of him."

"And came the day Cifelli did ask a favor," I prompted.

"The night of the murder. I was there that night—despite my telling you otherwise."

"So Lefcourt told the truth . . ."

"There was good reason for me to lie, I'll get to that by and by—unless I get cold feet."

I topped off the gin again. She smiled, knowing what I was doing.

"Keep your throat lubricated."

"And my lips flapping. Okay. Don't think I don't want to get it off my chest. The favor Mr. Cifelli wanted was for Mr. Lefcourt to set up Mr. Pagani. Mr. Pagani had made a dope deal with Mr. Cifelli and the whole thing blew up, with Mr. Pagani unable to produce the money or return the dope. It might not even have been his fault, but it made Mr. Cifelli very angry."

"Surprisingly."

"Time had run out. If he couldn't get either the merchandise or his money back, Mr. Cifelli wanted vengeance. Mr. Lefcourt's job was to locate Mr. Pagani and inform Mr. Cifelli when and where. 'When' was the night Rita Rose was murdered, and 'where' was the studio."

"Pagani couldn't get the money from Rita . . ."

"I would guess."

"And maybe Lefcourt wasn't too subtle, so Pagani knew he was in deep shit, excuse me, trouble . . ."

"Deep shit's more like it."

"So he had to really disappear, right away, get out, and get out without being seen."

"Absolutely. In fact, to tell you the truth, I made sure he understood that. Because it was one thing for Mr. Lefcourt to do business with Mr. Cifelli. Not my affair. But if I kept quiet about what was supposed to happen, I'd be a silent partner to murder, and that I wasn't willing to do."

"So you tipped him off. Then what did you do?"

"We were actually doing inventory, as Mr. Lefcourt said, so it took a while before I could get away. When I finally did, around midnight, give or take, and checked the cutting room, Pagani was already gone. But to be doubly sure, I went to Rita Rose's dressing room."

"Yes."

"She was dead."

"But you weren't the one reported it!"

"That was because—for the life of me I'll never understand why—on an impulse I've regretted for twenty-eight years, I stole a piece of her jewelry. The Sierra Tiara."

28

Mark Bradley

It took me hours before I connected with Goodman. Since in the eight days I'd known him he'd had only one semidate, with Julie at Nipper's, I figured he was probably out scratching an itch. As the old saying goes, a man's not made of stone. When he finally picked up his messages and got back to me, I learned he'd been having dinner with Miss Eldrege. Maybe some men *are* made of stone. Come to think of it, recalling the incidental intelligence Francie had gleaned from Julie re his indisposition, I hoped a seder dinner with Lefcourt's Grandma Friday didn't presage necrophilia.

At any rate we'd agreed, after he finished breaking matzo with the aforementioned Miss E., we'd meet at the Bel Age bar to exchange progress reports.

I'd arrived a little early and tried to seem reluctant as I declined the blandishments of a readily available lady or two—easier these days when they assumed you feared the Dreaded Disease rather than the gender itself—while succumbing to the house specialty, which was all-kinds-wodka.

The orange vodka had gone down so smoothly, and the lemon as well, I was about to sample the pepper vodka when a huffing, puffing, disheveled Goodman arrived.

"Sorry I'm late, it took me a while to find a parking space, and then I had a big climb up the hill."

Right, driving up and yielding his car to the valet would have taken an actual cash outlay.

"Principle, it's a matter of principle," he said, reading my mind. "Parking at a hotel ought to be free. It's just another one of our liberties they're trying to take away."

The waitress came over.

"I'd like a cup of coffee," said Goodman, flooring me. "And a Remy Martin," he added, putting everything right with the world again.

"Okay," he said, and gave me a rundown on his dinner with Miss Eldrege, including all the functional details about the various corporations Francie had discovered, and how Lefcourt was almost totally in hock to Harry, and how to get Harry off his back he'd let Cifelli in.

"Cifelli? That refined quiet gentleman we met at Harry's screening?"

"Right, that refined quiet extortionist, loan shark, blackmailer, dope dealer, murderer, and *Family* man."

"That's the one. Really?"

"Really. And, of course, once Cifelli and his band of bent noses were in, Lefcourt had less control than ever."

Then I learned about Pagani in detail, how he'd screwed up a deal with Cifelli, how Lefcourt was supposed to set him up for elimination, and how he'd had to get out of the studio to escape, and clearly was gone before the murder.

He also told me how Eldrege had stolen the tiara and hidden it all these years, and when Sally had told Harry she needed something really Spanishy for the Amigos affair, Harry had asked Eldrege to go shopping and find something suitable. In her slightly addled and guilt-ridden condition, Eldrege saw this as an opportunity to get rid of the Sierra Tiara, and so gave it to Harry, telling him she'd bought it. She "had" to take ten thousand dollars for it, or Harry would've gotten suspicious, she said. Which she now considered almost as dumb as stealing it in the first place, with which I agreed. But it did tend to further remove Harry from suspicion.

"We seem to be getting very good at finding people who didn't do it," I commented.

Then it was my turn. I told him about following his lead on Harley Williams to the Sunset Royale, and how I'd found Harley, only to have him turn tail and run like I had the plague. I knew Goodman was cognac-mellowed when he didn't lower to the occasion with a bad-taste remark at an opening like that.

"You know," he said, "if maybe Rafeel was telling the truth and he didn't attack Brian, could be—for whatever reason I don't know yet—that it was Harley. Then, say, after doing a number on Brian, he realized or was told he got the wrong guy. Now he's hanging around Sunset and all of a sudden sees you, who he probably recognizes, having likely seen a picture or two or twelve of you at your place. He had to figure you were there to bust him and the jig was up—in a manner of speaking. So he ran away."

"Yeah, could be. Could it be he was the killer, though?"

"Anything's possible, but again, seems hardly likely. As long as Rita was alive, he was doing all right. Even as a castoff husband, he could still hit her for enough money to live pretty good—she of the old basic heart of gold. Whereas Rita, dead, meant good-bye goodtimes, hello flophouse do this again," he said to the waitress without so much as a pause between addressing me and addressing her, pointing to the glass.

"And why would he want to beat me up? Rather why, since there was a stated motive—quit the book—would he *care* if I continued writing your story or not?"

"Hey, I don't know all the answers."

Or a lot.

Maybe he was thinking the same thing. At any rate, after a moment he continued, "You went to the airport?"

"I went to the airport," I replied.

"Well, sorry, it had to be checked out. There was an outside chance."

"Better than that," I said.

"I'm all ears," he replied, downing his Remy Martin in a single gulp. Clearly not all ears, a lot of throat.

"I got to the airport"—this was going to surprise him— "and I *wasn't* too late. The locker was still snug and locked. Of course it occurred to me it might have been cleaned out and rerented to somebody else, but I followed your instructions, on the off-chance, and staked it out. I got a newspaper and pretended to read standing against a post, the way they do in the movies. That seems so illogical—if you wanted to read, why wouldn't you sit down? Anyway, I was just about convinced it'd been already cleaned out when you'll never guess who came down the line, checking numbers, key in hand."

"Maria Shriver."

"Maria Shriver? Why her?"

"Just a wild guess. Probably takes a lot of planes."

"Guess again."

"I don't want to."

"You'll never in a mill—"

"I'll kill you!"

"Chief Edward Broward."

"Boy oh boy."

"Uh-huh—how about that?"

Clearly he hadn't expected this any more than I had.

"And did you see what was in the locker—an envelope?"

"No, a tote bag."

"Well, a tote bag could have some notes in it, I suppose. That's what I expected, Carkeys' backup information who the killer was. To protect herself from exactly what she wasn't able to protect herself from."

"Possibly that too, but I don't think so. It was something else altogether."

"You're gonna keep teasing me . . ."

"When Chief Broward lifted the tote bag out, it evidently had been left open, because some stuff fell out onto the floor."

"You're really flirting with serious injury . . ."

"*And*," I continued hastily, "what fell out was a bracelet and a necklace."

"Woo," said Goodman, whether turning Chinese or merely flabbergasted, I wasn't sure, but inclined toward flabbery.

"I had to duck out of the way when he turned toward me, and by the time I dared take another look, he was gone. I didn't see him anymore, and that's it."

Goodman furrowed his brow and closed his eyes, during which I was able to wave the waitress away when she came for "last call," on the not-unreasonable assumption that anybody who'd had the better part of a liter of gin and four Remy Martins might reasonably be considered to have had enough.

"Still, if the jewels were Carkeys', and we know Carkeys didn't do the murder, then the murder and the theft were two separate crimes. *And* there might still been some notes in the tote bag on who *did* the murder. So maybe Broward knows by now who did it and will be making an arrest soon. Which leaves only one big question."

"This is where I say, 'And that is?' "

"How did he know there was a key, and how did he know I had it?"

"That's two questions."

"And why did he have to bop me over the head to get it?"

"That's three. Would you have given it to him?"

"There's that—"

With which they flickered the lights in the bar, a polite hint we get the hell out and let them all go home.

Goodman was a mite unsteady on his feet so I offered to drive him home if he'd like to leave his car till morning.

The outrageous suggestion he might not be totally sober brought an instant transformation to a combination banshee and Mr. Hyde, and an unqualified challenge to fight me and any three others of my choice to see just who was drunk or not, buddy-boy. I respectfully declined.

"Not good enough," he bellowed. I apologized. "Too late for that!" he roared. By which time various employees of the hotel, plus gathering security forces, were actively involved in expediting his departure.

With the clarity of mind and perspicacity that so characterize the inebriated, he reflected on the quality of their hotel, their fruity vodka, their likely parentage, and was rewarded for his insightful observations by being barred for life from the Bel Age, its immediate environs, and/or corporate components worldwide.

I watched as he stumbled down the hill toward his car, got my own, pulled down and idled fifty yards behind him, saw him finally get started and pull up the hill toward Sunset. I made a U-turn, followed, in time to see him turn left, weave the few blocks to Doheny, turn up, and figured there wasn't too much he could hit on the side streets close to home, and let him go.

I turned down Doheny, left at Santa Monica, right at King's Road, and into my garage, the gate to which was open, followed by another tenant. I pulled up to our double parking spot, the other half of which was occupied by Brian's car, out of which Brian himself was this very moment decarring.

"Well, this is a nice time to be getting home," said I, after I got out myself.

"Let me go first," said Brian. "Where were *you* till twenty after two in the morning?"

"I was having a simply wonderful time keeping Rayford Goodman company and out of jail while he got drunk and abusive. In other words, working."

"Other people work from nine to five."

"Lucky them. And where were you, might I ask, if I may make so bold?"

"No, you may not! Inasmuch as you seem to think I'm going to just sit home buffing my nails and eating bonbons while you go traipsing about town—"

"With Goodman you don't traipse. You *reel*, maybe, but definitely don't traipse."

"—till all hours."

"The same hours, I might add, I'd like you to account for."

"Well, too bad. I don't have to account to you. And let me add one thing, loud and clear"—for sure. "If you keep spending twenty-four hours a day away from me, I'm not going to be spending those hours home alone!"

"Why don't we go upstairs and talk this over quietly?"

"Why don't we stay down here and *yell*?"

"Because I've already had yelling up to and beyond the kazoo. What I want now is quiet."

"I'll give you quiet!" he yelled.

I was definitely losing ground. However, there seemed to be a built-in hiatus forming as out of the car which had followed me in now appeared two well-dressed, near-yuppie-looking gentlemen, heading our way.

I say near-yuppie because, though well-dressed, neatly groomed, and mannered, they were incredibly well-built, with oak-width shoulders, waist-size thighs, and like that. I kept telling myself it was amazing how everyone was into working out these days and how they weren't, therefore, especially threatening. I kept telling myself, but I kept not believing it.

"Mr. Bradley?" said one.

"What can I do for you?" said I, hoping it was nothing I wouldn't *want* to do.

"A certain gentleman you recently met would like to have a conversation with you."

"It's two-thirty in the morning."

"At two-thirty in the morning."

"Well, look, why don't you just have him give me a ri—"

They each grabbed an arm. They were very good at grabbing—it had a lot of hurt in it.

"Now!"

"Now's good."

It had all happened so quickly, so politely understated, it hadn't quite registered on Brian, but now it was suddenly unmistakably clear, and he moved in to assist me.

"Stop that—let him go!" he said rather forcefully.

The gentlemen-hoodlums didn't find it all that forceful.

"No, no, Brian, I'll just go with them and find out what they want."

He clenched his fists, girding for battle.

"They can't do that," he said.

"I think they can."

He took a step forward.

"Don't do anything," said one of the mountains.

"Don't do *anything*," said the other as they began fast-walking me to their car.

There really wasn't anything he could do.

"I'll be back," I said over my shoulder, as much for myself as Brian.

"Probably," said the first mountain.

"That wasn't necessary," I said as he tossed me into the car as if I were a doggie bag. "No need to be cruel."

29

Rayford Goodman

It was hard to tell was it still the old concussion I was feeling, or the new hangover? Except it was very familiar. And I hadn't had all that many concussions.

There seemed to be an alarming lot of rusty water coming out the shower now. Looked like the days were numbered for putting off the Big Plumbing Sting they'd been threatening for three years.

Hey, the house was over twenty-five years old and the pipes designed to rot away after eighteen to twenty. So I hadn't done all that bad. It must have been hard for them to be so patient and use a metal took that long to rot—when cardboard would have fallen apart that much sooner. Motherfuckers.

On the other hand, with a little luck, maybe the rust came from the boiler. The boiler was designed to fall apart in only ten years. Which it had on schedule so far, this being my third. The good news, if it was the boiler, wouldn't cost an arm and a leg. Just an arm. Thieving shits.

I dried off—streaked off, really. Maybe it would look like a tan, and my hair pass for Grecian Formula with that cute red cast. Matched my eyes.

Externals aside, little by little I started to feel human. And with the first signs of recovery, cautiously optimistic. This was familiar pain, which meant maybe the concussion was getting better. I always was one to look on the brighter side.

There'd already been two calls on the answerphone, either while I was still zonked out or in the shower.

The first was from Brian, urgent. Right, I was sure real urgent. Probably wanted to read me off, keeping his boyfriend out all hours.

The other was from Curtis, the king of stolen auto parts. He was all antsy, warning me I better come through today or else. Terrorrr! But I did want to wrap that up, one way or the other. I'd have to make up my mind pretty soon. Was I going to drop the whole thing, so Luana wouldn't get hurt? Or do what I was hired to? Meaning bust not only Curtis but also Roger Meade, the guy who was filling my shoes, so to speak, with my ex-old-lady? I really hate crooks. Especially crooks named Roger.

Maybe it really was urgent. Brian.

I called. The line was busy.

I made some coffee. Called again. Still busy.

I copped a newspaper from my neighbor's lawn and speed-read it. And whatever happened to that, by the way—Evelyn Wood off in her mansion somewhere speed-counting her millions? But I could find no hint Chief Broward was about to make any arrests and/or at least report some progress solving the murders.

Even if Carkeys didn't leave any written clues, Broward had the tote bag with the jewels. They hadn't turned up at Carkeys', and then later, neither at Rollins'. Since the key did turn up with me and the only place I could have gotten it would have been Carkeys', he'd obviously been on the right track. Though even so, it was a reach for him to have known. Weird.

Now, he might still not know who did the murders, but at least there ought to be an announcement of recouping the jewels. Maybe it missed the first edition of the paper.

I turned on a local TV news—nothing there either.

I called Brian again. Still busy. Regular chatterbox.

I called Adderley, told him I was locking in on his problem, assuming I was still working for him. He said when and if he saw some results, he'd consider rehiring me. I said what about my car, how was the painting coming along? He said it was in limbo. The primer was on, but the paint was being held in abeyance. Pending determination of payment "or suitable remedies under law."

"Don't give me that mechanic's-lien crap, finish the goddamn car. One way or the other."

"Well, if we don't resume our association, the paint will come to twenty-one hundred dollars. Payable on completion, old bean."

"Great, fine, old potato," I said. What difference did it make if he asked five hundred or twenty-one hundred? Since I didn't have either, I was going to have to promote something. Poor-mouthing wouldn't help.

"Just get on with it. I promise you'll want to go with the original contract," I said, exuding confidence.

"The original contract didn't call for the total destruction of a vintage Rolls-Royce Silver Cloud II."

"Fortunes of war."

"It wasn't in connection with my case, old top."

"Not immediately obvious. But you can certainly take a *position* with your insurance company . . ."

"They are resisting."

"Well, whyn't we take it one step at a time? I'm about to break your case. That ought to save you more money than the Rolls was worth, being some people say vintage when it's plain old."

"Break the case and we'll talk."

"Paint the Caddy?"

"I suppose. It's not doing me any good taking up space."

We said good-bye and hung up.

I tried Brian one last time. Busy. Beginning to annoy me. So I locked up the house, which was something of a joke considering how easy everybody was getting in these days. Then I pulled up the garage door, popped into the rented Porsche, and headed down toward Beverly Hills and the Beverly Hills Police Department.

There was no legal free place to park at *our* police station. So I had to circle back across Little Santa Monica and regular Santa Monica to find a spot several blocks away.

The Beverly Hills police station's definitely no Fort Apache. It is, of course, a public building—but so's Versailles. At the moment it was a little less grand than usual, being it was under reconstruction. They were rebuilding from Moorish Nouveau Mucho to something a lot like kitchen moderne in the forties. But whether then, now, or in the future, the Beverly Hills police station was never the kind of place you were hit by that institutional Lysol smell. It was always squeaky clean and smelled a lot more like Giorgio's. Though the temporary quarters must have been quite an embarrassment to a force got its uniforms from Bijan.

Chief Broward was in a real good mood this morning. And why not, having broken an important robbery, not to mention the back of my head. Though I didn't figure he'd be admitting the latter. He not only agreed to see me but was downright pleasant.

"Well, well, Ray Goodman, what a surprise."

"Really?"

"Sure, really, how often do you come visiting?"

"I try to drop in whenever I get a bump on the head."

"Oh, have you been assaulted?"

"Yeah, it's just terrible with this criminal element running loose. I was robbed too."

"Ah. You must report it. I'll get an officer to take your statement." He reached for the intercom in slow motion, expecting me to stop him. When I didn't, he quit reaching.

"What, exactly, were you robbed of?"

"Well, you know, that's funny. Didn't take my TV. Didn't take my hi-fi. Just an old keepsake. Really hardly any value to anybody but me . . . or maybe you—someone like us. A key."

"A key, eh?"

"Yeah, eh, that's why I was kind of expecting some sort of action from this office. An announcement of some sort."

"What sort did you have in mind?"

"That there were developments . . ."

"Developments."

"Progress in the case."

"Goodman, I don't know what you're talking about."

"The jewels?"

"Hey, if you have any information to offer, by all means let's have it."

"I don't think I have any information you don't have."

"Then I don't understand this whole meeting," he said, ending the friendly bantering. He got up out of his chair, the standard kiss-off. "If you'll excuse me, I have work to do," he said.

"I thought you'd been doing it."

"Good-bye, Goodman."

So.

Maybe Broward wasn't solving crimes.

Maybe he was committing them.

Beverly Hills figured it didn't need phone booths on the streets. Hermès would let you use theirs with any purchase over a thousand dollars—which any purchase was.

Of course restaurants had them, but it always felt like they were doing you a favor because they weren't in the phone business, they were in the restaurant business. Which is why somehow you always tiptoed semi-guilty through a dining room to get to a phone. But La Famiglia didn't really seem to mind.

I picked up my messages. The first was from Brian saying please, please, right away, get in touch, he was home. The other was from Harley Williams and gave a number.

I called Brian. The line was still busy. If he wanted me to call back so urgent, why'n't he stay off the phone? So I called Harley Williams. He *had* been spooked by the sudden appearance of Bradley, figured right away he was in deep shit. What could he do to square the beef? I told him he could start off with the truth. He admitted he was the one beat up Brian.

I told him I didn't think that was a very nice thing to do.

He told me nobody ever accused him of being nice. Besides, it was a job, didn't I approve minority employment?

I asked who hired him, and he said it was unethical for him to give me that information.

I said I understood, but that only applied to people who were ethical. Or didn't mind spending long years in jail after they recovered from savage beatings.

He told me his employer's name.

He asked me if that meant he was off the hook.

I took another shot while I was at it and asked what

time he'd left the studio the night Rita Rose was killed. And if he was alone. He told me that too. Then he asked again now was he off the hook.

I said I personally didn't have any plans at the moment to hurt him, but I thought it might be better if he tried living on Corfu.

Then I called Brian one last time. And when it was still busy, got the operator and told her it was an emergency, and to cut in. And then found out his phone was out of order.

"Just relax, you're acting crazy," I told him after racing to his apartment, and Francie, after peepholing me and un-Fox-police-locking the door, had let me in.

"I am crazy, and totally beside myself. This is absolutely insane. Two weeks ago we had a nice normal life, with nice normal hours and a nice normal future ahead of us."

I thought under the circumstances I wouldn't challenge what he meant by "normal."

"How do you know Mark's been kidnapped?"

"Well, I got a *clue* when two bozos the size of Cleveland surrounded him, lifted him up, and carried him off to their car! It was right out of *The Untouchables*! I tried to stop them, but I couldn't fight my way through the *garlic*, let alone them."

"Did they say anything?"

"They said a certain gentleman Mark'd recently met wanted to have a conversation."

I had a pretty fair idea who "a certain gentleman" he'd recently met was.

"Francine," I said, "you've come across Armand Cifelli's name popping up on the board of directors of several corporations."

"That's right."

"Why would he do that? Why would a mobster let them put his name someplace it could be found?

"Because they're legitimate companies, doing legitimate things. Being associated with them gives *him* legitimacy. If anybody wants to know what he does, he doesn't have to say 'kill people and extort money.' He can say, 'I'm in the convalescent-home business; I'm in the shopping-mall business,' and so forth. It gives him respectability."

"And you figure he might know we've been poking around the computer files?"

"No doubt."

"So what does that mean?" asked the still near-hysterical Brian. "That you know who kidnapped Mark?"

"Think so. Even more, I probably know why, too."

"And do you also know how we're going to get him back?"

"That part I haven't figured out yet."

I did manage to calm him down a bit. I told him I didn't think Cifelli would really hurt Bradley. He just wanted some information. What I didn't tell him was if the information why we were butting into Cifelli's personal business didn't *satisfy* him, it could get deadly messy.

"So, what're you going to do?" croaked Brian.

"First, check my messages. Can I use the phone?"

"Why is it people you wouldn't trust to change a five dollar bill always *ask* if they can make a call that doesn't even cost anything?"

"Is that a yes?"

"You can't, it's out of order," he reminded me.

"Mark's car," suggested Francie, ever the practical one.

I knew there was a reason people had phones in their cars—for the once in twelve years their house phones went out of order.

"Don't panic, it'll work out," I told Brian.

"Please," he answered softly. Surprised myself, I was really touched.

Francie kept me company down to the garage. And showed me how to work the phone. I called my house.

Sometimes even the people who create the problems help you solve them. There was a message on my answerphone from a "representative of the gentleman you met the other night in company of Mr. Bradley." Cifelli was contacting me. That meant one of two things. Either everything was okay, and I could arrange to get him back. Or else Bradley fucked up so bad they wanted to include me in the package for disposal.

The voice suggested we have a little "sit-down" over lunch at Chianti, a very nice Italian restaurant on Melrose. Good, I hadn't had Italian in over a week.

"The setup?" asked Francine, doing nothing to quiet my nerves. "The old Italian restaurant rub-out?"

"Them to know and me to find out."

"You're going to go?" asked Brian.

"Hey, could be just lunch," I replied. "It's not as if they said meet them at a barber shop."

30

Mark Bradley

Help!

31

Rayford Goodman

Wild horses couldn't drag it out of me, but the truth is, I was so nervous I figured I better make use of the time till lunch—or I'd go nuts. So I left Brian and Francine and headed for the Valley again to nail old Roger. I guess I had sort of decided. That way I could at least get my car back from Adderley.

Daylight didn't do anything too wonderful for Sunswept, as you might imagine. It was every bit as grungy—more. But after all, not everybody could afford living in Beverly Hills. Me, for example. And the Valley was the only other game in town—or out of town. It definitely cost less. Only you paid with an extra five to ten degrees in heat and five to ten years in life, breathing industrial-strength smog. But besides money, a lot had to do with personality. Some kinds just felt more comfortable in the Valley—motorcycle nuts, check-kiters, crack manufacturers, people with pickup trucks.

And illegal auto-repair merchants.

I made the last turn on Sunswept Drive (Drive, yet), pulled up at the bottom of Roger Meade's driveway, and got out of the Porsche. I could have driven up the hill, but there was always the chance surprise would give me some advantage. I certainly hoped so, because if it was a tough climb at night, it was a killer by day.

Dusty, the sweat running off me, I finally got to the top and peeked in on the open bay he used for work. It was deserted. Except for the sleeping dog which opened one eye and decided he was off-duty. The house, too, seemed awful quiet. I looked in at the living room, nothing there. A den off to one side ditto. The bedrooms were I guess around back. I light-footed it there, the effort a lot compromised when I kicked an empty bucket

262

and sent it crashing down the hill. I froze, listening for some reaction, but nothing. So I inched along till I came to a window, where I stopped to catch my breath.

I guess the internal noise of my breathing kept me from hearing the footsteps. It sure didn't get in the way of feeling the cold steel suddenly pressed against my neck. I'd really lost my edge—which not booking enough work will do for you.

"Looking for something?" came the voice.

I held my hands out in plain sight in the universal I-surrender, no-trouble-from-me position, and slowly turned.

"Hi ya, Rog, how's the boy?" I said to the guy wearing the Jockey shorts and the Colt .45.

"Mr. Goodman?"

"Right, you want to put that gun away?"

"What are you doing here? Luana's not here."

"Right, you want to put that gun away?"

"I'm all alone, I swear."

"Put the gun away."

"Oh, yeah, sorry." He lowered the gun.

"Who is it, honey?" came a voice from inside, followed by a figure outside. Pretty near naked, far as I could see. Which was pretty far. So much for being alone. Or swearing.

"He's a friend of mine," said Roger.

"Don't get carried away," I said. "Acquaintance," I explained to the seminude lady. "We have a friend in common."

"This is, uh, Didi. Didi, Mr. Goodman."

"How do you do, sir?"

"Haii."

"Why don't you go make breakfast, Didi—I'll be in in a minute."

"All right, babe," she said, wrapping her body around him and eating half his face off with what I guess was just a friendly kiss. Don't mind me. I mean, I didn't think they were auditioning for Outstanding Pornography in a San Fernando Setting. But you never know.

She came up for air and headed back inside. Didi seemed to have some extra parts. There certainly was a lot of meshing. It was something to see, and didn't she know it. (Sir!)

"Not bad, huh?" said Roger the grease donkey.

The funny thing is, I found myself angry. Who the hell was he to be stepping out on Luana? I mean, how could you trust your car to a guy cheated on your wife?

"Look, if you came to talk about Luana," he said, "I don't think it's a very good idea. You're divorced, what she does is her own—"

"I didn't come here to talk about Luana, shmuck, I came to talk about auto repairs."

"What auto repairs?"

"I'm Benjamin Franks."

"Benjamin Franks?"

"The guy with the Rolls needs fixing. Curtis?"

"Oh, hey, yeah, great. Lemme just throw on some pants—"

"No, no, no—see, I'm *really* a private investigator. I was hired to find out who was stealing parts and customers from Beverly Hills British Motors."

"Well, I don't work there, I just free-lance."

"Right, you just receive stolen goods."

"Well, that's a very narrow way of looking at it."

"No narrower than I think the D.A. would look at it."

"You're mad at me 'cause I boffed your old lady."

"I'm mad at you 'cause you're a thief, a gonif, and you're un*faith*ful to my old lady."

Didn't seem to faze him.

"Hey, look, you're not official cops, right? There must be some way we can work this out. How about, say, I fix your car free?"

"It wasn't my car, it was just a prop. To scam you guys."

"Well, then, I guess, I see, uhm, you want money? I don't have much money . . ."

"There's nothing dumber than a crook doesn't have much money. What's the point stealing if not money? For a hobby?"

"Well, I have a lot of expenses."

Right, I thought, big overhead, looking at about eleven dollars' worth of furniture.

"Listen," he continued. "There must be some way we could work this out."

He got calculating—not a pretty sight. "Hey, Didi!" he said finally, his eyes narrowing. "You like Didi?"

"Try not to be a total snake. Here's the way it's gonna be: first, you're out of the stealing-from-Beverly Hills British Motors business."

"Oh, yeah, hey, sure."

"And Curtis is gone."

"No problem."

"Which leaves only the question of jail."

"Oh, man . . ."

Melrose Avenue sure changed. What used to be dingy, dirty, and dying had changed to lively, trendy, and hot. There were scores of new stores, specialty restaurants, esoteric boutiques (Whips of All Nations), the whole a sort of acid-deco-updated Carnaby Street.

I got to Chianti early. First, there was no one-upman-ship dealing with a heavy hitter like Cifelli. No time for games, keeping him waiting. And second, I wanted to seat myself with my back to the wall. Clichés are clichés for a reason.

Somehow a bullshot sounded more fortifying than a Bloody Mary, and fortified is what I wanted to be. Two bullshots were even more fortifying. I was starting to feel a little more confident as the minutes went by. After all, I was invited here to talk. I was good at talk. It would be all right. It would be better with just one more bullshot.

I was still debating whether I wanted another piece of celery or not. It wasn't the alcohol got you, it was the vegetables. That was the point a smiling Armand Cifelli sauntered in. Nonchalant, perfectly at ease—why not, he wasn't on the spot—he beamed his way to my table. And acted like we were the best of friends about to indulge ourselves in the great pleasure of each other's company.

"Ray, how good to see you. So nice of you to come."

I rose and shook hands, hoping the hell he wasn't going to hug me and maybe give me a Sicilian kiss or two.

"Mr. Cifelli, good to see *you*."

"Sit down, sit down." He light-footed it around to the

other side of the table. Not called the Dancer for nothing. Then, without even a look, started sitting, sure
somebody'd be holding the chair for him. Somebody was.
It seemed like at least three people were holding the one
chair.

Another came up with what looked like a perfectly
chilled Gibson—no stock red wines for this guy—and put
it before him. He smiled with satisfaction, and the room
exhaled with relief. The waiters and maîtres d' withdrew
to a discreet distance.

"So, now, you know what you want?" he asked.

"To eat?"

"Certainly to eat," he replied, still smiling. "You're
funny."

"I hope so," I said.

With which I scanned the menu, picked piccata. Cifelli
didn't have to call out, snap his fingers, didn't even have
to look. He simply moved his head a millimeter, and a
couple captains materialized. I ordered. The house evidently knew what Cifelli wanted. The crew backed away.
Cifelli was used to having people back away. And back
down, no doubt.

There was a bit of sizing-up going on. I hadn't really
checked him out that night at Harry's, but I knew him.
I knew all the hims from a lifetime experience. This one
was a slicker, more refined model, with taste, and hopefully reason. It didn't mean he was any less ruthless. Just
whatever he did would be for a purpose, and not for
pleasure. And for damn sure wouldn't dirty his shoes. I
actually sort of liked him.

The smile seemed relatively fixed in his smooth-
skinned face. The teeth had been capped, maybe only
bonded, the forehead and eyes a shade too free of wrin-
kles for a man over fifty, but he had kept the prominent
nose—with which I agreed. It was a grand proboscis and
added a noble touch. Thick brown hair flecked with gray
was set off by the whitest shirt I'd ever seen. The rich
have great ice cubes and really white shirts. The fawn
Brioni suit didn't hurt either. I felt pretty sure lunch was
on him.

I knew well enough not to try steering the conversation
any way or at any time. It was his party. I had a feeling

it was *always* his party. So, while we ate the tasty treats and drank the odd bullshot and the perfect Gibson, we chuckled over the latest fat/less-fat frustrations of Tom Lasorda, considered the chances for the Lakers to regain the championship, agreed we didn't much care how the Angels did—certain guys were just plain National Leaguers—and even less about the Kings, Clippers, and Afghanistan.

And we got through lunch.

"Shall we talk?" he asked after the longest meal.

I nodded.

"Why don't you tell me what's going on?"

"Exactly in what way?"

"In the way I want to know," he said, the smile shrinking. "This girl has been making inquiries that concern me. I understand she works with this boy—who's staying with us. My further understanding is he works for or with you?"

"Yeah, yeah."

"And the whole idea is . . . ?"

"The book, he's helping me write my autobiography."

"But how is it possible that's involving me?"

"I assure you, Mr. Cifelli, that was never anybody's intention. Basically, we're doing research on the Rita Rose murder. Certain people came into it. Their names were raised in connection with what happened at the time. Purely without meaning to, we also happened to learn you were associated with some of them—Mr. Lefcourt, Mr. Light. In a strictly legitimate way, of course. Now, none of this figures in the book, I assure you."

"I'm glad to hear that. I respect your assurances. You're a man, I'm sure, who knows that when someone gives me his word, he is obliged to keep it."

"Right."

"So, tell me, what have you learned?"

"About Rita Rose?"

"All right."

"Well, for one thing, we got the wrong guy, as much as I hate to admit it. It looks very much like Danny Pagani didn't do it."

"Ah, see, right away, we have a conflict of interest."

"Beg your pardon?"

"You're a man of discretion, I know. Let me tell you a secret."

"If you want to," I said, wishing like hell he wouldn't. Sharing a secret with Cifelli could be hazardous to your health.

"I had some business dealings with Mr. Pagani at that time. I imagine you might have heard."

"There was talk. I don't—"

He held up a hand. I stopped waffling. "Right, I heard."

"Well, the truth is, Mr. Pagani made a rather costly error. He was supposed to sell something for me, as you know. I gave him merchandise worth a hundred and fifty thousand dollars, which in 1963 was more than just leg-breaking money."

"Right."

"And he lost it. So I wound up with neither money nor merchandise *and* a large amount of embarrassment before my associates."

"Uh-huh."

"So, what it boils down to is, I have no objection if you and Mr. Bradley write this book, which I'm absolutely certain will contain no references to me. But what I would like is for the record to stand the way it is."

"That Pagani's guilty? Not that he was framed?"

"See, what it is is justice. Mr. Pagani misbehaved. He deserves punishment. I'm sure you can understand we can't publicly complain he ripped us off on a dope deal. So let his punishment be to continue being known as the brutal slayer of one of America's most beloved performers."

"Uhm . . ."

Cifelli smiled, leaned in close, and fixed me with a pair of very cold eyes.

"Capish?" he said.

He had one of his "associates" drive my Porsche as I joined him in the understated Mercedes limousine he favored and we headed off, I figured toward wherever he was stashing Bradley.

But looked like not right away, as the driver made his way up to Sunset and west toward UCLA. To get there, you turn left on Hilgard. No surprise, we weren't going to UCLA, instead turned right on Copa De Oro—which was a detour route for Stone Canyon—the part under repair. Then to Bellagio, and from there connected to Stone Canyon, where it developed we were en route to the Bel Air Hotel, than which nothing is more old-money and elegant in these parts.

We pulled up to the beautiful old hotel and were immediately surrounded by half of Mexico showing an intense desire to perform every possible service for Cifelli's car.

Two or three other guys fought for the privilege of opening the door. Cifelli got out, and motioned me to do the same. I followed him through the lobby, which acted a lot like the Red Sea to Charlton Heston. Nobody else existed might remotely inconvenience him. And, of course, whither he went, wenteth I. In sort of a formation. He led, with one associate preceding, one following, me. They didn't need rifles for me to get the idea there wasn't a whole lot of freedom of choice.

A moment before we got to his suite, the point associate rushed ahead and unlocked the door. I was led through the living room, to a bedroom, through a bathroom, on the far side of which was another locked door. That, too, was now unlocked, opened, and I was gently shoved. Once in, I saw a figure across the room get up slowly from a chair and turn to face me. It was Bradley!

"The last place," I said.

Cifelli smiled. "You surely didn't think I'd keep him in an abandoned warehouse, did you?"

"I should have guessed you'd come up with something better."

"Goodman," said a very nervous Bradley, "is it 'Thank God you're here' or 'My God they got you too'?"

It was a good question. I didn't actually know for sure. I turned to Cifelli.

"No, no, no—no such thing. This was all just a misunderstanding, as I've explained to Mr. Goodman. For which I most humbly apologize. I'm very, very sorry if you were inconvenienced."

Bradley stared dully, not yet sure Cifelli wasn't being sarcastic.

"I really do apologize," said Cifelli.

"I accept, I accept," said Bradley.

"If there's anything . . ."

"No, no," said Bradley.

"You're sure?" insisted Cifelli.

"Yeah, yep, real sure, absolutely, no question."

"All right, then." He pointed toward the inside of the suite, and his henchmen stepped aside. "Feel free to go."

"Just go?" said Bradley, wanting to be double sure he didn't break any rules.

"Please."

We started cautiously out.

"Oh, there is one thing you can do for me," said Cifelli.

Bradley froze. Here it came!

"Yes?" he said in a shaky voice.

"Give some thought to whether it might not be a good idea for *me* to have an autobiography."

32

Mark Bradley

Shake, rattle, and roll—mostly shake. I felt like I was doing one of those rubber-leg acts where the guy can't stand and seems to have about twelve joints in each limb. Dick Van Dyke used to do it, pretending he was drunk. Only he was funny; I was pathetic.

We were back in my apartment, and the full force of relief from the fear that'd consumed me since late last night was setting off some incredibly violent physical reactions.

"Hey, take it easy," said Goodman, noticing my eyes about to roll back. "Here, sit down."

I sat. "Whew, there's just so much going down. I'm not used to all that much excitement."

"Who is?" said Brian. "This is getting ridiculous. It was bad enough when the amateurs were harassing us, but when we start having to deal with professional mobsters . . ."

"Are there any amateur mobsters?" said Goodman.

"You know what I mean," said Brian. "The whole thing gives me the heebie-jeebies."

"Please, Brian," I said, momentarily perking up. "Not the heebie-jeebies, the Hebrew Jebrews." At which point a wave of weakness overwhelmed me again.

"I can't seem to shake this combination of incredible relief and an almost uncontrollable desire to babble like a baby."

"I know," said Goodman. "It's like getting out of combat. You've been stressed and going on nerve, and once you're safe and relax, you fall apart. Very normal—just go with it."

So I went with it and began to cry. I still felt embarrassed to be doing that in front of Goodman, but I couldn't seem to help it.

He truly understood. In fact, to my amazement, he put his arms around me.

"Okay, it's okay, Bradley," he said, patting my back.

"Well, no way do I think it's okay," said Brian. "*Kid*-napping you? What have we gotten ourselves into? It's totally outrageous, and I for one take umbrage—"

"You're setting me up, right?" I replied through the shaking and the crying. "Like if you've had even the teensiest *bite* of umbrage . . ."

"I think it's time we faced up to something here," continued Brian, unwilling to be joshed out of it. "This is not just a job anymore. The whole situation has gotten completely out of hand! I want you to give up the damned book!"

"I've got to see it through. I'm a journalist," I said, determined to stop reacting, already.

"The biographer of Bambi Blain is a journalist?"

"Don't get bitchy. I can't quit, and I'm sure you know why."

"Of course I know why," said Brian. "Because you're a Leo."

"Guys, guys," said Goodman. "I think we're overdramatizing here. True, we had a bit of a scare, but let's keep it in perspective. It's also true no real harm."

"I say quit," said Brian.

"And I say tomahto," I said.

At which point the doorbell rang. I peeped through the peephole, enlivened the dead bolt, defoxed the Fox, opened the door, admitted Francie, and closed the door. Only the door wouldn't close, a big brogan was in the door—attached to a large fellow. A significantly ominous large fellow.

"He's with me," said Francine—by the way, wearing the biggest, darkest sunglasses I ever saw. "I mean, he followed me in."

No puppy.

"Yes?" I said, feeling that thing in the legs again.

"Package for Mr. Bradley." Mr. Bradley didn't want a package—boy, did Mr. Bradley not want a package.

Though I felt pretty sure they had subtler ways of delivering bombs.

"Okay," I said, a little short on dialogue, which tended to happen when the saliva dried up.

The Big Bozo snapped his fingers. A second B.B. popped into the frame, holding a huge—extraordinarily huge—bouquet of exquisite flowers. Thank God at least it wasn't in the shape of a horseshoe.

"Compliments of a friend," said the first guy, snapping his fingers, prompting the second guy to hand them to me. They weighed a ton.

"There's a card," he added. Both left.

"Thanks," I mumbled weakly after them, closing the door with difficulty, and, struggling under the weight and bulk, returned to the living room.

"So what did *you* do last night," said Francine suggestively.

"Nothing to warrant this, I assure you," I replied, finding the card.

"Read it out loud," said Brian.

"If you dare," said Francine.

"The card says, 'Welcome to the wonderful world of omertà.'"

Goodman started to laugh. "Not too often the mob has a sense of humor," he observed.

"A very pretty way to tell you to keep your mouth shut," said Francine.

"Not the worst idea I've heard today," added Brian.

"I am not going to give up the book," I said.

"I don't think he meant you necessarily have to," said Goodman.

"Or have anybody dictate how it gets written."

"That may be another story," he added.

Francine let out a moan.

"I didn't know you cared that much about the book," I said.

"It wasn't about the book," she said.

"Then what's the matter?"

"Nothing."

"I distinctly heard an oi."

"It was nothing. Lots of people say oi from time to time."

"Not unless there's pain or cossacks."

"All right, it's pain—random pain."

"Come on—why're you wearing those dark glasses?"

"Does anybody ask Madonna why she's wearing dark glasses?"

"No, they probably figure she ran into Sean Penn again and he bopped her in the eye for old times' sake."

"Oh, aren't you the perceptive one."

"You went out with Sean Penn?" said Brian.

"No, I think it's the bopped-in-the-eye part," I said, reaching for the shades. She dodged.

"You never heard of conjunctivitis?"

"Lemme see." She resisted for another moment, then shrugged and let me take the glasses off. She had one prize shiner. Really pretty, all those purples and blues.

"You *did* go out with Sean Penn," said Brian. At which point the phone rang, and he went to answer.

"What happened?" I asked Francine.

"Child abuse."

"Come on."

"All right, all right—try to have some privacy around here. I made the mistake of accepting a date with Ferdie."

"Who's Ferdie?" asked Goodman.

"My coke connection."

"You mean a dope dealer was less than honorable with you?" said Goodman facetiously.

"The thing is, it's not like grass, where you pay and they sell and it's business. With coke you always have to pretend like you're really friends and he's sort of doing you a favor to sell you the stuff."

"Unbelievable," said Goodman.

"So he said he wanted to go out with me, and since he was such a buddy, I said yes."

Brian dashed over, a broad smile on his face, and interrupted impatiently.

"Hey, guess what, that was my agent—you know how long it's been since I heard from my agent?"

Like never, that's how long it's been. It'd been so long since even his last bit part, we almost forgot he was an actor, which made it pretty understandable for him to be that excited.

"Yes, tell us, Brian," I said. "What did your agent want?"

"Are you ready for this? I'm up for a part in *All for the Family*."

"*All in the Family?*" said Francine. "The television show? That's been off the air for years."

"No, *All* for *the Family*—it's a movie about, you know, like Godfather Five, or something. An independent. Lefcourt Productions. They called up and specifically asked for me, is that fantastic? The agent's going to call back and tell me what time I go for a reading."

I looked at Goodman, who looked back, raising an eyebrow.

"That's great," I said.

God, even as friends they could be so diabolical. How could I ask Brian to refuse what in effect was Cifelli's offer when it would mean so much to him? Yet here I'd be setting myself up for the day Cifelli would call and say: "Remember the movie? Well, I'd like you to do *me* a favor—there's this little package I want you to pick up in Colombia . . ."

"That's great," said Goodman. "I'll keep my fingers crossed."

After which there was sort of a heavy silence. Brian, I'm sure, didn't notice it, he was so self-absorbed and excited. But Goodman and I were not at all happy. Francine, on the other hand, like nature, abhorred a vacuum.

"So after you twisted my arm and *forced* me to bare my soul, this is all we're going to talk about is my black eye?" she said, clearly feeling neglected.

"Tell us more about your black eye," I said.

"Never mind."

"No, please, go ahead—we're listening."

"Well, Ferdie was his usual wired self, which I took to be an ordinary, normal overdose of cocaine. But he was really wild and I only belatedly realized he'd been mainlining meth for about three days straight, absolutely no sleep, just pop pop pop—and turned into your basic one-man Indianapolis Five Hundred."

"Yeah?"

"Well, you know about speedos."

"No, *you* know," said Goodman. "I'm just learning."

"Just, real speed freaks are all crazy. I mean, sooner or later they get like psychotic. It's a well-known medical fact."

"But *you* take uppers," said Goodman.

"*Some*times, a little—that's a different thing, I'm not whacked out on them."

"Right, you're a regular Miss Moderation."

"Well, I *am*, compared to some. I don't go overboard. I may take a little grass, an occasional black beauty, a toke of coke . . ."

"Or a gross of Quaaludes," I added helpfully.

"I don't drink much," she said.

"And hardly ever heroin."

"Birthdays, New Year's Eve maybe."

"But tell me about meth, speed, whatever you call it," said Goodman. "Is that a figure of speech, 'crazy,' or did he really go crazy?"

"If you'd seen it, you'd know—definite, clinically crazy. I consider myself lucky to've gotten away with only the eye—he just flipped out totally. And the argument was over nothing. I don't even know what it was set him off. One minute we were grooving, the next it's *Halloween Twelve*. And that's not the worst of it."

"Yeah? What else?"

"Now I'll have to get myself another connection."

The phone rang again. Brian dashed to answer.

"I don't suppose it would do any good to point out to you—" began Goodman.

"Any more than it would for me to point out to *you*," replied Francine. "Booze isn't exactly mother's milk."

"I have a feeling," I said, "neither of you is very likely to reform the other."

Brian meanwhile completed his phone call and returned, beaming from ear to ear.

"Guess what?"

"You just won an Evinrude outboard motor by correctly identifying Willie Nelson's headband size," said Francine.

"Not at all, where the hell did you come up with that?"

"You said guess, I took a shot."

"The *call*," continued Brian, "was from my agent. I

don't even have to audition, I got the part! Isn't that fantastic?"

"Fantastic," I said.

Goodman nodded knowledgeably.

"Somebody up there likes me!" said Brian.

"That's not the one we have to worry about," said Goodman *sotto voce*. "It's the somebody down here."

"I know," I said. "I'm just not sure which is more dangerous, having Cifelli for an enemy or having him for a friend."

33

Rayford Goodman

Well, there certainly was a lot to consider. Though if I had any brains there wouldn't be. Everything and everybody pointed just one way to go—stick with the story. Pagani got what he deserved. Maybe not even enough, considering Carkeys and Rollins, at least possibly. There were all those nagging little things didn't fit that *I* knew. But against that was nearly everybody's wanting me not to rock the boat. And even Broward, it sure looked like now, wouldn't do any rocking. So why'd it bother me? Whyn't I just forget it?

I guess because it was a mystery I hadn't figured out yet. And figuring out mysteries happened to be what I did.

I, and everybody else, started out with the clear idea this was a murder. With maybe some jewels robbed on the side. Who figured so much else was involved—corporations, mafiosi, police, cassettes, residuals, payoffs, frame-ups, and last but not least, my book. And that, of course, included, no longer so incidentally, my gay caballero collaborator. And *his* whatchamacallit. Which made for wheels within wheels within wheels.

Yet, the more layers I peeled, the more complicated it got, and the more people it upset. Also, the more I felt certain I was gaining on it.

But there was only just so much you could bite off without doing some digesting. The thing now was give it a rest.

Only I was making that decision the most awful time of day, midafternoon, which is too late for a health walk and too early for cocktail hour.

So I figured I'd go home and maybe do a few chores around the house. Which I did. Well, go home.

I'd never been one to keep a lot of lists of *things to do*. That can get pretty discouraging if you're not a person likes *things to do*. But even just considering those off the top of my head was such a downer. Like straighten up the yard, clean out the garage, do something about the pool, get somebody out to fix a couple appliances, get faucets fixed, sprinklers, garden, roof . . . I just wasn't a management person, *I* needed management. Hell, I still half wondered what I was gonna be when I grew up.

But on the plus side, I didn't run out of mixes, and I never forgot to make ice. There might be a lot of empties didn't get taken out, but there were always fulls when I wanted them. That's management, I'd say.

By the time I thought all this, and considered what, if anything, should be done, and in what order, or if by myself or a pro, it was too late to do anything anyway. Didn't management include not wasting energy? So I fixed a drink—which is the one exception to "if it ain't broke, don't fix it."

There were three messages on the answerphone. The first was from Curtis, the slimy limey, groaning and moaning something fierce. I guess Roger Meade had given him the word. That brightened my day. Seems I was taking the food off his table, "depryvin' me and moine of the bare necessities," without even giving him a chance to offer me a bribe, "like any decent bloke woulder."

The second was from Ackerman-Benson, an advertising agency wanting to use my garage to shoot a commercial for Quaker State Motor Oil. They'd only need it for an afternoon, to shoot a car driving in, with the "view" in the background. They'd give me five hundred bucks for the privilege. For five hundred bucks they could've *bought* the garage. Plus, they'd probably have to clean it up in order to use it. So good thing I hadn't wasted my energy doing that!

The third call was from Luana, out of sorts. I called her back and made a date for dinner. The combination being almost flush from almost renting my garage and her sounding so low brought out the reckless in me and I found myself saying I'd take her to L'Orangerie.

L'Orangerie was a terrific restaurant on La Cienega looked like a Swiss clinic. The food was great, but it was basically the sort of place charged the kind of prices I only had any right to spring for if I were getting married. And then only if we went Dutch. Maybe the Quaker State folks would pop for seven-fifty.

I got the car washed—wouldn't do to embarrass the parking attendants at L'Orangerie—and picked up Luana. She looked marvelous in a gray Armani jacket she told me was on sale for eleven hundred dollars— proving how thrifty she was—and a plain black gabardine skirt that was admittedly a teensy overpriced at four-twenty. Don't you love those prices? Not four hundred, four-twenty. "This little dinner dress is nine thousand thirty-five." But did I have any idea how impossible it was to find a plain black skirt at any price? I was beginning to. And by then I could see the crocodile shoes at four-seventy were a real steal.

"Lookin' good, Lu," I said. It was her money, after all, in a manner of speaking. If she wanted to squander it on clothes, wasn't my business. Nothing about her was still my business.

So how come she still had several digits of my number and I had none of hers?

"And you're looking nice too," she replied. "I've always liked that suit. Through the decades."

She obviously wasn't totally depressed.

"You always liked my father's tie too," I reminded her.

The thing is, what with wearing her ash-blond hair my favorite way, parted in the middle, drawn back into a bun—like a negative picture of a ballet dancer—she looked really stunning. No matter what I wore, she would look too good for me.

I always said she had a truckload of class.

So why was it I was just the least bit miffed she chose to dress rich instead of sexy? Not that I wanted to go to bed with her. Just that I wanted it to be a possibility she'd give *some* thought to.

First she'd worn her hair the way I like—and knew darn well. On the other hand, dressed totally hands-off.

There went those confusing signals. There always was that tendency with Luana for me to be so busy thinking and trying to figure what she had in mind that I didn't *feel* what to do or how to do it. And, too, always the possibility she wasn't outthinking me so much as having an instinct for the jugular. On the other hand, lots of times it occurred to me I might be giving her credit—or blame—for scheming and plotting when all she might have in mind was whether to wear the dark nail polish or the medium. But if the extramarital activities weren't to punish me but because she just simply *wanted* to, didn't that say something about my importance in her life and maybe failure to *hold* her? Or on the *third* hand, it could be because she just *liked* it—the way I do . . . did.

Then we were inside and had our drinks and ordered some of the cute little things that were so picturesque. The *trois carottes* shaped like a snowflake and the sliver-cut string beans "raining" on top of them, surrounding two bites of veal—all in the name of *nouvelle cuisine* and *votre santé*. After I established it wasn't really going to cost the whole five hundred—mostly because we weren't having wine—I sat back and lit a cigarette. That was when I knew whatever was on her mind was fairly heavy because she didn't jump all over me about killing myself and everybody within secondary sidesmoke or whatever the hell they called it. I had to confess, I really did like the place. It was grand, elegant, roomy, and Johnny Carson was only a brioche away—looking good. He even smiled, figuring he might know me. I smiled back—I knew *him*. Or was he smiling at Luana?

"Rayford," she said finally, "I want to tell you I think it was terribly sweet of you to ask me out."

"Sweet" was a left-handed, girl way to say "nice"—and insult you at the same time. I was, I think, as introspective as the next guy—if the next guy happened to be Lyle Alzado. I knew I had qualities, but sweet just wasn't one of them. When a woman called me that, I tended to think she was about to explain the reason she didn't want to sleep with me. And if I was "*such* a sweet guy" she not only didn't want to sleep with me but also wanted my okay that the one she *was* going to sleep with was my best friend. That way I sort of wouldn't be losing her so much as gaining a couple.

I mumbled something to show just how sweet I was.

"I was just feeling kind of lonely, and wanted to be with someone I felt comfortable with."

Old shoes and torn Levi's came to mind.

The most gorgeous young man you ever saw in your life brought the salad. The most gorgeous young men— who naturally wanted to be actors—often waited on tables at places where the likes of Johnny Carson and their producers ate. Those who'd already given up that particular goal—or couldn't remember food in French— learned to dance and worked Chippendales.

The limp salad wasn't really my first choice. I personally liked iceberg lettuce. But I knew from experience it would only embarrass Luana if I was déclassé enough to order anything *crisp* in the rabbit department. I toyed with asking for ketchup with the veal, but I had too much invested to chance it.

What the hell did she mean, felt comfortable with? We hadn't hardly exchanged a civil word in years.

"It was nice of you to ask me," she said.

"Nice" I can live with, though I didn't realize I'd done the asking. Well, I had, but I'd been maneuvered.

"Hey, anytime," I said, gracious on top of sweet and nice.

And finally we got down to it. Or close. First, did I think she was looking her age? Of course not. What age did I think she looked? Nine. The hands, the hands gave it away, right? Her hands were swell. Her boobs were swell. A little sag was hip, it made people know they weren't phonies. And the tiniest, dearest tear leaked out the corner of her eye.

"He dumped me," she said. "That guy you met the other night, Roger Meade?"

"Yeah, good-looking fellow, nice caps."

"If you're going to be unsympathetic . . ."

"I'm going to be sympathetic as hell. What happened?"

"He said he had to concentrate on his work and wouldn't have time to socialize for a while."

"Ahh," I said sympathetically.

"He might even have to go away for a while."

True.

"But I don't believe that. If you really love somebody, you don't have to concentrate on your work or go away for a while. You have to be with that person."

"Well, maybe it's a little different these days. You know, the younger generation."

"Don't get shitty."

Far be it from me.

"You don't, I suppose, know anything about this?"

"Me? What would I know about it? What was his line of work?"

"Transportation."

"I don't have anything to do with transportation."

"Well, I don't think it was very nice."

"I wasn't all that impressed with Roger. Maybe you're better off without him."

"Maybe so, but I'd a lot rather have come to that conclusion by myself."

She didn't say like she did with me.

"You're sure you didn't . . . ?" she said again.

"Of course I'm sure. Eat your *haricots*."

So far, so good. He was no kind of guy for her anyway. And considering what hell on wheels she'd been during our divorce—and marriage—I didn't want to even think what she'd do if I embarrassed her by sending him to jail. Life sure was a big conflict of interest.

I gave her the whole range of sympathy from he didn't deserve her to how much better life would be now she was free to seek her own level. Like champagne.

She told me my suit wasn't all that bad.

We finished the veal and I was fingering the flan when she got to the other reason for her call.

"The more I think about Harry and the Sierra Tiara, the more upset I get."

"I meant to ask you," I said. "How come you recognized this Sierra whatever and Sally didn't?"

"I don't know. My guess is since she had a big fight with Harry because he made other plans for the night of the Amigos affair, it's possible she just barely looked at it."

"Jewelry that expensive?"

"I don't know. One way or another, it still doesn't get me past the fact Harry *had* it."

"Well, maybe I can set your mind a little at ease there," I replied. "I happen to know Harry did *not* take that tiara from Rita's room."

"How can you know that?"

It was privileged information, in a way. Besides, I didn't see any reason to bust Miss Eldrege when she'd been so helpful. But before I could make up a convincing lie, Luana cut in:

"After all, Harry *was* making it with Rita."

"You know that for a fact?"

"I know Sally knew. And I know that while Harry and Rollins left her to go out for something to eat, Harry didn't really go, just Rollins. Harry went back to be alone with Rita."

"How can you be so sure?" I asked.

"*I* can't be sure, but Sally is. She says Rollins was supposed to beard for him by pretending they both went to get a bite. But she said Rollins told her he actually ate alone."

Sneaky little snitch.

"Look," I said, "take my word for it. Harry did not steal the tiara. I know that absolutely, because I know who did. I can't tell you, but it's true. As far as Harry is concerned, he bought it legitimately for Sally."

"Well, that's a big relief," she said. "Not that I could really believe it might be Harry who actually murdered Rita. It's still a big relief."

For her. But for me, she'd reopened a whole area. If what she said was true, two of the people who'd vouched for each other were alone sometime in the evening and either could have done it. Only one was already dead, which tended to eliminate him, and the other I didn't want to think about.

But before I went off half-cocked, I had to check the alibis one step further. I could do that by going over the log at the studio gate that night. To see who really went where at what time. That was definitely my next step.

Next after next. My *next* step was paying ye olde *l'addition*—sans la grande upchuck.

34

Mark Bradley

Maybe it was my imagination, but Goodman seemed to be at least as much optimistic as hung-over this morning, which either meant the date with his ex-wife had gone well or she'd succeeded in keeping him from drinking too much. I doubted the latter, since she hadn't managed it while they were together. He allowed it had gone well, but not necessarily in the way I thought.

He also elected to be mysterious about the day's occupation, saying only that it would be a good time to observe the varied ways an expert operative operatived.

We headed east across Santa Monica Boulevard, past the seamy sexual sights, nude-model joints, and other porno pits, the pathetic cruisers of various ilks, and progressed to the relative sunlight of hockshops, Okidog superfast-food stands, plumbing-supply stores, screen-repair shops, and all the other wondrous retail establishments that so brightened and enlivened the avenue.

But finally the neighborhood improved as the flotsam, jetsam, and sexam enterprises gave way entirely to the large boxy studio buildings, and with them better restaurants, stores, and studio parking lots. I noted Producers' Lot No. 1 had the sign so identifying it dented and defaced—expressing Lord only knew what hostility and anger—leading me to the conclusion a producer's lot was not a happy one. He at last turned north, pulling up and into the gate at Pinnacle Studios, which was located next to the Cinevision Facility—née Desilu, née RKO—on Gower Gulch in Hollywood.

A drive-on pass had been left for Goodman, indicating we were expected.

I mentioned that the guard hadn't said exactly where to park. Goodman explained that a drive-on pass never afforded you an actual parking spot, since all spots in the always overcrowded studios were assigned. It merely gave you license to usurp somebody else's place, and you could fight it out from there. Usually, your best shot was to take the spot of someone famous, since the odds were they wouldn't be in to the office provided for them, as one of the perks for having a contract. Norman Nobody needed his spot, he had a job to do, whereas Paul Newman was apt to be elsewhere.

As he drove about looking for just such, I indicated George Hamilton's spot.

"He'll either be jetting somewhere *fabulous* with Elizabeth or out getting a tan."

That seemed to settle it for Goodman, who pulled in.

We went up to Lefcourt's office, which surprised me, since I didn't imagine he'd be trying to interview the old man again. He wasn't; he'd come to see Miss Eldrege.

"Okay, Ray," she said, "I've arranged for the storage cellar to be opened for you. It's downstairs, bin twelve, section C, near as I can tell—the records are a little vague. There's a custodian waiting for you who'll unlock the door."

"Thanks, Miss E., you're a peach," said Goodman.

"Either that or a fink," she responded just a touch uncertainly.

And we went downstairs, and there was a custodian, and he was expecting us, and he did unlock bin twelve, Section C, and we went inside.

"What're we looking for?" I finally asked, confronted by box after box of temporary files.

"We're looking for the gateman's log of August one, August two, 1963."

Ah hah.

So we looked through the zillion dusty files. And the system was evidently pretty good, for we were, after no more than about forty-five minutes, able to locate the logs for 1963. It took only another couple of minutes to find those for August.

We spent another twenty, though, being absolutely certain those for August 1st through 2d were missing.

Goodman didn't consider this a setback. As far as he was concerned, it only meant we were getting hotter and hotter. And to a certain extent, that was true. The problem was, while we were obviously on the right track, someone kept removing the horses. So, to continue beating a dead metaphor, how were we going to boot home a winner?

Goodman had a notion about that.

But first he wanted to wrap up his "walking-around-money" case, so we went back west on Santa Monica till we came to Beverly Hills British Motors. Goodman turned the rented Porsche into the driveway and brought it to a stop next to the office. He honked loudly, which is the only way you can honk inside a totally concrete building, thereby eliciting the enmity of every employee within echo earshot.

He got out of the car, indicated I should also, and we both crossed to the by-now-open door of the office, at which stood a livid Adderley.

"I shoulda known it'd be you. Come in."

We entered. Goodman introduced me as his "associate"—shades of Armand Cifelli.

"So, wot's up?" said Adderley, "other than that, 'for pers'nal reasons,' my best mechanic, Curtis Smith-Buffington, has tendered his resignation suddenly and without suitable notification?"

"That'll give you a clue I've been working."

"And what have you achieved, other than cutting my work force?"

"I think we can consider the case closed. You won't have any more stealing or lose any more customers. Both inside and outside is taken care of."

"For the fact?"

"For the fact—*a* fact," Americanized Goodman.

"And who goes to prison?" asked Adderley.

"Well, that's kind of a problem," said Goodman. "I've, uh, opted for a sort of settlement, whereby everybody goes *away* in exchange for nobody going away up the river."

"*You've* opted. And suppose I don't fancy lettin' to-whom-it-may-concern get off free as air?"

"I'd suggest you don't concern yourself with that."

"But I do."

"Try not to, 'cause there's nothing I can do about it,"

he said. "There's no hard evidence, really. Just they know I know, and anytime they tried anything again, I'd nail them. I think that's the best you're going to get."

"And can I know who the other half of 'they' is? So at least I know not never to get involved with him?"

"That seems fair. The other guy who's 'not never' going to bother you, I promise, is a man named Roger Meade."

Uh-huh! Roger Meade was that hunk I met at Harry's screening, who was squiring Goodman's ex-wife, Luana. And apparently Goodman wasn't going to turn him in.

"Not putting these thieves in jail leaves me with a bitter taste, I can tell you."

"I know."

"Just don't sit right."

"Well, you gotta be philosophical. It's just the way the scones crumble," said Goodman, handing over an itemized bill, with a hideous attempt at an ingratiating smile.

Adderley looked at the bill, and was obviously none too pleased. "Hello, this is a bit steep, innit?"

"Justice comes high."

"I don't quarrel with your daily stipend, it's the bloody expenses. I say, look at all that petrol—with additives, and at full-service prices. And all the washes . . ."

"I had to maintain appearances," said Goodman. "Who'd believe I owned a Rolls if they saw me at a self-service pump?"

"I still say I'd feel a lot better knowin' justice had taken its true course if we sent those blighters to the pokey."

"Well, didn't work that way. Anyway, case closed," said Goodman. "Except for your check and my car."

Adderley bridled a moment longer, then said, "Far as I'm concerned, and I'm tryin' to be fair about this, you only did half the job."

"So you're only going to pay half the bill."

"Strikes me as fair."

"In which case you won't be wanting me for the free follow-up to make sure it doesn't happen all over again, in case, say, old Curtis happens not to throw away the duplicate key he obviously has, or something like that?"

"I see what you mean."

"Come on, you got your money's worth. You had a problem, I solved it. End of story. Except for my car."

"Oh, that's done—been done a week, don't you know. Came out right nice, it did."

The upshot was Goodman got about two-thirds. I learned later this often happened, clients willing to pay anything before a problem was solved, felt "anything" didn't mean "that much" after. Then he reclaimed the Caddy convertible—which did look "right nice" in anthracite gray, though now that the paint was fresh, it kind of missed having a new top—and followed as I drove the Porsche back to the rental agency, where he turned it in, endorsing Adderley's check and picking up some cash in the bargain.

Evidently Goodman noticed the raggedy roof too, because even though it was a bit nippy, he took the top down as I climbed in and we headed off toward Benedict Canyon—mine not to question why.

"So it turned out this Curtis guy was getting the customers and stealing the parts and that Roger Meade was doing the actual repairs."

"Right."

"It's the same Roger Meade, I take it, we met at Harry's?"

"Uhm."

"So you sort of had a private reason for not letting Adderley press charges."

"It seemed the best way to go about it."

"Also the best way not to embarrass your ex-wife. I think that was really rather nice of you, Ray."

"It wasn't anything of the kind. Just straight-ahead self-interest. I didn't want to go through all the shit she'd put me through if I sent him away."

"Sure."

We twisted and turned, as did Benedict Canyon— which is *why* we twisted and turned—and pulled up into a circular whitewashed-stone-bordered driveway leading to a typical "cottage"-style house. It was the sort that had shutters and Dutch doors, painted blue and white, partly ivy-covered, and mostly cutesy. And in this neighborhood would turn out to be surprisingly expensive.

Also, many of these houses were foolers, with more backyard than you'd think. Most had pools and many also mini orange groves. *All* had extravagant custom-built barbecues and picnic tables. As you might guess, definitely not my taste, but equally definitely no ghetto by several hundred thousand.

"And the name of the person who lives here . . . ?" I said.

"Sonny Moss."

"That's an oxymoron, I think. And Mr. Moss is . . . ?"

"A retired security guard at Pinnacle Studios. You don't need a lot of brains for that," said Goodman, getting out of the car and heading for the Dutch doors.

I didn't need to be told he would turn out to be the guard who was on duty the night of August one through August two in the year of our Lord nineteen hundred and sixty-three—no oxymoron I.

It was also no surprise that Sonny Moss had a knotty-pine den in this knotty-pine house with the fun bar that had the drunk leaning against the miniature streetlight. And behind the bar and filling a complete wall were photos of Sonny Moss with every known celebrity of the last three decades. Each was autographed, mostly attesting to his being "a great guy," "a terrific gatekeeper," and "a fine American"—this last inscribed on a photo taken with Lyndon Baines Johnson. Evidently Moss was even more beloved than the legendary studio shoeshine boy, Everet "Spit" Wallace ("Errol Flynn had the mos' itty-bitty feet . . .").

"The reason I wanted to talk to you in person and ask you about it," Goodman was saying, "is the log has gone missing."

"Well, I wouldn't know about that," said Moss in a way that immediately convinced you he definitely knew about that.

"I'm not suggesting anything, Sonny. It's too bad the log's missing, but I guess those things happen."

"Sure."

"I don't suppose you remember. Nah, you couldn't possibly remember . . ."

"Well . . ."

"Something such a long time ago? Anyway, your memory's probably none too good anymore."

"My memory's as good as the next guy's. Better."

"Well, sure, about say who won the Series last year and like that, but no way even a young guy'd remember all the comings and goings a night that long ago. Let alone someone your age."

"Maybe not your average person my age, or about an ordinary night, but hey, that wasn't your ordinary night. Then again, probably best I don't talk about all of that."

"Why's that, Sonny?" asked Goodman. "Whoever paid you told you not to say anything about it?"

"Who's saying anybody paid me anything?"

"Well, just an idea. Hard to imagine you bought this house on a security guard's pension."

"Listen, I had real estate, I did all right."

"Right, that's why you got special permission from Lefcourt himself to stay on and work five years past the mandatory retirement age. And used as a reason, or maybe threat, that you had such a fantastic photographic memory."

"I don't have to even talk to you."

"Of course not, Sonny. And, look, if you cashed in and made a few bucks on the deal, more power to you. I'm no choir boy, you know."

"Right."

"So, forget that, I got nothing against the little guy getting a taste of the good life."

"I worked hard for my money all my life."

"Damn right. But, like, suppose someone said, 'All right, Sonny, here's a nice big house for you, you're a swell guy. All you gotta do is lose the log for that night.' No big deal to lose one log out of all those years."

"I don't say I did."

"I don't say you did either. And I'd *never* say you did. This is just the three of us talking. Totally off the record."

The three of us weren't talking, only the two of them were talking. I was listening, and not a little impressed by Goodman's incredible ability to make people talk who had no intention of talking.

"The point is, *I* don't remember things happened twenty-five, thirty years ago. Hardly likely *you* could."

"I could remember plenty."

"No way. I'd bet, say . . . fifty dollars you couldn't."

"You wouldn't know it to look at me, maybe, but I *do* have a photographic memory. It's all like pictures to me. I can see the log like it was an open book in front of me."

"Get out of here. Hundred dollars."

"I'm telling you."

"All right, let's see: Harley Williams leaving . . ." led Goodman.

"You bet a hundred."

"That's the bet," replied Goodman, holding his hand out to me to be filled with Penny's bucks. Sonny eyed the money and rolled his eyes back in recall.

"Ten-fifty-five," he said. "Williams."

"Carkeys?"

"Which time?"

"Tell me."

"Eleven-ten with Williams, back at eleven-thirty-five. Out again eleven-fifty, back twelve-ten. For good twelve-twenty."

"That's a lot of in-and-out."

"It is what it is."

"Symington Lefcourt."

"Mr. Lefcourt, ten-forty."

"Dubie Dietrich?"

"Twelve-fifteen."

"Rollins and Harry Light."

"Out at eleven, Harry right back almost immediately. Rollins back at twelve-oh-five. Both Mr. Rollins and Mr. Light out for good at twelve-forty."

"Miss Eldrege?"

"Twelve-twenty-five."

"Mama Rose?"

"Nine-thirty."

"That's real impressive."

"You wanna know the Dodgers' batting average for 1948?"

"Hey, I can see you got an outstanding memory. Convinced me," said Goodman. But he didn't quite hand over the money yet. Shades of Columbo, he turned instead and as an obvious "afterthought" said, "Armand Cifelli?"

"Not in, not out," said Moss, then seemed to suddenly realize he hadn't intended to reveal all this. "And that's all I'm going to say." He grabbed the hundred.

"Two guys that looked like they worked for Mr. Cifelli?"

"Uh-uh, nothing doing."

"Two guys you never saw before?"

"Uh-uh. I mean it, that's all. You got me going pretty good there, didn't you?"

"Hey, no harm, pal—just doing a job."

"You're a smooth article, Ray Goodman."

"So I've been told. Come on, Bradley, we've taken up enough of Sonny's time."

"Not at all," said Moss. "Stay as long as you like. I got no job anymore these days. We could split a beer."

"I'll have to take a rain check, podner. I *do* have a job," said Goodman, leading me to the door. Then, another little Columbo move, as if he hadn't for a moment calculated it all along: "Oh, Sonny, let me take a guess. You don't have to say yes or no, I'm just curious. The one who paid you to lose the log, Harry Light?"

"You're not tricking me," said Sonny.

"But it was him, right?"

"You said it, I didn't," said Sonny, not being tricked.

Back in the car, heading down Benedict Canyon, Goodman was in hog heaven.

"That's about it," he said.

"What's about what?"

"It's practically solved."

"I don't see how you figure that."

"Well, maybe that's why I'm a detective and you're just a writer."

"A writer isn't just a 'just,' " I said, annoyed. Which may be why it took a moment to sink in. "You *know*?"

"Pretty much."

"Just when everything was falling apart, you *really* think you pulled it out?" I asked.

"Jawed from the snatch of defeat," he responded.

35

Rayford Goodman

I can't stand it, you gotta tell me," said Bradley.

"I said I had it *practically* worked out. Not totally."

"Then tell me practically."

"Patience. I need to figure a few things yet. But I'm ninety percent sure."

"So what now?"

"Now I drop you off wherever you want, and I go home."

"Why're you going home?"

"Because there's five hundred dollars waiting there. This afternoon the Quaker State people shoot their commercial about the car pulling into my garage at sunset."

"But you don't have to be there for that, they can shoot it without you."

"They can shoot it without me, but I can't get the five hundred without *getting* the five hundred. Anyway, I'm a responsible homeowner. I want to make sure there's no damage I don't get reimbursed for."

"I can't believe this. You don't feel any pressure?"

"The case waited all these years. Another couple hours isn't going to make all that much difference."

"But you won't do it without me."

"Wouldn't dream of it."

"Okay, take me back to the office."

So I headed back toward his office, but I could see my calm was driving him bananas.

"Just give me a hint."

"No way."

"All right, how about this: you going to assemble a whole bunch of people and keep us all guessing right down to the last minute?"

"What whole bunch of people?"

"All the suspects."

"Why would I do that?"

"I don't know, you're the detective. That's what they do."

"Don't be silly."

"Well, what *are* you going to do?"

"That's one of the things I have to figure out yet."

I could see the guy was about to pop with frustration. We finally got to his office. I pulled over. He opened the door, started out.

"You really have a mean streak," he said.

"You may be right," I answered. He let off an angry breath and stalked away. I smiled to myself, then noticed he'd left his tote bag.

"Hey!" I called. But he never even looked back. Just raised his right hand and extended that certain finger.

The Ackerman-Benson folks doing the Quaker State commercial had explained to me it was an easy shoot. Just a car driving into the garage, with one setup inside catching the entrance.

I figured a cameraman, an assistant, one or two other people just to pad things out, the car, and a can of oil.

What there was was four large trucks, with about seventy tons of equipment. Then came a caterer, with three in help, a director, a cameraman, a script supervisor— this with no dialogue or sound—and a lawyer with the release I had to sign before I could get the check. And finally, between thirty and forty other people, all needing to use the bathroom constantly. This meant either poor bladder control or good cocaine. I was beginning to understand why they'd come five hours early to catch one shot at sunset. Compared to moviemaking, detecting was an exact and efficient science.

I watched a little while—enough to at least cop a free lunch from the caterer's table. But eventually I got bored with the exciting cinematic life and went inside.

Enough stalling. I knew what I had to do. I didn't know exactly how it'd play, but there was really only one way to go. Confrontation.

I called the studio, got Miss Eldrege, and asked if Harry Light was there. She told me he wasn't, honest, and wouldn't be. I asked for his home number, which had been changed since I last called. She said she couldn't give me that. I said she knew I could get it, it would just be a pain in the neck. I'd have to go be nice to someone at the phone company. And as long as I could get it eventually, why not give it to me and save me the trouble being nice to strangers? Plus she might want to spend another holiday with a horny guy like me sometime who had this fantastic thing for older women. She told me blarney wouldn't melt in my mouth. I said there must be a Jewish word for it. She said yes, "bullshit." She also gave me the number.

Harry had an answering machine on with what I guessed was the joke of the day. Today's: "Why did the Mexican schools give up sex education? . . . The donkey died. This is your old buddy, leave a message."

"This is *your* old buddy, Ray Goodman. I'd like to get together with you real soon to discuss a real serious problem. Give you a clue: I know who was behind the Pagani parole."

I sifted through my notes, getting everything straight in my mind, then, after an hour, called again. "Me again. I know about Rafeel. I also know who sent Rafeel out to scare me off."

The Quaker State folks continued to set up, mill about, consider the angles. Pass another hour.

I called again. "I know about Harley. I also know who sent Harley out to warn Bradley off and got Brian by mistake."

Still no response. I held off having a drink, though. I wanted to be at the top of my game when we got around to talking.

I called again. "I know who pensioned Sonny Moss off. Shall we talk?"

The callback came under five minutes. I had to figure he'd gotten the other calls before and was just figuring out how to play it.

"Rayford . . ."

"Yeah."

"I think you're right, we ought to talk. But I just got a call from Frank, asking me to fill in for him at the

Homeless Benefit in San Francisco tonight. I've got to leave in an hour and a half."

"Why don't I pop on over now?" I said.

"Now's good," Harry replied.

"And maybe you ought to see if you can't get somebody to fill in for *you*, for San Francisco."

"Just come over. I'm sure I can answer all your questions and satisfy you."

"On my way."

I still hadn't fully decided exactly what I was going to do. I knew I would confront him. But after that, I'd have to see. In order to have a little insurance, though, I was going to wire myself to be sure whatever he had to say would be recorded.

I stripped off my shirt, taped the wire in place, slipped the mike under my collar, hung the machine on my waist, and said, "Testing, one two three." I played it back. It went, "Tessssstiii, wwwwwwwwwwwwwnnnnn," and stopped. Dead batteries.

Play it by ear.

I called Bradley at the office, got Francie.

"He left about twenty minutes ago, Ray. Anything I can do?"

Since I was pressed for time, I considered having her get me a battery and meet me, but it wasn't practical. In order to work she'd have to go stash it in a strange bathroom, where we couldn't have a prearranged place. Then I'd have to follow, find it, and insert it. All too complicated. And too risky.

"Thanks, Francine, I don't think so. Would Bradley be at home?"

"That's where he was heading. Brian's car broke down and he has to go to the studio for a fitting on the picture. So Mark's going to take him. But you might still catch him."

I thanked her and hung up, dialed Bradley.

"You have reached 8464. We're both out at the moment, but in case you're a crook, the Westec Security people are on the case, not to mention our two killer guard dogs, Eichmann and Gidget. At the tone please leave your message."

When the beep sounded, I said, "If you want to see

the way a master detective winds up a case, the minute you hear this, head straight over to Harry Light's. I'll have you cleared at the gate."

I hung up, threw on my jacket, and headed for the door.

Outside there was a guy sitting behind the camera, another holding the cable leading to the portable generator, another looking at a TV monitor, another with a slate, and another holding a can of Quaker State. Looked like they were getting close to doing some actual work. Wrong, they were *doing* actual work as this jazzy hundred-thousand-dollar bomber pulled into my garage and the director screamed "Cut" and glared at me.

"You ruined my shot," he yelled.

It seemed I'd walked into the picture. Hell, I was just coming out my kitchen door.

"Sorry," I said. "I was just leaving."

"Please, it's getting late. Come on, gang, we're losing the sunset," implored the director. "Let's go again."

I crossed to the Cad, told one of the twelve guys hanging around I'd appreciate if someone would move the van blocking my way out, and got in. Bradley's tote bag was on the seat, where he'd forgotten it. While I waited for them to move the van, I opened the thing. Detectives are naturally curious. Snoopy, maybe, but that's the way you find out things. Like now. I found out the guy sure traveled with a lot of stationery, for one thing.

But not the only thing.

I popped out of the car, turned back, just as the red super-hot Quaker-Stated zoomer pulled back into the garage, almost running me down.

"Cutttt!" yelled the director.

"I know, I know, I'm really sorry," I said, backing off and tripping over a cable which must not have been connected too good, since it killed several bulbs lighting the interior of the garage.

"You're really beginning to piss me off," said the director.

"I am sorry," I said. "But I wonder, could I ask you one little favor and I'll get out of your hair?"

"Anything, what, quickly."

"I see you've laid down that border of flowers. Could

you possibly spare a bunch for me, I'd really appreciate it."

"Give him some fucking flowers," he screamed.

"Thanks."

And as a greensman—greenboy, greenskeeper?—went to get me a bunch, I heard the cameraman say, "I'm afraid by the time we get the car back down the hill and turned around and headed back up here and into the garage, we'll have lost the sunset."

The director looked at me with such hatred I almost cringed.

"See what the hell you did? You've ruined the whole day's shooting. We lost the sunset. I don't think they ought to pay you."

"Wait, wait, you can still get your shot."

"Oh, look at Mr. Hollywood, and just how are we supposed to do that?"

"Instead of losing your last few minutes having the car go all the way down the street, turn around, and come back up, why don't you just start rolling, have him back out, and back down, and then run the film backwards?"

He looked at me for a minute. I couldn't tell whether he thought I was a genius or it was the dumbest idea he ever heard.

That issue got settled when he said, "Hurry up, roll 'em, cue the car, get ready to back out, this is a take—action!"

I stood carefully to one side, well out of the way, as they got the shot.

Then I grabbed my check from the lawyer, took the flowers from the greenie, and headed for my car, keeping well out of the way of the bestboys and the gaffers—whoever they were. To my surprise, the entire crew applauded me. I took a big bow, got in, and drove off down the hill, hoping nobody'd notice the airplane flying backward in the background when they reversed the film.

There'd always been a lot of security at Harry's. Understandably so. I'd never been searched before. It'd always been enough that I was me and I was expected. So I guess it was just as well I didn't bring a gun—which in any event I didn't own. It was bad enough they found the wire taped to my chest and ripped it out, together with most of my bodily hair.

"Hey," I said by way of lame explanation, "I was just coming from work."

"Mr. Light is expecting you," said one of the Mormons. For some reason the Mormons had a lock on certain kinds of security. Maybe they're the only ones fit those C&R suits. "Upstairs, in his office."

I was escorted to the base of the stairs and watched up. There was no free-lance roaming around in Harry's place. I must say I did wonder whether getting out wouldn't be even tougher than getting in.

The door to his office was open, as was a door on the other side, leading to the master bedroom. Harry was waiting for me, standing beside a packed overnight bag. On that was his Joel McCrea beat-up Burberry trench coat and a khaki trilby hat, trademarks from his many trips to entertain "our boys overseas"—and get cheap specials for our TV networks back home. He looked more tired than I'd ever seen him. In fact, I think it was the first time I'd ever seen him not smile.

"Well, Ray," he said. "I got a feeling we got some problems here."

"Looks that way, Harry."

"Hey, can't be too bad, you brought me flowers."

"Not really. I got 'em from my garden, for Sally. You might say in sympathy."

"Well, I imagine with goodwill and good intentions, we ought to be able to find a solution to any problem."

"I don't know."

"Though I must say, it's not exactly friendly of you to come in here wearing a wire."

"It's not a friendly call."

"I still say I gotta believe two men like us can work something out, especially when one of us is rich and the other one's not yet."

"I don't think this is one of those things where that works."

"Try me. What do you think you know?"

He pointed me to a leather couch, while he took the chair opposite, selected and lit a custom-made cigarette.

His chair was slightly higher, but that kind of show-business one-upmanship wasn't going to play here.

I sat. The couch was like his ice cubes, a cut above what the world even knew about. It was a buttery cream, the softest leather I'd ever seen, and must have been made from foreskins. It sure would be nice to be that rich. But not so nice right now. Another thing I felt bad about was Bradley missing this, but you had to take your shots when you could. I took a deep breath and started.

"Harry, I'd give a lot not to have to do this."

"No, you'd *get* a lot."

"But I have to. I know. I figured it all out, and I know."

"What exactly?"

"What went down the night of August first through August second, 1963."

"All right, let's hear what you think you know."

"Let's start with what we both know and agree on. We both know Dubie didn't do it, and we both worked hard to get him off the hook. Or so it seemed. And you, at least, are still taking care of him."

"No guilt to that, I take care of lots of people. I believe it's the Christian thing to do."

"Right. Okay, number two, I was wrong, but *you* knew Pagani didn't do it. He was a bad guy, did lots of terrible things, slime. Nobody really cares if he got a bad rap, since he had it coming twenty-two other ways. But after all this time, your Christian conscience bothered you. So you did what you could—which was plenty, with Mama Rose, your own political contacts—to get him paroled. Enough was enough. Scratch Dubie, scratch Pagani—neither one murdered Rita Rose."

"*You* say, the guy who nailed him in the first place. I don't necessarily admit that. All right, I helped get him paroled. Maybe I think he could be redeemed."

"Let's get back to that night and see who else we can eliminate."

"What does any of this have to do with me?"

"In time, Harry. In time."

"I'm on a tight schedule here."

"You may have more time than you think."

"You wouldn't be threatening me in my own home?"

"What, threatening? We're merely discussing the results of my investigation. An investigation you tried pretty hard and pretty violently to stop."

"Well, if your call's any indication, you know something about the reasons for that. The kind of job you did in sixty-three, well, that was a company wash. Maybe you didn't know it, but I wouldn't be surprised if even if you did, you'd've gone along."

"That we'll never know."

"But now's another thing altogether. Now people tell. Now people bust people. Now we have a bunch of Woodwards and Bernsteins and Kitty Kelleys who don't go along, no matter what. If it was just you writing your book, I'd figure maybe okay. If you stumbled on anything, I'd take a chance. But with Bradley too, it got sticky. You got into actually investigating things. So, you found out about my supporting Mama Rose, no crime. About my owning a lot of Lefcourt, just business . . ."

"And Cifelli owning a lot of you."

"That was news to me; that I didn't know. Lefcourt did that to get around me. The big thing I wanted to stop was you finding out about Rafeel."

"Yes, it wouldn't do to have it known America's top Christian hyphen comic had an illegitimate son in 1963, while deeply married to the dearest and finest woman on earth."

"Times were different. Even now, when every young actor has kids out of wedlock, sometimes on purpose, it's different for *me*. I have an image. I have a role to play."

"And that role didn't include fathering a bastard son, who also happened to be half-black."

"Hey, I'm an equal opportunity boffer," Harry said, the joke falling very flat. "*I* never cared what color people were. My public's maybe another thing."

"So you had Rafeel fire some shots at me and take a couple of pokes. I didn't like that a whole lot, Harry."

"You weren't supposed to get hurt. And you didn't, don't forget."

"Yeah? And what about Brian? What about your hiring Harley Williams to go beat up Brian?"

"He wasn't supposed to beat up Brian."

"Right, he was supposed to beat up Bradley."

"To scare him off if you wouldn't be. It was supposed to be a scare. Harley fucked up. I'm sorry about that. Maybe, you know, some compensation . . ."

"It might all be possible if what we were talking about here was just sweeping old Rafeel under the carpet. We're still talking Rita Rose."

"What about Rita Rose? So maybe it wasn't Pagani, but maybe it was, since who else, really, once you think about it? Had to be either a maniac or someone with a motive. What does that possibly have to do with me? You don't think I had a motive because of Rafeel? There was no problem there. Nobody knew, he was stashed away in Jamaica. And besides Rafeel, I had nothing to hide."

"Well, let's look at the log for that night. If you didn't have something to hide, why would you have bought off Sonny Moss? Why would you have had him destroy the log? The answer had to be in the times people came and went that night."

"You can't prove I had Sonny destroy the log. You're just winging it."

"No, I can't prove it. But I don't have to. I *know* that's where the answer was, so all I have to do is look at the timing."

"But you can't know the timing."

"I do. The murder was around midnight."

"Give or take."

"Within half an hour, the coroner said. So let's start narrowing down who had the opportunity, whether or not they had a motive. First to cross off, Mama Rose. She left the studio around nine-thirty. Plus of course she had no reason to do it."

"Of course Mama Rose didn't do it. Forget this tease, what do you think happened?"

The intercom buzzed. One of the Mormons said, "Mr. Light, you should be leaving for the airport." Mr. Light looked at me, then said tell them to hold the plane, he was running late. I thought he was running very late.

"Okay, okay, you were saying?"

"Let's start with Pagani. We know he was a punk. We know he shot a porno of Rita before she made it. And we know he was blackmailing her to sit on it. Bank records, canceled checks, studio logs, all point to a steady, regular payoff. He was a small-time pusher and operator, more or less getting by with a little of this and a little of that. Came a day he got a little too ambitious. He took on getting a big load of dope for Cifelli and company and one way or another managed to lose both the dope and the money. He'd run out of stalls, and out of time. Lefcourt, who was in bed with the mob, as you know—at least now—was forced to finger Pagani for a hit. Miss Eldrege knew about it, and warned Pagani. Later, when she went to check if he got out, she instead found the body. She originally lied about being there at all, for another reason—which I don't think I'll tell you."

"I could do without this whole conversation, for that matter," said Harry.

"I'm getting ahead of myself. Earlier Lefcourt dropped into Rita's dressing room about ten o'clock and knocked off a quick piece. I guess part of their deal. When Pagani showed up, Lefcourt took off to go tip Cifelli, then immediately left the lot, eliminating him as a suspect.

"Pagani, by this time, was desperate. He knew from Eldrege it was a question of hours, or maybe minutes. There was only one person who could possibly give him enough money to buy off Cifelli, and that was Rita. But Rita wouldn't. No way she was going to come up with any hundred and fifty thousand dollars. He tried roughing her up. Didn't work. Tough girl, remember. Carkeys, always somewhere nearby, tried to help out. Pagani knocked her out of the way. When he turned back to Rita, Carkeys quickly called her brother, Harley Williams, Rita's ex-husband, and told him get right over to the studio."

"How could you possibly know all that?"

"I don't exactly know. Some of it's guesswork, but it adds up. Listen: after spending more time pleading, begging, threatening, which still got him nowhere with Rita, he got really ugly. And this time really started doing a serious number on her. By now it's, say, close to eleven when Harley gets to the studio. That I know because Lefcourt saw him come in. Harley finds Pagani beating up on a badly hurt Rita, and takes him apart, including breaking his right arm. This I'm guessing, but some-how—maybe Sonny Moss?—the word gets to the dress-ing room Cifelli's men are on the lot. Pagani begs them to save his life. In spite of the fact Rita's seriously in-jured, there is that street-people bond, so she has Harley smuggle Pagani off the lot in the trunk of his car. Carkeys leaves with Harley, maybe to get bandages and stuff, Pagani stashed in the trunk. It's eleven-ten. Scratch Har-ley and Pagani as suspects, they never return that night."

"And Carkeys did?"

"Yes, at eleven-thirty-five. Here I admit it's guess-work, but it makes sense. I think Dubie shows up, likely stoned, he usually was, and finds Rita badly beaten. He tries to "help" with a shot of something or other, taking one himself. But it's bad shit, or too strong (they found major traces), and instead of bringing her around, they both pass out. I think when Carkeys returned and saw the two of them out cold, she was terrified. So she went to you, the one person she knew Rita could always count on. Only you weren't in your office, you were out with Arthur Rollins—or so you later claimed. Not true. You'd checked back in. At any rate, you weren't there, we'll get to where later. She was afraid to hang around while Cifelli's men were looking for Pagani, and scared the police would be called and she'd have to get involved. So she left you a note telling you what happened, grabbed up the various dope and incriminating crap she had, and got the hell out of there. It was ten minutes of twelve."

I found my mouth dry; I'd been talking nonstop pretty long.

"How do you like the story so far?" I asked.

"Fascinating," said Harry. "I don't see it as a series, maybe a one-shot. It is a good story. Nothing anybody could possibly prove, but a good story."

"Well, lots of bits and pieces I *could* prove, you'd be surprised. I didn't just make it up, you know. I don't suppose you'd have a drink around here?"

"How long is this going to go on?"

"Long enough if I were you, I'd be calling somebody for San Francisco."

He thought for a moment, called in his private secretary, told her to put the plane on hold, check Johnny Carson and see if he could do him *and* Frank a big favor, and ordered me a vodka-rocks, and a double Scotch for himself.

I took out a cigarette.

"Don't smoke that crap, have one of these," he offered. "They're made for me special in Switzerland. Absolutely safe, just too expensive for mass production."

I took one of the-rich-don't-have-to-get-cancer cigarettes. He picked up a lighter heavy enough to give you gold-elbow and lit it for me. He still thought it was all going to work out! Why not? It always had.

"Tastes good," I admitted, taking a puff.

"I can order them for you."

"Want to go on?"

He nodded wearily. "So, ten minutes to twelve. Then what?" he asked.

"Then I think the murderer, tipped what to expect, went to Rita's dressing room, saw Dubie and Rita out cold, saw Rita already half-wasted, saw the perfect opportunity. Knew Dubie's record with the dog, knew Pagani had a broken right arm, knew there'd never be a better chance with Rita unconscious and unable to fight back, plunged the knife—either on purpose lefty or because the killer *was* lefty—over and over, brutally, savagely, murdering her."

"And all this, uh, while I was out getting a bite to eat with Artie Rollins."

"All this while you *said* you were out getting a bite with Rollins. But which the log said differently."

"The log which is missing."

"Uh-huh."

"So, let me see if I understand you. You're saying what, exactly?"

"I'm saying we've already eliminated Lefcourt, Harley, Pagani. Now we know Carkeys is gone, Rollins is off the lot—who does that leave?"

There was your basic awkward pause; your basic gigantic awkward pause.

The secretary came in to tell him Johnny couldn't make it but got Jay Leno instead, and that our drinks would be up momentarily. She left.

"So what you're saying is, you think I did it," said Harry.

"Is that what I'm saying?"

"Well, if everybody else's been eliminated, I guess it has to be me."

"*If* everybody else's been eliminated," came a new voice, a familiar voice, the voice of Sally Light.

She'd entered from the bedroom, where I guess she'd been for some time, listening. She looked so girlish, with her pretty head tilted becomingly, arms clasped behind her back. She wore a soft chiffony dress that clung so subtly to her figure it seemed *you* were vulgar to find it sexy.

"I don't think you should get into this," said Harry.

"But, darling, I *am* into it. You certainly can't think I intend to stand by and let this man accuse you of murder."

"Accusing and convicting are worlds apart," said Harry.

"I don't think we want to take that chance," said Sally, bringing her hands from around back. In one of them was the most beautiful custom-made pearl-handled thirty-eight-caliber pistol I, or anybody else, had ever seen. Even their *guns* were gorgeous.

"Darling, I don't think this is the way to go about it," said Harry. "He can't convict me."

"He can't convict you for a couple of reasons. One, you didn't do it, and two, I'm going to kill him just to make sure."

36

Mark Bradley

I was certainly glad Brian got the job. Though I wasn't exactly thrilled his car broke down and I had to drive him all the way to the Valley just for a damn *fitting*. Considering he was a perfect forty anyway and they wouldn't have to alter a *thing* for this one-day role he'd have in this fourth-rate flick. *And* that I *had* told him you were supposed to top off your oil every decade or so, or your motor tended to swan out. I really did have more important things to do than shlep him to Universal, whose wardrobe Lefcourt was renting, and wait an hour and a half till they found out, *yes*, he was a forty, and *yes*, maybe his own suit *would* look better. *And* then later that, no, his car wouldn't be ready in the foreseeable future or necessarily ever.

We drove back in silence. He hadn't appreciated my constructive criticism. Somehow he had seen fit to return my doing him a favor by getting angry with me. Men—you couldn't live with them, and you couldn't live without them.

It was getting too late to return to the office. So I decided to pack it in for the day and take my loss. I pulled into the garage, parked, and now, in angry silence, followed Brian upstairs to our place. And that's when one of Goodman's several messages caught up with me.

Oh, no, if I missed out on the Big Finish I'd kill myself! I just had time to take a quick leak, daub a little cold water on my face, and get going. But something stopped me, I don't know, ESP? Shirley MacLaine? I reached into my bureau drawer, found what I wanted under my sweat socks, and got going.

Less than fifteen minutes later I was at the front gate of Harry Light's house. I saw Goodman's Caddy and parked behind it, then crossed to the gate and pressed the intercom.

I looked up and smiled at the TV, was identified and buzzed through.

At the door, the security man said I was expected, go right up. They were in Mr. Light's office at the top of the stairs, to the left.

I went up the stairs, turned left, and knocked at the closed door.

There was a brief pause; then I heard Harry say, "That'll be the drinks I ordered." Then, louder, "Come in."

I wasn't the drinks he ordered, but I came in anyway.

Goodman was sitting stiffly on the couch, Harry opposite him, and Sally standing in the doorway to the bedroom, her arms behind her.

"Sorry you could make it, partner," said Goodman.

"Why, what's up?"

"Hands, for one thing," said Sally, revealing a gun.

"That won't be necessary," said Harry.

"Just don't make any funny moves," said Sally.

"A lot of my funny moves I can't help," I said.

"I wouldn't try for humor," said Goodman.

"Old Rayford here's been accusing me of murder. And my wife's sort of taken exception to it," said Harry.

"Now, Harry, that's not exactly true," said Goodman. "I didn't say you did it."

It was clear I'd missed an awful lot of the good stuff.

"In fact, I know you didn't," said Goodman.

"We all do, darling. So, Rayford, what *do* you know?"

"Well, I guess you heard. We were at the point with Dubie and Rita both unconscious, Rita all beat up . . ."

"You don't mind going back a little bit?" I asked.

"Later, I'll tell you later," at which point he looked at Sally, pointing the gun. "If things work out." He took a deep breath, continued. "Carkeys went to tell Harry, but no Harry. He was supposed to be out for a snack with Rollins, but he wasn't."

"If I wasn't, where was I?"

"Well, to me, one of the key things was whether you and Rollins actually left together, which you did. But you came right back—otherwise, why go to the trouble of having Moss destroy the log? Unless it was to alibi a third person. After all, you'd all alibied each other, and if you were all really apart, any one of you could have done it. Well, not Rollins, since he was off the lot. As to where you were, I think you went to the dressing room, expecting to get a little action from Rita. That was the plan—Rollins your beard, giving you an alibi. But seeing the shape she was in, that was out. You couldn't help her because you weren't supposed to be there, and you couldn't go back to your dressing room or you'd bust yourself to Sally, here. So my guess is you just plain took a walk, got scarce on the back lot, waiting for Rollins to get back. You figured you'd send him to help Rita. But you missed when he came back too. I'll get to that in a minute."

"Wait, wait," I said. "Go back, Carkeys did what?"

"She saw Rita and Dubie both unconscious—I'll explain later . . . *maybe*—and went to Harry for help, knowing about Harry and . . . Rita."

Harry started to protest; Sally quieted him. "Don't be silly, Harry, you think I didn't know?"

"But since Harry wasn't there, Carkeys left a note saying Rita'd been beat up by Pagani, who himself was beat up by Harley, who also broke his right arm. What she didn't know, there was somebody else there. Sally. Probably in the bathroom. Sally saw the note, had for years been steaming about Harry's affair with Rita, plus probably knew, too, being a resourceful woman, that Harry had fathered Rita's child, Rafeel. Something must have snapped, as they say, and she made up her mind once and for all to get rid of the woman she felt was ruining her marriage and, worse, might cause a major scandal any time.

"So after she read the note, she ran over to the dressing room, I'd say very shortly after midnight, and found Dubie and Rita both unconscious on the floor, Rita brutally beaten. She got a knife from the kitchen, and using her left hand, to implicate Pagani, slashed and stabbed poor Rita, killing her. She wiped off her prints, dropped the knife, and dashed back to Harry's dressing room before anybody missed her."

"Holy cow!" I said.

"Not bad," said Sally.

"Sally, I wouldn't say anything, please," said Harry. "Maybe we can work things out. You know, Rayford here hasn't really had the material rewards in life he deserves. I wouldn't be surprised if he might not be joining our firm in a really big executive position, with a salary you never in your wildest—"

"Won't work, Harry, there has to be some kind of fall. We can't just let killers roam the streets. Even though it might be safe in Beverly Hills, since nobody else is ever *on* the streets."

"So, what're you going to do, put old Harry on trial and destroy everybody's faith in Hollywood?"

"Why would I put you on trial?"

"Because no way we're going to put her on. At worst, I'd confess. You've established I had the opportunity. I had the motive too, in a way, you could say—if I claimed Rita was blackmailing me, threatening to reveal—"

"Harry, Harry, stop that, it's not going to be that way," said Sally, brandishing the gun.

"You can't," said Harry. "Even if I let you kill Rayford, now there's whatsisname . . ."

"Mark," I offered.

"Mark too—where would it end?"

"You closed your eyes before. It was self-defense. They cooked up a scheme, tried to blackmail you, they—"

"Stop it," said Harry.

"I'd like to know about the rest of it," I said, amazed how calm I was. That I was, in fact, more curious than frightened. As they turned to look at me, I continued, "You know, Carkeys, Rollins."

"Well, the way I see it—" started Goodman, at which time there was a discreet knock on the door.

Harry looked at Sally. She put the gun behind her back. He said to come in. The door opened, and a houseman entered with a tray carrying a vodka on the rocks and a double Scotch.

"Ahhh," said Goodman. "A pause in the day's occupation, known as the Children's Hour."

Meanwhile, with Sally's gun no longer in a threatening position, I considered making a move. But inasmuch as the houseman was also one of the security guards, and Goodman was quietly shaking his head, I didn't.

"Thank you," said Harry.

"Cook wants to know, since you'll be staying in town, was there anything special you'd enjoy?"

"Tell you the truth," said Harry, "for some reason or other, I'm not terribly hungry. Whatever, cold cuts, not now."

"Very good, sir," said the houseman. They really did talk like that. Probably said "Good day" too. "Will there be anything else?"

"Considering how long it takes, you can rustle up a refill on this," said Harry.

"Me too," I said. I liked to think I'd be having a drink later, much later.

"As you wish," said the flunky, virtually bowing out. Under other circumstances I'd really have enjoyed this.

"Carkeys, Rollins?" I repeated.

"I figure Carkeys decided to come back after she'd dumped the dope and whatever. The log said she'd returned again at twelve-ten. She couldn't leave Rita in such terrible condition. Only, when she returned, she saw Rollins leaving Rita's dressing room. He'd probably gone there to pick up Harry after he was supposed to finish humping Rita. Only they missed connections because Harry got out earlier once he saw Rita and Dubie were both unconscious. But by this time Rita was dead, and Rollins saw a chance to do himself a bit of good, so he stole the jewels. Only, Carkeys saw him leaving with the jewels. When Rollins connected with Harry, he knew Harry hadn't done it—he didn't even know it'd *been* done. Being a confidant of Sally's, he knew she knew all about Harry's affair, and rightly figured *she'd* killed Rita. Rollins was one of those old queens who adore women, and he adored Sally. She knew it and counted on his loyalty. Plus, he had the jewels, was way ahead of the game, and Sally was sure to take very good care of him.

"Meanwhile, a few minutes later, Dubie must have come to, gone absolutely bananas at what he saw, and gotten the hell out, not knowing if he'd done it or what. But he was off the lot at twelve-fifteen.

"Now, the only fly in the ointment for Sally was Carkeys, who, also knowing Rita and Harry were making it, and having been convinced by Rollins *he* didn't do it, would correctly figure Sally must have. She'd taken off and stayed hidden a long time, knowing she was dealing with ruthless people wouldn't hesitate to off her. But eventually there came a time she needed money—as it did to all junkies—and she decided to risk it with Rollins. She demanded a payoff. He poor-mouthed it. She said then she wanted the jewels. Rollins went to Sally for advice. Sally said give Carkeys the jewels and they'd take care of that threat once and for all. She'd be found dead, with one of the jewels—the ring—and the rest gone, which they would've taken back. Robbery would be the motive, and certainly nobody would suspect them. But the ring that was supposed to be found on her finger was—I admit I'm guessing—lopped off by Dubie."

"How can you possibly know that?"

"I said I'm guessing."

"Not only about Dubie, you're also guessing about the rest."

"No, I'm very sure of that."

"Really?" I said involuntarily.

"You notice nobody interrupted me. Because it follows. Look, Sally had access to inside information and could influence events. So what does she do? She gets Harry to get Lefcourt to get Dubie out of the booby hatch on furlough. She has Rollins give Carkeys the jewels. Carkeys, looking for insurance, contacts me and we agree to meet at Nipper's. But what happens? She takes one look and aborts the meet. Why? *I* was there. I didn't bring any cops, nothing was suspicious. What spooked her? She saw *Sally*, and Sally was the one person she was afraid of most in the world.

"So she stashes the jewels in the airport locker and takes Lefcourt's offer to stay at Dubie's old house in Laurel Canyon. Exactly how Sally did it, I don't know. Maybe she got Rollins to drug Carkeys first—not too hard to do with her, and that *was* his car I saw near the scene. Anyway, Sally traps her there, and copycats the first murder, gore and all, which she knows how to do exactly. I'd guess, too, Rollins sprang Dubie from Lefcourt's pool house—remember the 'man from the studio' who visited him?—and brought Dubie 'home' in time to take the fall.''

"Jesus," I said. But I noticed nobody was protesting too much. "And Rollins?"

"Well, Rollins was losing out. He'd 'lent' the jewels to Carkeys, Sally promising he'd get them back. But Carkeys had been too quick. She'd gotten rid of them, and both missed picking up on the key. Now, my guess is Rollins wanted Sally to replace his loss, after his long and faithful service. Sally could see he was the one remaining loose end. Even though she'd bought him that big rock he'd flashed at the screening, she knew she'd never be totally safe with him alive. So, since Dubie was back in Ojai, and she had no way of knowing where Pagani was, to possibly take the rap, she couldn't copycat this one. Instead, she merely took that nice pearl-handled thirty-eight—I just bet ballistics will confirm it—and popped him right between the eyes."

"Exactly as I'm going to do with you," said Sally, raising the pistol and leveling it at Goodman, disdainfully turning her back on me.

"I don't think so," I said. I wanted to say, "I wouldn't try that if I were you, shweetheart," but, you know . . . To make sure there was no misunderstanding, I pressed the cold steel of my brand-new gun against her neck.

"Well, look at you!" said Goodman in amazement. "Where'd you get that?"

"I got it at Guns R Us. Whatta you mean where'd I get it?"

"You bought it?"

"Of course I bought it."

"I just don't see you with a gun. *I* don't even have a gun."

"You weren't kidnapped and thrown into a dungeon."

"Some dungeon, a suite at the Bel Air Hotel."

"Nevertheless, considering all the assorted mayhem you've brought into my life, I thought I ought to do something to protect myself. Now, would you mind relieving the lady of her weapon?"

Goodman took away Sally's gun. She grew perceptibly less menacing.

There was a knock at the door.

"Yes?" said Harry wearily. He, too, was seemingly drained of energy.

"Your drinks, Mr. Light," came the response.

"Not a moment too soon," said Goodman, positively beaming.

37

Rayford Goodman

But of course we couldn't exactly hold a gun on them forever. Bradley said to call the police. I said no hurry, they weren't going anyplace.

Sally threw a big yawn and said in that case would we mind if she went to the bathroom?

I asked were we boring her? She said no. I said stay where she was.

With which she went into a yawning fit, the same time scratching herself.

"I want to go to the bathroom," she whined.

"You can't," I said.

Harry said she didn't exactly want to go to the *bathroom*, she needed a shot. Big news.

Too bad, I said, she could just start learning to do without.

"I've got to go to the bathroom!" she yelled, sweating heavily. "Don't you understand, I've *got* to go!" And now she was practically tearing the skin off her face.

"Please," said Harry. "She has to go. She needs her medicine."

"It's not medicine, it's fucking dope," I said.

"Right, I know, you're right. The damn stuff. That's the whole problem, the only problem," Harry said.

Putting it a little mildly. Some "problem"—a person goes around killing and mutilating. Francine certainly knew what she was talking about when she told me people on speed eventually became stone psychotics. Case proved.

"Please," she cried. "Please, please!"

"Okay," I said, giving in. "But leave the door open. Go get your dope. You watch her, Bradley."

He followed her to the bathroom and saw her through

her fix. After which she returned—a different woman—and we all settled back down.

With the weapons put away, and the tension eased, Harry started to feel like Harry again. He said something to the effect when you think of it, all this pulling guns on each other and making big threats was just one person's word against another. Or two people's words against two people. In fact, chances were his security folks would deny anyone *with* a gun could've possibly got by them. Which also reminded him somebody's ass needed firing.

"How *did* you get in here with a gun, anyway?" he asked Bradley.

"You mean did anybody search me?"

"Right."

"Why would anybody search a gay writer? Who could be more harmless?"

"I don't know, you looked pretty tough in there to me," I said. "You almost maybe saved my life."

"Yeah, but against a girl?" said Bradley.

"Don't be a chauvinist pig. You did good."

"Listen," said Harry. "If you can stop patting each other on the back for a minute, think about this. While a lot's been said, and even admitted here today, if you were to check back tomorrow, who's to say anybody really said any of those things? Nobody saw anything, nobody heard anything—it's your basic tree falling in the forest making no noise."

"Not exactly," I said, reaching for the flowers I'd brought. "When this tree fell, Memorex was listening." With which I pulled out the tape recorder I'd found in Mark's tote bag and stashed in the bouquet I'd gotten from the Quaker State folks.

"Boy, I *do* have to fire some people," said Harry. "Just can't get good help." Then, nobody laughing, "So what happens now?"

"We call the cops and the district attor—" started Bradley. I stopped him.

"*We* know, and they know we know. Plus we've got it on tape."

"Which I'm sure isn't admissible," said Harry.

"Maybe not, but it'd certainly get their attention.

And with a really sincere investigation, no reason the police wouldn't eventually find what I found. But what I think is, let's sleep on it. You're not going anywhere and we're not going anywhere."

"Why?" demanded Bradley.

"In the fullness of time," I replied. And since I was beginning to feel a letdown from release of tension and there didn't seem any more drinks forthcoming, I suggested we get ourselves the hell out of there.

Outside, Bradley was the exact opposite of me—big surprise!—bursting with energy and a million questions.

"Not now," I said, trying to hold him off. "I'm dead on my feet. All I want to do now is sleep. I have to sleep. A lot."

"Well, when *can* we talk? When do we decide what to do?"

"Tomorrow night. On me, eight o'clock, Chasen's."

"You're going to keep me waiting with all these questions till then?"

"Longer, if you don't let me go home and sleep."

"Okay."

"And listen, you think Francine might care to come along? You know, go out with me? Like a date?"

"I wouldn't be surprised, why don't you ask her?"

"Yeah, why don't I?" I said, then added, "Why don't you get a girl too?"

"Why would I do that, when I've got a perfectly good boy?" he answered.

"Whatever," I said.

The garage looked great. The movie folks'd really cleaned it up, although Bradley's flowers seemed to be gone. And they say show business is sentimental.

I took a fond look at the Caddy. It sure looked terrific in gray. Though of course it wasn't technically classic anymore, since it hadn't come in that color at the time. But who's to judge? It was great. And next time I got a few bucks, a new top, for sure.

I went inside, poured a drink, ran a tub. It ran rusty too. Maybe it was the boiler. I hadn't taken a bath in years. I always took showers. But somehow I was all aches and pains and wanted to soak. Strange, there was

no sense of victory, either. I was almost sad, I *was* sad—
and I didn't understand that. I didn't often get too philosophical about things. Things were the way they were.
In my business it was often messy, and even when you
won, it usually meant someone had to go down. Unless
it was someone you were actual enemies with, there
wasn't any great pleasure in it. It was the way it was.
The way it was supposed to be. So?

I settled into the steamy tub and felt myself relax. I
hadn't realized just how knotted up I was. A sudden
wave of depression hit me. What the hell was this? Getting old? *Sorry* you won?

Drink more, think less.

Do.

I pulled the phone over to the tub, called Francine, and
asked if she'd like to have dinner tomorrow at Chasen's.

"You mean you've got some more research for me?"

"I mean I'd like to have dinner with you. Period."

"Yeah? Why?" she said.

"Well, I figured I had to eat anyway—what the hell
you mean, why? I need a reason to think I'd enjoy your
company?"

"Enjoying my company's a good reason. I'd like to."

"Good, we'll double-date with Bradley and Brian."

"All right."

"And that way if we don't exactly hit it off, we're not
stuck with each other the rest of the evening."

"Hey, you romantic fool, you."

"I didn't mean . . . I meant you too, it could work
both ways."

"I think I'll take my life in my hands and risk having
a dinner with you."

"You mind the guys pick you up and meeting me there?"

"You're not going to overwhelm me with attention,
are you? Sure, that's fine."

"Good, then I'll see you at eight."

We said good-bye and hung up.

I felt better.

Next morning I took the walk, and walked briskly,
which is not something I usually did. But you were going
to exercise, the idea was get some value out of it.

I saw the Old Cockers, waved—they waved back. I saw the post-stroke guy, nodded—he palsied back. And the Fast Walker, who I crossed the street to keep from hearing his spiel about the wonderful breakthrough sneakers. It was good to see them.

I cut almost three minutes off my best time, got myself all out of breath and my pulse pounding. Good news, all out of breath, heart pounding—which everybody used to think meant you were dying. Now means you're getting healthy! Then I popped up the hill, got home, actually cleaned up the yard, showered—still rusty—made a call, made an appointment, kept the appointment.

I was treated like it hadn't been a couple of years since I'd been to Chasen's. Seated in my favorite spot near the bar, at my favorite table; an old and valued customer. Maybe everything in life wasn't turning to crap.

Brian and Bradley looked sharp in designer suits, that gray nubby stuff the kids all seemed to be wearing, with shoulder pads the size of interior linemen's. Plus artistically prewrinkled shirts and ties looked like they came in a box of Cracker Jack. I wondered did they still have Cracker Jack and still have gifts inside? I had to admit it added up—for them. Their skin was tight, their eyes were clear, and they sported matching sunburns.

"Took tanning lessons," explained Bradley.

Francie was . . . very much there. She seemed to have done something about her body heat. Or else maybe I never noticed before. Her skin seemed to have a thin mist of perspiration that didn't seem part of the external environment. Sitting next to me, she seemed to give off an almost feverish heat. Aglow. Her hair was all piled up top of her head, sort of loose and flyaway, rumpled, like she just got out of bed. She had opted for a lush boobs-on-parade low-cut number, soft, a print of some sort, maybe a copy or relic of the forties? Hard to tell with them, they sometimes dressed to be funny. This wasn't funny. It was all really nice and sexy in a nubile-milkmaid sort of way. Very different from last time and the leathers and feathers tough chic. She was somehow being an old-fashioned girl for an old-fashioned guy. Or else putting me on and they'd all have a big laugh later, pick one. Anyway, she made a very good second impression.

We ordered drinks, talked about Chasen's and the old days. Or *I* talked about Chasen's and the old days, since I was the only one likely to remember it. But they were interested.

The drinks came. The drinks got drunk. Other drinks got ordered and came. We ordered dinner.

"I hope you don't mind," said Bradley, "but I played them the tape."

"I don't mind. But you have to understand, it's confidential. You've got a right to share it because you were part of it, but that's as far as it goes."

They agreed.

"But we all have questions," said Brian.

"Shoot."

"Who blew up your car?"

"And who tried to run you down at the cleaners?" added Francie.

"I'd say Arthur Rollins to both questions."

"Why?" asked all three.

"To stop the book. Practically all those moves were for that. The others—Rafeel and Harley—were protecting Harry. They didn't want us nosing around for fear we'd find out about Rafeel and Harry's affair with Rita. Rollins was working for Sally, trying to protect her and keep us from finding out she was the killer."

The salad came. I stopped the questions till we finished the salad, to give me a chance to think. That wasn't made any easier as I was more and more aware of the heat from Francie's thigh brushing up against mine.

"How come," the thigh owner asked, salad over, "Luana"—saying the dreaded L word—"recognized the Sierra Tiara and Sally didn't?"

"I think Sally *did* recognize it too and was scared stiff Harry had somehow got onto the jewels—not realizing at the time Harry'd known all along she was the murderer and was protecting her. She figured if she made a fuss, she'd have to face up to God knows what. So the best thing was play dumb and accept the gift from Harry

at face value. Fairly easy since they were fighting and
didn't go to the Amigos affair anyway."

"But didn't your ex-wife tell her she recognized the
tiara?"

"No, the whole thing scared her too much. She told
me, and once I told her I knew Harry'd gotten it on the
up-and-up, that was good enough for her. She wasn't
about to open any can of worms on her own. Nobody
ever said Luana wasn't smart."

"I've got a question," said Bradley. "Did you really
know, in advance, when you went over to Harry's, that
it was Sally?"

"That's who we nailed."

"But did you *know*?"

"Sometimes you *know*, and sometimes you *think*, and
sometimes you sort of luck out."

This got them going again. But the main course arrived, and I called time.

There must have been hundreds of new restaurants
through the years, come and go. But Chasen's was still
Chasen's—almost. As much as any of us were still us.
Food tasted real good; people were real nice; it all
looked great; smelled great. A bit of the old. We finished
the entrée.

"So what happened to the jewels?" asked Bradley.
"And why hasn't Broward gone public? In fact, how did
Broward know you had the key? How did he know there
even *was* a key?"

I sighed. This part wouldn't come easy.

"The truth is, I think I underestimated Broward all
along. I think he actually solved this thing. The first time.
I think, long ago, he went to Harry and told him what
he knew. I think Harry put the fix in with him. For that
Broward needed two things. One, to profit—no problem
with Harry—and two, a fall guy."

"We're talking originally," Bradley said.

"Originally," I went on. "I think Harry agreed to
both. First, for the fall guy, Harry gave him Dubie. Remember, we found out Harry really hated Dubie—
'loathed,' Sally said at the screening. Plus, being so
whacked-out, Dubie was a natural for the part—the perfect patsy. But I came along and proved it couldn't *be*

Dubie, so they had to change the script and settle for my candidate, which was Pagani."

I took a sip of water.

"Harry being Harry," I went on, "he then became Dubie's chief protector and ally."

"The jewels?" asked Francie.

"Well, it wasn't hard for Harry to figure out Sally didn't have them. So who was closest to Sally? Had to be Carkeys or Rollins. With Carkeys they'd certainly have surfaced in no time flat. So that left Rollins. Good enough, let him keep them. Which Rollins did, all these years. But then Carkeys came back into the picture. So Sally pressured Rollins to cough 'em up temporarily—in exchange for the big diamond he 'treated himself to'— to set up Carkeys. But she was too smart for that and stashed them first, which of course still didn't stop her getting murdered."

"All right," said Bradley, not totally convinced. "But I still don't exactly—"

"Just stay with the fact Broward was onto it, step by step. He'd never been able to nail Rollins, but with Carkeys back in town, figured it had to do with the jewels, and greedy bastard that he is, figured to take a shot at them too. But when he didn't find them at the murder scene, or for that matter, even a handbag of Carkeys', and I'd been there—he figured . . ."

"Cherchez le Goodman," said Francie.

"Something like that."

"So he tossed your house," said Bradley. "Which didn't come up with anything either."

"Till I walked in."

"Till you walked in. He bopped you over the head, searched you, and there was the key!"

"Didn't take a rocket scientist to figure what would be in the locker. He went to the airport, opened it, found the jewels."

"And *kept* them," said Bradley, outraged. "What a story!"

"Yeah," I said in a voice that everyone noticed wasn't exactly at the same level of enthusiasm.

"We *are* going to put that in the book," said Bradley.

"Of course," said Brian.

"You've got to," said Francie.

"Well, now, that's kind of a hard prove," said me. "It'll look suspicious, eventually, in a year or two when it'll turn out he 'got lucky in the market' and decides to retire. But I still don't think we'll be able to prove anything."

"Well, so we'll hint at it. Enough that people'll know. What can he do?" said Bradley. "He's not about to sue and open himself up to the chance we can prove it. What a book this is going to be!"

"Ah, the book," I said.

"Oh, wow," said Bradley. "I'll have to revise a lot of the chapters I've laid out. But no problem. What a sensation; we'll knock them on their keister. We're talking best-seller, mini-series, the whole enchilada!"

"Still, you heard Richard Penny. That's not what he wants."

"Oh, well, sure he said that before. But wait'll he finds out what you did and what happened, it's a tremendous story. He'll have to go along."

"Even if it means losing one of his best sources, Harry Light?"

"Well, sure, even Penny's enough of a publisher, he's got to be thrilled to come up with this kind of hot stuff."

"Right," I said quietly.

"Of course!" said Bradley noisily.

"Of course," I said, *very* quietly.

Which is when Brian noticed I wasn't waxing all that enthusiastic.

"What is it, what's the matter?" he said.

"Wait till after dessert," I said.

"No, now," said Bradley. "Right now."

"You sure? They have wonderful desserts."

"Now!"

"Okay, here's the way it goes. You did a great job; Francine did a great job; we all did."

"Is this a concession speech?" asked Francie suspiciously.

"In a way. This is the deal we cut—"

"What do you mean, 'the deal we cut'?" said Bradley.

"You want to listen? Goes like this: Sally's to go to

a maximum-security private Shady Acres forever—the deal is *forever*."

"Nooo!" wailed Bradley.

"She gets away with *murder*?" said Brian.

"Not getting away, she *does* get punished."

"Yeah," said Francie, "no more Bistro Gardens for lunch."

"Locked up *forever*," I reminded.

"Let's hear it all," said Bradley, clearly dreading it. "Bottom line, Goodman."

"All right, bottom line: Sally's gone; Brian gets the second lead in Harry's next picture; you get to write it; Francine gets to co-produce, and I get a big guest shot for big bucks on his next special, coincidental with the book coming out."

"Fucking sellout!" said Brian.

"You could say that," I said.

"You sound like an agent. The book, what about the book?" wailed Bradley. "How could you do this, what are we going to say in the book?"

"We're going to say how Rita got killed, and how Dubie was falsely accused. Then how they called me in and I proved it wasn't Dubie at all—the movies' second-most-beloved comic being an innocent victim. And how the foul deed was done by this rat Danny Pagani, a known porno king, wife beater, child molester, and dope peddler."

"Hey, he doesn't sound *all* bad," said Francine.

"Who also, incidentally, can't then sue you for five million dollars," said Brian.

"What're you, trying to say it's all selfish? There's power here. There's certain realities. I can't call all the shots. I can only make the best deal I can, given there're a lot of other considerations."

Bradley rolled his eyes. "So that's what it's going to be. Porno king, dope peddler . . ."

"And how," I continued, "just when it looked like Hollywood was going down for the count with another terrible scandal, old Ray Goodman stepped in and saved the day."

"It's awful," cried Bradley.

I know, I thought. But that way we don't have to

destroy an American institution, Harry Light. And that way Cifelli doesn't do us grievous bodily harm. And that way Penny actually publishes the book."

"It's just god-awful," cried Bradley again.

"Try to think of it more as 'That's Hollywood,' " I said.

There was a long, painful silence. Then Brian said, "How big is this second lead?"

It was a big disappointment to me too. Did they think I liked shaving the points? Did they think I wouldn't rather have a world where good triumphed and truth prevailed?

But it wasn't all bad.

For example, Francie came home with me.

She seemed to like the house; said the yard looked nice, enjoyed her dinner, thought there was a lot more to me than she had at first.

I was a little gunshy about heading for the sack—and given my "condition." So I found myself stalling at the bar, having just one more for the road—that long road to the bedroom. She lit a joint and smoked it noisily. Filthy habit.

"I really don't understand how a smart, attractive girl like you—"

"Woman like me."

"—woman like you can keep on doing all those terrible things to herself."

"Someone has to."

"I mean it."

"So do I." She came close. I felt like kissing her. I wanted to. But I didn't know where it would lead. Or *if* it would lead. I smiled, turned back to my cognac.

"You don't like my using drugs."

"Right."

"Tell you what," she said. "On a money-back, trial basis: I'll give up drugs . . ."

"Yeah?"

". . . if you give up impotence."

Out, right out in the open. Holy shit! Where did she get that? Could she tell? Did it show? Outfuckingrageous!

"Did it ever occur to you maybe you're not my type?"

"Well, I was sort of hoping for someone living, my-self," she said.

"I'm living . . . just not very well."

She reached out her hand.

"Would you like to try for better?"

I took her hand, came around the bar, and together we went inside. She said it was nice inside. That sounded inviting. Enough so we took off our clothes. And I held in my stomach long enough to get a laugh and some interest as we moved toward each other. And she had that pussycat heat. And we embraced, and she had that skin, that touch-and-you'll-die skin I remembered from so long ago. And it was so good. And then we went to bed. And hell, I wasn't out to set any records. I just wanted to go the distance, in no particular hurry—well, *some* hurry—and I did. It was easy, really. You might almost say natural.

"Okay?" she said.

"Hey, it all comes back," I said. "Like riding a bike."

She punched me. Not too hard.

Thanks to Donald Von Wiedenman,
who, oddly, inspired the even chapters.
And my wife, Victoria . . .
in case you were wondering.

Don't miss
Shot on Location,
the terrific new
Goodman/Bradley mystery
by Stan Cutler

PROLOGUE

The house was, at best, a gigantic mistake. A melange of disparate elements, it might have been the mutant offspring of an architectural misalliance between a South Pacific potentate and an Iranian lottery winner.

Situated between Malibu and Point Dume on a bluff overlooking its own private beach, it had been built in a defilade created to protect its privacy (and coincidentally the sensibilities of others with better taste) and afford added structural integrity against the ocean's vagaries and occasional hurricanic violence.

Thus, it was mercifully invisible both from the Pacific Coast Highway to the east and its neighbors to the north and south.

It was huge, yet because of its design and geography possessed less a look of solitary splendor than that of a building shunned. The original intent to render an earth-clinging refuge, hunkered down against the forces of nature and space, had instead, on execution, produced an effect more closely resembling an enormous wreck disgorged from the sea, cringing on the beach in embarrassment.

At three-forty A.M. a figure detached itself from the shadow of the main house and was vaguely silhouetted in the waning moonlight silently padding toward the guest house. It was that of the Outsider, a name self-designated, but for good and sufficient reason.

The main building was loosely connected to the guest

house by a pathway of scattered flat stones. These were assiduously avoided, as each foot instead was carefully and soundlessly placed on the sand between.

None of the various security appliances had been tripped; none of the dogs barked. Had anyone chanced to observe, such movement would not have been considered remarkable, the traffic to and from the guest cottage adhering to no particular pattern or time frame. In fact, the blare of rock music, even now alternately audible with the sound of waves crashing on the beach, was unexceptional, at this or any hour. (In fairness, it could as easily have been jazz, or even classical—being a house of eclectic tastes.)

Though no conversation could be heard, that, too, indicated little. Besides the likelihood of being overwhelmed by the music and the ocean's noises, the absence of conversation could as easily signify the occupants were asleep (inured by aural conditioning to ignore such sound), awash in sexual activity, or simply zonked out. In any event, prudence dictated caution, to avoid prompting the attention of a potential witness. Or alerting one's prey.

The Outsider, of course, knew the workings of the compound intimately. (And most especially the location of all its occupants this night.) One could possess intimate knowledge without being an intimate. This was an establishment where one could even reside and remain an Outsider. For there was, despite all the people living here and their varying degrees of acceptance, only one significant, indisputable Insider—and that was the house's owner and master: three-time Oscar winner, actor Stacy Jaeger.

Given the hour and custom, the Star was undoubtedly asleep in his huge master suite atop the main building, also undoubtedly alone, since his interests in things carnal had long since yielded to things gastronomic.

In any event, he had also long since distanced himself from any interest in what went on in the guest cottage, or in the lives of its occupants.

In fairness, his disinterest extended beyond this immediate circle to embrace most of the world, its works, woes, and functions. Though in all, he maintained a contrary *appearance* of avid interest. Women, politics—even the more than casual observer would consider him an advocate—he *was* an actor (and did have public relations people).

But at the gut level, figuratively and literally, food, food, food was his monomaniacal preoccupation. The hardest addiction.

He no longer made movies, he made meals. Indeed, it was only in their contemplation and consumption that Jaeger these days became fully alive. Not since the time of the late Orson Welles had such a giant allowed his accomplishments to be eclipsed by such a singular failing.

And as Jaeger presumably slept in sated exhaustion, the Outsider proceeded on cautious feet toward the guest house. Its occupants of record being Stacy, Jr., the star's first son, though namesake alone was no guarantee of preference, the Outsider would know in intimate detail; Carey—second born, with good and sufficient complaints of his own; and Iris, third child and most apparent beloved—though at such an emotional remove as to derive little benefit from the fact.

To the official company could be found, at various times, girlfriends for the boys—boyfriends for the girl. None of which, save one, was the shadowy wraith expecting to find in attendance, having with considerable effort established as much.

So now it was that the Outsider stopped, with heightened senses sniffing the wind for any lingering hint of danger, nourishing courage with air, and with each breath gathering rage to transmute into energy, the better to prepare for what lay just ahead.

Outsider, Insider—irrelevant terms of remote interest only to the individuals concerned. Only one real relationship obtained—that of servant to master. Service to the Star remained always at the core. It was what the compound, its occupants, the entire direction of its personnel and accoutrements thereto were designed to provide.

And now, the Outsider, personal feelings, resentment, neglect aside, would render another, most outstanding service, even though it had not been sought. But, indeed, wasn't it part of the job to anticipate the needs, whether he knew it or not, of Him From Whom All Goodness Flowed?

But it was remarkable, nonetheless, that the Star somehow tolerated all the unremitting abuse visited upon his favorite child; that he so little protected her from immediate dangers. It was as if he had determined that somehow her madness had caused it to happen, and that it was enough she visit serially the most costly—and often mercifully remote—sanitoria of the world for protracted periods of time. That he was thus discharging his paternal responsibility, but that any quotidian intervention was too personal and painful to be involved in. This, while her current victimization was so apparent to everyone else.

Well, he was a Star, whose eyes dwelt mostly on his own image, and even when turned outwardly, saw only what he wanted to see. And there was little doubt he would never appreciate in any significant or even conscious way the favor he was about to receive. But of course, that's what made the doing so wonderful—it would be without overt compensation. At least from him. But it *would* be in the Star's interest, no question of that. A surcease from the pain, or minimally, distraction. A setting of priorities with the family put in its proper perspective, and he free to pursue his calling—indeed, *forced* to render obeisance to that genius with further accomplishment.

Three forty-seven.

The Outsider crossed the remaining distance, eased open the always unlocked door, and entered the building. Crossing the living room, silencer-equipped pistol in hand, and momentarily pausing at the bedroom door of the Favored Child. Oh, how one yearned to enter that door and lie on that bed.

The world would soon enough be told that Iris, poor misbegotten child, and the sole potential witness, having taken her customary two Halcions, had slept through it all—no doubt attired in a pair of her trademark-color purple pj's.

The door was open. A nightlight on. The target was elsewhere—as reconnaissance had indicated.

With a cautious tread, breath withheld—no time to blow it now—the Outsider tiptoed over to the kitchen.

And there, as planned and expected, sprawled asleep with his head on the table (by arrangement, design, and chemical aid), was Wesley Crewe—bringer of bruises, causer of contusions—the Favored Child's lover.

All the pieces were in place, all the players on their figurative marks. Just beyond Crewe's outstretched hand was an overflowing ashtray, full of cigarette butts and marijuana roaches. An overturned glass was mired in sticky amber fluid, over which several flies hovered stuporously, sharing an interest in its potent remains.

The Outsider took three deep yoga breaths to clear the lungs and concentrate necessary energy. Then, focusing on the predesignated target area, calmly pumped three silencer bullets into Crewe's head.

Which, incidentally, the Outsider couldn't help noticing, sounded exactly like someone spitting out cherry pits.

Three fifty-two.

ABOUT THE AUTHOR

STAN CUTLER is a Los Angeles–based TV screenwriter. *Best Performance by a Patsy* is his first Rayford Goodman/Mark Bradley mystery. He is at work on the next.